KRAKATIT

KRAKATIT

KAREL ČAPEK

Translated by Edward Lawrence Hyde

Edited and Revised by John Betancourt

Introduction by Karl Wurf

WILDSIDE PRESS

Story first published in 1922.
English translation by Edward Lawrence Hyde, 1925.
Edited and Revised by John Betancourt for Wildside Press.
Introduction copyright © 2025 by Karl Wurf.
Published by Wildside Press LLC.
wildsidepress.com

INTRODUCTION

KARL WURF

Karel Čapek (1890–1938) was a Czech novelist, playwright, and journalist, born in Malé Svatoňovice in the Austro-Hungarian Empire. Čapek emerged as one of the most influential literary voices in Europe during the early 20th century, famed for his visionary works that cleverly blended science fiction with social and ethical commentary. He remains best remembered today for introducing the word "robot" to global culture in his groundbreaking play *R.U.R. (Rossum's Universal Robots)* (1920). This inventive play showcased his talent for combining gripping stories with deep philosophical questions about humanity and technology.

Although primarily remembered for his science fiction, Čapek was notably versatile, writing mystery, satire, and philosophical novels. His wide literary interests often centered around humanity's struggle with ethical dilemmas and the moral implications of scientific advancement. Čapek's works frequently delved into the complexities of human nature, politics, and society, making him a powerful voice not just within science fiction but across multiple literary genres.

His novel *Krakatit* (1922, English translation 1925) occupies a significant place in the early history of science fiction, blending elements of thriller and political intrigue. At its core, the novel explores the dramatic consequences of unchecked scientific ambition. Following the scientist Prokop, who discovers an explosive powerful enough to destroy entire cities, Čapek expertly weaves a tense narrative of espionage, ethical uncertainty, and personal struggle. *Krakatit* resonates strongly with themes of scientific responsibility, political power struggles, and humanity's capacity for both innovation and destruction, making it profoundly relevant today. Its compelling mix of suspense, vivid characterizations, and thoughtful analysis of ethical issues remains immensely appealing to modern readers.

In his own time, Čapek was celebrated not only as a gifted storyteller but also as a thoughtful critic of society and politics. Today, his reputation endures due to his visionary perspectives on technology's impact on society and his warnings about humanity's potential for self-destruction—concerns increasingly relevant in contemporary discourse.

Čapek profoundly influenced later generations of speculative fiction authors, including Ray Bradbury, Philip K. Dick, and Isaac Asimov. Modern readers, rediscovering Golden Age fiction, now increasingly turn to Čapek's works, finding in them insights remarkably prescient for our own technologically driven age.

Recommended Reading

Books by Karel Čapek:

The Absolute at Large

Hordubal

R.U.R.

War with the Newts

CHAPTER I

With the evening the fog of the cold, damp day grew thicker. You felt as if you were making your way through some thin, moist substance which closed behind you again for good. You wished you were at home. At home by your lamp, in a box of four walls. Never before had you felt so forsaken.

Prokop felt his way along the embankment. He was chilled and his forehead was damp with the sweat of weakness; he wanted to sit down on that wet seat but he was afraid of the policemen. He felt as if he was twisting round; yes, near the Old Town mill, a man made a detour to avoid him as though he were a drunkard. He exerted all his strength to walk straight. And now there came another man, walking towards him with his hat drawn down over his eyes and his collar turned up. Prokop set his teeth, furrowed his brow and strained all his muscles in the attempt to pass him successfully. But when he was just a step away from the other, there was suddenly a darkness inside his head and the whole world began to revolve with him; suddenly he saw ever so near a pair of penetrating eyes which were fixed on him.

He struck against someone's shoulder, murmured a word of apology and moved away with a sort of convulsive dignity. A few paces further he stopped and looked round. The other man stood regarding him fixedly. Prokop pulled himself together and moved off a little more quickly; but it was no good, he was obliged to give another glance back. The man was still standing and watching him, sticking his head out of his collar like a tortoise. "Let him look," thought Prokop uneasily, "now I shan't turn round again." And he went on as best he could. The man with the turned-up collar followed him. It seemed that he was running. Prokop took to flight in terror.

The world again began to revolve around him. Breathing heavily, with chattering teeth, he leaned against a tree and closed his eyes. He felt horribly ill and was afraid that he would fall, that his heart would burst and that the blood would spurt out of his lips. When he opened his eyes he saw the man with the turned-up collar standing right in front of him.

"Aren't you Engineer Prokop?" asked the man, as though repeating the question.

"I... I haven't been there," answered Prokop, trying to lie.

"Where?" asked the man.

"There," said Prokop, and indicated with his head some place in the direction of Strahov. "What do you want of me?"

"Don't you know me? I'm Thomas. Thomas from the Polytechnic. Don't
you know, now?"

"Thomas," repeated Prokop, utterly indifferent to what the name might
signify. "Yes, Thomas, of course. And what do you want from me?"

The man with the turned-up collar seized him by the arm. "Wait, first of
all you must sit down. Do you understand?"

"Yes," said Prokop, and allowed himself to be led to a seat. "I… That is
to say… I'm not well, you see." He suddenly drew out of his pocket a hand
bound up with a piece of dirty rag. "Wounded, see? A confounded business."

"And doesn't your head ache?" asked the man.

"It does."

"Now listen, Prokop," said the other. "You've got a fever or something
of the sort. You must go to the hospital, see? Anyone can tell you're in a bad
way. But at least do remember that we know one another. I'm Thomas. We
did chemistry together. My dear fellow, do remember!"

"I know Thomas," echoed Prokop weakly. "That rotter. What about
him?"

"Nothing," said Thomas. "He is talking to you. You must go to bed, see?
Where do you live?"

"There," Prokop attempted to say, and made a gesture with his head.
"Near…near Hybsmonka." Suddenly, he attempted to stand up. "I don't want
to go there! Not there! There—there is…there is…"

"What?"

"Krakatit," breathed Prokop.

"What's that?"

"Nothing. I shan't say. No one must go there. Or… Or…"

"What?"

"Ffft, bang!" said Prokop, and threw his hand up in the air.

"What's that?"

"Krakatoe. Kra-ka-tau. A volcano, see? It…tore off my finger. I don't
know what.…" He stopped and added slowly: "A frightful thing, you know."

Thomas watched him carefully as if he were waiting for something.
"And so," he began after a moment, "you're still on explosives?"

"Yes, always have been."

"With success?"

Prokop gave a strange kind of laugh. "You'd like to know, eh? No, my
friend, it won't do that way…not that way," he repeated, swaying his head in
a drunken manner. "My friend, by itself—by itself—it…"

"What?"

"Kra-ka-tit. Krakatit. Krrakatitt. And by itself—I only left a little powder on the table, see? All the rest I c-c-collected in a snuffbox. There was only a l-l-little powder left on the table, and suddenly…"

"It exploded."

"Exploded. Only a trace, only the powder that I had dropped. It was hardly visible. Then the electric light globe—a kilometre away. It wasn't near that. And I—in the armchair, like a bit of wood. Tired, you know. Too much work. And suddenly…*crash!* I was thrown on to the floor. The window was blown out, and the globe wasn't there. A detonation like—the explosion of a lyddite cartridge. Terrible energy. I… I thought at first that it was the por-porcel-por-ce-lain, polcelain, porcelene…the white insulator, you know, that had exploded. Aluminium silicate."

"Porcelain."

"Snuffbox. I thought it had exploded. So I strike a match and there it is unharmed, unharmed, unharmed. And I stay there like a post…until the match burns my fingers. And then—across country—in the dark to Brevnov or Střešovice—and somewhere on the way the word Krakatoe, Krakatit came into my head. Kra-ka-tit. No, no, it wasn't l-l-like that. When it went up, I fell on the floor and shouted out, 'Krakatit. Krakatit.' Then I forgot it. Who's that there? Who—who are you?"

"Thomas."

"Thomas, aha! That lousy fellow! We used to lend one another our notes. He never gave me back a chemistry notebook. Thomas, what was his first name?"

"George."

"I know now, George. You're George, I know. George Thomas. Where's my notebook? Wait a moment and I'll tell you something. If the rest goes up there'll be trouble. Man, it'll flatten out the whole of Prague. Wipe it away. Blow it off the Earth—ffft! When that por-ce-lain box explodes, see?"

"What box?"

"You are George Thomas, I know. Go to Karlin or to Vysocany and watch it explode. Run, run!"

"Why?"

"I made a hundred-weight of it. A hundred-weight of Krakatit. No, about three ounces. Up there, in that porcelain box. When it explodes, man—but wait a minute, that's impossible. It's senseless," mumbled Prokop, clutching his head.

"Well?"

"Why—why—why didn't it explode also in the box? If the powder exploded by itself—wait a moment, on the table there's a sheet of zinc—why did it explode on the table? Wait, be quiet, be quiet," said Prokop. His teeth chattered, and he rose up unsteadily.

"What's up with you?"

"Krakatit," muttered Prokop. He made a twisting movement with his whole body and fell on the ground unconscious.

CHAPTER II

The first thing of which Prokop was conscious was that everything in him was being shaken and rattled and that someone was holding him firmly round the waist. He had a terrible fear of opening his eyes; he had an idea that everything would collapse on top of him. And when this didn't happen, he opened them and saw in front of him a vague square about which were moving misty balls and strips of light. He was unable to explain it; confusedly he watched the phantom shapes as they jumped about and slid away, having patiently resigned himself to anything which might be in store for him. Then he realized that the rattling was that of the wheels of a cab and that outside lights were slipping past in the fog. Exhausted by this act of observation he again closed his eyes and allowed himself to be carried away.

"Now lie down," said a quiet voice above his head; "swallow an aspirin and you'll be better. In the morning I'll fetch a doctor, yes?"

"Who's that?" asked Prokop sleepily.

"Thomas. You're lying down at my place, Prokop. You've a fever. Where does it hurt you?"

"Everywhere. I feel giddy. So, you see…"

"Just lie quiet. I'll boil you some tea and you'll go off to sleep. It's the result of excitement, see? A sort of nervous fever. It'll be gone before morning."

Prokop knitted his brows in the effort to remember. "I know," he said carefully, after a moment. "Listen, someone must throw that box into the river. So that it won't explode."

"Don't worry. Now stop talking."

"Perhaps I could sit up. Aren't I heavy?"

"No, lie down."

"—and you've got my chemistry notebook," Prokop remembered suddenly.

"Yes, you'll get it back. But now stay quiet, do you hear?"

"My head's so heavy."

Meanwhile, the cab was rattling up Ječná Street. Thomas was softly whistling a tune and looking out of the window. Prokop was breathing heavily and moaning quietly. The fog made the pavements damp and insinuated itself under one's coat with its cold, wet slime. It was late and the streets were deserted.

"Here we are," said Thomas loudly. The cab bumped more noisily over a square and turned off to the right. "Wait, Prokop, can you manage a couple of steps? I'll help you."

With an effort Thomas dragged his guest up to the second floor. Prokop seemed to himself to be without weight, and allowed himself to be quickly wafted up the stairs; but Thomas was breathing heavily and wiped the sweat from his forehead.

"See, I'm like a thread," said Prokop, surprised.

"Well," said Thomas, panting, and opened the door of his flat.

Prokop felt like a little child while Thomas was undressing him. "My mother," he began, "when my mother, ever so long ago…father sat at the table, and mother carried me to bed, see?"

Then he was in bed, covered up to the chin, his teeth chattering and watching Thomas rapidly making a fire. He could have cried from self-pity and weakness, and he babbled the whole time; then a cold compress was placed on his forehead and he quieted down. He looked about the room; there was a scent of tobacco and women.

"You're a rogue, Thomas," he exclaimed seriously, "always having women."

Thomas turned round. "Well?"

"Nothing. What exactly are you doing just now?"

Thomas gestured in despair. "It's bad, my friend. No money."

"You womanize."

Thomas only shook his head.

"And it's a pity, you know," began Prokop, with concern. "You could have—look, I've been at it for twelve years."

"And what have you got out of it?" retorted Thomas sharply.

"Well, something here and there. I sold some explosive dextrine this year."

"For how much?"

"For ten thousand. But that's nothing. Rubbish. Only an explosive for mines. But if I had wished to…"

"Do you feel better now?"

"Fine. I've found out some methods for you! Nitrate of cerium, there's an excitable monster for you, man; and chloride, chloride, tetrachloride of nitrogen, that's exploded by light. You turn on the light, and bang! But that's nothing. Listen," he exclaimed, suddenly sticking his thin, terribly mutilated hand out of the bedclothes, "when I take anything in my hand, so…I feel the vibration of the atoms. Just like ants. Each kind of substance creeps differently, see?"

"No."

"That's power, see? Power in matter. Matter is terribly powerful. I... I feel it moving. It holds together…with an enormous effort. Once you loosen it inside, it disintegrates. Bang! Everything is an explosive. Every thought is a sort of explosion inside the head. When you give me your hand I feel as if something is exploding inside you. I've an extraordinary touch, man. And hearing. Everything is bubbling like effervescent powder. Tiny explosions again. There's a noise going on in my head.…Ratata, like a machine gun."

"Yes?" said Thomas. "And now swallow this aspirin."

"Yes. Ex-explosive aspirin. Perchlorated acteylsalic acid. That's nothing. Man, I've discovered an exothermic explosive. Water. Water is an explosive. Every material is really an explosive. The feathers in a feather bed are explosives. At present, you see, this has only a theoretical significance. And I've discovered atomic explosions. I—I—I—I've made alpha explosions. It disintegrates into plus electrons. No thermochemistry. Des-truc-tion. Destructive chemistry, man. That's a tremendous thing, Thomas, purely scientific. At home I've got tables.… If only I had apparatus! But I've only eyes…and hands.… Wait, let me write it down!"

"Don't you want to sleep?"

"I do. Today—I'm—tired. And what have you been doing all this time?"

"Nothing. Life."

"Life is an explosive, see? Bang, and a man is born and then, bang, he falls to pieces. And we think it lasts some years, see? Wait a moment, I've got something mixed, haven't I?"

"It's all right, Prokop. Tomorrow, perhaps, we'll make an explosion. That is, if I haven't any money. But it's all the same, just go to sleep."

"I'll lend it to you, if you like."

"No, thanks, it wouldn't be enough. Perhaps my father—" Thomas waved his arm.

"So you've still got a father," said Prokop after a moment with sudden gentleness.

"Well, yes. A doctor in Tynice." Thomas stood up and began to walk up and down the room. "I'm up against it. But don't worry about me. I—I'll do something. Sleep!"

Prokop quieted down. Through his half closed eyes, he watched Thomas sit down at the table and rummage among some papers. It was somehow delicious to listen to the rustling of paper and the quiet noise of the fire in the stove. The man bent forward over the table, supported his head with his hand and, it seemed, was hardly breathing; and to Prokop it was as if he was at home and looking at his elder brother, Joseph, studying electrical engineering in preparation for the examination the next day. He fell into a feverish sleep.

CHAPTER III

He dreamed that he heard a noise made by innumerable wheels. "It's some factory or other," he thought and ran up the steps. All at once he found himself standing in front of a large door, on which was a glass plate with the name: Plinius. Inordinately delighted, he went in. "Is Mr. Plinius in?" he asked of a girl sitting at a typewriter. "He'll be here in a moment," she answered, and directly afterward there appeared a tall, clean-shaven man with enormous circular spectacles. "What can I do for you?" he asked.

Prokop glanced inquiringly at his extraordinarily expressive face. His mouth was of the British variety, his forehead was covered with lines and had a wart the size of a sixpence, his chin was that of a cinema artist. "Are y-y-you Mr. Plinius?"

"Please," said the tall man, and with an abrupt gesture, he indicated the way to his study.

"I am extremely... It's a great honour for me," stammered Prokop, taking a seat.

"What is it you want?" the tall man interrupted him.

"I've disintegrated matter," announced Prokop.

Plinius remained silent; he only played with a steel key and, behind his spectacles, closed his heavy lids.

"It's like this," began Prokop impetuously. "E-e-everything is disintegrating, you understand? Matter is fragile. But I can make it disintegrate all at once, *bang!* An explosion, if you comprehend me? Into smithereens. Into molecules. Into atoms. And I've also broken up atoms."

"A pity," said Plinius after consideration.

"Why a pity?"

"It's a pity to break anything. Even an atom. Well, go on."

"I...break up the atom. I am aware that Rutherford has already... But that was only donkey work with radiation, you know. That's nothing. The thing must be done *en masse*. If I were asked to, I could explode a ton of bismuth in that way. It would blow up the whole world. Would you like me to?"

"Why would you do it?"

"It's...scientifically interesting," said Prokop, confused. "Wait, how shall I... It's amazingly interesting." He clutched his head. "One moment, my he-he-head's splitting; it will be scientifically enormously interesting, eh?

Aha!" he burst out, relieved. "Now I can explain. Dynamite—dynamite smashes up matter into pieces, lumps, but benzoltriozonide reduces it to dust; it makes only a small hole, but it disintegrates matter into submicroscopic fragments, see? That's through the quickness of the explosion. Matter hasn't time to get out of the way, it can't even b-b-break up, see? But I... I've accelerated the speed of detonation. Argonozonid. Chlorargonozonide. Tetrargon. And so on and on. And suddenly, after a certain speed, the power of explosion increases terribly. It increases...quadratically. I watch it as if I were an idiot."

"Where does it come from, this energy?" demanded Prokop feverishly. "Tell me."

"Well, perhaps from the atom," suggested Plinius.

"Aha," cried Prokop exultantly, and he wiped the sweat away from his face. "That's the amusing part of it. Simply from the atom. It throws the atoms together...and t-t-t-tears off the Beta layer...and the core disintegrates. It's an Alpha explosion. Do you realize who I am? I am the first man, sir, who has overcome the coefficient of compressibility. I... I have extracted tantalum from bismuth. Listen, do you know the amount of power there is in one gramme of mercury? Four hundred and sixty-two millions of kilogramometres. Matter is frightfully powerful. Matter is a regiment which is marching without moving: one two, one two; but give it the right order and the regiment will attack. *En avant!* That's the explosion, you understand? Hurrah!"

Prokop was pulled up by his own exclamation. The beating in his head was so loud that he ceased to understand anything.

"Excuse me," he said, in order to cover his confusion, and with a shaking hand felt for his cigar case. "You smoke?"

"No."

"Even the ancient Romans used to smoke," Prokop assured him and opened his case. Inside was nothing but some heavy fuses.

"Light up," he urged, "this one's a small Nobel Extra." He himself bit off the end of a tetryl cartridge and looked round for matches. "Never mind," he said, "but have you ever heard of explosive glass? A pity. Listen, I can make you explosive paper. You write a letter, someone throws it into the fire, and *crash!* The whole of the place collapses. Would you like that?"

"What for?" asked Plinius, raising his eyebrows.

"Well, I don't know. Power must out. I'll tell you something. If you were to walk on the ceiling, what would happen to you? To begin with, I have no use for the theory of valency. Everything is possible. Listen, you hear that noise outside? That's the grass growing; nothing but little explosions. Every seed is an explosive cartridge which goes off. *Poof,* like a rocket. And those fools think that there is no such thing as tautomerism. I'll show them such merotropy that they'll go off their heads. Pure laboratory experience, my dear sir."

Prokop suddenly had a dreadful feeling that he was babbling nonsense. He tried to extricate himself from his position, but only jabbered all the more quickly, mixing everything up. Plinius nodded his head seriously and finally inclined his body forward more and more, as if he were bowing. Prokop gabbled confused formulae, unable to stop himself, his eyes fixed on Plinius who was swinging backwards and forwards with increasing speed, like a machine. The floor began to move and lift under him.

"But stop it, man," roared Prokop, terrified, and woke up.

Instead of Plinius, he saw Thomas, who grunted, "Don't shout, please," without turning round from the table.

"I'm not shouting," said Prokop, and he closed his eyes. Inside his head, the blows had become faster and more painful.

It appeared that he was moving with the minimum velocity of light; in some way his heart was compressed. But that was only the Fitzgerald-Lorentz contraction, he explained to himself; soon he would become as flat as a pancake. And suddenly there appeared in front of him countless glass prisms; no, they were only endless, highly polished planes which intersected at sharp angles like models of crystals. He was thrown against the edge of one of them with terrible speed. "Look out!" he shouted to himself, for in a thousandth of a second he would be smashed to pieces; but at that moment he flew at an enormous speed towards the apex of a huge pyramid. Thrown back from this like a beam of light, he was cast against a wall as smooth as glass, slid along it, whizzed madly along walls set at angles, was hurled back against he knew not what. Cast away again he was falling on to a sharp angle, but at the last moment was thrown upwards again. Now he struck his head on a Euclidean plane and now fell headlong downwards, downwards into darkness. A sudden blow, a painful shuddering of his whole body, but he immediately picked himself up and took to flight. He tore along a labyrinthine passage and heard behind him the noise made by his pursuers; the passage became narrower and narrower, its walls came together with a frightful and inevitable movement; he became as thin as an awl, held his breath and dashed along in horror, so as to escape before the walls crushed him. They crashed behind him with a stony impact, while he whirled into a chasm. A frightful blow, and he lost consciousness. When he awoke he was in black darkness; he groped along the slimy stone walls and cried for help, but no sound came from his lips. Such was the darkness.

Shivering with fear, he stumbled about the bottom of the pit. He came upon a path along the side and followed it. Actually it consisted of steps, and above, an incredible distance away, there gleamed a tiny opening, as in a mine. Then he ran up endless and terribly steep stairs; but at the top there was nothing but a platform, a light metal platform which trembled above the dizzy abyss, and downwards there descended endless spiral steps of iron plates. And again he heard behind him the panting breath of his pursuers. Beside himself with fear he dashed down the twisting stairs, and behind him the steps of his enemies clanged upon the iron. Suddenly, the spiral steps ended sharply in a void. Prokop shrieked, extended his arms and, still turning, fell into the gulf. His head spun, he saw and heard nothing; with legs that seemed to be bound he ran he knew not whither, dominated by a blind and terrible impulse to reach some place before it was too late. He ran more and more quickly along an endless vaulted corridor; from time to time the number changed on a semaphore, and always higher: 17, 18, 19. Suddenly, he realized that he was running in a circle and that the numbers represented the circuits he had made. 40, 41! He was seized with the intolerable fear that he would never get away; he whizzed round at an insane speed, so that the semaphore moved like telegraph poles seen from an express train; and still more rapidly! Now the semaphore ceased to move and recorded at a lightning speed thousands and tens of thousands of revolutions, and still there was no exit from this tunnel, and the tunnel was smooth and polished and, as well, was itself rotating. Prokop sobbed with fear. This was Einstein's universe and he must get there before it was too late! Suddenly, there resounded a frightful cry. Prokop was aghast; it was the voice of his father, whom somebody was murdering. He tried to run still more quickly, the semaphore disappeared and everything was dark. Prokop felt along the walls and discovered a closed door, and behind it he again heard desperate wails and the noise of furniture being thrown about. Crying out with horror, he dug his nails into the door, scratched it and tore it into pieces, to find behind it the familiar stairs which led him every day to his room when he was little. And upstairs his father was being suffocated, someone was strangling him and dragging him along the floor. Prokop flew upstairs, saw the familiar pail, his mother's breadbox, and the half opened door into the kitchen, and there, inside, his father was making a rattling noise in his throat and begging someone not to kill him. Prokop wished to go to his aid, but some blind, mad force obliged him again to run in a circle, faster and faster, laughing convulsively, while the wailing of his father slowly died away. Incapable of escaping from this dizzy, senseless circle, he suddenly burst into a laugh of horror.

He woke up, covered with sweat, his teeth chattering. Thomas was standing over him in the act of laying another cold compress on his burning forehead.

"That's good, that's good," mumbled Prokop, "now I shan't sleep any more." And he lay quietly and watched Thomas sitting near the lamp. George Thomas, he said to himself, and then Duras, and Honza Buchta, Sudik, Sudik, Sudik, and who else? Sudik, Trlica, Trlica, Pesek, Jovanovic, Madr,

Holoubek, who wears spectacles, that was our year at chemistry. God, and who's the other? Aha, Vedral, who was killed in 'sixteen, and behind him there sat Holoubek, Pacovsky, Trlica, Seba, all the men of the year. Then he suddenly heard the words: "Mr. Prokop to be examined."

He became terribly frightened. At the desk sat Professor Wald, pulling with a dry hand at his beard, as usual. "Let's hear," said Professor Wald, "what you know about explosives."

"Explosives, explosives," began Prokop nervously, "their explosiveness lies in the fact that—that—that—that a large volume of gas is suddenly liberated which—which expands from the much smaller volume of the explosive mass… I beg your pardon, that's not right."

"What?" asked Wald severely.

"I—I—I've discovered *alpha* explosives. The explosion takes place, that is to say, through the disintegration of the atom. The parts of the atom fly… fly."

"Rubbish," the professor interrupted him. "There are no such things as atoms."

"There are, there are, there are," said Prokop through his teeth. "Please, I'll demonstrate to you…"

"An obsolete theory," said the professor gruffly. "There are no such things as atoms, only gumetals. Do you know what a gumetal is?"

Prokop sweated with fear. He had never heard the word in his life. Gumetal?

"I don't know," he said in confusion.

"There you are," said Wald dryly. "And yet you presume to offer yourself for examination. What do you know about Krakatit?"

Prokop stopped uneasily. "Krakatit," he whispered, "that is…that is…a completely new explosive, which…which up to the present…"

"How is it ignited? How? How does it explode?"

"By Hertzian waves," croaked Prokop with relief.

"How do you know?"

"Because the Krakatit which I prepared exploded for no reason at all. Because…because there was no other reason. And because…"

"Well?"

"…I synthesized it…du-du-during high-frequency oscillation. This isn't yet explained, but I think that…that there were some sort of electromagnetic waves."

"There were. I know. Now write down the chemical formula for Krakatit."

Prokop took up a piece of chalk and scribbled his formula on the board.

"Read it."

Prokop read the formula aloud. Then Professor Wald stood up and suddenly said in a voice which was somehow completely different: "How does it run?"

Prokop repeated the formula.

"Tetrargon?" inquired the professor rapidly. "How much Pb?"

"Two."

"How is it prepared?" inquired the voice, this time extraordinarily close. "The method! How is it prepared? How? How do you prepare Krakatit?"

Prokop opened his eyes. Thomas was bending over him with a pencil and notebook in his hand and breathlessly watching his lips.

"What?" mumbled Prokop uneasily. "What do you want? How...is it prepared?"

"You've got some strange idea into your head," said Thomas and hid the notebook behind his back. "Sleep, man, sleep."

CHAPTER IV

"Now I've blurted something out!" Prokop realized with the fragment of his brain that was most clear; but otherwise he was completely indifferent on the subject; all he wanted was to sleep, to sleep inordinately. He saw in front of him a sort of Turkey carpet, the pattern of which continually changed. It was nothing important and yet it somehow agitated him. Even in sleep he yearned to meet Plinius again. He tried to rid himself of his image; instead, he saw before him an abominable grinning face, which ground its yellow, rotten teeth until they were crushed, and then spat them out in pieces. He wanted to get away from this picture. The word "fisherman" came into his head, and *presto* there appeared to him a fisherman sitting above some grey water with a net full of fish. He said to himself "scaffolding," and he actually perceived scaffolding to the last hook and rope. For a long time he amused himself by thinking of words and looking at the pictures which they called up; but then not even by exerting all his powers could he recall a single one. He made the most strenuous efforts to remember at least one word or thing, but in vain; and then through the horror of impotence he came out in a cold sweat. He decided that he must go to work methodically; he must begin from the beginning or he was lost. Luckily he remembered the word "fisherman"; but now there appeared before his eyes an empty petroleum tin. It was horrible. He said to himself "chair," and he saw with astonishing clearness the tarred fence of a factory with a patch of dreary, dusty grass and some rusty hoops. This is insanity, he said to himself with cold clearness; this, gentleman, is typical madness, hyperofabula ugongi dugongi Darwin. This technical term for some unknown reason appeared to him to be excruciatingly funny. He positively gulped with laughter and woke up.

He was covered with sweat and had kicked off his bedclothes. With feverish eyes he watched Thomas, who was moving quickly about the room and throwing a few things into a suitcase; but he did not recognize him. "Listen, listen," he began, "here's a funny thing, listen, wait a moment, you must listen—" He wanted to tell him as a great joke this extraordinary technical designation, and was already smiling in anticipation; but for the life of him he was unable to recall how exactly it had run. He became annoyed and was silent.

Thomas put on an ulster and a cap; but when he had already picked up the suitcase he hesitated and sat down on the end of Prokop's bed. "Listen, old chap," he said with concern, "I've got to go away now. To my father, in Tynice. If he doesn't give me any money I shan't come back, see? But don't be worried about that. The doorkeeper's wife will come in the morning and bring you a doctor, yes?"

"What's the time?" asked Prokop indifferently.

"Four. Five past four. Perhaps... There's nothing you want, is there?"

Prokop closed his eyes, resolved to take no further interest in anything in the world. Thomas covered him up carefully and all became quiet.

Suddenly, he opened his eyes again fully. Above him he perceived an unfamiliar ceiling round the edge of which there ran an ornament which he had not seen before. He stretched out his hand for the table at his bedside, but groped in the air. Frightened, he turned round and saw, in the place of his laboratory desk, some sort of table with a small lamp. Where there used to be a window there was a screen; in the place of the washstand some door or other. This confused him enormously; he could not understand what was happening to him, or where he was. Conquering his giddiness, he sat up in bed. Slowly he realized that he was not at home, but could not remember how he got to be where he was. "Who is that?" he asked aloud on chance, controlling his tongue with difficulty. "Drink," he said, after a moment, "drink." It was painfully quiet. He got out of bed and, a little unsteadily, started to look for water. On the washstand he found a carafe and drank from it greedily; but when he was returning to the bed his legs gave way and he sank into a chair, unable to do any more. He sat there for a good hour, perhaps; then he began to shiver with cold, and became overwhelmed with self-pity, thinking that he was in some strange place, that he was not capable of even reaching the bed, and that he was alone, helpless, and without anyone to give him counsel. Suddenly, he began to cry convulsively like a child.

When he had cried in this way for a bit his head became clearer. At last he was able to get to the bed and lie down with his teeth chattering; no sooner had he got some warmth into his body than he went off into a deep, swoon-like, dreamless sleep.

When he woke up the grey light of day was coming through the window; someone had pulled up the blind and created a certain amount of order in the room. He was unable to comprehend who had done this; but, on the other hand, he remembered the explosion of the day before, Thomas, and his departure. His head was splitting, he felt a weight on his chest, and he was tortured by a tearing cough. That's bad, he said to himself, that's really bad; I ought to have gone home and gone to bed there. He got up and began to dress himself with long pauses. He felt as if something was exercising a horrible pressure on his chest. Then he sat down, indifferent to everything and breathing heavily.

Suddenly, the bell rang briefly and lightly. With an effort he remembered himself and went to open the door. Outside was standing a young girl with a veil over her face.

"Does…Mr. Thomas live here?" she asked rapidly and confusedly.

"Please," said Prokop and made way for her. When, hesitating a little, she had passed close by him into the room, he became conscious of a faint and elegant perfume which he inhaled with delight.

He gave her a seat by the window and sat down opposite her, holding himself as straight as he was able to. He felt that through this very effort he must appear to be severe and frozen, which embarrassed both the girl and himself exceedingly. Behind her veil she bit her lip and cast down her eyes; oh, the delicious smoothness of her face, oh, what small hands and how extraordinarily excited! Suddenly, she raised her eyes and Prokop held his breath with ecstasy, so beautiful did she seem to him.

"Mr. Thomas isn't at home?" asked the girl.

"Thomas has gone away," said Prokop, with some hesitation. "Last night."

"Where?"

"To Tynice, to his father."

"And he will return?"

Prokop shrugged his shoulders.

The girl bent her head down, her hands pulling at something. "And did he tell you why…why?"

"He did."

"And you think that…that he will do it?"

"What?"

"That he will shoot himself."

In a flash, Prokop remembered that he had seen Thomas put a revolver into his suitcase. "Tomorrow, perhaps, we'll make an explosion," he again heard him mutter through his teeth. He did not wish to say anything. He looked very serious.

"Oh my God!" said the girl, "but this is terrible. Tell me…"

"What?"

"If only somebody could follow him! If only somebody could say— could give him—you understand, don't you, that he mustn't do it! If only somebody could go after him today—"

Prokop looked at her hands which were twisting desperately.

"I will go there for you," he said quietly. "As it happens I've got to go somewhere in that direction. If you wish it I—"

The girl raised her head. "Could you really?" she cried joyfully, "could you…?"

"I'm an old…colleague of his, you see," explained Prokop. "If you would like to send him a message…or send… I would willingly…"

"You are really very good," breathed the girl.

Prokop reddened a little. "That's nothing," he defended himself. "As it happens…I've some free time… I should like to go away somewhere and also, generally speaking—" He waved his hand in embarrassment. "It's not worth talking about. I will do anything that you wish."

The girl blushed and looked quickly in another direction. "I really don't…know how to thank you," she said in confusion. "I am really very sorry that…you…. But it is so important—you're his friend. Don't you think perhaps that I myself—" Then she got control of herself and turned her clear eyes on Prokop. "I must send him something. From somebody else. I cannot tell you."

"There is no need to," said Prokop quickly. "I shall give it to him and that's all there is about it. I am so glad that I am able…that I can help him…. Is it raining then?" he asked suddenly, looking at the drops of moisture on her fur.

"Yes, it is."

"That's good," said Prokop. He was actually thinking how pleasantly cool it would be if he could put his forehead against the fur.

"I haven't got it with me," she said, standing up. "It will only be a small parcel. If you could wait… I'll bring it you in two hours' time."

Prokop bowed; and in doing so he was afraid of losing his equilibrium. In the doorway she turned round and gave him a direct look. "*Au revoir.*" She was gone.

Prokop sat down and closed his eyes. The drops of rain on the fur; a thick and bedewed veil; a curiously distant voice; scent; uneasy hands in small tight gloves; a clear and disturbing glance from beneath firm, elegant eyebrows; her hands on her lap; the soft folds of her dress over her strong knees. Oh, little hands in tight gloves! Scent, a dark and vibrant voice, a smooth, pale face. Prokop dug his teeth into his quivering lips, sad, and confused and brave. Blue-grey eyes, eyes clean and full of light. Oh God, how her veil pressed against her lips!

Prokop groaned and opened his eyes. "And she's Thomas's girl," he said to himself, with blind fury. "She knew the way; it wasn't the first time she had been there. Perhaps here…here in this very room…" Prokop dug his nails into his palms in intolerable agony. "And I, like a fool, suggest that I shall go after him! I, idiot that I am, am to take him a letter! What…have I to do with her?"

Then he had a saving thought. I will dash off home to my laboratory at the top of the house—and she—let her come here! Let her do what she wants to! Let…her go after him herself, if…it's so important to her—

He looked round the room; he saw the tumbled bed and straightened it a little as he was accustomed to at home. Then it seemed to him that it was not tidy enough, so he did it again, smoothed it and then set about cleaning up the whole place, even trying to arrange the curtains in nice folds. After which he sat down with a dizzy head and a chest which was thumping painfully, and waited.

CHAPTER V

It seemed to him that he was walking about in an enormous kitchen garden. All around was nothing but cabbage heads, not simply heads, but heads which grinned and were slimy from the creatures which had crawled over them; gibbering heads, blear-eyed, monstrous, watery, pimpled and swollen. They were growing on cabbage stumps, and creeping over them were repulsive green caterpillars. And now across the garden there ran towards him the girl with the veil over her face. She raised her skirts a little and jumped over the heads. But under each of them there suddenly sprouted bare, horribly thin and hairy hands, which clutched at her feet and her skirts. The girl screamed in fear, and raised her skirts still higher, above her strong knees, showing her white legs, and tried to spring out of the way of these grasping tentacles. Prokop closed his eyes; he could not bear the sight of her white strong legs and was nearly mad with dread lest those green heads should defile her. He cast himself on the ground and chopped off the first head with his clasp-knife. It squeaked like an animal and snapped at his hand with its rotten teeth. Now the second and the third head. Christ! Would he be able to mow the enormous field before the girl reached the other end? Springing madly about, he trampled them down and kicked them; his feet became entangled in their thin suckerlike claws, he fell, was seized, torn and suffocated. Then everything disappeared.

Everything disappeared in whirling confusion. And suddenly he heard quite near the veiled voice: "I have brought you the parcel." He sprang up and opened his eyes, and before him stood the girl from Hybsmonka, squint-eyed and pregnant, her stomach damp, and gave him something wrapped up in a damp rag. "It's not her!" groaned Prokop painfully, and suddenly he saw before him the tall, dreary saleswoman who used to stretch his gloves for him on wooden sticks. "It's not her!" Prokop repeated, and there appeared before him a puffy child on legs bent with rickets who…who shamelessly offered herself to him! "Go away," cried Prokop, and then he saw an overturned can in the middle of a dried-up lawn and some cabbages covered all over with the traces of snails, and this picture would not disappear in spite of all his efforts to banish it.

At that moment the bell rang quietly, with a noise like the piping of a bird. Prokop dashed to the door and opened it. In the passage was standing the girl with the veil, pressing the parcel to her breast and panting for breath. "So it's you," said Prokop gently and, without knowing why, was profoundly touched. The girl came in, brushing him with her shoulder as she went past. Her scent moved Prokop painfully.

She remained standing in the middle of the room. "Don't be angry, please," she said quietly and somehow hastily, "that I have given you such a commission. You see you have no idea why…why I—if it's really causing you any trouble—"

"I will go," said Prokop in a hoarse voice.

The girl turned her clear serious eyes on him. "Don't think anything bad of me. I am only afraid that Mr.…that your friend may do something which would drive a certain person to death. I have so much confidence in you…. You will save him, won't you?"

"I shall be ever so glad to," said Prokop softly in an uncertain voice which was not his own; to such an extent was he overcome with excitement. "I…what you wish.…" He turned his eyes away; he was afraid that he would blurt something out, that perhaps she would hear the loud beating of his heart. He was ashamed of his uncouthness.

And the girl also was infected by his confusion; she blushed terribly and did not know what to do with her eyes. "Thank you, thank you," she tried to say in a voice which was also somehow uncertain, and she gripped the sealed packet which she held in her hand. There was a silence, a silence which induced in Prokop a sweet and painful dizziness. He felt feverishly that the girl was watching his face askance; and when he suddenly turned his eyes on her he saw that she was looking down on the ground, waiting till she was able to endure his look. Prokop felt that there was something which he ought to say to save the situation; instead he only moved his lips uneasily and trembled with his whole body.

Finally, the girl touched his hand and whispered, "That parce—" Then Prokop forgot why he was holding his right hand behind his back and reached out for the large parcel. The girl turned pale and recoiled. "You are wounded," she burst out. "Show me!" Prokop hastily hid his hand again. "It's nothing," he assured her quickly; "I just got a slight…slight wound."

The girl, quite pale, drew in her breath sharply as if she herself felt the pain. "Why don't you go to a doctor?" she said abruptly. "You mustn't travel anywhere! I… I will send somebody else!"

"It's healing already," said Prokop, as if something precious were being taken away from him. "Really it's almost…right again, only a scratch, and anyway what nonsense! Why shouldn't I go? And then, in such matters…you can't very well send a stranger. Really it doesn't even pain me—look!" And he shook his right hand.

The girl made a movement of sympathy which was yet severe. "You mustn't go! Why didn't you tell me? I....don't allow it! I don't want—"

Prokop became extremely unhappy. "Look here," he said hotly, "it really is nothing; I am used to such things. Look here," and he showed her his left hand, almost the whole of the little finger of which was missing, while another had a twisted scar on the joint. "That's the sort of occupation I have, you see?" He did not even notice that the girl shrank away from him with pale lips and was looking at a deep scar on his forehead stretching from the eyes to the hair. "There's an explosion and there you are. Like a soldier, I get up and run off as fast as I can, you understand? Nothing can happen to me now. Give it to me!" He took the parcel out of her hand, threw it into the air and caught it again. "No need for anxiety. I'll go like a gentleman. Do you know, it's a long time since I have been anywhere. Do you know America?"

The girl remained silent and watched him with a pained expression.

"It's all very well for them to say that they have new theories," muttered Prokop feverishly through his teeth, "but wait; I'll show them something when I have finished my calculations. It's a pity that you don't understand that sort of thing; I could explain it to you. I trust you, I trust you but not him. Don't trust him," he said earnestly, "take care. You are so beautiful," he breathed enthusiastically.

"Up there I never speak to anybody. Only a sort of hut made of planks, you understand? Ha ha! How frightened you were of those heads! But I won't give you up! Don't be frightened of anything! I won't give you up."

She looked at him with eyes distended with horror. "But you simply must not go!"

Prokop grew dispirited and became suddenly weak. "No, you mustn't take any notice of what I'm saying. I've been talking nonsense, haven't I? I simply wanted you not to think about that hand. So that you shouldn't be frightened. It's all over now." He got control of himself again and became stiff and almost sulky through his very concentration. "I shall go to Tynice and find Thomas. I shall give him the parcel and say that it comes from a young lady whom he knows. Is that right?"

"Yes," said the girl with some hesitation, "but really you must not—"

Prokop tried to muster a supplicatory smile. His heavy scared face suddenly grew beautiful. "Leave it to me," he said quietly, "it's...for you."

The girl blinked her eyes; a sharp feeling had suddenly driven her nearly to tears. She inclined her head silently and gave him her hand. He raised his shapeless left hand. She looked at him interrogatively and pressed it warmly. "Thank you so much," she said quickly. "Good-bye!"

In the doorway she stopped as if she wished to say something. Twisting the handle, she waited.

"Am I to…to convey any greeting to him?" asked Prokop with a wry smile.

"No," she said quietly and gave him a quick glance. "*Au revoir.*"

The door closed behind her. Prokop looked after her and suddenly he felt mortally heavy and weak, his head began to swim, and it cost him an immense effort to take a single step.

CHAPTER VI

At the station he had to wait an hour and a half. He sat down in the corridor shivering with cold. His wounded hand pulsated painfully. He closed his eyes and immediately it seemed to him that this aching hand was growing, that it was as big as a head, as a gourd, as a cauldron, and that all over it the flesh was twitching feverishly. At the same time he felt oppressively faint and a cold sweat kept on breaking out on his forehead. He did not dare to look at the dirty, muddy floor covered with spittle—his stomach would have risen. He tore off his collar and fell half asleep, gradually overpowered by an infinite indifference. He had the impression that he was a soldier, lying wounded in the open field; where…where are they fighting all the time? Then there sounded in his ears a loud ringing, and someone shouted… "Tynice… Duchcov… Moldava! Take your seats!"

Now he was sitting in the railway carriage next to the window and feeling inordinately gay, as if he had got the better of somebody or had escaped from them; yes, now he was on the way to Tynice and nothing could stop him. Almost giggling with delight he settled down in his corner and began to observe his fellow-travellers with amazing eagerness. In front of him sat some sort of a tailor with a thin neck, a slight dark woman, and then a man with an extraordinarily expressionless face; next to Prokop was a terribly fat gentleman whose stomach could not settle down between his legs, and, further away, somebody else, but that didn't matter. Prokop did not dare to look out of the window—it made him feel giddy.

Ra-ta-ta-ra-ta-ta the train thumped out, vibrating and rattling with the feverishness of its movement. The head of the tailor swung to the right, to the left, to the right, to the left; the dark lady in some curious fashion bounced stiffly up and down on the same spot, the expressionless face vibrated and jerked like a bad film in a cinema. And his fat neighbour was simply a heap of jelly which jumped, shook and hopped in the most extraordinarily entertaining manner. *Tynice, Tynice, Tynice,* scanned Prokop to the beat of the wheels; faster, faster! The train grew heated through its haste; it became warm in the carriage, and Prokop began to sweat; the tailor had now two heads on two thin necks; both heads shook and knocked against one another until they rattled. The dark lady jumped up and down on her seat in the most amusing and yet offensive way; she deliberately put on the expression of a wooden doll. The expressionless face disappeared; in its place there sat a body with its arms folded in a dead manner on its lap. The hands jumped about, but the body had no head.

Prokop exerted all his strength in order to see it properly. He pinched his leg, but it was no use; the body remained headless and lifelessly responded to the vibration of the train. Prokop became horribly uncomfortable. He nudged his fat neighbour with his arm; but the neighbour only quivered still more like a jelly. It seemed to Prokop that the fat body was voicelessly tittering at him. He was unable to look at it any longer; he turned to the window, but there, out of the void, appeared a human face. At first he could not make out why it disconcerted him so; he stared at it with wide-open eyes to realize finally that it was another Prokop whose eyes were fixed on him with terrible earnestness.

"What does he want?" said Prokop, terror-stricken. "My God! Have I left that parcel in Thomas's room?" He hastily went through his pockets and found the parcel in the inside one of his coat. Then the face in the window smiled, and Prokop felt better. Finally, he plucked up courage to look at the headless body and saw that all that had happened was that the man had pulled over his face a coat that was hanging from the rack and was asleep behind it. Prokop would have done the same but was afraid that someone would take the sealed package out of his pocket. And yet it was important for him to sleep. He was intolerably tired; he would never have been able to imagine that it was possible for him to be so tired.

He dropped off, awoke with a start, and dropped off again. The dark lady had one head bobbing on her shoulder and held the other in her lap with both hands; and as for the tailor, instead of him there were sitting empty, bodiless clothes, out of the top of which projected a porcelain pestle. Prokop fell asleep but suddenly started up with a feverish conviction that they were already in Tynice. Somebody outside had shouted the name out, or the train had stopped.

He rushed out and saw that it was already evening; two or three people were getting out at a tiny station with blinking lights behind which was an unknown and foggy darkness. They told Prokop that he could only get to Tynice by a postwagon, if there was still room in it. The postwagon proved to consist of a coachbox behind which was a trough for packages, and the postman and some passenger or other had already taken their seats.

"Will you take me to Tynice, please?" said Prokop.

The postman shook his head in infinite dejection. "Can't be done," he answered after a moment.

"Why…how is that?"

"There's no more room," said the postman, having considered the matter.

Tears of self-pity came into Prokop's eyes. "How far is it…on foot?"

The postman reflected sympathetically. "Well, an hour," he said.

"But I...can't walk it! I've got to get to Dr. Thomas's!" protested Prokop, crushed.

The postman thought for a moment. "Are you...going...as a patient?"

"I feel bad," mumbled Prokop; actually, he was trembling with weakness and fever.

The postman again considered the matter and shook his head. "But it can't be done," he said finally.

"If only you could make...a little room..."

On the coachbox there was no sound. The postman pulled at his beard; then, without saying a word, he got down, did something at the side and silently went off to the station. The passenger on the coachbox remained motionless.

Prokop was so exhausted that he was obliged to sit down on the edge of the pavement. "I shall never get there," he felt desperately; "I shall remain here until...until..."

The postman returned from the station bringing with him an empty tub. Somehow he attached it to the platform of the coachbox and looked at it reflectively. "Sit down there," he said finally.

"Where?" asked Prokop.

"Well...on the coachbox."

By some superhuman effort, as if some magical power were lifting him up, Prokop got on to the coachbox. The postman did something with the reins and there he was sitting in the tub with his legs hanging down over the side. "Hey," said he.

The horse made no movement, but only trembled.

The postman made another thin, guttural "*R-r-r.*" The horse whisked its tail. "*R-r-r-r-r-r-r.*"

The post-wagon moved off. Prokop convulsively gripped a railing at his side; he felt that it was beyond his strength to keep his place on the coachbox.

"*R-r-r-r.*" It seemed that this high, whirring note somehow galvanized the old horse. It limped along, twitching its tail.

"*R-r-r-r-r-r-r.*" They were going along an avenue of bare trees. It was pitch dark, save where the flickering strip of light from the lantern moved over the mud. Prokop clung to the railing feeling that he had already completely lost control of his body, that he must be careful not to fall, that he was infinitely weak. Some lighted window or other, an avenue, a dark field. "*R-r-r.*" The horse trotted along, moving its legs stiffly and unnaturally, as if it had already been dead for a long time.

Prokop cast a surreptitious glance at his fellow-traveller. He was an old man with a scarf wrapped round his neck. All the time he was chewing something, rolling it about in his mouth and periodically spitting. And then Prokop remembered that he had seen this face somewhere before. It was the loathsome face from the dream, which ground its rotten teeth until they crumbled and then spat them out in fragments. It was wonderful and horrible.

"*R-r-r-r-r.*" There was a turn in the road, they climbed up a hill and then descended again. Somebody's estate—the barking of a dog—a man passing along the road and wishing them good-night. The houses increased in number; they were reaching the top of the hill. The post-wagon swung round, another high "*R-r-r-r-r*" and it suddenly drew up.

"This is where Dr. Thomas lives," said the postman.

Prokop wished to say something but was unable to do so. He wanted to let go of the railing, but could not. His fingers were frozen.

"Well, here we are," said the postman again. Once more he called out, and Prokop slipped down from the coachbox, trembling with his whole body. As if performing a remembered action, he opened the gate and rang at the door. Inside there was to be heard a fierce barking and a young voice called out: "Honzik, quiet!" The door opened and, scarcely able to move his tongue, Prokop inquired, "Is the doctor at home?"

A moment of silence; then the young voice said, "Come in."

Prokop stood in the warm sitting-room. On the table was a lamp, supper was laid, there was a smell of beech wood. An old gentleman with his spectacles pushed up on to his forehead rose from the table, came over to Prokop and said: "Well, what can I do for you?"

Prokop tried to remember, dully, what exactly it was that he had come for. "I…that is to say…" he began, "is your son at home?"

The old gentleman looked at Prokop attentively. "He isn't. What do you want with him?"

"George…" mumbled Prokop, "I'm…his friend and I am bringing him… I have to give him…" He hunted about in his pocket and found the sealed package. "It's…an important matter and…and…."

"George is in Prague," the old gentleman interrupted him. "But do sit down."

Prokop was profoundly astonished. "But he said…he said…that he was coming here. I m-m-must give him…" The floor began to sway beneath his feet, and he started to slip forward.

"A chair, Annie," shouted the old gentleman in an extraordinary voice.

Prokop still had time to hear himself cry out before he collapsed on to the ground. A boundless, darkness swept over him and then there was nothing.

CHAPTER VII

There was nothing; only when the mist lifted, as it were, for a time, there appeared the pattern which was painted on the walls, the carved cornice of a cupboard, the top of the curtains or the frieze on the ceiling. Or somebody's face bent over him as if over the mouth of a well; but its features were not to be discerned. Things were happening, somebody from time to time moistened his hot lips or raised his helpless body, but everything disappeared in snatches of dreaming which continued to drift away from him. And there were landscapes, patterns of carpets, differential calculations, balls of fire, chemical formulae. From time to time something rose to the surface and took the form for a moment of a clearer dream, but immediately afterward it dissolved again into the wide current of unconsciousness.

Finally, there came moments when he awoke fully. Then he saw above him the warm ceiling with its stucco pattern; his eyes lighted on his own thin, deathly white hands, resting on the coloured coverlet. Beyond there appeared the frame of the bed, the cupboard and a white door; everything somehow pleasant, quiet and already familiar. He had not a notion where he was. He wanted to consider this problem; but his head was hopelessly weak. Everything began to grow confused again and he closed his eyes and rested, resigning himself to his weakness.

The door opened gently. Prokop opened his eyes and sat up a little in bed, as if something had raised him up. And there at the door was standing a girl, slender and bright, with clear eyes with an extraordinarily astonished look in them, lips half open with surprise, and holding to her breast a pile of white linen. Embarrassed, she remained motionless, only moving her long lashes, while her rosy face began shyly and uncertainly to smile.

Prokop's face darkened. He made an effort to find something to say, but his head was completely empty. He moved his lips voicelessly and looked at the girl with severe eyes that were trying to recall something.

"I supplicate thee, O Queen," came from his lips rapidly and involuntarily in Greek, "if indeed thou art a goddess of them that keep the wide heaven; to Artemis, then, the daughter of great Zeus, I mainly liken thee, for beauty and stature and shapeliness. But if thou art one of the daughters of men who dwell on earth, thrice blessed are thy father and thy lady mother, and thrice blessed thy brethren. Surely their souls ever glow with gladness each time they see thee entering the dance, so fair a flower of maidens."

The girl made no movement. As if she were turned to stone, she listened to this greeting in an unknown language. On her smooth forehead there was so much confusion, her eyes blinked so childishly and with so much apprehension that Prokop continued with increased warmth to deliver the speech of Odysseus when cast on the shore, himself only vaguely realizing the meaning of the words.

"But he is of heart the most blessed," he continued quickly, "beyond all other who shall prevail with lips of wooing, and lead thee to his home. Never have mine eyes beheld such an one among mortals, neither man nor woman; great awe comes upon me as I look on thee."

The girl blushed deeply as if she understood the greeting of the Greek hero. An invincible and delightful embarrassment held her limbs. Prokop, twisting his hands on the coverlet, spoke as if he were praying.

"Yet in Delos," he continued rapidly, "once I saw as goodly a thing; a young sapling of a palm tree springing by the altar of Apollo. For thither too I went, and much people with me, on that path, where my sore troubles were to be. Yea, and when I looked thereupon, long time I marvelled in spirit for never grew there yet so goodly a shoot from ground—even in such wise as I wonder at thee, lady, and am astonished and do greatly fear to touch thy knees, though grievous sorrow is upon me."

Yes, he was terribly frightened; but the girl was frightened too, and continued to press the linen to her breast without taking her eyes from Prokop, who hastened to continue his invocation.

"Yesterday, on the twentieth day, I escaped from the wine-dark deep, but all that time continually the wave bare me, and the vehement winds drove, from the isle Ogygia. And now some god has cast me on this shore, that hereto, methinks, some evil may betide me; for I trow not that trouble will cease. The gods ere that time will yet bring many a thing to pass."

Prokop sighed deeply and raised his wasted hands in fear. "But, Queen, have pity on me, for after many trials and sore to thee first of all am I come, and of the other folk, who hold this city and land, I know no man. Nay, show me the town, give me an old garment to cast about me, if thou hadst, when thou camest here, any wrap for the linen."

Now the girl's face became a little brighter, her moist lips opened. Perhaps Nausicaa was speaking, but Prokop still wanted to bless her for the cloud of sympathy which made her face so rosy. "And may the gods grant thee all thy heart's desire; a husband and a home, and a mind at one with his may they give—a good gift, for there is nothing mightier and nobler than when man and wife are of one heart and mind in a house, a grief to their foes and to their friends great joy, but their own hearts know it best."

Prokop scarcely more than breathed the concluding words. He himself only understood with difficulty what he was saying; effortlessly it flowed out from some forgotten corner of memory. It was almost twenty years since he had heard that sweet melody of the Sixth Book. It afforded him almost physical relief to let it reel itself off in this manner; his head became lighter and clearer, he was almost in ecstasy in this pleasant weakness. An embarrassed smile trembled on his lips.

The girl smiled too, made a slight movement and said: "Well?" She made a step towards him and then burst out laughing. "What did you say?"

"I don't know," said Prokop uncertainly.

Then the door, which had not been completely closed, was burst open and there dashed into the room something small and shaggy which whined with delight and jumped on to Prokop's bed.

"Honzik!" cried the girl apprehensively. "What are you doing?" But the little animal was already licking Prokop's face and in excited joy had snuggled down into the coverlet. Prokop wiped his face with his hand and was disconcerted to find that he had a full beard. "B-b-but," he stammered, and became silent with surprise. The dog was in the seventh heaven; with overflowing devotion he bit at Prokop's hands, yelped, and snorted, thrusting his wet muzzle up to his chest.

"Honzik!" cried the girl, "you're mad! Leave the gentleman alone!" and she ran to the bed and took the dog in her arms. "Honzik, you *are* stupid!"

"Leave him alone," said Prokop.

"But you've got a bad hand," objected the girl with great seriousness, pressing the struggling dog to her breast.

Prokop regarded his right hand doubtfully. Across the palm there stretched a broad scar covered with a new, thin, red membrane which was pleasantly itching. "Where—where am I?" said he in surprise.

"At our house," said the girl, as if it were the most self-evident thing in the world, and Prokop was reassured at once. "At your house," he said with relief, although he had no idea where that might be. "And how long?"

"Three weeks. And all the time—" She wanted to say something but stopped herself. "Honzik has been sleeping with you," she added hurriedly, and for some reason or other blushed, holding the dog as if it were a little child. "Do you know about it?"

"I don't," replied Prokop. "Have I been asleep?"

"All the time," she said quickly. "You've slept the whole time." Then she put the dog down on the ground and drew nearer to the bed. "Do you feel better? Do you want anything?"

Prokop shook his head; he could think of nothing which he wanted.

"What's the time?" he asked doubtfully.

"Ten. I don't know what you are allowed to eat; wait till father comes.... Father will be so glad.... Don't you want anything then?"

"A mirror," said Prokop hesitatingly.

The girl burst out laughing and ran off.

There was a humming in Prokop's head; he was continually trying to recall what had happened and it was continually escaping him. And now here was this girl again, she said something and handed him a mirror. Prokop tried to lift his hand; but it couldn't be done. The girl placed the handle between his fingers but the mirror fell on to the coverlet. Then the girl suddenly became pale, grew anxious, and held the mirror in front of his eyes herself.

Prokop looked and saw a face covered with hair and almost unrecognizable. He looked and was unable to understand, and his lips began to tremble.

"Lie down, lie down again at once," she ordered him in a tiny voice, almost crying, and quickly her hands placed the pillow ready for him. Prokop let himself fall on to his back and closed his eyes. Just for a moment he would doze, he thought to himself, and then there would be a deep, lovely silence.

CHAPTER VIII

Someone pulled at his sleeve. "Well, well," said this someone, "we mustn't sleep any more, eh?" Prokop opened his eyes and saw an old gentleman with a pink-bald head and a white beard, gold spectacles up on his forehead, and an extraordinarily bright look in his eyes. "No more sleep, my friend," he said. "You've done that long enough; you don't want to wake up in the next world."

Prokop looked darkly at the old gentleman; he wanted to dream on a little longer. "What do you want?" he said finally in an irritated tone. "And... with whom have I the honour...?"

The old gentleman burst out laughing. "Dr. Thomas, if you please.... You haven't yet deigned to recognize me, eh? But don't bother about that. What may your name be?"

"Prokop," said the invalid ungraciously.

"Well, well," said the doctor contentedly. "I thought that you were the Sleeping Beauty. And now, Mr. Engineer," he said energetically, "we must have a look at you. Don't get cross." He whisked a thermometer from under Prokop's armpit and made a self-satisfied noise. "Ninety-nine. You're like a fly, man. We must feed you up, what? Don't move."

Prokop felt on his chest a bald pate and a cold ear, which moved from one shoulder to the other and from his stomach to his neck, accompanied by an animated grunting.

"Well, thank God," said the doctor finally, and settled his spectacles on his nose. "We'll fix up that little wheezing in the chest, and the heart—well, that'll adjust itself, eh?" He bent over Prokop, poked his fingers through his hair and raised and lowered his eyelids with his finger. "No more sleeping, see?" he said, and at the same time looked at the pupils of his eyes. "We'll get some books and do some reading. We'll eat a little, drink a glass of wine and keep still. I shan't bite you."

"What's the matter with me?" asked Prokop timidly. The doctor drew himself up. "Well, nothing now. Listen, where did you come from?"

"What?"

"We picked you up from the floor, and...where did you come from, man?"

"I don't know. From Prague, perhaps," Prokop recalled.

The doctor shook his head. "By train from Prague! With the membrane of your brain inflamed? Were you mad? Do you know what it is?"

"What?"

"Meningitis. The sleeping form of it, and added to that inflammation of the lungs. 104, eh? My friend, one doesn't go out on expeditions when one has that sort of thing. And do you know that—well, show me your right hand, quick!"

"That…was only a scratch," Prokop justified himself.

"A nice sort of scratch. Blood poisoning, you understand? When you are well I shall tell you that you were…an ass. Forgive me," he said with dignified warmth. "I very nearly said something stronger. An educated man, and he doesn't know that he's ill enough for three! How were you able anyway to keep on your feet?"

"I don't know," whispered Prokop, ashamed.

The doctor wished to go on talking but instead grunted and waved his hand. "And how do you feel?" he said sternly. "A little drunk, eh? No memory, eh? And," he tapped his forehead, "a little weak, eh?"

Prokop remained silent.

"And now, Mr. Engineer," said the doctor, "don't do anything about it. It will last for some time. You understand me? You mustn't overwork your head. No thinking. It'll come back…in bits. Only a temporary disturbance, a slight loss of memory, you see?"

The doctor shouted, sweated and grew agitated as if he were struggling with a deaf-mute. Prokop continued to watch him and then said quietly, "Shall I remain always weak-minded?"

"But no, no, no," said the doctor excitedly. "Completely out of the question. Simply…for a certain time…a disturbance of the memory, disassociation, exhaustion and certain symptoms, you understand me? Irregularities in coordination, see? Rest. Quiet. Do nothing. You must thank God, my friend."

"Survived," he went on after a moment and in his delight blew his nose loudly. "Listen, I've never had such a case before. You arrived here completely delirious, crashed on to the ground and *finis!* What was I to do with you? It's a long way to the hospital and the girl howled so much, and besides you came as a guest…to see George, eh? So we left you, you understand? Well, it didn't bother us. But I've never had such an entertaining guest before. To sleep for twenty days! When my colleague cut your hand open you didn't even stir, what do you think of that? A quiet patient, upon my soul. But that's nothing, the great thing is that you are out of it." The doctor slapped his thigh. "But, for God's sake, no more sleeping! My friend, you might have gone to sleep for good and all, do you hear? For goodness' sake try and get yourself under control! Drop it, see?"

Prokop nodded his head weakly; he felt as if a curtain had been drawn between him and actuality, a curtain which shrouded, disturbed and muted everything.

"Annie!" came an agitated voice. "The wine! Bring the wine!"

Some quick steps, a conversation which seemed to be going on underwater, and cool wine caressed his throat. He opened his eyes and saw the girl bending over him.

"You mustn't sleep," she said excitedly, and her long hair trembled as if to the beating of her heart.

"I won't sleep anymore," said Prokop submissively.

"I should like you not to," said the doctor gruffly from the end of the bed. "A specialist is coming from the town for a consultation. We'll let him see that we provincial medicos know something, too, eh? You must behave yourself nicely." With unexpected dexterity, he lifted Prokop up and thrust a pillow behind his back. "There, now you can sit up; and you won't want to sleep until after dinner, what? I must go to my patients. And you, Annie, sit down now and gossip about something or other. Generally your mouth goes like a wheelbarrow, eh? And if he tries to sleep, call me. I shall know how to deal with him." In the doorway he turned round and grunted.... "But...I'm glad about it, see? So be careful!"

Prokop's eyes wandered to the girl. She sat a short distance away, her hands in her lap, and for the life of her could not think what to talk about. Then she raised her head and opened her lips slightly. One heard that she was saying something, but she was confused, gulped, and lowered her head still more. Her long eyelashes trembled on her cheeks.

"Father is so abrupt," she said finally. "He's so used to shouting.... to scolding.... the patients." Here, unfortunately, she ran out of material; on the other hand—as if by a happy inspiration—she became conscious of her apron between her fingers, and began to arrange it in all sorts of interesting folds, her eyelashes still trembling.

"What's that noise?" asked Prokop after a long pause.

She turned her head to the window; she had beautiful light hair and her lips were attractively moist. "It's the cows," she said with relief. "There's a yard there, you see? Father has a horse and cart there.... His name is Fritz."

"Whose?"

"The horse. You've never been to Tynice, have you? There's nothing here. Only avenues and fields.... When mummy was still alive, it was more cheerful; George used to come here.... But he hasn't been here for over a year. He had a quarrel with father and...he doesn't even write. We aren't even allowed to speak of him—do you see him often?"

Prokop shook his head decidedly.

The girl sighed and became reflective. "He's… I don't know. Funny, somehow. He did nothing but go about with his hands in his pockets, yawning. I know that's nothing, but yet… Father is so glad that you are with us," she concluded quickly and somewhat disconnectedly.

Somewhere outside, a young cock began to crow hoarsely and comically. Immediately afterward, all the chickens became very excited, and one could hear a wild "ko-ko-ko" and the triumphant yelping of a dog.

The girl sprang up. "Honzik is chasing the chickens!" But she sat down again at once, having resolved to leave them to their fate. It was pleasantly silent.

"I don't know what to talk about," she said with the most beautiful simplicity. "Would you like me to read you the paper?"

Prokop smiled. She fetched the paper and started confidently on the leading article. The financial equilibrium, the Budget, uncovered credits… Her charming and uncertain voice quietly read out these extraordinarily important items, and Prokop, who simply was not listening at all, was better off than if he had been soundly asleep.

CHAPTER IX

And now Prokop was able to get out of bed for an hour or so every day; so far he was only capable of dragging his legs along somehow and there was not much question of talking to him. Whatever you said to him, he answered in a niggardly manner, excusing himself with a weak smile.

At mid day—it was the beginning of April—he sat down on a seat in the garden. Next to him the wiry-haired terrier Honzik grinned for all he was worth, obviously proud of his function as companion, and through sheer delight he licked himself, and blinked his eyes when Prokop's scarred left hand smoothed his warm, shaggy head. About this time the doctor usually ran out of his consulting room, his skullcap slipping about his bald head, squatted down on his haunches and planted vegetables in the garden. With his short fat fingers he worked the heaps of soil and carefully arranged the beds for the young buds. Every now and then he became excited and grunted; he had stuck his pipe into the ground somewhere and was unable to find it. At this point Prokop arose and with the astuteness of a detective (for he spent his time in bed reading detective stories) went straight to it. Whereat Honzik shook himself noisily.

About then also Annie used to come and water her father's flowerbeds. Her right hand carried the can, her left swung in the air. A silver stream of water hissed into the new soil, and if Honzik happened to be near he caught it on his back or on his stupid, good-natured head, which led him to yelp desperately and seek protection with Prokop.

The whole of the morning patients kept on arriving at the consulting-room. In the waiting-room they coughed or were silent, each one thinking about his own suffering. Sometimes a terrible cry was to be heard when the doctor was pulling out the teeth of some little boy. Then Annie in a panic took shelter behind Prokop, pale, and quite beside herself, her long lashes trembling in her anxiety, waiting until the frightful affair was over. Finally, the boy ran off wailing, and Annie awkwardly apologized for her tender-heartedness.

It was different when there drew up before the doctor's house a cart on the bottom of which straw had been spread and two old men carefully carried a seriously wounded man up the steps. He had a crushed hand or a broken foot, or his head had been split open by the kick of a horse. A cold sweat poured down his terribly pale forehead and he was quietly groaning with heroic self-control. A tragic silence descended upon the whole house; something serious was silently taking place in the consulting-room. The fat, jovial servant went about on the tips of her toes. Annie's eyes were full of tears and her fingers trembled. Then the doctor would burst into the kitchen and shout for rum, wine, or water, and with redoubled gruffness cover up his acute sympathy. And the whole of the next day he would be silent, fly into rages, and slam the doors.

But there was also a holiday, the splendid annual function of the provincial doctor, the inoculation of the children. A hundred mothers nursed their squalling, yelling, or sleeping children; they filled up the consulting-room, the passage, the kitchen, and the garden. Annie was wildly excited and wanted to nurse, swaddle, and play with all these toothless, downy children in an ecstasy of exuberant motherhood. The doctor's bald pate seemed to shine more than ever. From early in the morning he went about without his spectacles, so as not to frighten these scamps, and his eyes were filled with exhaustion and happiness.

Sometimes, in the middle of the night the bell would ring excitedly. Then voices were heard in the doorway, the doctor grumbled and Joseph had to harness the horse. Somewhere in the village, behind a lighted window, a new being was about to enter the world. It was already morning when the doctor returned, tired out, but contented, and strongly smelling of carbolic. Annie liked him best of all like that.

There were other people about the place; the fat, garrulous Nanda in the kitchen, who sang and chattered the whole day and was always being doubled up with laughter. Then the serious, whiskered coachman, Joseph. A historian, he was always reading history books and was delighted to expound on the Hussite wars or the historical secrets of the country. Then the gardener from the castle, a great one for the girls, who appeared every day in the doctor's garden, pruned roses, clipped bushes, and convulsed Nanda with laughter. Then the above-mentioned shaggy and excited Honzik, who followed Prokop about, chased flies and chickens and, best of all, liked to sit on the doctor's coachbox. Fritz was an old horse, a little grey, a friend of the rabbits, good-natured and reliable. It was the height of pleasantness to smooth his warm and sensitive nostrils. Then a dark-haired boy who helped in the yard, in love with Annie, who, together with Nanda, made fun of him mercilessly. The foreman, an old fox who played chess with the doctor and often became excited, and often grew angry and always lost the game. And other local characters, among whom an extraordinarily tedious surveyor with political interests who bored Prokop on the strength of being also a professional man.

Prokop read a lot, or at least pretended to. His scarred, heavy face did not reveal much, especially nothing of his desperate secret struggle with his disturbed memory. The last few years of study had particularly suffered; the most simple formulae and processes were lost, and Prokop jotted down in the margin of his book fragments of formulae which came into his head when he was least thinking of them. Then he would leave the book and go to play billiards with Annie, since this was a game during which one had no need to talk. Annie was impressed by his leathery and impenetrable seriousness. He played with concentration, aimed with his eyebrows severely drawn together, and when the ball, as if on purpose, went in the wrong direction he opened his mouth in astonishment and indicated the proper destination with a movement of his tongue.

Evenings by the lamp. Most talkative of the three was the doctor, an enthusiastic scientist without any knowledge of the subject. He was especially fascinated with the deeper mysteries of the universe: radio activity, the boundlessness of space, electricity, relativity, the origins of matter and of prehistoric man. He was an out-and-out materialist, and just for this reason experienced a sweet and secret fear when confronted with unsolved problems. Occasionally Prokop could not contain himself and corrected the German *naïveté* of his views. The old gentleman listened piously, and began to have an inordinate admiration for Prokop, especially when he could no longer understand what he was talking about—potentials of resonance or the quantum theory. Annie sat quietly, resting her chin on her hands. She did not even blink and, large-eyed, looked at Prokop and her father in turn.

And the nights, the nights were wide and quiet, as everywhere in the country. Now and then one could hear the rattle of chains from the cowshed or, nearer or farther away, the barking of a dog. A falling star flashed across the sky, the spring rain hissed in the garden or water dropped with a silver note into the deserted well. A clear, deep cold came in through the open window and one fell into a blessed sleep, untroubled by dreams.

CHAPTER X

Now things were better. Life returned to Prokop day by day. He felt a dullness in his head and he was always a little as if in a dream. There was nothing to do but to show his appreciation of the doctor's services and go on his own way. He announced this decision one day after supper but everybody received it in stubborn silence. Then the old man took Prokop by the arm and led him into the consulting-room. After a certain amount of beating about the bush he said gruffly that Prokop must not leave, that it was better for him to rest, that the battle was not yet won—in short, that he was to remain. Prokop vaguely defended himself; the fact was that he did not yet feel himself in the saddle and that he was a little demoralized by comfort. All talk of going away was postponed indefinitely.

Every afternoon the doctor shut himself up in his consulting-room. "Come in and see me, eh?" he said to Prokop casually. And Prokop found him surrounded by all sorts of bottles, crucibles, and powders. "There's no apothecary in the town, you know," explained the doctor, "I have to prepare the medicines myself." And with his fat, trembling fingers he laid some powder on the pan of the small balance. His hand was uncertain, the scales twisted and jumped about; the old gentleman became agitated, wheezed, and small drops of sweat appeared on his nose. "I can't see as well as I used to," he said, excusing his old fingers. Prokop watched for a moment and then, saying nothing, took the scales from him. Two little taps and the powder was weighed to a milligram. And a second and a third powder in the same way. The delicate balance simply danced in Prokop's fingers. "Just look at that," said the doctor with admiration and watched Prokop's crushed, knotty hands with their shapeless knuckles, broken nails, and short stumps in the place of one or two missing fingers. "Your fingers are wonderfully nimble, man!" In the course of a few moments Prokop had spread some ointment, measured off some drops of liquid, and heated a test-tube. The doctor glowed with pleasure, and stuck on the labels. In half an hour all the medicines were ready, and, in addition, there was a pile of powders in reserve. In a few days Prokop could read the doctor's prescriptions and make them up. *Bon!*

One evening the doctor was poking about in the garden in the loose soil. Suddenly, there was a frightful report in the house, and a moment after the noise of falling glass. The doctor dashed indoors and in the passage ran into the terrified Annie. "What has happened?" he cried.

"I don't know," replied the girl. "In the consulting-room."... The doctor ran there and found Prokop on all fours picking potsherds and pieces of paper off the floor.

"What have you been doing?" cried the doctor.

"Nothing," said Prokop, and got up guiltily. "A test-tube burst."

"And what, in God's name, does this mean?" thundered the doctor, stopping suddenly; a stream of blood was pouring from Prokop's left hand. "How did you tear your finger?"

"Only a scratch," Prokop protested and hid his left hand behind his back.

"Show me," cried the doctor and dragged him to the window. Half of one finger was hanging by the skin. The doctor rushed to the cupboard for his scissors and in the open door saw Annie, deathly pale. "What do you want?" he rapped out. "Be off, quick!" Annie did not move; she pressed her hands to her breast and looked as if she might swoon away any moment.

The doctor turned to Prokop. To begin with he did something with some wadding and then snapped the scissors. "Light," he shouted to Annie. Annie dashed to the switch and turned it on. "And don't stay here," roared the old gentleman, dipping a needle into some benzine. "What can you do here? Some thread, quick!" Annie sprang to the cupboard and gave him a box full of thread. "And now away with you!"

Annie looked at Prokop's back and did something else instead; she stepped closer, took the wounded hand and held it in both of hers. The doctor at the moment was washing his hands; he turned to Annie and was going to burst out with something but instead grunted: "All right, hold it firmly! And nearer the light!" Annie held the hand, her eyes blinking. When there was nothing to be heard but the doctor's heavy breathing she ventured to raise them. Below, where her father was working, all was bloody and revolting. She hastily glanced at Prokop; his face was turned away and twitched with pain. Annie shivered and swallowed her tears.

Meanwhile, Prokop's hand grew larger and larger; quantities of wadding, silk, and a good kilometre of bandages; finally an enormous white lump. Annie continued to hold the hand. Her knees shook; it seemed to her that this terrible operation would never be over. Suddenly, her head began to swim and the next thing that she heard was her father saying: "Drink this quickly!" She opened her eyes and found that she was sitting in the armchair in the consulting-room and that her father was handing her a glassful of some stuff or other while Prokop was standing behind him, smiling and holding his bound hand, which looked like a huge doll, across his chest. "Drink it up," repeated the doctor through his teeth. She swallowed the contents of the glass and nearly choked with coughing; it was murderously strong cognac.

"And now you," said the doctor, and gave the glass to Prokop. Prokop was a trifle pale and valiantly awaited the scolding which was due to him. Finally, the doctor himself drank, cleared his throat and said, "What exactly have you been doing?"

"An experiment," said Prokop with the twisted smile of a guilty person.

"What? What experiment? Experiment with what?"

"Something with potassium chlorate."

"What were you making?"

"An explosive," whispered Prokop with the humiliation of a sinner.

The doctor's eyes moved to his bandaged hand. "And you've paid for it, my friend! It might have torn your hand off, eh? Does it hurt? But it suits you," he added bloodthirstily.

"But, father," said Annie, "leave him alone now!"

"What's that to do with you?" grunted the doctor and caressed her with a hand which smelt of carbolic and idioform.

After that the doctor kept the key of the consulting-room in his pocket. Prokop ordered a parcel of scientific books, went about with his arm in a sling and spent the whole day in study. The cherries had already begun to blossom, the sticky young leaves were glistening in the sun, the golden lilies were putting out heavy buds. Annie went about the garden with a buxom girl friend, their arms round one another's waists, laughing all the time. They put their red faces together, whispered something, burst out laughing and began to kiss one another.

At last Prokop felt bodily well again. Like an animal, he basked in the sun, blinking his eyes. Then he would sigh and sit down to work, but would at once feel an inclination to move about and wander far into the country, passionately giving himself up to the joy of breathing. Sometimes he would meet Annie about the house or in the garden and try to say something. Annie would look at him out of the corner of her eye and not know what to do. Prokop would be equally at a loss and covered his embarrassment by speaking in a gruff voice. He felt better, or at least more sure of himself, when he was alone.

In the course of his studies he noticed that there was a great deal that he had missed. There were all sorts of new developments, and he was obliged to orientate himself again. Chiefly he was afraid of not being able to remember his own work, for it was in connection with this that his memory suffered most. He worked like a mule, or else gave himself up to dreaming. He dreamt of new laboratory methods, and at the same time he was fascinated by bold and delicate theoretical calculations. When his dull brain proved incapable of splitting the thin hair of a problem he would grow angry with himself. He was conscious of the fact that his laboratory "destructive chemistry" opened up the most marvellous vistas in the theory of the constitution of matter.

He came up against unexpected correlations, immediately afterward to be oppressed by the laboriousness of his methods. Disgusted, he would throw everything down and plunge into reading some stupid novel; but even here he was haunted by the atmosphere of the laboratory. Instead of words he read only chemical symbols, mad formulae full of elements hitherto undiscovered, which disturbed him even in his sleep.

CHAPTER XI

That night he dreamed; it seemed to him that he was studying a highly technical article in the *Chemist*. He came across the symbol *An Ni* and did not know what to make of it. He reflected, bit his knuckles and suddenly realized that it stood for Annie. And then he saw her in the room, smiling, with her arms clasped at the back of her head. He went across to her, took her in his arms and began to kiss her on the lips. Annie fought wildly with her elbows and knees while he held her brutally and with one hand tore her clothes into long strips. He already had his hands on her young flesh. Annie struggled desperately, her hair fell over her face, and now, now she suddenly became weak and drooped.... Prokop threw himself upon her; but instead found in his arms nothing but long rags and bandages. He tore them and ripped them up, trying to disengage himself from them, and then he woke up.

He was exceedingly ashamed of his dream, dressed quietly, sat down at the window and waited for the dawn. There is no frontier between night and day. The sky becomes the slightest bit pale; there is still neither light nor sound; but the signal has been given to nature to awake! Now, while it is still night, morning has begun. The cocks crow, the animals move in their sheds. The sky turns to pearl, grows brighter and then rose-coloured; the earliest red streak appears in the east; the birds begin to chirp and the first man to go to work sets out with a swinging step.

The man of science also sat down to work. For a long time he bit his penholder, and then decided to set down the first words. For this was to be a big affair, the result of twelve years of experiment and reflection, work really paid for with his own blood. Of course this would only be a rough draft, or rather a sort of physical philosophy or poem, or a confession of faith. It would be a picture of the world composed of figures and equations. But these figures of an astronomical order measured something other than the sublimity of the firmament; he was calculating the instability and destructibility of matter.

Everything that exists is a dull, latent explosive; but whatever the index of its inertia may be, it represents only an insignificant fraction of its explosive power. Everything which takes place, the movement of the stars, tellurian work, entropy, active and insatiable life itself, all this is only on the surface, while invisibly and incalculably there is gnawing beneath it that explosive force which is called matter. Consider now that the cord which binds it is nothing more than a cobweb on the limbs of a sleeping titan. Give him strength to disturb it and he will tear the surface off the globe, and hurl Jupiter on to Saturn. And you, humanity, you are only a swallow which laboriously builds a nest under the roof of the cosmic powder magazine; you twitter in the eastern sun while in the casks beneath you there vibrates silently the terrible potential of explosion…

Naturally Prokop did not write these things down; to him they were only a secret melody, which lent wings to the heavy phrases of the technical exposition. For him there was more phantasy in a bare formula and more blinding beauty in an index of explosiveness. And so he wrote his poem in symbols, figures, and the frightful jargon of scientific terminology.

He did not come down to breakfast. Annie came in and silently brought it to him. He thanked her, and then remembered his dream and was somehow unable to look at her. He stared obstinately into a corner. God knows how it was possible, but he nevertheless saw every golden hair on her bare arms. He had never noticed them so much before.

Annie was standing quite near him. "Are you going to write?" she asked in some uncertainty.

"I am," he muttered and wondered what she would say if he were suddenly to put his head on her breast.

"The whole day?"

"The whole day."

She was moving off, greatly impressed. She had firm, small and broad breasts, a fact of which she was probably unaware. But what did it matter!

"Is there anything you want?"

"No, nothing."

It was silly. He would have liked to bite her arm or something. Women never seem to realize how much they disturb men.

Annie shrugged her shoulders, a little offended. "All right then." And she was gone.

He got up and began to walk up and down the room. He was angry with himself and with her; and, the chief thing, he did not want to write any more. He collected his thoughts; but it simply would not go. He grew annoyed, and, in a bad frame of mind, strode from wall to wall with the regularity of a pendulum. One, two hours. Downstairs there was a rattling of plates; they were preparing lunch. He sat down at his papers again and put his head in his hands. A moment afterward the servant came in and brought him his meal.

He pushed the food away almost untouched and cast himself irritably on the bed. It was clear that they had already had enough of him, that he also was tired of it all and that it was time to depart. Yes, the very next day. He made a few plans for his future work, without realizing why the process was so painful, and why he felt ashamed, and ended by falling into a deep sleep. He woke up late in the afternoon, with his soul clogged and his body demoralized by abominable slothfulness. He wandered about the room, yawned and, unable to think, became infinitely bored. It grew dark, and he did not even light the lamp.

The servant brought him his supper. He left it to grow cold and listened to what they were doing downstairs. He heard the chink of forks, the doctor grumbling and, directly after supper, slam the door of his room. All became quiet.

Convinced that he would meet nobody, Prokop pulled himself together and went into the garden. It was a moist and clear night. The lilac was already in blossom; Beetius stretched his starry arms across the sky; it was quiet but for the distant barking of a dog. Something white was leaning against the stone wall in the garden. Of course it was Annie.

"It's a beautiful night," he remarked, in order to say something, and leant against the wall next to her. Annie said nothing but only turned her face away and her shoulders trembled in an anxious and unaccustomed manner.

"That's Beetius," said Prokop hoarsely. "And above it…the Dragon and Cepheus, and over there is Cassiopeia, those four stars together. But you must look higher."

Annie turned away from him and rubbed something away near her eyes. "There, where it's clear," said Prokop hesitatingly, "is Pollux, one of the twins. You mustn't be angry with me. Maybe I was a bit rough with you, eh? I'm…something was worrying me, you see? You mustn't take it to heart."

Annie sobbed loudly. "And what's…that one over there?" she said in a quiet, timid voice. "The brightest one of all, low down."

"That's Sirius, in the Great Dog. They also call it Alhaboa. And there right away to the left are Arcturus and Spica. There's a falling star. Did you see it?"

"Yes. Why were you so angry with me this morning?"

"I wasn't. I'm perhaps…sometimes…a bit crude; but I've had a hard life you know, too hard; always alone and…like an outpost. I can't even talk properly. Today I wanted…to write something beautiful…a sort of scientific prayer, so that everybody should understand it. I thought that…that I'd read it to you; and then, everything dried up in me—one becomes ashamed of getting so excited. Or at least one should be able to say something. I'm stale, so to speak. You understand? I'm already growing grey."

"But it suits you," said Annie softly.

This aspect of the question took Prokop by surprise.

"Well, you know," he said, in confusion. "It isn't pleasant. It is already time…to bring one's harvest home. What wouldn't another do with all that I know! And I've got nothing, nothing, nothing from it all. I'm only…

'*berühmt*' and '*célèbre*' and '*highly esteemed*'; and nobody here…knows anything about me. I think, you know, that my theories are pretty bad; I haven't got a head for theory. But what I have discovered isn't without value. My exothermic explosives…diagrams…and explosions of atoms…have a certain worth. And I have only published about a tenth of what I know. What wouldn't another have done with it! I…don't even understand their theories; they are so subtle, so rich…they only confuse me. My spirit is that of the kitchen. Put some stuff under my nose and I can tell by smelling it what to do with it. But to realize what follows from that…theoretically and philosophically, that I can't do. I only know…facts; I *create* them; they're my facts, do you understand? But still… I…feel some sort of truth in them; a great general truth…that changes everything…until it explodes. And this great truth is hidden in facts and not in words. And so one must go for facts, even if both one's arms are torn off.…"

Annie, leaning against the wall, was scarcely breathing. Their gloomy guest had never said so much before—and, principally, had never spoken about himself. He had to struggle hard with words. There was wrestling within him an enormous pride, but also pain and shyness; and even when he spoke in terms of integral numbers Annie understood that something interior and humanly lacerated was taking place before her.

"But the worst of it is," mumbled Prokop, "that sometimes…and especially now, it all seems to me to be stupid…and worthless. Even this final truth…in fact everything. It's never happened to me before. Why…? Perhaps it would be wiser to give in…to everything"—(he indicated with his hands something surrounding them). "Simply to Life. A man mustn't be happy; it softens him, you understand? Then everything else appears to be useless, small…and senseless. The best things…the best things are done by a man through desperation. Through anger, loneliness, being stunned. So nothing's enough for him. I used to work like a maniac. But now, now I've begun to be happy. I've now learnt that perhaps…there's something better than thinking. Here one only lives…and sees that it is something tremendous just to live. Like your Honzik, like a cat, like a chicken. Every animal understands that… and it seems to me so terrific, as if I have never lived before. And so…so I've again lost twelve years."

His deformed right hand, sewn up God knows how many times, trembled on the wall. Annie was silent; she was resting her arms on the brick wall and looking up at the stars. Then something rustled in the shrubbery and Annie became frightened; she threw herself on Prokop's shoulder. "What's that?"

"Nothing; probably a marten; they come right into the yard after the chickens."

Annie was reassured. Her young breasts, full and soft, were resting against Prokop's right hand. She, perhaps, did not realize the fact herself, but

Prokop was more aware of it than of anything else in the world. He was terribly afraid of moving his hand, for, in the first place, Annie would think that he had put it there on purpose, and in the second place, she would draw away from him. Curiously enough, as a result of this circumstance, he was unable to talk any further about himself and his wasted life. "I've—" he stammered in confusion, "I've never been so glad…so happy, as I am now. Your father is the finest man in the world, and you…you are so young…"

"I thought that you found me…too stupid," said Annie quietly and happily. "You never spoke like that with me before."

"True, never before," said Prokop gruffly. Both became silent. He felt against his hand the light rising and falling of her breasts. He kept perfectly still and held his breath, and she, it seemed, was also holding her breath and trembling quietly, her eyes fixed on some spot in the distance. Oh, to caress and embrace her! Oh, the ecstasy of touching her for the first time! Involuntary and burning delight! Had you ever any adventure more intoxicating than this unconscious and self-sacrificing devotion? Timid and delicate body, like a drooping bud! If you could realize the agonizing tenderness of this rough youth's hand which, without moving, is caressing and holding you!

Annie suddenly drew herself up with an unnatural movement. "Ah! Girl, you haven't realized anything!"

"Good night," said Annie quietly, her face pale and indistinct, and rather stiffly she gave him her hand.

He stretched out his own faintly, as if it were broken, and stared fixedly in another direction. Didn't she really wish to linger a little? No, she was already going. She hesitated; no, she stood still and pulled at the edges of some leaves. What more was there to be said? Good night, Annie, and sleep better than I shall.

For there was certainly no question of going to bed now. Prokop threw himself down on the seat and put his head in his hands. Nothing, nothing had succeeded. Annie was pure and unconscious as a young doe, but enough of that; he was not a raw lad. Then a light showed in a window on the first floor. It was Annie in her bedroom.

Prokop's heart beat wildly. He knew that it was shameful to watch her secretly; certainly as a guest he should not do such a thing. Finally, he attempted to cough so that she should hear him; but somehow he found this to be false, and sat motionless like a statue, unable to take his eyes from the golden window. Annie moved to and fro, bent down, took a long time to do something or other. Aha! She was making her bed. Then she stood at the window, looking into the darkness, her hands behind her head exactly as he saw her in his dream. Now, now he would so gladly have liked to call to her; why did he not do so? But it was too late. Annie turned away and began to move about again. She was still there; no, she was sitting with her back to the window and slowly and reflectively taking her shoes off. Now, at least, he might depart, but instead he climbed up on to the seat, so as to see better. Annie turned round, already half undressed; she raised her bare arms and began to comb her hair. She moved her head and it all fell over her shoulder, gave it a shake and all this wealth of hair tumbled over her face and she set to work with the comb and brush until her head was as smooth as an onion.

Annie, a white virgin, stood motionless, with bent head, and braided her hair into two plaits. Her eyes were lowered and she whispered something to herself, smiled, and became ashamed. The strap of her chemise threatened to slip down. Plunged in reflection, she rubbed her white shoulder with a sort of delight, trembling with the cold.

The shoulder strap slipped still more dangerously, and the light was extinguished.

Never had he seen anything more white, more beautiful than that lighted window.

CHAPTER XII

Early in the morning he found her scouring Honzik in a trough full of soap-suds. The little dog struggled desperately; but Annie, inexorable, laughing and splashed with water, soaped him energetically. "Look out!" she cried when Prokop was still some way off, "he will splash you!"

She looked like a young, enthusiastic mother. Oh God, how simple and beautiful everything is in this sunny world!

Even Prokop was unable to bear continued idleness. He remembered that the bell was out of order, and went off to repair the battery. He was just scraping some zinc when she softly approached him. Her sleeves were turned up above the elbows and her hands were wet from washing. "It won't explode?" she asked with anxiety. Prokop was obliged to smile. She also smiled and splashed him with soapsuds; then with a serious face she came over to him and rubbed the splashes of soap off his hair. The night before she would not have ventured to do such a thing.

At mid day she and Nanda carried a basket of washing into the garden to be bleached. Prokop shut his book with relief; he would not allow her to carry the heavy watering-can. He possessed himself of it and began to sprinkle the linen. The thick stream bubbled joyously on to the folds of tablecloths, white coverlets and the widely spread arms of shirts; the water hissed, guttered and formed little fiords and lakes. Prokop began to water white petticoats and other interesting things; but Annie took the can out of his hands and did it herself. Meanwhile, Prokop sat down on the grass, inhaling with delight the damp smell and watching Annie's beautiful and active hands.

Σοί δέ θεοί τόα δοῖεν, he remembered piously, σέβας μ'ἔχει εἰσορόωντα.

Annie sat down on the grass next to him. "What were you thinking about?" She blinked her eyes happily, dazzled by the brightness of the sun, blushed, and for some reason was inordinately happy. Plucking a full handful of fresh grass, she tried exuberantly to throw it on to his hair; but for some reason or other she suddenly felt a sort of shyness before this shaggy hero. "Have you ever been in love?" she asked inconsequently and quickly looked in another direction.

Prokop laughed. "I have. And you surely have already loved somebody?"

"I was silly once," said Annie, and against her will grew red.

"A student?"

Annie only nodded and sucked a blade of grass. "It was nothing," she said quickly. "And you?"

"I once met a girl who had the same sort of eyelashes that you have. Perhaps she was rather like you. She sold gloves or something of the sort."

"And what else?"

"Nothing. When I went there again to buy some gloves, she was gone."

"And…were you fond of her?"

"I was."

"And…did you ever…?"

"Never. Now my gloves are made by someone else."

Annie concentrated her attention on the ground. "Why do you always hide your hands from me?"

"Because…because they are so knocked about," said Prokop, and the poor fellow grew red.

"They are just as nice that way," whispered Annie with her eyes cast down.

"Din—*ner*! Din—*ner*!" called Nanda from the house.

"Goodness, already?" said Annie, and she reluctantly got up.

* * * *

After dinner, the old doctor rested for a bit. "You know," he excused himself, "I've been slaving this morning like a dog." And a moment afterward he was snoring away. They signalled to one another with their eyes and left the room on tiptoe; and even in the garden they spoke quietly, as if they respected his repose.

Prokop was obliged to narrate the story of his own life. Where he was born, where he grew up, that he had been as far as America, the poverty which he had endured, what he had done and where. It did him good to go over his life in this way; he was astonished to find that it was more wonderful and complicated than he had imagined; but there was much which he was silent about, especially certain emotional experiences since, in the first place, they were of no significance, and, in the second, every man has certain things of which he cannot speak. Annie was as quiet as a mouse. It seemed to her somehow curious and amusing that Prokop had once been a child and a youth and something different from the gruff and extraordinary person by the side of whom she felt herself to be so small. Now she ceased to be afraid of touching him, tying his cravat and combing his hair. And for the first time she became conscious of his thick nose, his heavy and severe lips and his sombre, bloodshot eyes. It all seemed to her extraordinarily wonderful.

And now it was her turn to speak of her life. She had already taken breath and opened her lips; but suddenly she burst out laughing. What could she say about such an insignificant life, especially to a person who had once been buried by a shell for twelve hours in the War, had been in America, and who knows what else? "I have nothing to say," she said directly. But is not such a "nothing" as valuable as the experience of a man?

It was late in the afternoon when they set off together on a sun-warmed path across the fields. Prokop was silent, and Annie caressed the prickly heads of the wheat with her hand as she went along. She brushed him with her shoulder, lingered and stopped—and then set off again two steps in front of him, pulling at the wheat with some curious compulsion to destruction. This sunlit solitude finally weighed her down and made her nervous. We shouldn't have come here, they both thought secretly, and in this oppressive disharmony they dragged out a shallow, fragmentary conversation. Finally, here was their objective, a little chapel between two ancient lime trees. It was late in the afternoon, the time when the herdsmen begin to sing. In front of the chapel was a seat placed there for pilgrims; they sat down and became more silent than ever. A woman was kneeling on the steps of the chapel and praying, certainly for her family. Scarcely had she left when Annie knelt in her place. There was in this action something obviously and eternally feminine. Prokop felt himself to be very young by the side of the mature simplicity of this timeworn and sacred gesture. Finally, Annie stood up, grew more serious, as it were ripened, having decided something, reconciled herself to it; it was as if she had become aware of something, as if she were heavy-laden, preoccupied, changed in some way. She carried something new within her; when they wandered back home in the twilight she answered only in monosyllables in a sweet and hushed voice.

During supper neither she nor Prokop spoke. Perhaps they were wondering when the old gentleman would go away to read his newspaper. The old gentleman muttered and scrutinized them over his spectacles; something had put him out, was not as it should be. The evening dragged on and on until the bell rang and a person from Sedmidoli or Lhota called for the doctor to attend a confinement. The old man was far from delighted, and finally forgot even to grumble. When already in the doorway with his bag in his hand he hesitated and said tersely… "Go to bed, Annie."

Without a word she got up and slipped away from the table. For a long, long time she was occupied with something in the kitchen. Prokop smoked nervously, and was already about to go away. Then she returned, pale, as if frozen, and said with heroic self-control: "Would you care for a game of billiards?"—which meant that there was no question of going in the garden that evening.

It was a wretched game. Annie was terribly formal, played blindly, forgot her turn and scarcely spoke at all. And when she had missed a particularly easy shot Prokop showed her how she should have played…the left hand so, the cue held nearer the end. In showing her he touched her hand with his. Annie gave him a sharp, dark look, threw the cue on the ground, and ran out of the room.

What should he do? Prokop walked up and down the room, smoked and became annoyed. A curious girl; and why should she confuse him? Her stupid mouth, her narrow eyes, her smooth and burning face—well, a man isn't made of wood. Why should it be wrong to stroke her face, to kiss her red cheeks, stroke her hair, her delicate hair at the nape of her young neck—a man isn't made of wood. To caress her, take her in one's arms, and kiss her reverently? How stupid, thought Prokop, annoyed; I'm an ass; I ought to be ashamed of myself—such a child, who never thinks of such things—Good; Prokop considered that he had dealt with this temptation, but it was not to be managed so quickly.

He stood still in front of the glass, sombre, biting his lips and bitterly considering his age.

Go to bed, old bachelor; you've saved yourself from being insulted; this young, stupid girl would laugh at you. More or less decided in his mind, Prokop stumped upstairs to his bedroom; the only thing which oppressed him was that he was obliged to go past Annie's door. He went on tiptoe; perhaps the child was already sleeping. And suddenly he stopped with his heart beating wildly. The door of Annie's room…was not closed. Inside there was darkness. What could this mean? And then inside he heard something like weeping.

He had an impulse to rush into the room; but something stronger sent him hurriedly downstairs and out into the garden. He stood in the thick shrubbery, pressing his hand to his heart, which was beating hard. Thank Christ that he did not go in to her! Annie was certainly kneeling, half dressed and crying into her pillow; why? And if he had gone in what would have happened? Nothing; he would have smoothed, smoothed her bright hair, already loose on her shoulders—O God! Why did she leave the door open?

A light shadow glided out of the house towards the garden. It was Annie. She was dressed and her hair was not loose, but she pressed her hand to her temples to cool her burning forehead; and she was still sobbing from her recent crying. She went past Prokop as if she had not seen him, but made no resistance when he took her by the arm and led her to the seat. Prokop mustered a few words of consolation (but, in God's name, on account of what?) Then suddenly he felt her head on his shoulder; once more she cried convulsively and in the midst of her sobs assured him that "it was nothing." Prokop put his arms round her as if he were her uncle and not knowing what to say muttered something to the effect that she was a good girl and wonderfully lovable; upon which the sobs changed to long sighs (he felt somewhere on his arm a hot dampness) and it was all right. O Night, Queen of heaven, you lighten the breast of the afflicted and loosen the heavy tongue; you quicken, bless, endow with wings the quietly beating heart, oppressed and silent; the thirsty can drink of your endlessness. At some tiny point of space, somewhere between the pole and the Southern Cross, the Centaur and Lyra, something tender is taking place; some man for no reason at all feels himself to be the sole protector of this girl, with her face moist with tears, strokes her head and says—what exactly?—that he is so happy, so happy, that he loves so dearly, so terribly dearly this creature which is sobbing on his shoulder, that he will never leave her, and so on, in that vein.

"I don't know what happened to me," said Annie through her tears. "I—I so wanted to talk to you before…"

"And why did you cry?" asked Prokop.

"Because you took such a long time to come to me," ran the surprising answer.

Something in Prokop weakened, the will or something of the sort. "Do… you…love me?" he said with difficulty, and his voice was as confused as that of a boy of thirteen. The head buried itself in his shoulder quickly and nodded.

"Perhaps… I should have come to you," whispered Prokop, crestfallen. The head shook decidedly. "Now… I feel better," sighed Annie after a moment. "Here it is so beautiful!" Most people would find it difficult to understand what there was attractive about a man's shabby coat, smelling of tobacco; but Annie thrust her head into it and for nothing in the world would she have turned to look up at the stars, so pleasant was it in this dark and smoky resting place. Her hair tickled Prokop under the nose and had about it an exquisite fragrance. Prokop smoothed her drooping shoulders, smoothed her young neck and breast, and encountered nothing but palpitating devotion; then, forgetting everything, he roughly and brutally seized her head and began to kiss her on her moist lips. And, lo! Annie defended herself wildly, became quite paralyzed with fear and gasped out "No, no, no!" She again buried her face in his coat and he could almost hear the frightened beating of her heart. Prokop suddenly realized that she had probably been kissed for the first time.

Then he became ashamed of himself, grew extraordinarily serious and did not venture to do more than smooth her hair. This one may do… God, she's still just a child and quite *naïve!* And now not a word that might besmirch this innocent young creature; not a thought which would coarsely interpret the confused emotions of this evening! In truth he did not know what he was saying; it had a crude melody and no syntax; it touched in turn upon the stars, love, God, the beauty of the night and some opera or other the name of which Prokop was quite incapable of recalling, but the notes of which were sounding intoxicatingly in his head. A few moments after it seemed to him that Annie had fallen asleep; he remained silent until he felt again on his shoulder the exquisite breath of sleepy attention.

At last Annie drew herself up, folded her hands in her lap and became reflective. "I can't believe it, I can't believe it," she said. "It seems to me impossible that it should have happened."

Across the sky a star fell in a streak of light. There was a scent of honeysuckle, the peony slept closed up in a ball, a heavenly breath rustled through the tops of the trees. "I should like to stay here," whispered Annie.

Once more Prokop had a silent struggle with temptation. "Good night, Annie," he said. "If…your father were to return…"

Annie obediently stood up. "Good night," she said and hesitated; and they stood opposite one another, not knowing what to do or how to come to an end. Annie was pale, her eyelids fluttered in agitation and she looked as if she were preparing herself for some heroic deed; but when Prokop, this time completely losing his head, took hold of her elbow she recoiled apprehensively and left him. He followed her along the garden path about a yard behind; when they reached the place where the shadow was darkest they evidently lost the way or something of the sort since Prokop struck somebody's forehead with his teeth, kissed a cold nose and finally found with his mouth a pair of desperately closed lips. Forcing them apart, he violently kissed their moaning, burning moistness. Then Annie tore herself out of his arms, ran to the garden gate and began to sob. Prokop dashed after her to comfort her, covered her ears, hair and neck with kisses, but it was of no avail; she asked to be released, and turned to him a moist face, eyes full of tears, and a sobbing mouth. He kissed and caressed her and suddenly saw that she had ceased to resist him, that she had given herself up to whatever might come and perhaps was crying because of her own abruptness. Prokop became filled with masculine gallantry and, infinitely moved, kissed nothing but her desperate fingers, trembling and damp with tears. Now, now it was better. Now she again rested her face on his rough paw and he kissed her soft, hot mouth and she was reluctant for him to cease.

And now he held his breath, overcome with painful tenderness.

Annie raised her head. "Good night," she said softly, and quite simply offered him her mouth. Prokop bent down and implanted on it the most delicate kiss of which he was capable. He did not dare to accompany her farther but stood quite still for a moment and then took himself off to the other end of the garden, untouched by any ray of light from her window. There he remained motionless as if he were praying. But he was not praying; it was only the most wonderful night of his life.

CHAPTER XIII

When it grew light he found it impossible to stay in the house…he thought he would go out and pick some flowers; then he would lay them outside Annie's door, and when she came out… On wings of delight Prokop crept downstairs while it was still hardly after four o'clock. Outside, it was beautiful; every flower sparkled like an eye (she has large, calm eyes like a cow) (she has also long lashes) (now she is sleeping, her eyelids are as delicate in color as pigeons' eggs) (God! If I could know her dreams) (if her hands are crossed on her breast they will rise and fall with her breathing; but if they are under her head then certainly her sleeve has fallen back and one can see her rosy elbow) (she said the other day that up to now she has been sleeping in the green bed she had when a child) (she said that she would be nineteen in October) (she has a birthmark on her neck) (how is it possible that she loves me?—it is so wonderful); in fact there is nothing more beautiful than a summer morning, but Prokop looked down at the ground, smiled as far as he was able to do so, and made his way to the river, still full of his reflections. There appeared—but near the other bank—the buds of some waterlilies. Scornful of all dangers he undressed, threw himself into the muddy torrent, cut his feet on some insidious stump and returned with an armful of the plants.

The waterlily is a poetical flower, but it exudes an unpleasant liquid from its juicy stalks. Still Prokop ran home with his poetic booty and wondered how he could make an attractive bouquet out of the flowers. He saw that the doctor had left a copy of yesterday's *Politika* on the seat in front of the house. Fiercely he tore it into pieces, casually noticing something about a mobilization in the Balkans, a crisis in some Ministry or other, the notice, framed in black, of somebody's death, bemoaned of course by the whole nation, and wrapped up the wet stems in these items of news. Just as he was preparing, however, to gaze with pride at his work, he got a sudden shock. At the back of the paper he discovered one word, It was KRAKATIT.

For a moment he stared, stupefied, unable to believe his own eyes. Then with feverish haste he unrolled the paper, scattering all the glory of the lilies on to the ground, and finally found the following announcement: "KRAKATIT! Will Eng.P. send his address? Carson, Poste Restante." Nothing more. Prokop's eyes bulged, and he read again. "Will Eng.P. send his address… Carson." What in heaven's name!… Who is this Carson? And how on earth can he possibly know…? For the fiftieth time Prokop reread the mysterious announcement…. "KRAKATIT! Will Eng.P. send his address?" and then "Carson, Poste Restante."

Prokop sat down as if he had been struck with a club. Why—why did I ever take that cursed paper into my hands? flashed desperately through his head. How did it run? "KRAKATIT! Will Eng. P. send his address?" Engineer P., that meant Prokop; and Krakatit, that was the cursed place, that foggy place somewhere in his head, that morbid swelling in his brain which he did not like to think about, which led him to go about running his head into walls, that which had ceased to have a name—what was it there? "KRAKATIT!"

Prokop's eyes again grew wide through the interior blow which he had received. Suddenly, he saw…a certain lead salt, and in a flash there unrolled before him the film that had become blurred in his memory; a desperate, unduly protracted contest in the laboratory with this heavy, dull, apathetic substance; blind and foolish attempts when everything failed him, a corrosive feeling when, in his anger, he triturated it in his fingers, a sticky taste on the tongue and a caustic smoke, exhaustion, so that he had dropped off to sleep in his chair, cold; and suddenly—perhaps in his sleep, or at least it seemed like it—a final inspiration, a paradoxical and miraculously simple experiment, a physicist's trick which he had never employed before. He saw thin, white crystals which he finally collected in a porcelain box, convinced that he would be able to explode them finely the next day when he had buried the box in a hole in the sand out in the open fields where he had his thoroughly illegal experimental station. He saw the armchair in his laboratory, out of which there stuck wire and pieces of stuffing. He curled up in it like an exhausted dog and evidently dropped off to sleep, for it was completely dark when, to the accompaniment of a frightful explosion and the jingle of falling glass, he was thrown out of the chair on to the ground. Then came that sharp pain in his right hand, for something had cut it open; and then—then—

Prokop furrowed his brow painfully in the act of recollecting all this. There the scar was across his hand. And afterward, he had tried to turn on the light, but the electric bulb had been broken. Then he had felt about in the darkness to see what had happened; the table was covered with debris and there, where he had been working, the sheet of zinc covering the desk was torn to pieces, twisted and fused, and the oak table split as if it had been struck by lightning. And then he came across the porcelain box and found it—intact, and this gave him a fright. Yes, that was Krakatit. And then—

Prokop was unable to remain seated; he strode over the scattered lilies and ran about the garden, nervously gnawing at his fingers. Then he had run somewhere or other, into the open country, over ploughed fields, several times fell over—God! Wherever did he go? At this point the sequence of his recollections was definitely broken; the only thing which he could remember with certainty was the terrible pain in his forehead and some affair or other with the police, after which he spoke with George Thomas, and walked to his place—no, took a cab. Then he was ill and George looked after him. George was all right. My God, what a long time ago that was! George Thomas said that he was going here, to his father, but he did not do so; now that's odd; after that he slept or something—

Then the bell rang, briefly and gently; he went and opened the door and outside was standing a girl with a veil over her face.

Prokop groaned and covered his face with his hands. He forgot completely that he was sitting on the very seat where the night before he had been caressing and consoling somebody else. "Does Mr. Thomas live here?" she asked, out of breath; probably she had been running, her fur was covered with rain drops and suddenly, suddenly she raised her eyes—

Prokop nearly cried out with pain. He saw her as she had been that evening; hands, little hands in tight gloves, drops of moisture from her breath on her thick veil, a clear glance, full of suffering; beautiful, sad and brave. "You will save him, won't you?" She looked at him with serious, troubled eyes, and all the time was gripping in her hand some sort of a package, a sealed package, pressing it to her bosom agitatedly and trying to keep control of herself.

It was as if Prokop had received a blow in the face. *Where did I put that package? Whoever that girl may be, I promised her that I would take it to Thomas. While I was ill… I forgot everything; because I…or rather…he did not like to think about it. But now—now I must find it, that's clear.*

He rushed up to his room and pulled out all the drawers. No, no, no, it's not here. For the twentieth time he rummaged through all his possessions, piece by piece; then he sat down in the midst of the frightful disorder that he had created, as above the ruins of Jerusalem, and corrugated his brow. Perhaps it had been taken by the doctor or by the guffawing Nanda; how else could it have disappeared? When he had discovered, however, that this was not the case he experienced a sort of compulsion or confusion in his head, and, as if in a dream, made his way to the stove, groped in the recess behind it and pulled out…the missing parcel. And as he did so he had a vague impression that some time or other he must have put it there himself, some time when he was not yet…completely well; he also remembered that in that condition of swooning and delirium he had insisted on having it in the bed with him the whole time and fell into a rage when they tried to take it away from him, and that at the same time he had been in a painful state of anxiety about it. Evidently, with the astuteness of the madman, he had hidden it from himself, so as to be left in peace. But it was impossible to penetrate these secrets of his unconsciousness; anyway, here it was, this carefully packed parcel with five seals, on which were written the words, "for Mr. George Thomas."

He tried to deduce something more from this inscription but instead saw before him the veiled girl, holding the parcel in her trembling fingers; now, now she was again raising her eyes…he passionately smelt the package. There clung to it an evanescent and remote fragrance.

He put it down on the table and began to walk up and down the room. He would have given a lot to know what it contained under its five seals; certainly some weighty secret, some fateful and urgent relationship. She certainly said…that she was doing it for somebody else; but she was so agitated—

But that she could love Thomas was incredible. Thomas was a good-for-nothing, he assured himself with blind fury. He was always getting what he wanted from women, a cynic. All right, he would find him and give him this love letter, and that would be the end of it.

Suddenly, a thought flashed through his head. There must be some connection between Thomas and that—what was his name—that cursed Carson! Because nobody else had ever heard anything about Krakatit, only George Thomas and this other.

A new picture introduced itself uninvited into the blurred film of his memory: he, Prokop, was muttering something in his fever (it must have been in Thomas's room), and George bent over him and wrote something down in a notebook.

"Without the slightest doubt that must have been my formula!" he cried. "He wheedled it out of me, stole it, and probably sold it to that Carson!"

Prokop grew cold at the thought of such treachery. Christ! And that girl had fallen into the hands of a man like him! If anything in the world was clear it was that she must be protected at any cost!

Good! To begin with, he must find Thomas, that criminal. He would give him the sealed package, and in addition, he would smash his face for him. Also, he would get him in his power. Thomas would have to tell him the name and address of that girl and promise—no; no promises from such a waster. But he would go to her and tell her everything. And then he would disappear from her eyes forever.

Satisfied with this cavalier decision, Prokop got up. Ah, to find out—that was the only thing—where the girl lived! He saw her again, standing elegant and strong. Nothing in her glance betrayed any contact with Thomas. Was she capable of lying with such eyes…?

Then, drawing in his breath with pain, he broke the seals and tore off the paper and string. Inside was a letter and some banknotes.

CHAPTER XIV

Meanwhile, Doctor Thomas was sitting at breakfast grunting and puffing after working hard at a difficult delivery. From time to time he threw anxious and inquisitorial glances at Annie, who sat motionless, neither eating nor drinking, simply unable to believe that Prokop had not yet put in an appearance. Her lips were trembling and she was evidently about to cry. Then Prokop came in, with inappropriate buoyancy, pale, and incapable even of sitting down, as if he were in a hurry. He greeted her perfunctorily, giving her a casual glance as if he had never seen her before, and immediately asked with impulsive impatience: "Where's your George?" The doctor swung round, disconcerted... "What?"

"Where is your son now?" repeated Prokop, and devoured him with threatening eyes.

"How should I know?" grunted the doctor. "I don't want to hear of his existence."

"Is he in Prague?" insisted Prokop, clenching his fists. The doctor was silent but within him something was working swiftly.

"I must see him," said Prokop incoherently. "I must, do you hear? I must go and see him now, at once! Where is he?"

The doctor made a chewing movement with his jaws and walked towards the door.

"Where is he, where does he live?"

"I don't know," shouted the doctor in a voice which was not his own, and slammed the door.

Prokop turned to Annie. She sat frozen and looked into the distance with her large eyes. "Annie," said Prokop feverishly, "you must tell me where your George is. I—I must go and see him, do you understand? that is to say... it's a question of... To cut it short, it's to do with... I... Read this," he said quickly, and stuck in front of her eyes the crumpled fragment of newspaper. But Annie saw nothing but some circles or other.

"That's my discovery, do you see?" he explained nervously. "A certain Carson is looking for me—where's your George?"

"We don't know," whispered Annie. "It's two...quite two years since he wrote to us—"

"Ah!" growled Prokop and angrily crushed the paper into a ball. It was as if the girl had turned to stone, only her eyes grew larger and between her half closed lips she breathed out something confused and painful.

Prokop would have liked to sink through the ground. "Annie," he said at last, breaking the painful silence, "I shall come back. I...in a few days.... You see, this is a very important business. A man...after all must consider... his work. And he has, you know, certain...certain obligations...." (God, how he had botched it!) "Consider that... I simply must," he cried suddenly. "I would rather died than not go, you see?"

Annie only nodded her head slightly. Ah, if she had moved it more it would have sunk on the table and she would have burst out crying; but, as it was, her eyes only filled with tears.

"Annie," cried Prokop in desperation, and took shelter near the door, "I won't even take leave of you; look, it isn't worth it; in a week, a month I shall be here again...see—"

He could not help watching her; she sat perfectly still, with relaxed shoulders; he could not see her eyes; it was painful to look at her. "Annie," he tried again, and again was unable to go on. The last moment in the doorway seemed to him to be endless; he felt that there was still something which he should say or do, but instead he forced out of himself an "*Au revoir*" and stole miserably away.

He left the house like a thief, on tiptoe. For a moment he hesitated outside the door behind which he had left Annie. Inside all was quiet, a fact which caused him unspeakable agony. In the porch he stopped short like a person who has forgotten something and went softly to the kitchen—thank God, Nanda was not there!—and picked up the *Politika*. "...ATIT!...address Carson, Poste Restante." Thus it ran on a fragment of newspaper which the cheerful Nanda had used for covering a shelf.

Prokop left a handful of money in return for her services and made off.

Prokop, Prokop, you are not the only man who intends to return in a week!

"We're off, we're off," beat the wheels of the train. But its noisy, vibrating pace did not suffice for human impatience; human impatience desperately twisted about, drew his watch out of his pocket and nervously kicked his feet about. One, two, three, four...telegraph posts. Trees, fields, trees, a watchman's house, trees, the bank of a river, a fence and fields, Eleven-seventeen. Fields of turnips, women in blue aprons, a house, a little dog which took it into its head to race the train—fields—fields—fields. Eleven-seventeen. God, how the time stood still! Better to think of something; to close one's eyes and count up to a thousand; to recite a *paternoster* or repeat some chemical formula. "We're off, we're off!" Eleven-eighteen. God! What is one to do?

Prokop started. "KRAKATIT" stared him in the eyes, until he grew frightened. Where was it? Aha! The man opposite was reading a paper and on the back was that announcement. "KRAKATIT! Will Eng. P. give his address? Carson, Poste Restante." I wish that Mr. Carson would leave me alone, thought Eng. P.; all the same at the next station he bought all the papers which his country produced. It was in all of them and in all of them the same. "KRAKATIT! Will Eng. P. give his address? Carson, Poste Restante."

"My Godfathers!" said Eng. P. to himself, "there's some demand for me! But what does he want me for, when Thomas has sold him the secret?"

But instead of solving this fundamental problem he looked to see if he was observed, and then, perhaps for the hundredth time, drew out the familiar package. With all possible delays, delays which gave him acute pleasure, after all sorts of reflections and hesitations, he pulled out of it the sealed-up money and that letter, that priceless letter, written in a mature and energetic hand.

"Dear Mr. Thomas," he again read with excitement, "I am not doing this for you, but for my sister. She has been nearly off her head since you sent her that terrible letter. She would have sold all her clothes and jewels in order to send you money; I had to use all possible force to prevent her from doing something which she would afterward have been unable to hide from her husband. What I am sending you is my own money; I know that you will take it without making unnecessary difficulties and beg you not to thank me for it—L." Then a hasty postscript: "For the love of God, after this leave M. in peace! She has given all that she has; she gave you more than what belonged to her; I am horrified to think of what would happen if it all were discovered. I beseech you not to abuse your terrible influence over her! It would be too base if you were to—" The rest of the phrase was struck out and there followed still another postscript: "Please convey my thanks to your friend, who is bringing you this. He was unforgettably kind to me at a time when most of all I needed human help."

Prokop was simply overpowered by an excess of happiness. So she was not Thomas's! And she had nobody to whom she could turn! A brave and generous girl. She got together forty thousand to save her sister from…evidently from some humiliation. Thirty thousand of it was from the bank; it still had a band round it as when she had drawn it—why the devil didn't the band have on it the name of the bank? And the other ten thousand she scraped together nobody knows how; for it was made up of small notes, miserable, soiled five-crown notes, tousled rags from God knows whose hands, shabby money from women's purses. God! What a frightful time she must have had before she got this handful of money together! "He was unforgettably kind to me…." And that moment Prokop would have pounded Thomas to death, that low, shameless scoundrel; but at the same time he somehow forgave him…

since he was not her lover! She did not belong to Thomas…that certainly signified at the least that she was a pure and beautiful angel; and it was as if some unknown wound suddenly healed in his heart.

Yes, to find her; before everything…before everything he must return her her money (he was not in the least ashamed of forming such a pretext) and say that…that, in short…she could depend on him…. "He was unforgettably kind." Prokop clasped his hands…. God! What would he not do to earn such words from her—

Oh, how slowly the train was going!

CHAPTER XV

Directly he arrived at Prague he made for Thomas's rooms. Outside the Museum, he pulled himself up…curse, where exactly did Thomas live? He walked, yes, he walked, shaking with fever, along the road by the Museum; but from where? From which street? Swearing, Prokop wandered round the Museum looking for the most probable direction; he found nothing and went to the Inquiry Office of the police. George Thomas; the dusty official looked through a number of books. Engineer Thomas, George, that, please, is Smichov, such and such a street. Evidently an old address. Nevertheless Prokop flew into Smichov to such and such a street. The caretaker shook his head when he asked for George Thomas. He certainly used to live here, but more than a year ago; where he lived now nobody knew; incidentally he had left all sorts of debts behind him—

Crestfallen, Prokop wandered into a coffee-house. "KRAKATIT" hit him in the eyes from the back of a paper. "Will Eng. P. give his address? Carson, Poste Restante." Well, this Carson will certainly know about Thomas…there must be some connection between them. All right then… "Carson, Poste Restante. Be at such and such coffee-house tomorrow at mid day—Eng. Prokop." Directly he had written this a new idea came into his head…the debts. He rushed off to the courts, the Inquiry Department. Yes, they knew Mr. Thomas's address very well…a whole pile of undelivered circulars, official reminders, etc.; but it appeared that this Thomas, George, had disappeared without leaving a trace, and, especially, had furnished no one with his new address. All the same, Prokop dashed off to the new address.

The caretaker's wife, encouraged by an adequate tip, at once recognized Prokop, who on one occasion had spent the night there. She informed him quite voluntarily that Mr. Engineer Thomas was a crook and a good-for-nothing. Further, that on that occasion he had gone off in the night and left him, the gentleman, in her care; that she had come upstairs three times to ask whether he needed anything, but that he, the gentleman, remained asleep and kept on talking to himself, and finally disappeared. And where on earth was Mr. Thomas? That night he had gone off and left everything lying about and had still not returned. All he had done was to send her some money from somewhere abroad, but he was still in debt for the new quarter. She had heard that they were going to sell his effects in the State Lottery if he didn't report by the end of the month. He was nearly a quarter of a million in debt, so they said, and had made off.

Prokop subjected the worthy woman to a cross-examination... Did she know anything about a certain young lady who was supposed to have relations with Mr. Thomas, who—came to his rooms and so on?

The caretaker's wife could not tell him anything; as far as women went, as many as twenty came to the place, some with veils over their faces and others "made up," and all sorts. It was a scandal for the whole street. Prokop paid for the new quarter himself and in return obtained the key of the flat.

Inside, there was the musty smell of rooms which have long been unoccupied and from which almost all life has departed. Only now did Prokop realize that he had wrestled with his fever amidst the most extraordinary luxury. Everywhere Bokhara or Persian carpets, on the walls tapestries and nude studies, a divan, armchairs, the dressing-table of a *soubrette*, the bathroom of a high-class prostitute—a mixture of luxury and vulgarity, lewdness and dissoluteness. And here, in the middle of all these abominations, she had stood pressing the package to her bosom, her clear, woeful eyes cast on the ground. And now, my God! She raised them in brave devotion.... What on earth could she have thought of him when she found him in this den? He must find her at least...at least to return her her money. Even if it was for nothing else, for nothing more important...it was absolutely necessary to find her!

That is easy enough to say, but how? Prokop bit his lips in obstinate reflection. If he only knew where to look for George, he said to himself.

Finally, he came upon a pile of correspondence which was waiting there for Thomas. Most of it consisted, naturally, of commercial letters, obviously chiefly bills. Then a few private letters which he turned over and sniffed with some hesitation. Perhaps in one of them there was a clue to his whereabouts, an address or something of the sort, which would enable him to find him... or to find her!

He heroically repressed the inclination to open at least one letter; but he was alone there behind dirty windows, and everything seemed to exhale an atmosphere of base and secret corruption. And then, quickly overcoming all his scruples, he began to tear open the envelopes and read one letter after the other. A bill for Persian carpets, for flowers, for three typewriters; urgent reminders regarding goods given on commission; some mysterious transaction relating to a horse, foreign currency, and twenty wagons of wood somewhere near Kremnice.

Prokop could not believe his eyes. According to these documents, Thomas was either a smuggler on a large scale, or an agent dealing in Persian carpets, or a speculator on the Exchange—and very probably all three. In addition, he did business in motorcars, export certificates, office furniture, and, obviously, all sorts of things. In one letter there was something about two million crowns, while in another, soiled and written in pencil, there was a threat of a complaint regarding some antique or other which he had wheedled from somebody. Everything together pointed to a long succession of deceptions, embezzlement, and falsifications of export documents. As far as Prokop was able to understand, it was simply amazing that it had not all come out. One solicitor intimated briefly that such and such a firm had brought an action against Mr. Thomas for embezzling forty thousand crowns; it was in Mr. Thomas's own interest to appear at his office, etc.

Prokop was horrified. If it were all once found out, what would not be the ramifications of this unutterable turpitude? He thought of the quiet house in Tynice and of the girl who had stood in the very room, desperately determined to protect that third person.

He took up all Thomas's commercial correspondence and ran to burn it in the stove, which he found full of charred papers. It was evident that Thomas himself had simplified conditions in this way before he left.

Good; that dealt with the commercial papers; there remained a few purely private letters, tender or dreadfully scrawled, and over these again Prokop hesitated in burning shame. But what on earth else was he to do? He was suffocating with embarrassment, but he boldly opened the remaining envelopes. "Darling, I remember," "a further meeting,"—and so on. A certain Anna Chvalova stated with the most touching orthographical mistakes that Jenicek had died "of an eruption". Somebody else intimated that "he knew something that might interest the police but that he would be willing to discuss the question," and that Mr. Thomas "certainly knew the price of his discretion"; there followed an allusion to "that house in Bret Street where Mr. Thomas knew whom to speak to if the affair was to be kept secret." Then something about some business or other, the sale of some bills, signed "your Rosie." The same Rosie stated that her husband had gone away. The same handwriting as in No. 1, a letter from a watering-place, nothing but bovine sentimentality, the unbridled passion of a fat and mature blonde, sweetened all over with reproofs, and lofty sentiments, apart from "sweetheart" and "ducky" and other abominations. Prokop positively felt bilious. A German letter, signed "G," a deal in foreign currency, "sell these papers, I await your reply, P.S. Achtung, K. aus Hambourg eingetroffen." The same "G"; a hasty and offended letter, the frigid use of the second person plural. "Send back that ten thousand, sonst wird K. dahinter kommen." H'm. Prokop was deeply ashamed at having to penetrate into the malodorous obscurity of these disreputable affairs, but it was no good stopping now. Finally, four letters signed M.; tearful, bitter and miserable, from which emerged the passionate history of some blind, airless, servile love. There were passionate demands, crawlings in the dust, desperate incriminations, frightful offerings of the writer's self and more terrible self-torture; references to the children, the husband, the offer of a further loan, obscure allusions and the all too clear wretchedness of a woman at the mercy of passion. So this was her sister! To Prokop it was as if he saw before him the cruel and mocking lips, the taunting eyes, the aristocratic, proud, self-confident head of Thomas; he would have liked to smash it with his fist. But it was of no use; the miserable love of this woman told him nothing about…about this other one, who was for him so far without a name and whom he must seek out.

Nothing was left but to find Thomas.

CHAPTER XVI

To find Thomas…as if that were a simple matter! Prokop again made a general examination of the whole flat; he rooted in all the cupboards and drawers, finding old bills, love letters, photographs and other relics of Thomas's youth, but nothing which was likely to help him with his quest. Well, it was natural enough that a person who had brought down so much on himself would have to disappear very definitely!

He again cross-questioned the caretaker's wife; he certainly learnt all sorts of stories, but nothing which put him on Thomas's trail. He tried to find out from the caretaker from where Thomas had sent the money from abroad. He had to listen to a whole sermon from an ungracious and rather unpleasant old man, who had suffered from every possible sort of catarrh and who enlarged upon the depravity of the young men of today. At the price of superhuman patience Prokop finally learnt that the money in question was not sent by Mr. Thomas but by an agent of the Dresdner Bank "Auf Befehl des Herrn Thomas." He dashed off to the solicitor who had a claim prepared against the delinquent. The solicitor withdrew to an unnecessary extent into his professional secrecy; but when Prokop stupidly blurted out that he had some money to give to Thomas, the solicitor became more alive and demanded that he should hand it over to him. It cost Prokop a good deal of trouble to get away.

This taught him not to search for Thomas among people who had any sort of commercial connection with him.

At the next corner he stopped; what now? There remained only Carson. An unknown quantity who knew something and wanted something. Good. Carson then. Prokop found in his pocket the letter which he had forgotten to post and ran off to a letterbox.

But once there his hand dropped. Carson, Carson—yes, but he…what he wants is hardly a trifle. Devil take it, that fellow knew something about Krakatit and had got something up his sleeve—God knows what. Why was he looking for *him?* Evidently Thomas didn't know everything, or he didn't want to sell everything, or he laid down impossible conditions, and he, Prokop, like an ass, had to sell himself more cheaply. It must be something like that; but (and here Prokop for the first time grew terrified at the extent to which he was involved) what could he do with Krakatit when he got it? To begin with he must know very well what the substance is for, how it is handled, etc. Krakatit, my friend, is not snuff or a sleeping-powder for children. And in the second place, in the second place it was…too strong a tobacco for this world. Just imagine what could be done with it…let us say in a war. Prokop began to get frightened of the whole business. What devil was bringing that cursed Carson here? On all accounts he must stop, cost what it may—

Prokop clutched at his head so markedly that passersby stopped to look at him. For he remembered that up there in his laboratory shed in Hybsmonka he had left nearly four ounces of Krakatit! That is to say enough to blow off the earth I don't know what—the whole district! He became frozen with horror and ran for a tram. What did not hang upon these few minutes! He went through hell before the tram took him across the river; then he climbed the street as fast as he possibly could and finally reached the shed. It was locked up and Prokop vainly hunted in his pockets for something resembling a key; then, taking advantage of the twilight like a burglar, he broke open the window, pulled back the bolts and crawled home through the window.

He only needed to strike a match to see that the place had been plundered in the most methodical way possible. Certainly the bedding and a few sticks of furniture remained; but all the flasks, test-tubes, crushers, mortars, dishes and apparatus, spatulas and balances, all his primitive chemical kitchen, everything which had contained material upon which he had experimented, anything on which there might be left the slightest sediment or trace of any chemical, had disappeared. There was missing also the Porcelain box containing Krakatit. He pulled out a drawer of the table; all his papers and notes, every scrap of paper on which he had scribbled, the smallest relic of twelve years of experimental work, all had gone. Finally, even the spots and splashes had been scraped off the floor, and his overall, that ancient, ragged covering, positively encrusted with chemicals, had also been taken away. He found himself nearly crying.

Until late in the night he remained sitting on his soldier's palliasse and blankly stared at his looted workroom. At moments he consoled himself by thinking that he would remember everything that he had made a note of in the course of twelve years; but when he tried to repeat some experiment in his head he found, in spite of his most desperate efforts, that it was impossible; then he gnawed his mutilated fingers and groaned.

Suddenly, he was awakened by the rattling of a key. It was fully light, and as if it were the most ordinary thing in the world a man came into the room and made towards the table. He sat down with his hat still on, muttering and scratching at the zinc on the table. Prokop cried out from the palliasse: "What do you want here, man?"

Extraordinarily surprised, the man turned around and looked at Prokop without a word.

"What do you want here?" repeated Prokop excitedly. The man said nothing; to crown everything he put on his spectacles and gazed at Prokop with enormous interest.

Prokop ground his teeth, for there was prepared within him a fearful insult. But at this point the man glowed with the most human feeling, sprang out of the chair and suddenly looked as if he were joyfully wagging his tail. "Carson," he said rapidly introducing himself, and added in German: "God, I am glad that you have come back! You undoubtedly read my announcement?"

"I did," answered Prokop in his stiff and ponderous German. "And what do you want here?"

"You," said his guest completely delighted. "Do you know that I've been chasing you for six weeks? All the newspapers, all the detective institutes—ha, ha, my dear sir, what do you say to that? Herr Gott, I am glad! How are you? Well?"

"Why have you stolen my things?" said Prokop gloomily.

"What do you mean, please?"

"Why have you stolen my things?"

"But, Mister Engineer," said the cheerful little man, not in the least put out, "what are you saying? Stolen! Carson! That's good, aha!"

"Stolen," repeated Prokop meaningfully.

"Tut, tut, tut," protested Mr. Carson. "It's all carefully stored. I arranged everything in order. My dear sir, how could you possibly leave it lying about like that? Anybody might have stolen it from you—what? Of course they could, my dear sir. They could have stolen it, sold it, made it public, eh? That goes without saying. They could have done that. But I've stored it for you, do you understand? Honestly, I have. That's why I have been looking for you. You shall have everything back. Everything. That is," he added with some hesitation and something steely flashed under his shiny spectacles, "that is… if you will be reasonable. But we shall come to an understanding, eh?" He added quickly: "You must become qualified. A wonderful career. Atomic explosions, disintegration of elements. Magnificent! Science, before everything science! We shall come to an understanding, eh? Honestly, you shall have everything back. So."

Prokop was silent, overpowered by this avalanche of words, while Mr. Carson waved his arms and circulated about the laboratory inordinately delighted. "I've preserved everything, everything," he said exuberantly. "Every fragment from the floor. Sorted out, stored away, ticketed, sealed. Aha! I could have gone off with everything, eh? But I'm honourable, my dear sir. I shall return everything. We must come to an understanding. You trust. Carson. A Dane by birth, formerly a lecturer in Copenhagen. And I've also studied theology. What does Schiller say? *Dem Einen ist sie—ist sie*—I've forgotten, but it's something to do with science. Amusing, eh? But don't thank me. Later. So."

Prokop had had no idea of thanking him, but Mr. Carson glowed like a self-righteous benefactor.

"In your place," Mr. Carson said enthusiastically, "in your place I should get—"

"Where is Thomas now?" Prokop interrupted him.

Mr. Carson gave him a searching look. "Well." he said through his teeth after consideration, "we know about him. Oh, yes," he said quickly, "you should provide yourself...provide yourself with the largest laboratory in the world. The very best instruments. The World's Institute of Destructive Chemistry. You are right, a university chair is a stupidity. They only repeat old facts, eh? A waste of time. Institute a laboratory in the American style. An enormous laboratory, a brigade of assistants, everything that you want. And you mustn't worry about money. Where do you *déjeuner?* I should so much like you to be my guest."

"What do you really want?" Prokop burst out.

Then Mr. Carson sat down on the palliasse next to him, took him extraordinarily warmly by the hand and said suddenly in quite a different voice: "Keep cool. You can make millions and millions."

CHAPTER XVII

Prokop looked at Mr. Carson in amazement. He was surprised to find that his face was no longer an insipid one, glowing with kindliness; it had grown serious and severe, the eyes of this zealous man had disappeared behind his heavy lids and only for an instant now and then did they flash out sharply. "Don't be foolish," he said emphatically. "Sell us Krakatit and the thing is done."

"But how do you know…?" said Prokop hoarsely.

"I'll tell you everything, honestly everything. Mr. Thomas came to us; he brought four ounces and the formula. Unfortunately he was not able to tell us the process. Neither he nor our chemists have so far been able to discover it, to discover how to make the stuff. Some sort of a trick, eh?"

"Yes."

"H'm. Maybe we may come upon it without your assistance."

"You won't."

"Mr. Thomas…knows something about it, but keeps it a secret. He worked for us behind locked doors. He's a terribly bad chemist, but more artful than you are. At least he doesn't blurt out what he knows. Why did you tell him? All he knows is to cadge money out of people. You should have come yourself."

"I didn't send him to you," muttered Prokop.

"Aha!" said Mr. Carson, "extremely interesting. Your Mr. Thomas came to us—"

"Where exactly?"

"To us. Factories in Balttin. Do you know it?"

"No."

"A foreign concern. Marvellously up to date. An experimental laboratory for new explosives. We make keramit, methylnitrate, and such things. Chiefly military, you see? You'll sell us Krakatit. Yes?"

"No. And is Thomas still with you?"

"Aha! Mr. Thomas; wait, that's amusing. Now he comes to us and says: This is the legacy of my friend, Prokop, a chemist of genius; he died in my arms, and with his last breath, aha! He bequeathed it me. Aha! Magnificent—what?"

Prokop only smiled wryly. "And is Thomas still…in Balttin?"

"Wait a moment. Naturally, to begin with we kept him…as a spy. We get hundreds of them, you know. And we had this powder, Krakatit, tested."

"And the result?"

Mr. Carson raised his hands to heaven. "Magnificent!"

"What's the speed of detonation? How did you find Q? And t? The figures!"

Mr. Carson let his hands fall, so that they slapped on his knees and opened his eyes very wide. "What figures, man! The first attempt…fifty percent starch…and the crusher gauge was blown to smithereens. One engineer and two assistants…also in smithereens. Would you believe it? Attempt No. 2…a Trauz block, ninety percent Vaseline, and bang! The roof went up and one workman was killed; nothing of the block remained but a fragment. Then we let the soldiers have a go at it; they laughed at us…said we knew as much about it as…a village blacksmith. We gave them a little; they rammed it into a gun with a lot of sawdust. Splendid results. Seven gunners blown up including a N.C.O.…they found one leg three kilometres away. Twelve dead in two days, there's figures for you. Aha! Magnificent, eh?"

Prokop wanted to say something, but gulped it down. Twelve dead in two days—the devil!

Mr. Carson rubbed his knees and glowed with pleasure. "The third day we gave it a rest. It makes a bad impression, you know, when…you have many such incidents. Then we only took a little Krakatit…about three decigrams…in glycerine and that sort of thing. The idiot of a lab boy left a pinch lying about in the night when the laboratory was shut, and—"

"It exploded?" cried Prokop.

"Yes. At ten thirty-five. The laboratory chemist was torn to shreds, not to speak of a couple of blocks of buildings.… About three tons of methylnitrate went up with it—in short, about sixty killed. Naturally enough, a tremendous investigation and all the rest of it. It turned out that nobody had been in the laboratory and that evidently it must have exploded—"

"By itself," interrupted Prokop, scarcely breathing.

"Yes. Was it the same with you?"

Prokop nodded gloomily.

"There you are," said Carson quickly. "And not without a reason. Terribly dangerous stuff. Sell it to us and you won't have to worry anymore. What would you have done with it?"

"And what would *you* have done with it?" said Prokop through his teeth.

"We've…made arrangements about that. What does it matter ,blowing up a few fellows—but it would be a pity if you were to suffer."

"But the Krakatit in the porcelain box didn't explode," said Prokop, still obstinately reflecting.

"Thank God, no. I should think not!"

"And it was at night," Prokop reflected further.

"At ten thirty-five, precisely."

"And…those few grains of Krakatit were lying on a zinc…on a metal plate," Prokop went on.

"It was nothing to do with that," burst out the little man with a worried expression, and he bit his lips and started pacing up and down the laboratory. "It was…perhaps only oxidization," he said after a moment. "Some sort of chemical process. It didn't explode when mixed with glycerine."

"Because it isn't a conductor," jerked out Prokop. "Because it doesn't ionize—I don't know."

Mr. Carson stopped and stood over him with his hands behind his back. "You're very astute," he said appreciatively. 'You deserve to get a lot of money. It's a pity you're stuck here."

"Is Thomas still in Balttin?" asked Prokop, exerting all his strength so as to appear indifferent.

Something flashed behind Mr. Carson's spectacles. "We've got our eye on him," he said evasively. "He certainly won't come back here. Come to us… You may find him—if you want him so very badly," he said slowly and emphatically.

"Where is he?" repeated Prokop obstinately, making it quite clear that he would talk of nothing else.

Mr. Carson waved his hand airily. "Well, he's made off," and he gave Prokop an inscrutable glance.

"Made off?"

"Faded away. He wasn't supervised carefully enough, and he was an artful bird. He undertook to prepare Krakatit for us. Experimented with it… about six weeks. Cost us a frightful amount of money. Then disappeared, the rotter. Didn't know what to do—what? Knows nothing."

"And where is he?"

Mr. Carson bent over Prokop. "A rotter. Now he is offering Krakatit to some other state. And at the same time, he stole our methylnitrate, the swine. Now he is playing the same trick on them."

"Where?"

"Mustn't say. Honestly, I mustn't. And when he bolted, I went, *aha!* To visit your grave. Piety—what? Chemist of genius, unknown to anyone here. That was a job, if you like. Had to keep on advertising in papers like an idiot. Naturally, the others got on to it, see? You understand me?"

"No."

"Come and have a look," said Mr. Carson briskly, and he crossed to the opposite wall. "Here," he said and tapped the boarding.

"What is it?"

"A spyhole. Someone came here."

"And who shot at him?"

"Well, I did. If you had crept through the window the same way a fortnight ago, someone...would have let fly at you."

"Who?"

"That's all the same, this or that state. A good many foreign powers, my friends, have been knocking at this door. And meanwhile, you were somewhere, *aha!* catching fish, eh? Marvellous fellow! But listen, my dear sir," he said with sudden seriousness, "kindly give up coming here. Never, do you understand?"

"Rubbish!"

"Wait. You won't find a grenadier waiting for you. Very unpretentious-looking people. Nowadays, this sort of thing...is done very discreetly." Mr. Carson stopped near the window and drummed on the glass with his fingers. "You cannot believe how many letters I got in answer to my advertisement. About six Prokops introduced themselves.... Come and look, quick!"

Prokop came over to the window. "What is it?"

Mr. Carson silently pointed at the road with his short finger. On it, a young man was twisting about on a bicycle in a desperate attempt to maintain his equilibrium, each wheel exhibiting a strong inclination to go in a different direction. Mr. Carson looked at Prokop inquiringly.

"Apparently learning to ride," said Prokop doubtfully.

"Frightfully inept, eh?" said Mr. Carson and opened the window. "Bob."

The youth on the bicycle stopped instantly: "Yessir."

"Go to the town for our car!" said Mr. Carson in English.

"Yessir." And the young cyclist whisked off towards the town.

Mr. Carson turned away from the window. "An Irishman. Very smart lad. What was I going to say? *Aha!* About six Prokops appeared—meetings in different places, especially at night—amusing, eh? Read this."

"Come to my laboratory at ten o'clock tonight, Eng. Prokop," read Prokop as if in a dream. "But this is...practically...my handwriting!"

"You see," said Carson with a grin. "My friend, things are warm. Sell the stuff and be left in peace!"

Prokop shook his head.

Mr. Carson gave him a heavy, fixed look. "You can ask...let us say... twenty million. Sell us Krakatit."

"No."

"You will get everything back. Twenty million. Sell it, man!"

"No," said Prokop heavily. "I don't want anything to do...with your wars."

"What's your position here? A chemist of genius...and you live in a wooden hut! That's the way your countrymen appreciate you! I know. A great man has no countrymen. Don't let yourself be worried! Sell it and—"

"I don't want to."

Mr. Carson stuck his hands into his pockets and yawned. "Wars! Do you think they can be stopped? *Pish!* Sell it and don't worry. You're a scientist… what does the rest matter to you? Wars! Don't be silly. As long as people have nails and teeth—"

"I shan't sell it," said Prokop through his teeth.

Mr. Carson shrugged. "As you like. We shall discover it ourselves. Or Thomas will. Good."

There was a moment of silence.

"It's all the same to me," said Mr. Carson. "If you prefer it, we'll offer it to France, to England, wherever you like, even to China. Together, see? No one would buy it here. You would be a fool to sell it for twenty million. Trust Carson, eh?"

Prokop shook his head decisively.

"Character," said Mr. Carson appreciatively. "All honour to it. I like that sort of thing enormously. Listen, I'll tell you an absolute secret. I swear it."

"I'm not asking you for your secrets," muttered Prokop.

"Bravo. A discreet fellow. Just my type, my dear sir."

CHAPTER XVIII

Mr. Carson sat down and lit a very fat cigar, after which he reflected for a time. "Tchah!" he said at last. "So it exploded with you also. When was that? The date?"

"I can't say now."

"The day of the week?"

"I don't know. I think…two days after Sunday."

"Tuesday then. And at what time?"

"About…some time after ten in the evening."

"Correct." Mr. Carson thoughtfully blew out some smoke.

"With us, it exploded…as you were pleased to express it, 'by itself'…on Tuesday at ten thirty-five. Did you notice anything at the time?"

"No. I was asleep."

"Aha! It also explodes on Fridays, about half-past ten. On Tuesdays and Fridays. We tested it," he explained in answer to Prokop's fascinated look. "We left a milligram of Krakatit lying exposed and watched it day and night. It exploded on Tuesday and Friday at half-past ten. Seven times. Once also on a Monday at ten twenty-nine. So."

Prokop was inwardly horrified.

"A sort of blue spark appears on it," added Mr. Carson, absorbed, "and then it explodes."

It was so quiet that Prokop could hear the ticking of Carson's watch.

"Tchah!" sighed Mr. Carson and rummaged desperately with his hand in his brush of red hair.

"What does it mean?" Prokop burst out.

Mr. Carson only shrugged his shoulders. "And what did you," he said, "what did you think yourself when it exploded…'by itself,' eh?"

"Nothing," replied Prokop evasively. "I didn't speculate…so far."

Mr. Carson mumbled something uncomplimentary.

"That is," Prokop corrected himself, "I thought that perhaps…it was done by electromagnetic waves."

"Aha! Electromagnetic waves. We thought so, too. A splendid idea, only idiotic. Unfortunately, completely idiotic. So."

Prokop was completely at a loss.

"To begin with," continued Mr. Carson, "wireless waves don't pass over the world only on Tuesdays and Fridays at half-past ten! And secondly, my friend, you must imagine that we at once experimented accordingly. With short, long, all possible waves. And your Krakatit didn't alter that much," and he indicated a minute spot on his own nail. "But on Tuesdays and Fridays at half-past ten it conceived the idea of exploding 'by itself.' And do you know what besides?"

Prokop of course did not. "This. For some time...about six months or something of the sort...the European wireless stations have been horribly annoyed. Something is interfering with their conversations, you know. Really. And as it happens...always on Tuesdays and Fridays at half-past ten in the evening. What did you say?"

Prokop had said nothing, but only rubbed his forehead.

"Well, on Tuesdays and Fridays. They call it disturbed conversations. Something begins to crackle in the telegraphists' ears, and there we are; it's enough to send the fellows off their heads. Sad, eh?" Mr. Carson removed his spectacles and began to clean them with extreme care. "To begin with...to begin with they thought it was magnetic storms or something of the sort. But when they found that its office hours were always Tuesday and Friday...to cut the story short, Marconi S.F. Transradio, and various Ministries of Posts and Marine, Commerce, the Interior and I don't know what, have agreed to pay twenty thousand pounds sterling to the smart fellow who can find out the cause of it." Mr. Carson replaced his spectacles and smiled broadly. "They think that there is some illegal station in existence which amuses itself by interfering with conversations on Tuesdays and Fridays. Rubbish! A secret station which uses up twenty kilowatts for a joke! Fie!" And Mr. Carson spat contemptuously.

"On Tuesdays and Fridays," said Prokop, "that is, regularly..."

"Extraordinary, eh?" leered Mr. Carson. "I've got it written down: on Tuesday on such and such a date at ten thirty-five and so many seconds a disturbance at all stations from Reval onwards, and so on. And a certain amount of your Krakatit explodes at the same instant 'by itself,' as you are good enough to express it. Eh? What? The same the next Friday at ten twenty-nine and a few seconds; a disturbance and an explosion. The next Tuesday at ten thirty-five explosion and disturbance. And so on. As an exception, not in accordance with the programme as it were, a disturbance on Monday at ten twenty-nine minutes, thirty seconds. Ditto explosion. Comes on the second. Eight times in eight cases. A joke, eh? What do you think about it?"

"I d—don't know," mumbled Prokop.

"There's one thing," said Mr. Carson after reflecting for a long time. "Mr. Thomas was working with us. He has no knowledge, but he has got hold of something. Mr. Thomas had a high frequency generator installed in his laboratory and shut the door in front of our noses. A rotter. It's the first time I've heard of high frequency machines being used in ordinary chemistry, eh? What's your idea?"

"Well...naturally," said Prokop doubtfully, with an uneasy glance at his own brand-new generator in the corner.

Mr. Carson did not fail to notice this. "H'm," he said. 'You've the same sort of toy, eh? A pretty little transformer. What did it cost you?"

Prokop grew sullen, but Mr. Carson began to glow. "I think," he said with growing expansiveness, "that it would be a magnificent thing if one could produce in some substance...let's say with the help of high power currents...certain vibrations, set it in violent motion, loosen its interior structure so that one only had just to tap it, from a distance...with some waves or other...by an explosion, oscillations, or the devil knows what, and it would fly to pieces—what? Bang! From a distance! What do you say to that?"

Prokop said nothing, and Mr. Carson, pulling at his cigar in delight, feasted his eyes on him.

"I'm not an electrician, you know," he began after a moment; "it was explained to me by an expert, but I'll be damned if I understood it. The fellow was all over me with electrons, ions, elementary quanta and I don't know what; and, to finish up with, this professorial luminary stated that, to make a long story short, the thing was impossible. My friend, you've made a howler! You've done something which according to the greatest authorities is impossible...

"I tried to explain it myself," he continued, "but not like that. Let us suppose that someone takes it into his head to...to make an unstable compound...from a certain lead salt. The salt in question does not behave as it should; it refuses to combine, eh? Then this chemist of ours tests everything possible...like a madman; and then remembers, let us say, that in the January number of the *Chemist* there was something about the said phlegmatic salt being a first-class coherer...a detector of electric waves. He gets an inspiration. An idiotic and sublime inspiration—that perhaps by the use of electric waves he can bring that cursed salt into a better frame of mind, eh? A man gets his finest inspirations through being stupid. So he gets hold of some comic transformer and sets to work; what he did is at present his secret, but in the end...he will achieve the synthesis he wants. He'll achieve it. Or at least, the oscillation will do it. Man, I shall have to go down on all fours and start learning physics in my old age; I'm talking rubbish, eh?"

Prokop muttered something completely unintelligible.

"That doesn't matter," said Mr. Carson calmly. "As long as it holds together. I'm dull and I imagine that it has some sort of electromagnetic structure. If this structure is disturbed, then...it disintegrates, eh? Luckily about ten thousand regular wireless stations and several hundred illegal ones preserve in our atmosphere the sort of electromagnetic climate, the sort of—eh—eh—oscillatory bath which suits this structure. And so it holds together…"

Mr. Carson reflected for a moment. "And now," he began again, "imagine that some devil has a means by which he can thoroughly disturb electric waves. Obliterate them or something of the sort. Imagine that—God knows why—he does this regularly on Tuesdays and Fridays at half-past ten o'clock at night. At that minute and second all wireless communication is interrupted all over the world; but at that minute and second something also happens in this unstable compound, in so far as it is not isolated…. In a porcelain box, for example; something in it is disturbed…cracks, and it…it…"

"…explodes," cried Prokop.

"Yes, explodes, disintegrates. Interesting—what? One learned gentleman explained to me that—hell, what did he say? That—that—"

Prokop sprang up and seized hold of Mr. Carson's coat. "Listen," he burst out, violently excited, "if one were to…sprinkle…some Krakatit about… here, let us say…or simply about the place…"

"…then the next Tuesday or Friday at half-past ten it would explode. Ha! Don't strangle me, man."

Prokop released Mr. Carson and paced up and down the room gnawing his fingers in consternation.

"That's quite clear," he muttered, "that's quite clear! Nobody must prepare Krakatit—"

"Besides Mr. Thomas," suggested Carson sceptically.

"Leave me alone," said Prokop. "He won't be able to prepare it!"

"Well," said Mr. Carson doubtfully, "I don't know how much you told him."

Prokop stopped as if rooted to the ground. "Imagine," he said feverishly, "imagine, for instance…a war! Anyone who possessed Krakatit could… could…whenever he liked…"

"At present only on Tuesdays and Fridays."

"…blow up…whole towns…whole armies…everything! All that is necessary is to sprinkle—can you imagine?"

"I can. Magnificent!"

"And therefore…for the sake of the world… I shall never, never give it up."

"In the interest of the world," repeated Carson, "do you know, in the interest of the world the first thing is to get on the track of that—"

"What?"

"That cursed anarchist wireless station."

CHAPTER XIX

"Do you mean to say," stammered Prokop, "that...that perhaps..."

"*We know,*" Carson interrupted, "that there exist various transmitting and receiving stations. That regularly on Tuesdays and Fridays they certainly say something more than good-night. That they have at their disposition certain forces at present unknown to us: explosions, oscillations, sparks, rays or some other cursed things. Or certain counter-waves, counter-oscillations or whatever they may be called, something which just obliterates our waves, you understand?" Mr. Carson glanced about the laboratory. "Aha!" said he, and took up a piece of chalk. "It may be like this," he went on, drawing a long arrow on the floor with the chalk, "or like this," and he scribbled over the whole of the board and added, by wetting his finger, a dark streak. "So or so, you understand? Positive or negative. They either send new waves into our medium or interfere with ours at fixed intervals, you see? In both cases they can do without our control. Both systems are at present though technically and physically...a pure mystery. Hell!" said Mr. Carson and in a sudden access of anger broke the chalk into pieces, "that's too much! To send secret messages by secret waves to a secret addressee who is doing—what do you think?"

"Perhaps the Martians," said Prokop, forcing himself to jest; but he was certainly not in the mood for doing so.

Mr. Carson looked at him with hostility and then neighed exactly like a horse. "Let us say the Martians. Magnificent! But let us rather say somebody on the earth. Let us say that some earthly power is sending out its secret instructions. Let us say that it has extremely serious reasons for escaping human control. Let us say that there exists some sort of...international service or organization, or the devil knows what, and that it has at its disposal certain mysterious forces, secret stations and the rest. In any case...in any case we have the right to be interested in those secret messages, eh? Whether they are from hell or from Mars. It's simply in the interests of human society. You can imagine.... Well, my dear sir, they certainly won't be wireless messages about Little Red Riding Hood. So."

Mr. Carson moved rapidly up and down the shed. "One thing is certain to begin with," he said loudly, "that the transmitting station in question is somewhere in Central Europe, approximately in the middle of the areas where these disturbances occur, eh? Relatively, it's not very strong, as it only talks at night. All the worse; there's no difficulty in finding the Eiffel Tower or Nauen, eh? My friend," he shouted suddenly and stood still: "Imagine that in the very heart of Europe something extraordinary is being prepared. The organization has branches and offices, and the branches are in touch with one another; it has technical devices unknown to us, secret powers and, that you may know," roared Mr. Carson, "it has also Krakatit, so!"

Prokop jumped up like a madman. "What!"

"Krakatit. Nine grammes and thirty-five decigrammes. All that we had left."

"What did you do with it?" said Prokop fiercely.

"Experiments. We handled it as carefully as if…as if it were something very precious. And one evening—"

"What?"

"It disappeared. Including the porcelain box."

"Stolen?"

"Yes,"

"And who—who—"

"Obviously the Martians," grinned Mr. Carson. "Unfortunately through the base collusion of a lab. boy who has disappeared—of course with the porcelain box."

"When did that happen?"

"Well, just before they sent me here in search of you. An educated man, a Saxon. He left us not even a grain of powder. Now you know why I came."

"And you think that it fell into the hands…of these mysterious people?"

Mr. Carson only snorted.

"How do you know?"

"I am certain. Listen," said Mr. Carson, jumping about on his short legs, "do I look like a timid person?"

"N—no."

"But I tell you that this frightens me. Honestly, I'm terrified. Krakatit… that's bad enough; and that unknown wireless station is still worse; and if they both fall into the same hands, then…good morning. Then Mr. Carson will pack his bag and go off to the cannibals of Tasmania. You know, I shouldn't like to see the end of Europe."

Prokop only rubbed his hands together between his knees. "Christ, Christ," he whispered to himself.

"Well, yes," said Mr. Carson. "I'm only surprised, you know, that nothing…nothing large has gone up in the air already. All you have to do is to press some button or other and two thousand kilometres away—bang! And there you are. What else do you expect?"

"That's clear," said Prokop feverishly. "Krakatit mustn't be given up. And Thomas—Thomas must be stopped…"

"Mr. Thomas," said Carson rapidly, "would sell Krakatit to the Devil himself if he paid him for it. At the present moment Mr. Thomas is one of the most dangerous people in the world."

"My God," muttered Prokop desperately, "what are we to do now?"

Mr. Carson waited for some time. "It's clear," he said finally. "Krakatit must be given up."

"N-n-no! Never!"

"Given up. Simply because it's a…deciphering key. It's the very moment to do so, my dear sir. For goodness sake give it to anybody you like, only don't make all this fuss about it. Give it to the Swiss or to the League of Aged Virgins or to the Devil's grandmother; it will take them six months to realize that you are not insane. Or give it to us. We've already set up a receiving apparatus at Balttin. Just consider…infinitely rapid explosions of microscopic fragments of Krakatit. Ignited by an unknown current. Directly they turn on the switch somewhere the whole business starts off: t-r-r-r ta ta t-r-r-r t-r-r-r ta t-r-r-r ta ta. And there you are. Decipher it and you have the message. If only one had Krakatit!"

"I won't give it up," Prokop replied, covered with a cold sweat. "I don't believe you. You would…make Krakatit for yourself."

Mr. Carson only pulled down the corner of his mouth. "Well," he said, "it's only a question of…we'll call a Conference. The League of Nations, the World Postal Union, the Eucharistic Congress or anything you like. For the sake of being in peace. I'm a Dane and have no use for politics. So. And you can give Krakatit to an International Commission. What's the matter?"

"I—I've been ill for a long time," Prokop excused himself, deathly pale. "I don't feel quite well…and… I haven't eaten for two days."

"Weakness," said Mr. Carson, sitting down next to him and putting his arm round his neck. "It'll soon pass. You must go to Balttin. A very healthy region. And then you must go after Mr. Thomas. You shall have as much money as a millionaire. You'll be a big man. Well?"

"Yes," whispered Prokop like a little child, and meekly allowed himself to be rocked.

"So so. Too much strain, see? That's nothing. The chief thing…is the future. You've had a lot of poverty, man, eh? You're a good chap, see? Now you're better." Mr. Carson smoked reflectively. "The future is something tremendous. You'll get tons of money. You'll give me ten percent, eh? An international custom. You need Carson as well…"

In front of the shed there resounded the horn of a motor-car.

"Thank God," said Carson with relief, "here's the car. Well, my dear sir, we'll be off."

"Where?"

"For the moment, to eat."

CHAPTER XX

The next day, Prokop woke up with a terribly heavy head and at first could not realize where exactly he was; he waited for the sound of the clucking of the chickens or the resonant barking of Honzik. Slowly he realized that he was no longer in Tynice; that he was in bed in the hotel to which Carson had brought him completely drunk, roaring like an animal. Only when he put his head under a stream of cold water did he recall the happenings of the evening and could have sunk through the ground with shame.

They drank even during the meal, but only a little, enough to make them both very red in the face, and then went somewhere in the car along the edge of some woods so as to clear their heads. Prokop chattered the whole time without respite while Carson chewed the end of his cigar, nodded from time to time and said: "You will be a big man." "Big man," "big man," echoed in Prokop's head like the note of a gong; if only in such glory he could be seen by…that girl with the veil! He nearly burst with importance in talking to Carson, who only nodded his head like a mandarin and added fuel to the flame of his insane pride. In his ardour Prokop nearly fell out of the car; he was explaining his conception of the World Institute for Destructive Chemistry, Socialism, Marriage, the Education of Children and other nonsense. But in the evening they began with a vengeance. Where it was they drank, God alone knows; it was terrible. Carson, his face inflamed and his hat pushed down over his eyes, paid for all sorts of strangers, while some girls were dancing. Somebody broke some glasses and Prokop, sobbing, told Carson about his terrible love for the mysterious woman. On remembering this, Prokop clutched his head with shame and mortification.

Then they put him, shouting "Krakatit," into the car. Heaven knows where they went; they dashed along endless roads, while beside Prokop there jumped up and down a fiery red spot which must have been Mr. Carson with his cigar. Mr. Carson, who hiccoughed "quicker, Bob" or something of the sort. Suddenly, at a corner two lights rushed at them, some voices cried out, the car swung off the road, and Prokop was thrown head first on the grass, which brought him to his senses. There was a sound of several violently disputing voices, accusations of drunkenness. Mr. Carson swore terribly and muttered "now we must go back," upon which, with thousands of precautions, they carried Prokop, as if he were seriously wounded, into the other car. Mr. Carson sat down next to him, and they set out for home, Bob remaining with the injured vehicle. Halfway back the seriously wounded man began to sing rowdily, and just before reaching Prague found that he was thirsty again. They were obliged to go with him to several bars before he quieted down.

Prokop studied his disfigured face in the glass with dark aversion. In this painful occupation he was interrupted by the hotel porter who, with due apologies, brought him a registration form to fill out. Prokop put down the necessary particulars and hoped that he had dealt with the matter; but scarcely had the porter read his name than he became excited and begged Prokop not to leave the room. A certain gentleman from abroad had asked him to telephone to him at his hotel the moment he learned that Eng. Prokop had arrived. If Mr. Eng. would allow it, etc. Mr. Eng. was so furious with himself that he would have allowed him to cut his throat. He sat down to wait, painfully resigning himself to enduring the pain in his head. In a quarter of an hour the porter was back and handed him a card. On it was printed:

SIR REGINALD CARSON

President of the International

Wireless Corporation

London

"Show him in," ordered Prokop, and he was extremely surprised that that fellow Carson had not told him the evening before about his honours and that today he should have arrived so ceremoniously; he was also a little curious to see how Carson would look after that wild night. Then his eyes simply started out of his head with astonishment. There came into the room a completely strange gentleman, a good foot taller than the Mr. Carson of yesterday.

"Very glad to see you," said the strange gentleman slowly, and bowed just as low as if he had been a telegraph pole.

Prokop made an indeterminate noise and gave him a seat. The gentleman sat down on it squarely and began very leisurely to peel off a pair of magnificent kid gloves. He was a very tall and extraordinarily serious gentleman with a horselike face with very precise lines on it. In his tie-pin was an enormous Indian opal, on his gold watch-chain an antique cameo. He had the enormous feet of a golf player, and was, in brief, every inch an English gentleman. Prokop was stupefied. "Please?" he managed to say finally, when the silence had become unbearable.

The gentleman was in no hurry. "Without doubt," he began slowly in English, "without doubt you must have been surprised when you first came across my announcement in the paper. I assume that you are Eng. Prokop, the author of some extremely interesting articles on explosives."

Prokop nodded silently.

"I am very glad to meet you," said Sir Reginald without haste. "I have been wanting to see you in connection with a matter of great scientific interest and practically of great importance for our company, the International Wireless Corporation, whose president I have the honour to be. It is of no less importance for the International Union for Wireless Telegraphy, who have been so good as to elect me as their General Secretary. You will certainly be somewhat astonished," he continued without being out of breath, "that these important concerns should have sent me to see you when your distinguished work is in quite another field. Allow me." With these words Sir Reginald opened his crocodile leather wallet and pulled out some papers, a writing block and a gold pencil.

"About nine months ago," he began slowly, putting a pair of gold pince-nez on his nose so as to see better, "the European wireless stations noticed the fact—"

"Pardon me," Prokop interrupted him, unable to control himself, "did you put those announcements in the papers?"

"Certainly I did. The stations became aware, then, of certain regular disturbances—"

"—on Tuesdays and Fridays, I know. Who told you about Krakatit?"

"I proposed to come to that later," said this venerable gentleman somewhat reproachfully. "Well, I will pass over the details, assuming that to a certain extent you are informed regarding our aims and oh—eh—ah—"

"—regarding a secret international conspiracy, eh?"

Sir Reginald opened his pale blue eyes very wide. "Excuse me, but to what conspiracy do you refer?"

"Well, to those secret messages at night, to the secret organization which sends them out—"

Sir Reginald cut him short. "Fantasy," he said regretfully, "pure fantasy. I am aware that the *Tribune* when our company advertised such a relatively large reward…circulated the report—"

"I know," said Prokop quickly, afraid that this leisurely gentleman would begin to discuss the point.

"Yes. Pure invention. The whole business has nothing but a commercial basis. It is in the interests of a certain person to demonstrate the unreliability of our stations, if you understand me. He wishes to undermine public confidence. Unfortunately our receivers and—ah—coherers are unable to discover the particular type of waves which bring this disturbance about. And since we have received reports to the effect that you have in your possession a certain substance or chemical which reacts in the most remarkable way to these disturbances—"

"Reports from whom?"

"From your colleague, Mr.—ah—Mr. Thomas. Mr. Thomas—ah." Sir Reginald extracted a letter from the bundle of papers he had brought with him. "'Dear Sir,'" he read with a certain amount of effort, "'I have seen in the newspapers an announcement of a reward, etc., etc. As at the present moment it is impossible for me to leave Balttin, where I am at work in connection with a certain discovery, and as a matter of such importance cannot be dealt with by letter, I beg you to seek out in Prague a friend of mine with whom I have worked for many years, Mr. Eng. Prokop, who is in possession of a newly discovered substance, Krakatit, a tetragonal crystal form of a certain lead salt, the synthesis of which is made by utilizing the effect of a high frequency current. Krakatit reacts, as various exact experiments have demonstrated, to certain mysterious disturbing waves by a powerful explosion, from which it follows that it will have decisive significance for determining the nature of the waves in question. In view of the importance of the matter I would suggest, on behalf of myself and my friend, that the reward offered should be considerably rai—'" Sir Reginald cleared his throat. "That is really all," he said. "We could discuss the question of the reward separately. Signed by Mr. Thomas in Balttin."

"H'm," said Prokop, possessed by a sudden serious suspicion, "that such a personal...unreliable...fantastic report should suffice for the International Wireless Corporation."

"I beg your pardon," retorted Sir Reginald, "needless to say we have received very precise reports regarding certain experiments in Balttin—"

"Aha! From a certain Saxon laboratory assistant, eh?"

"No. From our own representative. I'll read you it now." Sir Reginald again rummaged in his papers. "Here we are. 'Dear Sir, the local stations have so far been unable to overcome the disturbances in question. Attempts at using greater power for transmission purposes have completely failed. I have received a report from a reliable informant to the effect that the military works in Balttin have acquired a certain quantity of some substance—'"

There was a knock at the door. "Come in," said Prokop, and the waiter entered with a visiting card: "Some gentleman is asking—"

On the card were the words:

MR. CARSON

Balttin

"Show him in," said Prokop, suddenly violently angry and completely ignoring Sir Reginald's gesture of protest. A moment afterward the Mr. Carson of yesterday, his face bearing evident marks of lack of sleep, walked into the room and made towards Prokop, evidently delighted to see him again.

CHAPTER XXI

"One moment," Prokop stopped him, "allow me to introduce you. Mr. Carson, Sir Reginald Carson."

Sir Reginald drew himself up but remained seated with unruffled dignity; but Mr. Carson, whistling with surprise, sank into a chair like a man whose legs have suddenly failed him. Prokop leaned against the door and stared at both of them with uncontrolled hostility. "Well?" he asked finally.

Sir Reginald began to put his papers away in his wallet. "Undoubtedly," he said slowly, "it would be better for me to visit you some other time—"

"Please stay," Prokop interrupted him. "Excuse me, gentlemen, are you by any chance related?"

"Certainly not," said Mr. Carson. "On the contrary."

"Which of you is the real Carson?"

Nobody answered; there was a painful silence.

"Ask this gentleman," said Sir Reginald coldly, "perhaps he will show you his papers."

"With the greatest pleasure," hissed Mr. Carson, "but after the other gentleman has done so first. So."

"And which of you inserted that announcement in the papers?"

"I," said Mr. Carson without the least hesitation, "my inspiration, my dear sir, I see that even in our sphere one comes across the unheard-of depravity of exploiting someone else's idea. So."

"Allow me," Sir Reginald turned to Prokop with real moral indignation, "this is really too much. What would it have looked like if still another announcement had been made under another name! I was therefore obliged to accept the situation created by the other gentleman."

"Aha!" burst out Mr. Carson aggressively, "and so the gentleman assumed my name for his purposes!"

"All I want to say is," Sir Reginald defended himself, "that this gentleman is simply not named Carson."

"What is his name then?" asked Prokop quickly.

"…I don't know exactly," said Sir Reginald contemptuously through his teeth.

"Carson," said Prokop, turning to the engineer, "and who is this gentleman?"

"Competition," said Mr. Carson with bitter humour. "This is the gentleman who wished to trap me with false documents. He certainly wanted to make me acquainted with some very charming people."

"With the local military police," muttered Sir Reginald.

Mr. Carson's eyes flashed maliciously and he coughed warningly: "I beg you not to speak about it! Certainly—"

"Would the gentlemen like to explain anything to one another?" grinned Prokop from the door.

"No, nothing further," said Sir Reginald with dignity; so far he had not considered the other Carson worthy of a single glance.

"Now," Prokop began, "first of all I should like to thank you both for your visit. Secondly, I am extremely glad to hear that Krakatit is in good hands, that is to say, in my own; for if you had the slightest hope of getting hold of it otherwise I should not have been so much in demand, eh? I am extremely obliged to you for the information which you have involuntarily given me."

"Don't exult too soon," muttered Mr. Carson, "there remains—"

"—him?" said Prokop, indicating Sir Reginald.

Mr. Carson shook his head. "Good gracious, no! But a certain third person—"

"Excuse me," said Prokop, annoyed, "you don't surely think that I believe anything of what you told me last night?"

Mr. Carson shrugged his shoulders regretfully. "Well, as you like."

"Thirdly," Prokop continued, "I should be obliged if you would kindly tell me where Thomas is at present."

"But I told you already," said Mr. Carson quickly, "that I am not allowed to do so. Come to Balttin and there you are."

"And you, sir," Prokop turned to Sir Reginald.

"I beg your pardon," said the latter, "but I prefer to keep that to myself."

"Fourthly, I entreat you not to devour one another while I go out—"

"—for the police," said Sir Reginald. "Quite right."

"I am delighted that you share my opinion. Pardon my locking you in while I am away."

"Oh, please," said Sir Reginald politely, while Mr. Carson would have protested desperately.

Greatly relieved, Prokop locked the door behind him and further stationed two waiters outside it, while he himself ran off to the nearest police station; for he thought it best to let them know what had happened. It transpired that the matter was not to be arranged so easily. He was unable to accuse either of the strangers of having committed even any crime so unimportant as that of stealing silver spoons or playing faro; it cost him a great deal of effort to allay the suspicions of the official at the police station, who evidently regarded him as insane. Finally—probably for the sake of being left in peace—he allotted Prokop a shabby and taciturn plain clothes detective. When they reached the hotel they found both waiters still valiantly guarding the door, surrounded by a group consisting of the entire *personnel* of the establishment. Prokop unlocked the door and the detective, having blown his nose loudly, stepped quietly into the room as if he were going to buy a pair of braces. It was empty. Both the Carsons had disappeared.

The taciturn individual merely blew his nose again and made his way to the bathroom, which Prokop had completely forgotten. From there there was a window looking out on to the well of the hotel, and on the opposite wall was a window in the wall of the lavatory. The taciturn individual then proceeded to the lavatory. This led to another flight of steps. The door was locked, and the key had disappeared. The detective undid the door with a passkey and opened it; inside he found it empty, but there were footmarks beneath the window. The taciturn individual locked the door again and said that he would go and fetch his superior.

His superior, an active little man and a first-rate criminal expert, did not take long to grasp the situation. He spent a good two hours in trying to extract from Prokop an explanation of his relation to the two gentlemen. It appeared that he had a strong desire to arrest at least Prokop, who had become terribly embarrassed in his explanation of his dealings with the two foreigners. Then he questioned the doorkeeper and the waiters and instructed Prokop to report himself at the police station at six o'clock that evening, intimating that he would do better not to leave the hotel meanwhile.

Prokop spent the rest of the day in wandering about the room and reflecting with horror that he would probably be imprisoned; for how could he furnish an adequate explanation when he was determined not to mention Krakatit at any cost? The devil only knew how long such a detention might last; and then, instead of looking for her, the unknown one with a veil... Prokop's eyes were full of tears; he felt so weak and soft that he grew positively ashamed. Finally, he mustered all his determination and set out for the police station.

They led him at once into an office which was furnished with a thick carpet, leather armchairs and a large box of cigars—that of the president. Near the writing-table, Prokop was confronted with an enormous back like that of a boxer, inclined over some papers, a back which at the first glance inspired him with terror and submissiveness.

"Sit down, Mr. Engineer," said the back in a friendly tone, and there turned to Prokop a face no less monumental in build, appropriately placed on the neck of a wild bull. The powerful gentleman studied Prokop for a moment and then said: "Mr. Engineer, I will not force you to tell me what you have decided, after consideration, to keep to yourself. I know about your work. I have the impression that the matter had to do with a certain explosive prepared by you."

"Yes."

"The substance has a certain…shall we say military significance?"

"Yes."

The powerful gentleman got up and shook hands with Prokop. "I should just like to express my thanks to you, Mr. Engineer, for not selling it to foreign agents."

"Is that all?" breathed Prokop.

"Yes."

"Have you arrested them?" Prokop burst out.

"Why?" smiled the gentleman. "We have no right to do so. So far it is only a matter of your secret and not of one belonging to our army…"

Prokop took the delicate hint and became confused. "The matter…hasn't yet matured…"

"I believe you. I have confidence in you," said the powerful man and again shook his hand.

That was all.

CHAPTER XXII

"I must set to work methodically," Prokop decided. Good; and after reflecting for a long time and having a series of remarkable inspirations he evolved a course of action....

To begin with, he inserted the following announcement in all the papers: "Mr. Thomas. The messenger with a wounded hand asks the lady in the veil for her address. Very important. P. Write '40,000' to Box Office." This formulation of the inquiry seemed to him to be very ingenious; he certainly did not know whether the young lady read the newspapers, and especially advertisements, at all, but still, who knows? Chance is a powerful factor. But instead of chance, circumstances came about which could have been foreseen, but which Prokop had not anticipated. In answer to the advertisement he received piles of correspondence, consisting mostly of bills, reminders, threats and insults addressed to the missing Thomas: "Let Mr. Thomas in his own interest furnish his address..." and so on. Further, there wandered into the office of the paper a lean person who, when Prokop called for the answers to his advertisement, stepped up to him and asked him where Mr. Thomas lived. Prokop was as rude to him as the circumstances permitted, whereupon the lean person produced his authority out of his pocket and emphatically warned Prokop not to misbehave himself. It was a question of a certain embezzlement and other disreputable matters. Prokop was able to convince the lean person that he himself was inordinately desirous of knowing where Mr. Thomas lived; after this adventure and after studying the replies to his advertisement his faith in the efficacy of such a method was seriously weakened. In any case the replies steadily decreased in number, becoming on the other hand more threatening in tone.

The next thing he did was to go to a private detective agency. There he explained that he was looking for a mysterious girl in a veil and attempted to describe her. The agency was quite prepared to furnish him with perfectly discreet information regarding her if only he could tell them her name, or address. There was nothing for him to do but to go away.

Then he got an inspiration of genius. In the package, which never left him day or night, there was, besides a number of smaller banknotes, thirty thousand crowns done up in a wrapper, as is usually the custom when banks pay out large sums of money. The name of the bank was not on it; but it was at least highly probable that the girl had drawn the money from some institution or other the day that Prokop left for Tynice. Well, all he had to do was to find the exact date and then go round all the banks in Prague and ask them to give him the name of the person who on that day drew out thirty thousand crowns or something about that figure. Yes, to find the exact date; Prokop was certain that Krakatit had exploded on a Tuesday and it was probable that the girl had drawn the money on a Wednesday; but Prokop was uncertain of both the week and the month; it might have been in February or in March.

He made a tremendous effort to remember, or at least to calculate, when it was; but all his speculations were nullified by the fact that he had no idea how long he had lain ill. Good; they certainly must know at Tynice what week it was in which he descended upon them. Dazzled by this new hope, he sent a telegram to old Dr. Thomas: "Please telegraph date when I arrived at your house. Prokop." He had scarcely sent off the wire when he was overcome with a feeling of remorse at having behaved so badly. To the telegram he obtained no answer. Just as he was about to abandon this trail it occurred to him that the caretaker's wife at Thomas's flat might remember the date. He flew off there; but the caretaker's wife insisted that it was a Saturday.

Prokop became desperate; then he received a letter written in the large and careful characters of a schoolgirl, to the effect that he had arrived at Tynice on such and such a day but that "father mustn't know that I have written to you." Nothing more. It was signed by Annie. For some reason, Prokop's heart was torn by this couple of lines.

Now, having at last found the date he wanted, he rushed off to the nearest bank; could they tell him who on such and such a day had drawn, say, thirty thousand crowns? They shook their heads, saying that it was not the custom to furnish such information; but when they saw that he was completely disconcerted they consulted somebody behind and then asked him on whose account the money had been taken out; for certainly it had been drawn on a cheque, a deposit account or something of that sort. Naturally Prokop did not know. Further, they told him, it was possible that the person in question had only sold certain bills, in which case there would be no record of his name in their books. And when, finally, Prokop informed them that he had simply no idea whether the money was paid out by this particular bank or not they burst out laughing and inquired whether he was going round the two hundred and fifty-odd financial institutions, agencies and exchanges in Prague with the same question. So Prokop's marvellous inspiration proved a complete failure.

There only remained the fourth possibility, the chance that he would meet her. Prokop tried to introduce method even into this possibility; he divided the map of Prague into sections and examined each one twice daily. One day he calculated the number of people he would meet in this way in one day and arrived at a total of nearly forty thousand; bearing in mind the total population of the city it worked out that the chances were one in twenty that he would meet her. Even this small probability gave him hope. There were certain streets and places in which she was more likely to reside, or along which she was likely to be walking; streets with acacias in bloom, venerable old squares, intimate corners of deep and serious life. It was surely impossible that she should be found in the sort of noisy and dreary street along which one only hurried. Nor amid the symmetrical desolation of characterless flats. Why, was it not possible that she lived behind those large, dark windows beyond which was to be found a shaded and refined quiet? Wandering as if in a dream, Prokop realized for the first time in his life what there was to be discovered in this town in which he had spent so many years of his existence; God! How many beautiful spots, where life unrolls itself, peaceful and mature, and entices one when one is distraught!

Numberless times Prokop dashed off in pursuit of young women who gave him the impression from a distance, for some reason, of being she whom he had only seen twice. He ran after them with a wildly beating heart; what if it should prove to be she! Heaven knows what instincts of divination led him to go after them. They were certainly mysterious, sad and beautiful, absorbed in themselves and wrapped in some sort of inaccessibility. Once he was almost certain that it was she; he was so excited that he had to stop for a moment to take breath; and at that moment the woman got into a tram and disappeared. For three days afterward he waited near the stopping place, but never saw her again.

Worst of all were the evenings when, completely exhausted, he sat rubbing his hands on his knees and trying to evolve a new plan of campaign. God! He would never abandon the search for her; it may be that it was an obsession; that he was a lunatic, an idiot, a maniac; but he would never give up. The more she evaded him—the greater efforts would he make; it was… simply fate…or something.

Once he awoke in the middle of the night and it suddenly became inevitably clear to him that he would never find her in this way; that he would have to set out in search of George Thomas, who knew about her and could tell him what he wanted. Although it was the middle of the night he clothed himself, unable to wait until morning. He was unprepared for the incredible difficulties that awaited him in obtaining a passport; he could not understand what they wanted of him and alternately cursed and grew dejected in feverish impatience. Finally, finally the night came when an express carried him across the frontier. And now, to begin with, to Balttin!

Now it will be decided, Prokop felt.

CHAPTER XXIII

It was decided very differently from the way he imagined.

He had conceived a plan of seeking out in Balttin the person who had given himself out to be Carson and of saying to him something like this: "Whatever happens, I spit on your money; lead me at once to George Thomas, with whom I have business, and in return you shall get a good explosive, say fulminate of iodine with a guaranteed detonation of some eleven thousand metres per second, or a certain acid with a good thirteen thousand, my dear sir, and you can do with it what you like." They would simply be mad not to take advantage of such an offer.

From the outside the factory in Balttin seemed to him to be positively enormous; he was rather startled when, instead of a porter, he came upon a military sentry. He asked for Mr. Carson (of course that was not the fellow's real name!); but the soldier passed him on without a word to his N.C.O. The latter said little more and led Prokop to the officer. "We've never heard of Engineer Carson here," said the latter, "and what might the gentleman want with him?" Prokop announced that, strictly speaking, he wished to see Mr. Thomas. This made such an impression on the officer that he sent for the commandant.

The commandant, a very fat and asthmatic person, questioned Prokop in detail as to who he was and what he wanted; by this time there were at least five military persons in the office and they all stared at Prokop so hard that he simply sweated. It was evident that they were waiting for somebody, for whom they had meanwhile telephoned. When this somebody suddenly dashed into the room he proved to be nobody else but Mr. Carson; they addressed him as director, but Prokop never learned his real name. He cried out with delight when his eyes fell on Prokop, saying that he had been waiting for him for a long time and various other things. He at once telephoned to the "Castle" for the guest's suite to be prepared, took Prokop by the arm and conducted him all over the factory. It appeared that what Prokop had taken for the factory was nothing but the guard's and firemen's quarters at the entrance; from there they went along a long road, bordered on each side by a fence about thirty feet high. Mr. Carson led Prokop to the end of this road and only then did he realize what the Balttin factories were really like: a whole town of munition sheds, designated by numbers and letters, hillocks covered with grass which, he told him, were magazines, a little farther on a siding with cranes and ramps, and behind it a number of buildings made of wood. "You see that wood over there?" said Mr. Carson, pointing to the horizon. "Behind it are the first experimental laboratories. And there, where you see those sand hills, is the range. So. And here in the park is the castle. You'll open your eyes when I show you the laboratories. Absolutely up to date. And now we'll go to the castle."

Mr. Carson chattered on happily, but said nothing about what had happened or what was to happen in the future; they passed through the park and he showed him a rare variety of Amorphophallus and next to it a particular species of Japanese cherry; and then they came in sight of the Castle of Balttin, all overgrown with ivy. At the entrance, a quiet and gentle old man in white gloves named Paul was waiting. He led Prokop straight to the guest's apartments.

Prokop had never been in such surroundings in his life: parquet flooring, empire style, everything old and valuable, so that he was afraid even to sit down. And before he had had time to wash his hands there was Paul with eggs, a bottle of wine and a glass, which he set down on the table as carefully as if he were waiting on a princess. Beneath the window was a yard covered with pale yellow sand; a groom in top boots was training a large dapple-grey horse; beside him there stood a slight, dark girl who was watching the trotting of the horse through half closed eyes and from time to time giving the groom some sort of brief orders, after which she knelt down and felt the animal's hocks.

Mr. Carson then appeared with the swiftness of the wind, saying that he must now introduce Prokop to the general manager. He led him along a long white passage, adorned exclusively with antlers and lined with black carved chairs. A red-faced page wearing white gloves opened the door for them, Mr. Carson pushed Prokop inside into a sort of reception room and the door closed behind them. At a desk there was seated a tall old man, extraordinarily erect, as if he had just been taken out of a cupboard and prepared for the interview.

"Mr. Eng. Prokop, your Excellency," said Mr. Carson, "Prince Hagen—Balttin."

Prokop's brow darkened and he jerked his head angrily, a movement which he evidently regarded as constituting a bow.

"Very—pleased—to welcome you," said Prince Hagen and stretched out an inordinately long hand. Prokop again jerked his head.

"I—hope that—you will—enjoy yourself—among us," continued the Prince, and then Prokop noticed that he was paralyzed in half his body.

"Do—honour us—with your presence at dinner," continued the Prince, with evident anxiety on the score of his artificial teeth.

Prokop moved his feet nervously. "Excuse me, Prince," he said finally, "but I am unable to stay here; I—I must leave this very day—"

"Impossible, quite impossible," cried Mr. Carson from behind.

"I must leave today," repeated Prokop obstinately. "I only wanted…to ask you the whereabouts of Thomas. I should be…pleased to offer you in return—"

"What?" cried the Prince, and looked at Mr. Carson with eyes wide with complete lack of comprehension. "What—does he want?"

"Leave that for the moment," said Mr. Carson in Prokop's ear. "Mr. Prokop means to say, your Excellency, that he was not prepared for your invitation. That doesn't matter," he went on, turning quickly to Prokop. "I've arranged for that. We shall dine today out on the lawn, so there is no question of evening clothes; you can go as you are. I've telegraphed for a tailor; no need for anxiety, my dear sir. Everything will be arranged by tomorrow. So."

It was now Prokop's turn to open his eyes wide. "What tailor? What does this mean?"

"It will be—a particular honour—for us," the Prince concluded and gave Prokop his lifeless fingers.

"What does this mean?" raged Prokop when they were outside in the passage and seized Carson by the shoulder. "Tell me now, man, or—"

Mr. Carson neighed like a horse and slipped out of his grasp like a street urchin. "Or—what?" he laughed and flew off, bouncing like a ball. "If you can catch me I'll tell you everything, honestly."

"You clown," thundered Prokop, furious, and set off after him. Mr. Carson, still neighing, flew down the stairs and slipped past the row of armoured knights into the park. There he squatted down like a hare in mockery of his pursuer. "Well," he cried, "what will you do to me?"

"I'll smash you to a jelly," Prokop burst out, falling on him with his full weight. Carson slid away, squeaked with delight and leapt about the lawn like a hare. "Quick," he sang out, "here I am," and again he slipped out of Prokop's hands and cried "I see you!" from behind the stump of a tree.

Prokop again set off after him silently with clenched fists, as serious and threatening as Ajax. He was already panting for breath when, looking round, he saw the dark Amazon watching him from the castle steps with half closed eyes. He became exceedingly ashamed of himself, stopped, and had a sudden foolish fear that the girl would come across and feel his hocks.

Mr. Carson, suddenly quite serious again, strolled over to him with his hands in his pockets and said in a friendly manner: "Not enough training. You shouldn't spend the whole day sitting. Exercise your heart. So. *A-a-a-a*," he sang out, glowing, "haholihoo! The daughter of the old man," he added softly. "Princess Willy, that is Wilhelmina Adelaide Maud and so on. An interesting girl, twenty-eight years old, a great horsewoman. I must introduce you," he said aloud and dragged the protesting Prokop up to the girl. "Princess," he called when they were still some distance away, "let me introduce to you—to a certain extent against his will—our guest, Engineer Prokop. A terribly irate person. Wants to kill me."

"Good morning," said the Princess, and turned to Mr. Carson: "Do you know that one of Whirlwind's hocks is inflamed?"

"My God!" said Mr. Carson, horrified. "Poor Princess!"

"Do you play tennis?"

Prokop was frowning darkly and did not even realize that the remark was addressed to him.

"He doesn't," Carson answered for him and dug him in the ribs. "You must play. The Princess lost to Lenglen by only one set, eh?"

"Because I was playing against the sun," said the Princess, a little piqued. "What do you play?"

Again Prokop did not realize that he was being addressed.

"Mr. Prokop is a scientist," said Carson warmly. "He's discovered atomic explosions and that sort of thing. A marvellous mind. Compared with him, we're nothing but help in the kitchen. Scraping potatoes. But he," and Mr. Carson whistled with amazement, "he's a pure magician. If you want him to he'll prepare hydrogen from bismuth. So, madame."

The half closed grey eyes glanced casually at Prokop, who stood still, thoroughly embarrassed and furious with Carson.

"Very interesting," said the Princess and at once looked elsewhere. "Ask him to teach me about these things sometime. We meet again then at mid day, eh?"

Prokop bowed just in time and Carson dragged him off into the park. "Race," he said appreciatively. "That woman has breeding. Haughty, eh? Wait till you know her better."

Prokop stopped. "Listen, Carson, so that you will get it clear. I don't intend to get to know anybody better. I am going away today or tomorrow, you understand?"

Mr. Carson chewed a piece of grass. "A pity," he said. "It's very nice here. Well, it can't be helped."

"The long and short of it is, where is Thomas—?"

"Wait until you are leaving. How did you like the old man?"

"What interest have I in him?" growled Prokop.

"Well, yes, an antique. There for show. Unfortunately, he has a paralytic stroke nearly every week. But Willy's a marvellous girl. Then there's Egon, a hobbledehoy, eighteen. Both orphans. Then the guests, some second cousin, Prince Suwalski, all sorts of officers, Rohlauf, Von Graun, you know, Jockey Club and Dr. Krafft, the tutor, and various others. You must come and see us this evening. Drink, none of the aristocracy, our engineers and people of that sort, see? Over there in my villa. It'll be in your honour."

"Carson," said Prokop severely, "I want to speak seriously with you before I go."

"There's no hurry. Just rest yourself. Well, I must get back to my work. Do just what you like. No formalities. If you want to bathe, there's a lake over there. We'll talk seriously later. Make yourself comfortable. So."

And he was gone.

CHAPTER XXIV

Prokop wandered about the park, irritable and yawning through lack of sleep. He wondered what they wanted with him and contemplated with dissatisfaction his huge, ungainly boots and wornout trousers. Absorbed in these reflections, he very nearly walked on to the tennis court, where the Princess was playing with two girls in white dresses. He hastily turned aside and set off towards what he imagined was the end of the park. But in that direction the park ended in a sort of terrace; a stone balustrade and below it a wall nearly forty feet high. From the terrace one had a view of the pine woods and of a soldier who was pacing up and down below with a fixed bayonet.

Prokop then set off to the part of the park which sloped away from the castle. There he found a lake with some bathing sheds, but overcoming the temptation to bathe, he went on into a beautiful copse of birch trees. Here he came upon a lattice-work fence and a half effaced path leading to a gate; the gate was not completely closed and it was possible to pass through it into a pine wood. He walked quietly along over the slippery pine cones until he reached the edge of the wood. And there, damnation, was a fence surmounted by barbed-wire, a good twelve feet high. How strong, he wondered, was the wire? He tested it carefully with his hands and feet until he noticed that his conduct had begun to interest a soldier with a fixed bayonet who was standing on the other side.

"A hot day, eh?" said Prokop, to pass it off.

"You are not allowed here," said the soldier; and Prokop swung round and set off farther along the barbed-wire fence. The pine wood turned into scattered young trees, behind which were a few sheds and stables, evidently the yard belonging to the castle. He looked through the fence and inside there immediately began a frightful howling, yelping and barking, and a good dozen dogs, bloodhounds and wolfhounds, hurled themselves at the fence. Four pairs of unfriendly eyes looked out of four different doors. Prokop made some sort of greeting and wished to go farther, but one of the servants ran after him, saying that "You're not allowed here," after which he led him back to the gate at the end of the birch-wood.

All this put Prokop into a very bad frame of mind. Carson must tell him which was the way out, he decided; he was not a canary, to be kept in a cage. Making a detour to avoid the tennis court he made his way to the road through the park, along which Carson had first led him to the castle. No sooner had he reached it than a fellow in a flat cap, who looked as if he had stepped out of a film, came up to him and asked where the gentleman might be going.

"Outside," said Prokop shortly; but "You're not allowed here!" exclaimed the fellow in the cap; "this is the road to the munition barracks and anyone who wants to go along it must have a *laisser-passer* from the management. The gate leading outside directly from the castle is back there on the main road and to the left, please."

Prokop went along the main road and to the left, please, until he was brought up by a large gate with a grating in it. The old doorkeeper went forward to open it for him. "Have you a ticket, please?"

"What sort of ticket?"

"A pass."

"What sort of pass?"

"A ticket, giving you permission to go out."

Prokop became furious. "Am I in a prison, then?"

The old man shrugged his shoulders regretfully: "I was instructed this morning, please."

Poor wretch, thought Prokop, as if he could prevent anyone going out! A movement of the hand—

From the window of the doorkeeper's house there looked out a familiar face, recalling that of Bob. Prokop left his train of thought unfinished, turned back, and wandered again towards the castle. The devil, he said to himself, they're up to some curious tricks; it almost looks as if one were a prisoner here. Good; I'll discuss this with Carson. To begin with, I'm not going to take any notice of their hospitality and shan't join them at dinner. I'm not going to sit down with those young ladies who laughed at me behind my back on the tennis court. Infinitely dejected, Prokop returned to the rooms which had been assigned to him and threw himself down on a divan, giving himself up to his anger. A moment later Mr. Paul knocked at the door and asked with great kindness and concern whether the gentleman was going down to lunch.

"No, I'm not," growled Prokop.

Mr. Paul bowed and disappeared. In a minute he had returned, pushing before him a little table on wheels, covered with glasses, fragile porcelain and silver. "What wine, please?" he asked tenderly. Prokop muttered something so as to be left in peace.

Mr. Paul went on tiptoe to the door and there took from two white paws a large dish. "*Consommé de tortue*," he whispered and poured some out for Prokop, upon which the dish was borne away in the white claws. By the same route there arrived fish, meat, salad, and things which Prokop had never eaten in his life and did not even know how to deal with; but he was shy of exhibiting his embarrassment before Mr. Paul. To his surprise, his wrath had somehow disappeared. "Sit down," he ordered Paul, savouring the dry white wine with his nose and palate. Mr. Paul bowed considerately but remained standing.

"Listen, Paul," Prokop continued, "do you think that I'm in prison here?"

Mr. Paul politely shrugged his shoulders: "I am unable to say, please."

"Which is the way out?"

Mr. Paul reflected for a moment. "Along the main road and then to the left, please. Will the gentleman take coffee?"

"Well, perhaps." Prokop burnt his throat with the superior Mocha, after which Mr. Paul handed him all the perfumes of Araby, contained in a cigar-box and a silver lighter. "Listen, Paul," Prokop began again, biting the end of a cigar, "thank you. Did you ever know a certain Thomas here?"

Mr. Paul raised his eyes to heaven in an effort of recollection. "I didn't, please."

"How many soldiers are there here?"

Mr. Paul considered and made a calculation. "In the main guard about two hundred. That's the infantry. Then the field militia, I don't know how many. In Balttin-Dortum a squadron of hussars. Some gunners at the artillery ground in Balttin-Dikkeln."

"Why do they have field militia here?"

"This is a military camp, please. In connection with the munition factory."

"Aha! And there's only a guard just round this place?"

"Here there are only patrols, please. The chain is further away, behind the wood."

"What chain?"

"The protective zone, please. No one is allowed to go there."

"And if anyone wants to leave the place—"

"Then he must obtain a permit from the camp commandant. Does the gentleman require anything more?"

"No, thank you."

Like a satiated Eastern potentate, Prokop stretched himself out on the divan. Well, we shall see, he said to himself; so far things were not so bad. He wished to reflect on the matter but instead could only remember the way in which Carson had jumped about in front of him. Supposing he hadn't caught him? he thought and set off in pursuit. It was only a question of a jump of about fifteen feet; but Carson soared up like a grasshopper and flew smoothly over a clump of bushes, Prokop stamped his feet and rose after him, but he had scarcely raised his feet when he found himself skimming over the tops of the bushes. Another jump and he was flying God knows whither, not worrying any more about Carson. He glided about amongst trees, as light and as free as a bird; he tried a few movements with his legs and found himself rising higher.

This pleased him inordinately. With powerful strokes he circled up and up. Below him, like a beautiful map, there appeared the prospect of the castle park with its arbours, lawns and serpentine paths; one could distinguish the tennis courts, the pond, the roof of the castle, the birch wood; over there was the yard with the dogs, and the pine wood and the wired fence, and to the right began the munition sheds and behind them the high wall. Prokop made his way through the air over the part of the park which he had not yet visited. On the way there he saw that what he had regarded as a terrace was really the old fortifications of the castle, a powerful bastion with a moat, evidently formerly filled from the lake. He was principally interested in that part of the park between the main entrance and the bastion; there there were overgrown paths and wild bushes, and a wall a good nine feet high, beneath which was some sort of a rubbish heap; beyond was a kitchen garden and round it a wall in which was a green gate; the other side of the gate ran the main road.

"I'll have a look in that direction," said Prokop to himself, and descended a little. But at this point there appeared on the road a squadron of cavalry with drawn sabres, advancing directly upon him. Prokop drew his knees up to his chin, so that they should not slash at him; but through this movement received such an impulse that he once more flew up to a height like an arrow. When he looked down again he saw everything small as on a map; down on the main road there was moving a tiny battery of artillery, the polished muzzle of a gun was turned upwards, a small white cloud appeared and bang! The first shell flew over Prokop's head. They're firing at me, he thought, and quickly waved his arms so as to descend. *Bang!* Another shell whizzed passed Prokop's nose. He took to flight as quickly as he was able. *Bang!* A third shell struck away his wings and Prokop shot head downwards to earth and woke up. Someone was knocking at the door.

"Come in," cried Prokop, and sprang up, not knowing what it was all about.

There entered the room a white-haired aristocratic-looking gentleman in black, who bowed deeply.

Prokop remained standing and waited to see what the distinguished gentleman might say.

"Drehbein," said the minister (at least!) and bowed again.

Prokop bowed equally deeply. "Prokop," he introduced himself. "What can I do for you?"

"If you will kindly remain standing for a moment."

"Please," said Prokop, frightened as to what was going to happen to him.

The white-haired gentleman studied Prokop attentively for a moment; then he walked round him and became absorbed in the contemplation of his back.

"If you would kindly draw yourself up a little."

Prokop became as rigid as a soldier; what the devil—

"Allow me," said the gentleman, and knelt down in front of Prokop.

"What do you want?" gasped out Prokop, recoiling.

"To take your measure." And he drew out of his coat tails a tape measure and began to consider Prokop's trousers.

Prokop receded as far as the window. "Stop it, will you?" he said, irritated. "I've ordered no clothes."

"I've already received instructions," said the gentleman respectfully.

"Listen," said Prokop, recovering control of himself, "go to—I don't want any clothes and that's that! Do you understand?"

"Please," agreed Mr. Drehbein, and he squatted down in front of Prokop, lifted his waistcoat and began to measure the top of his trousers. "Two inches more," he noted, getting up. "Allow me." And he slipped his hand along to Prokop's armpit in a professional manner. "A little more free."

"Good," muttered Prokop and turned his back on him.

"Thank you," said the gentleman and smoothed out a crease on the back of his coat.

Prokop swung round, furious. "Take your hands away, man, or—"

"Excuse me," said the gentleman and gently passed his arms round his waist. Before Prokop had time to fell him to the ground he had loosened his waistcoat strap, had stepped back and was regarding Prokop's waist with his head on one side. "So," he said, completely satisfied and bowed deeply. "I beg to take leave of you."

"Go to the devil," cried Prokop after him, and "It won't be tomorrow now," he said to himself, after which he began to pace from one corner of the room to the other. "Holy smoke, do these people imagine that I am going to stay here for six months?"

Then there was a knock at the door and Mr. Carson entered with a completely innocent face. Prokop, his hands behind his back, stopped him and measured him with melancholy eyes. "Who are you, man?" he said sharply.

Mr. Carson did not even blink, crossed his hands on his chest and bowed like a Turk.

"Prince Aladdin," he said, "I am a djin, your slave. Instruct me and I will carry out your every wish. You've been to bye-byes? Well, your Excellence, how do you like it here?"

"Enormously," said Prokop, bitterly. "I should only like to know whether I'm a prisoner here, and if so, by what right."

"A prisoner?" said Mr. Carson, astounded. "Good heavens, surely nobody's been preventing your going into the park?"

"No, but going out of the park."

Mr. Carson shook his head sympathetically. "Unpleasant, eh? I'm terribly upset that you're dissatisfied. Did you bathe in the lake?"

"No. How do I get out?"

"By the main exit, of course. Go straight on and then to the left—"

"And there I've to show a pass, eh? Only that I have none."

"A pity," said Mr. Carson. "Such pretty country round about."

"Mostly masses of soldiers."

"A lot of soldiers," agreed Mr. Carson. "Well said."

"Listen," burst out Prokop and his forehead twitched with anger, "do you think that it's pleasant to come upon a bayonet or a barbed-wire entanglement every few yards?"

"Where's that?" said Mr. Carson, astonished.

"Everywhere at the edge of the park."

"And what in God's name is taking you to the edge of the park? You can walk about the middle; what more do you want?"

"So I am a prisoner?"

"God preserve us! So I shan't forget it, here's a pass for you. A *laissez-passer* to the factory, see? In case by any chance you would like to have a look at it."

Prokop took the pass from him and became amazed; on it was his photograph, evidently taken the same day. "And with this I can get outside?"

"No," said Mr. Carson quickly. "I shouldn't advise you to. Generally speaking, I should be careful if I were you, eh? You understand? Come and look," he said from the window.

"What is it?"

"Egon is learning to box. Phew, he's caught it! That's Von Graun, see? Aha! That kid's got some spirit!"

Prokop looked with revulsion into the yard, where a half naked lad, bleeding from the mouth and nose, and sobbing with pain and anger, was hurling himself again and again at an older opponent, to be thrown back every time more bloody and pitiful than ever. What he found particularly revolting was that the performance was being watched by the old Prince from a bath-chair, laughing for all he was worth, while Princess Willy was chatting calmly all the time with a magnificently handsome man. Finally, Egon collapsed into the sand completely stupefied and allowed the blood to pour from his nose.

"Brutes!" roared Prokop, addressing the remark to no one in particular, and clenched his fists.

"You mustn't be so sensitive here," said Mr. Carson. "Severe discipline. Life…as in the army. We don't treat anybody gently here," he added, so pointedly that it seemed like a threat.

"Carson," said Prokop seriously. "Am I here…as it were…in prison?"

"Good gracious, no! You're only in a facility which is under supervision. A powder factory isn't quite the same sort of thing as a barber's shop, what? You must adapt yourself to the position."

"I leave tomorrow," Prokop burst out.

"Ha, ha!" laughed Mr. Carson and slapped him on the stomach. "A great wag! You'll come and see us this evening, eh?"

"I won't go anywhere! Where's Thomas?"

"What? Aha! Your Thomas. Well, at the moment a long way away. Here's the key of your laboratory. Nobody will disturb you. I'm sorry I've no time."

"Carson!" Prokop wished to stop him, but he drew back before a gesture so commanding that he did not venture to come nearer; and Mr. Carson slid out of the room whistling like a trained starling.

Prokop made his way with his pass to the main entrance. The old man studied it and shook his head; the pass, he said, was only valid for exit C, the exit leading to the laboratories. Prokop went to exit C; the man out of the film with a flat cap examined the pass and pointed: straight ahead, then the third crossroad to the north. Prokop of course took the first road to the south; but after five steps he was stopped by a soldier: back and the third road to the left. Prokop ignored the third road to the left and went straight ahead across a meadow; in a moment three people appeared in front of him. He was not allowed to go this way. Then he obediently went along the third road to the north, and when he thought that there was no one watching him again turned off the road between some munition sheds. Here he encountered a soldier with a fixed bayonet who told him to go to crossroads No. B11 Road N.6. Prokop tried his luck at each crossroad; he was always stopped and sent back to road B11 N.6; finally he learned reason and realized that a pass on which were the letters "C3n.wF.H.A.V11. N6.barV.7.F.b!" had some secret and inescapable significance which he was bound to recognize. So he now went where they directed him. The munition sheds were left behind, and instead were small concrete structures, all marked with numbers, evidently experimental laboratories or something of the sort, distributed amongst the sand dunes and pine woods. His path led to a completely isolated hut numbered V.7. On the door was a brass plate marked "Eng. Prokop." Prokop brought out the key which Carson had given him and went inside.

He was confronted with a perfectly equipped laboratory for the chemistry of explosives—so complete and modern that Prokop held his breath with the delight of a specialist. On a nail there hung his old overall, in the corner was a military palliasse like the one he had had in Prague, and in the drawers of a magnificently appointed writing-table there lay, carefully classified and catalogued, all his printed articles and manuscript notes.

CHAPTER XXV

It was six months since Prokop had had any chemical apparatus in his hands.

He examined one instrument after another; everything of which he had ever dreamed was there, gleaming, brand-new and arranged with pedantic precision. There was a desk and a technical library, an enormous table covered with chemicals, cupboards containing delicate instruments, a chamber for experimental explosions, a room containing transformers, and apparatus of which he had never even heard. He had looked over about half these marvels when, following a sudden impulse, he rushed to the table for a certain barium salt, some nitric acid, a few other things, and began an experiment in the course of which he succeeded in burning his fingers, smashing a test-tube to fragments and burning a hole in his coat. Satisfied with this beginning he sat down at the writing-table and jotted down two or three notes.

Then he had another look round the laboratory. It reminded him rather of a newly instituted perfumery. Everything was arranged too carefully; but after changing the places of a few things it became more to his taste, more intimate. In the midst of the most intense work he suddenly stopped himself.

"Aha!" he said, "this is how they're trying to catch me! In a minute Carson will arrive and begin talking about becoming a big man and that sort of thing."

He sat down morosely on the palliasse and waited. When no one appeared he sat like a thief at the desk and began again on the barium salt. Anyway, he was here for the last time, he told himself. The attempt proved perfectly successful: the stuff burst with a long tongue of flame and cracked the glass case containing the balance. "Now I shall catch it," he said to himself guiltily, when he saw the extent of the damage, and crept out of the laboratory like a schoolboy who had broken a window. Outside, it was already dusk and a fine rain was falling. Ten paces in front of the shed stood a military guard.

Prokop slowly walked back to the castle along the road by which he had come. The park was deserted; a fine rain hissed in the branches of the trees, lights began to appear in the castle and the triumphant notes of a piano resounded in the darkness. Prokop made his way to a lonely part of the park between the main entrance and the terrace. Here all the paths had been overgrown and he plunged into the wet underbrush like a boar, every now and then stopping for a moment to listen and then making a way for himself again through the crackling bushes. At last he reached the edge of this jungle where the bushes stretched over an old wall not more than nine feet high. Prokop seized an overhanging branch so as to drop from it onto the other side of the wall; but under his solid weight the branch gave way with a sharp crack like a pistol shot, and Prokop fell heavily onto a sort of rubbish heap. He remained seated with a beating heart. Surely someone would come after him now. But he heard nothing more than the dripping of the rain. He picked himself up and noticed a wall with a green gate, as he had seen it in his dream.

It was just the same save in one detail; the gate was open. He was greatly disconcerted. Either someone had just gone out of it or was shortly returning; in either case it meant that there was a person in the vicinity. What should he do? Suddenly decided, Prokop kicked the gate open and came out on the main road; and, sure enough, there outside was stumping about a short man in a mackintosh, smoking a pipe. They stood opposite one another, somewhat embarrassed as to how to begin. Naturally the more agile Prokop was the first to take action. Having chosen instantaneously one of a number of possibilities, he threw himself with all his force on the man with a pipe, and, butting him like a goat, threw him into the mud. Then he pressed his chest and elbows into the ground, rather doubtful as to what to do next; for he could hardly wring his neck like a chicken's. The man underneath him never even let the pipe fall from his mouth and evidently was awaiting developments. "Surrender!" roared Prokop; but at that moment he received a blow from the man's knee in the stomach and another from his fist under the chin, as a result of which he rolled into a ditch.

When he began to pick himself up he was greeted with another blow, while the man with the pipe remained quietly watching him from the road. "Again?" he said through his teeth. Prokop shook his head. Then the fellow fetched out an extraordinarily dirty handkerchief and began to clean Prokop's clothes. "Mud," he remarked and rubbed him assiduously.

"Back!" he said finally, and indicated the green gate. Prokop weakly assented. The man with the pipe led him as far as the old wall, and bent down, his hands on his knees. "Climb up," he ordered. Prokop clambered on to his shoulders, the man drew himself up sharply with an "Up!" and Prokop, seizing an overhanging branch, found himself on the top of the wall. He was almost crying with shame.

And, to add to everything, when, scratched and swollen, and covered with mud, he crept humiliated up the steps of the castle to his suite, he met Princess Willy on the stairs, Prokop tried to pretend that he wasn't there, or that he did not recognize her, or something of the sort, omitted to salute her and dashed upstairs like a statue made of mud. But just as he was passing her he caught her astonished, haughty, highly offended look. He stopped stock still. "Wait," he cried and rushed up to her. "Go," he cried, "and tell them, tell them that…that I don't care twopence for them and that… I don't consent to be imprisoned, see? I don't consent!" he roared and brought down his fist on the banisters so that they rattled, after which he dashed into the park again, leaving the Princess behind him pale and dumbfounded.

A few moments later someone almost obliterated by mud rushed into the porter's house, knocked the old man over with an oak table, seized Bob by the throat and dashed his head against the wall so violently that he lost consciousness, after which he possessed himself of the key, opened the door and ran out. Outside, he came up against a sentry, who immediately challenged him and raised his rifle, but before he could fire somebody was shaking him violently, tore the gun out of his hands and broke his collar-bone with the butt. Then two sentries on duty near by ran up; the black being threw the rifle at them and slipped back into the park. Almost at the same moment the night guard at exit C was also attacked; something large and black, appearing from nowhere, suddenly began to hammer his lower jaw. The sentry, a blonde giant, was too astonished for a moment to whistle for assistance. Then this somebody, cursing terribly, let him go and ran back into the dark park. The guard was called out and a number of patrols began to search the grounds.

At about midnight, somebody demolished the balustrade on the terrace and threw stones twenty pounds in weight at the guard, which was passing thirty feet below. A soldier fired, producing from above a string of political insults—and then all was quiet. At that moment a detachment of cavalry arrived from Dikkeln, while the whole of the Balttin garrison were occupied in thrusting their bayonets into the underbrush. In the castle nobody attempted to sleep.

At one A.M., an unconscious soldier without a rifle was found on the tennis court. Shortly afterward, an exchange of shots was heard in the birch wood; luckily nobody was injured. Mr. Carson, with a serious and careworn expression, insisted on sending Princess Willy back to the castle. Trembling through the cold more than anything else, she had ventured, for some reason or other, on to the battlefield. But the Princess, her eyes unusually widely open, asked him to be so good as to leave her alone. Mr. Carson shrugged and let her have her own mad way.

Although people were gathered round the castle as thick as flies, somebody continued to break the windows methodically from the bushes. There was a panic, accentuated by the fact that at the same time three or four rifle shots were heard from the main road. Mr. Carson looked exceedingly anxious.

Meanwhile, the Princess was silently walking along an avenue of beech trees. Suddenly, there appeared before her an enormous black creature, which stood still for a moment, clenched its fists, muttered something to the effect that it was a shame and a scandal, and then dived into the bushes again. The

Princess turned back and stopped the patrol, saying that there was nobody there. Her eyes were wide and shining, as if she were feverish. A moment afterward firing was heard from the bushes behind the lake; according to the noise it came from shotguns. Mr. Carson grumbled, saying that if the yard boys mixed themselves up in it he would pull their ears for them. He did not know that at that moment somebody had thrown a heavy stone at a valuable Danish hound.

At dawn they found Prokop sleeping soundly on a bench in the Japanese summer-house. He was terribly scratched and befouled and his clothes hung in rags; on his forehead he had a lump as big as his fist and his hair was clotted with blood. Mr. Carson shook his head over the sleeping hero of the night. Then Mr. Paul shuffled forward and carefully covered the snoring sleeper with a warm rug, produced a basin full of water, a towel, some clean linen, and a brand-new tweed suit made by Mr. Drehbein, and went away on tiptoe.

Two inconspicuous persons in plain clothes, with revolvers in their hip pockets, strolled up and down in the neighbourhood of the Japanese summer-house until morning with the unconcerned air of people who are waiting to observe the sunrise.

CHAPTER XXVI

Prokop was waiting for all sorts of things to happen as a result of the night's activity; nothing took place, except that he found himself followed about by the man with the pipe—the one being whom Prokop for some reason or other feared. This person bore the name of Holz—a name which was very expressive of his quiet and observant nature. Wherever Prokop went, Holz was five paces behind him. This drove him nearly mad and he tormented his attendant for a whole day in the most refined manner, running hither and thither up and down a short path and waiting fifty and a hundred times for Mr. Holz to get tired of turning face about every few steps. Mr. Holz, however, did not get tired. Then Prokop took to flight and ran three times round the whole park. Mr. Holz silently followed him without even taking his pipe out of his mouth, while Prokop became completely out of breath.

Mr. Carson did not show himself that day. Evidently he was too angry.

Towards evening, Prokop collected himself and went to his laboratory, accompanied, of course, by his silent shadow. Once in the laboratory, he wanted to lock himself in; but Mr. Holz stuck his foot in the door and came in with him. And, since an armchair had been provided in the hall, it was evident that Mr. Holz would remain there. Well, good. Prokop busied himself with some secret business while Mr. Holz coughed shortly and dryly in the hall.

About two hours before dawn, Prokop sprinkled some sort of fabric with petroleum, lit it and dashed outside as fast as he was able. Mr. Holz instantly sprang out of the armchair and followed him. When they were a hundred yards away from the building Prokop threw himself into a ditch with his face on the ground; Mr. Holz remained standing over him and began to light his pipe. Prokop raised his head, and was about to say something to him, but stopped on remembering that conversation with Holz was forbidden on principle. Instead he stretched out his hand and pulled his legs from under him, "Look out!" he roared, and at that moment there was an explosion in the shed and fragments of stone and glass whistled over their heads. Prokop stood up, cleaned himself more or less and quickly, and ran off, followed by Mr. Holz. At the same moment there appeared the guard and a fire engine.

This was the first warning addressed to Mr. Carson. If he didn't come and negotiate now, worse things would happen.

Mr. Carson did not come; instead there arrived a new pass for another experimental laboratory. Prokop was furious. All right, he said to himself, this time he would show them what he could do. He ran off to his new laboratory, reflecting on the form which his protest would take. He decided for explosive potash, ignited by water. But, having arrived at the new laboratory, he found himself helpless. That Carson was a devil!

Adjacent to the laboratory were the quarters of the factory guard. In the garden a good dozen children were playing about in the dirt, and a young mother was endeavouring to appease a little red-faced creature that was yelling vigorously. On seeing Prokop's irate visage, it suddenly stopped. "Good evening," muttered Prokop, and wandered back with his fists clenched. Mr. Holz followed him five paces behind.

On the way to the castle he ran into the Princess on horseback accompanied by a whole cavalcade of officers. He would have turned off down a side path, but the Princess in a flash had ridden up to him. "If you would like to ride," she said quickly, and her dark face flushed, "Premier is at your disposition."

Prokop edged away from the careering Whirlwind. He had never been on a horse in his life, but would not have admitted this for anything in the world. "Thank you," he said, "but there is no need…to sweeten…my imprisonment."

The Princess frowned. It was certainly out of place to refer to the matter so directly in speaking to her; however, she controlled herself and, suavely combining a reproach and an invitation, answered: "I beg you not to forget that at the castle you are my guest."

"That doesn't matter to me," mumbled Prokop obstinately, watching every movement of the nervous horse.

The Princess, irritated, made a movement with her foot; Whirlwind snorted and began to rear. "Don't be frightened of him," Willy threw out with a smile.

Prokop, furious, struck the horse a blow on the muzzle; the Princess raised her whip as if she wished to slash at his hand. All the blood rushed to Prokop's head. "Look out," he said through his teeth, his bloodshot eyes fixed on the Princess's flashing ones. But at this point the officers became aware of the unfortunate incident, and cantered up to the Princess. "Hallo, what's up?" cried the one who was riding in front on a black mare and made straight for Prokop. Prokop saw the horse's head above him, seized hold of the bridle, and with all his force dragged it aside. The horse screamed with pain and reared up on its hind legs, while the officer flew into the arms of the tranquil Mr. Holz. Two sabres flashed in the sun; but quickly the Princess placed Whirlwind between Prokop and the officers. "Stop!" she ordered, "he is my guest!" and, giving Prokop a black look, she added: "Incidentally he is afraid of horses. Let me introduce you to one another. Lieutenant Rohlauf. Engineer Prokop. Prince Suwalski. Von Graun. The affair is settled, eh? When Rohlauf has mounted again we will go. Premier is at your disposition, sir. And please remember that here you are a guest. *Au revoir!*" The whips swished through the air, Whirlwind twisted round, and the cavalcade disappeared round the corner of the road. Only Mr. Rohlauf pranced round Prokop on his horse, fixing him with angry eyes, saying finally in a voice choked with anger: "You shall give me satisfaction, sir."

Prokop swung round on his heel, returned to his room, and locked himself in. Two hours later a message was carried by the fragile Paul from the guest's suite to the management. Immediately Mr. Carson ran to Prokop with a severe expression on his face; with a commanding gesture he pushed back Mr. Holz, who was quietly dreaming in an armchair outside the room, and went inside.

Mr. Holz took a seat in front of the castle and lit his pipe. From within there came a terrible roar, but Mr. Holz paid no attention to it; his pipe was not drawing properly. He unscrewed the stem, and in an expert manner cleaned it with a stalk of grass. From the guest's suite could be heard the growling of two tigers whose teeth were fixed in one another; both roared, there was a sound of furniture being overturned, a moment of silence, and then a frightful cry from Prokop. People appeared from the garden; but Mr. Holz waved them away, and continued to occupy himself with his pipe.

The uproar inside increased, both tigers roared still louder and threw themselves on one another in fury. Mr. Paul ran out of the castle as white as a sheet, lifting his terrified eyes to heaven. At that moment the Princess cantered up with her escort. When she heard the unholy turmoil in the guest's wing of the castle she smiled nervously, and quite unnecessarily gave Whirlwind a cut with the whip. Then the noise quieted down a little; one could hear the thundering of Prokop, who was threatening something and striking the table with his fist. Interspersed with this came the sound of a sharp voice, which threatened and commanded. Prokop shouted passionate protests; but the sharp voice answered quietly and decidedly.

"By what right?" cried Prokop's voice. The authoritative voice explained something with quiet and terrible emphasis. "But in that case, you understand, you'll all go up in the air," roared Prokop, and the uproar again became so terrific that Mr. Holz suddenly stuck his pipe in his pocket and ran into the castle. But again all became quiet. Only the sharp voice gave orders and enunciated clear phrases, to the accompaniment of a dark and threatening murmur; it was as if the conditions of an armistice were being dictated. Twice more there resounded Prokop's frightful roar; but the sharp voice remained calm, apparently sure of its victory.

An hour and a half later Mr. Carson burst out of Prokop's room, purple and covered with sweat, snorting and sombre, and hurried round to the Princess's apartments. Ten minutes afterward Mr. Paul, trembling with respect, announced to Prokop, who was gnawing at his fingers in his room: "Her Excellency."

The Princess entered in evening dress, deathly pale, her eyebrows drawn with anxiety. Prokop came forward to meet her, and wished, apparently, to say something; but the Princess stopped him with a movement of her hand that was full of command and protest, and said in a strangled voice: "I've come...sir, to apologize to you for striking at you. I am infinitely sorry that it happened."

Prokop flushed, and again wished to say something, but the Princess continued: "Lieutenant Rohlauf is leaving today. The Prince begs you to join us at dinner occasionally. Please forget the incident. *Au revoir.*" She quickly gave him her hand; Prokop touched the ends of her fingers. They were cold, and as if dead.

CHAPTER XXVII

The fight with Carson seemed to clear the air a little. Prokop certainly announced that he intended to escape at the first opportunity; but he solemnly undertook that until that time he would refrain from any resort to force or to threats. In recognition of this, Mr. Holz was removed to a distance of fifteen paces, and Prokop was allowed, accompanied by him, to move freely in a circle of three miles from seven in the morning to seven in the evening, to sleep in the laboratory, and to dine where he wished. On the other hand, Mr. Carson quartered a woman and two children in the laboratory (as it happened, she was the wife of a workman who had been killed by an explosion of Krakatit), as a sort of moral guarantee against any "carelessness." In addition Prokop was assigned a large salary, paid in gold, and he was left free to work or amuse himself as he wished.

Prokop spent the first few days after this adventure in studying the terrain within the three miles' limit with a view to the possibilities it afforded of escape. In view of the protective zone, which functioned quite perfectly, the chances were exceedingly poor. Prokop thought out a few methods of murdering Mr. Holz; but luckily he discovered that this dry and sturdy being was supporting five children besides a mother and a lame sister—and that, in addition, he had behind him three years' imprisonment for manslaughter.

It was a certain satisfaction to Prokop that he had won the passionate devotion of Mr. Paul, a retired butler, who was delighted that he again had someone to wait on; for the dear old man was very pained by the fact that he was considered too slow to wait at the Prince's table. Prokop at times became nearly desperate at his oppressive and respectful attention. Further, Dr. Krafft, Egon's tutor, who was as ruddy as a fox, and had been terribly unfortunate in his life, had also become attached to Prokop. He had received an unusual education, was a bit of a theosophist, and as well the most absurd idealist which it is possible to imagine. He approached Prokop with shyness, and admired him without shame, since he regarded him as at least a genius. He had been acquainted for some time with Prokop's technical articles, and had even based on them a theosophical theory of the lowest plane of manifestation, or, in more ordinary language, of matter. He was also a pacifist, and, like all people with too exalted views, a bore.

Prokop finally grew sick of wandering aimlessly about inside the protective zone and began to visit the laboratory more and more. He studied his old notes, filled up a lot of gaps in them, and prepared and afterward destroyed a large number of explosives, whose structure confirmed his most daring hypothesis. At this time he was almost happy, but in the evening he avoided people and languished under the calm glance of Mr. Holz, looking up at the clouds, the stars, and at the horizon.

One other thing interested him enormously. Directly he heard the beat of horses' hoofs he stepped to the window and watched the rider—whether it was a yard boy, some officer or other, or the Princess (with whom he had not exchanged a word since that day), with attentive eyes. He observed that the rider did not actually sit down as in a chair, but to a certain extent might be said to stand in the stirrups; that he used his knees and not his back; that he did not allow himself to be passively shaken about like a sack of potatoes by the movement of the horse, but actively adapted himself to it. Practically the process was probably very simple, but for the technical engineer who was watching the mechanism it appeared to be enormously complicated, especially when the horse began to rear, prance, or dance about in thoroughbred shyness. Prokop studied all this for hours, sheltered behind the window curtains; and one fine morning he ordered Paul to have Premier saddled. Mr. Paul became extremely disconcerted. He explained that Premier was a high-spirited and restless animal which had never been fully broken in, but Prokop merely repeated the order. His riding things were ready in the cupboard; he put them on with a faint feeling of vanity and went downstairs. Premier was already there, prancing about and dragging a groom round with him. Prokop endeavoured to appease the animal by stroking his nostrils, as he had seen other people do. The creature grew a little more calm, though his feet still dug into the sand. Prokop approached his side in a calculating manner, and was just raising his foot to the stirrup when Premier struck out like lightning with his hind legs, so that Prokop only just had time to get out of the way. The groom broke into a short laugh. That was enough. Prokop hurled himself at the horse, somehow got his foot into the stirrup and heaved himself into the saddle. For the next few moments he had no idea what was happening; everything spun round, somebody shouted, Prokop had one foot in the air while the other remained for some incredible reason in the stirrup. At last Prokop got established in the saddle, and gripped with his knees with all his strength. He did this just in time, for immediately afterward Premier suddenly bucked violently; Prokop hastily leant back and feverishly tugged at the bridle. As a result the beast stood up on his hind legs; Prokop tightened his knees like a vice and put his face forward right between the horse's ears, taking great care not to throw his arms around its neck, as he was afraid that this would appear foolish. He was practically only hanging on by his knees. Premier ceased to rear and began to twist round and round like a wolf dog; Prokop utilized this to get his other foot into the stirrup. "Don't squeeze him so tightly," shouted the groom; but Prokop was glad to feel the horse between his knees. The animal, more desperately than spitefully, made another attempt to throw his strange rider; he twisted and kicked, scattering the sand, and all the personnel of the kitchen ran out to watch this extraordinary circus. Prokop caught a glimpse of Mr. Paul, who was pressing a napkin to his lips in consternation, and then Dr. Krafft dashed out, his ruddy hair gleaming in the sun, and, at the risk of his own life, attempted to seize hold of Premier's bridle. "Leave him alone," shouted Prokop, inordinately proud, and dug his spurs into the horse's side. Premier, to whom this had never happened before, shot off like an arrow into the park. Prokop drew in his head, so as to fall lightly if it came to the worst; he stood in the stirrups inclined forward, involuntarily adopting the seat of a jockey. When flashing past the tennis court in this manner, he noticed there several white figures; this filled him with fury, and he began to belabour Premier's haunches with his whip. At this the animal completely lost his head. After a number of disturbing sidelong jumps he sat down on his haunches so that it seemed that he would fall over; but instead he got up and flew across the lawn. Prokop realized that everything now depended on holding his head, if they were not both to turn a somersault. He dragged at the bit for all he was worth. Premier stopped short suddenly, covered with sweat, and then began to move at a reasonable trot. Victory was secured.

Prokop was extraordinarily relieved. Now at last he was able to apply what he had studied so carefully theoretically. The trembling horse allowed himself to be directed as his rider wished, and Prokop, as proud as a god, rode him back along the twisting paths of the park towards the tennis court. He caught a sight of the Princess, racket in hand, the other side of a bush, and spurred Premier into a gallop. At the very moment the Princess clicked her tongue, Premier rose into the air and flew towards her like an arrow over the tops of some shrubs; and Prokop, completely unprepared for this advanced exercise, flew out of the saddle and descended on to the grass. He felt something go, and the next moment his senses were obliterated by pain.

* * * *

When he recovered consciousness he saw in front of him the Princess, and three men in the embarrassed position of people who do not know whether to laugh at a joke or run for assistance. Prokop tried to move his left leg, which lay underneath him, twisted in a surprising manner. The Princess was watching him with an inquiring and at the same time frightened expression on her face.

"Now," said Prokop firmly, "you've broken my leg for me." He was in great pain, and the shock had confused his mind; nevertheless, he tried to stand up. When, for the second time, he came to, he was lying in the Princess's lap, and she was wiping his sweat-covered forehead with a strongly scented handkerchief. In spite of the frightful pain in his leg, he was half in a dream. "Where is...the horse?" he babbled, and began to groan. Two gardeners lifted him on to a stretcher and carried him into the castle. Mr. Paul changed into everything in the world: an angel, a nurse, a mother. He ran about, arranged the pillows under Prokop's head, and poured cognac down his throat; then he sat down at the head of the bed and allowed Prokop to crush his hand in his spasms of pain. Dr. Krafft stood near with eyes filled with tears, and Mr. Holz, evidently touched, cut away Prokop's riding breeches and applied cold compresses to his thigh. Prokop groaned quietly, smiling for a moment now and then with his blue lips at Krafft or Mr. Paul. Then there appeared the regimental doctor, or rather butcher, accompanied by an assistant, who very soon started work on Prokop's leg. "H'm," he said, "compound fracture of the femur and so on; at least six weeks in bed, my friend." He produced two splints and then began a very unpleasant business. "Stretch his leg out," ordered the butcher of his assistant, but Mr. Holz politely pushed aside the excited beginner and himself seized hold of the broken member with all his strength. Prokop bit into the pillows so as not to scream with agony like an animal, and caught sight of the pained face of Mr. Paul in which was reflected all his own torture. "A bit more," said the doctor in a bass voice, feeling the fracture; Holz tugged silently and violently. Krafft ran out of the room gasping out something in complete desperation. Then the butcher quickly and adroitly fixed the splints in position, muttering something about putting the cursed leg into plaster the next day. At last it was all over; the pain was still terrible, and the stretched-out leg seemed to be dead, but at least the butcher had gone away. Mr. Paul still walked about the room on tiptoe, doing all he could to relieve the patient.

Then Mr. Carson dashed up in a car, and, mounting the steps four at a time, flew into Prokop's room, which became filled with his sparkling sympathy. He was gay and comradely, chattered all sorts of nonsense at a tremendous speed, and suddenly began to smooth Prokop's bristly hair in a friendly, and at the same time timid, manner. Prokop forgave his obdurate adversary and tyrant nine-tenths of his sins. Then something heavy was heard coming up the stairs, the door flew open and two lackeys with white gloves led in the crippled Prince. While still at the door he waved a preternaturally long and emaciated hand as if to prevent Prokop, out of respect for him, rising by some miracle and coming over to greet him; then he allowed himself to be placed on a chair and delivered himself of a few phrases of courtly sympathy.

Scarcely had this apparition disappeared than someone tapped at the door and Mr. Paul whispered something to a chambermaid. A moment after the Princess came in, still in her tennis things, her face expressing a mixture of obstinacy and repentance. She had come voluntarily to apologize for her clumsiness. But before she could say anything Prokop's homely, hard, rough-cast face broke into a childish smile. "Now," said the proud patient, "am I afraid of a horse or not?"

The Princess blushed so deeply that she became confused and angry with herself. But she soon regained her self-control, and at once became again the charming hostess. She told him that a distinguished surgeon was coming to see him, and inquired what he would like to eat, read, and so on, further instructing Paul to send a report on the patient's health twice a day. Then, after putting something straight on the bed, she left the room with a brief nod of the head.

When, not long afterward, the famous surgeon arrived in a car, he was obliged to wait for some hours, however much he might shake his head over it. Prokop had fallen into a deep sleep.

CHAPTER XXVIII

Needless to say, the distinguished surgeon did not recognize the work of the military butcher. He stretched out Prokop's leg again, put it into plaster, and concluded by saying that he would probably be lame for life.

There began for Prokop a succession of delightful and lazy days. Krafft read him passages from Swedenborg and Mr. Paul and others from the Court Calendar, while the Princess saw to it that the patient's bed was surrounded by a magnificent selection of volumes of world literature. Finally, Prokop got tired even of the Calendar, and began to dictate to Krafft a systematic work on destructive chemistry. Curiously enough, he became most fond of Carson, whose insolence and lack of consideration impressed him more and more, for beneath it he found the grandiloquent plans and crazy fantasy of an out-and-out international militarist. Mr. Paul was in an ecstasy of delight. He was now indispensable night after night, and could dedicate every breath and every step of his faltering legs to Prokop's service.

You lie encased in matter, like the stump of a tree; but can you not feel the crepitation of terrible and unknown forces in that inert matter which binds you? You luxuriate on magnificent pillows charged with more power than a cask of dynamite; your body is a sleeping explosive, and even the faded, trembling hand of Mr. Paul contains more explosive force than a capsule of melinite. You lie motionless in an ocean of immeasurable, unanalyzable, unutilized forces; you are surrounded not by the walls of the room, quiet people and the rustling branches of trees, but by an ammunition store, a cosmic magazine prepared for the most frightful deed. You tap matter with your finger as if you were testing casks of ekrasite to see if they are full.

Prokop's hands had become transparent through lack of use, but on the other hand they had acquired an extraordinary sense of touch. They felt and detected the potential power of detonation of whatever they encountered. A young body had an enormous explosive tension, while Dr. Krafft, an enthusiast and an idealist, had a relatively weak capacity for explosion. Carson's index of detonation approached that of tetranitraniline, and Prokop recalled with a shudder the cool touch of the Princess's hand, which revealed to him the terrible explosive power of this haughty amazon. He racked his brains in trying to decide whether the potential explosive energy of the organism depended upon the presence of certain enzymotic or other substances or on the chemical composition of the cells themselves, which constituted charges *par excellence*. Be that as it may, he would have liked to know how that dark proud girl would explode.

And now Mr. Paul wheeled Prokop about the park in a bath-chair. Mr. Holz proved superfluous, but was active, as he had revealed great talent as a masseur, and Prokop felt a beneficial explosive force flowing from his powerful fingers. If the Princess came across the patient in the park she said something with complete and precisely calculated politeness, and Prokop to his annoyance never understood how she managed to do it, for he himself was always either too rough or too friendly. The rest of the household regarded Prokop as a marvel; this gave them the right not to take him seriously, and allowed him to be as rude to them as he liked. On one occasion, the Princess drew up near him with the whole of her escort; she left the gentlemen to wait, sat down by Prokop's side, and asked him about his work. Prokop, wishing to be as obliging to her as possible, embarked on a long technical explanation, as if he were giving a lecture before an international chemical congress. Prince Suwalski and some cousin or other began to laugh and nudge one another, at which Prokop grew furious, turned to them, and said that it was not them whom he was addressing. All eyes turned on Her Excellency, for it was her task to put this unpolished plebeian in his place; but the Princess smiled indulgently, and sent them off to play tennis. While she was looking after them with eyes narrowed to a slit, Prokop scrutinized her out of the corner of his eye; for the first time he really noticed what she was like. She was rigid, thin, and with an excess of pigmentation in her colouring, strictly speaking, not beautiful. She had small breasts, ungainly legs, magnificent hands indicative of race, a scar on her proud forehead, deepset eyes with a sharp glance, dark brown under her sharp nose, full and haughty lips; well, yes, after all, almost pretty. What were her eyes really like?

Then she turned fully round and Prokop became confused. "They say that you are able to discover the character of things by touching them," she said quickly. "Krafft was talking about it." Prokop smiled at this feminine description of his peculiar chemotaxis. "Well, yes," he said, "one feels how much force a thing has; that's nothing." The Princess gave a quick glance at his hand, and then looked round the park; there was nobody about.

"Show me," muttered Prokop, and opened his scarred hand. She laid on it the smooth tips of her fingers; a sort of flash passed through Prokop, his heart began to beat violently, and the mad idea came into his head: "Supposing I closed my hands!" Then he proceeded to knead and press in his rough paw the firm, burning flesh of her hand. His head suddenly became filled with a drunken giddiness; he saw the Princess close her eyes and draw her breath sharply through her half open lips, while he also closed his eyes and, setting his teeth, whirled down into the swirling darkness. Her hand struggled feverishly and wildly with its thin sinuous fingers, fingers which were writhing to get free, which twisted like serpents, which dug their nails into his skin, and then suddenly pressed convulsively against his flesh, Prokop's teeth chattered with ecstasy; the trembling fingers played on his wrist, red circles appeared before his eyes, a sudden sharp and burning pressure, and the thin hand tore free from his grasp. Exhausted, Prokop opened his eyes; there was a noisy beating inside his head; the green and golden garden again presented itself to his eyes, which were blinded by the light of day. The Princess had grown deathly pale, and bit her lips with her sharp teeth; through the slits of her eyes there flashed a boundless resistance.

"Well?" she said sharply.

"Virginal, unfeeling, libidinous, proud and capable of violent anger—inflammable as tinder—and wicked. You are wicked; you are fiery through your very cruelty, arrogant and heartless; you are wicked and overcharged with excitability; inaccessible, filled with curiosity, hard, hard on yourself, fire and ice, ice and fire—"

The Princess nodded silently. "Yes."

"Of no use to anybody; haughty, incapable of loving, poisoned and burning—ardent, and everything around you leaves you indifferent."

"I must be severe with myself," whispered the Princess. "You don't know—" She waved her hand and got up. "Thank you. I will send Paul to you."

Having thus relieved himself of his personal offended bitterness, Prokop began to think of the Princess more kindly. Finally, he became annoyed that she now evidently avoided him. He prepared some friendly phrases to say to her at the first opportunity, but the opportunity did not offer itself.

At the castle there arrived Prince Rohn, known as *Mon Oncle Charles*, the brother of the late Princess, a refined and polished cosmopolitan, amateur of everything possible, *très grand artiste*, as they say. He had written a number of historical novels, and was an extraordinarily pleasant personality. He exhibited a particular liking for Prokop, and spent whole hours with him. Prokop profited a great deal from his contact with this charming old gentleman, acquired from him a certain finish, and realized that there were other things in the world besides destructive chemistry. *Mon Oncle Charles* possessed an enormous fund of anecdotes. Prokop turned the conversation on to the Princess, and heard with interest what a malicious, madcap, proud, and magnanimous girl she was, how on one occasion she had fired at her dancing master and on another had wanted to have a piece of her skin cut off for transplantation on to the limb of a nurse who had received some burns; when permission to do this was refused, in her rage she smashed a window of the most valuable glass. *Le bon oncle* also brought young Egon along to Prokop, whom he set up as an example to the young man with such extravagant praise that the unfortunate Prokop became as confused as Egon himself.

After five weeks he was going about on crutches. He visited the laboratory more and more, working like a madman until the pain in his foot began again, so that on the way home he literally hung on the attentive Holz. Mr. Carson glowed with pleasure when he saw Prokop again so peaceable and industrious, and from time to time threw out allusions to Krakatit; but this was a subject which Prokop positively would not hear about.

One evening, there was an important soirée at the castle. Prokop prepared a coup for this occasion. The Princess was standing in a group of generals and diplomatists when the doors opened and there entered—without a stick—the obstinate prisoner, who was thus making his first visit to the company in the castle. *Oncle Charles* and Carson ran forward to meet him while the Princess confined herself to giving him a quick, discriminating glance. Prokop had imagined that she would come to greet him, but when he saw that she remained with two old ladies, both of them with their dresses cut incredibly low, his brow clouded, and he retired into a corner, bowing with a bad grace to the distinguished personages to whom Carson introduced him as "a distinguished scientist," "our eminent guest," and the like. It was as if Mr. Carson had assumed the rôle of Holz, for he never left Prokop for a moment.

As the evening went on, Prokop became desperately bored; he retired still deeper into his corner and glowered at the whole world. Now the Princess was talking with various dignitaries, one of them an admiral and the other some famous foreign lion. The Princess glanced quickly in the direction in which Prokop was standing sullenly, but at that moment the claimant to some lost throne or other came up to her and led her off in the opposite direction. "Well, I'm off home," muttered Prokop, and decided in the depths of his dark soul that within three days he would make a further attempt to escape. Just then the Princess approached him and held out her hand, "I'm so glad that you are well again."

Prokop forgot all the education he had received from *Oncle Charles*. Making a heavy movement with his shoulders, which was intended for a bow, he said in a surly tone: "I thought that you did not even see me." Mr. Carson disappeared as quickly as if he had sunk through the earth.

The Princess wore a low-necked dress which had the effect of confusing Prokop. Whichever way he might look, he saw her firm swarthy flesh and smelt the fragrance of her delicate scent.

"I hear that you are working again," said the Princess. "What exactly are you doing?"

"Well, one thing and another," answered Prokop, "nothing particularly important." Here was a chance to repair his insulting behaviour when he had seized her hand, but what on earth could he say by way of expiation? "If you would like me to," he mumbled, "I could…make an experiment with your powder."

"What sort of experiment?"

"An explosive. You've enough on you to charge a cannon."

The Princess smiled. "I didn't know that powder was an explosive?"

"Everything is an explosive…if you treat it properly. You yourself—"

"What?"

"Nothing. A latent explosion. You are terribly explosive."

"When I am treated properly," smiled the Princess, and suddenly grew serious. "Wicked, unfeeling, violent, curious, and proud, eh?"

"A girl who wants to sacrifice her skin…for an old woman."

The Princess flared up. "Who told you that?"

"*Mon Oncle Charles*," babbled Prokop.

The Princess grew stiff and was suddenly a hundred miles away. "Ah, Prince Rohn," she corrected him dryly. "Prince Rohn talks a great deal. I'm glad that you are all right." A brief nod of the head and Willy glided across the room at the side of someone in uniform, leaving Prokop to rage in a corner.

Nevertheless, the next morning Mr. Paul brought Prokop something precious, which the Princess had sent by her *femme de chambre*.

It was a box of brownish powder with a penetrating scent.

CHAPTER XXIX

Prokop, bent over this box of powder, was disturbed and excited by this strong feminine scent; it was as if the Princess herself was in the laboratory and was bending over his shoulder.

In his youthful ignorance, he had never realized that powder was nothing but starch; he had regarded it as inorganic colouring. Well, starch is a magnificent thing, let us say, for damping too powerful explosives, because in itself it is dull and unresponsive; even more so when it becomes an explosive itself. He had no idea how to begin with it, and buried his head in his hands, pursued by the penetrating scent of the Princess. He did not leave the laboratory even at night.

The people at the castle whom he liked best ceased to visit him, as he was always shut off from them by his work and treated them impatiently, absorbed all the time in the cursed powder. What the devil was he to try next? After five days he began to see the light; he feverishly studied aromatic nitroamines, after which he began the slowest synthetic work which he had ever done in his life. One night the powder lay in front of him, unchanged in appearance and exuding its penetrating scent; a brown powder, reminiscent of a woman's healthy complexion.

He stretched himself out on the divan, completely exhausted. It seemed to him that he saw a placard with the inscription "Powderite, the finest explosive powder for the complexion," and on the placard was a picture of the Princess putting out her tongue at him. He tried to turn away, but two bare brown arms stretched out from the placard and, medusalike, drew him towards her. He pulled a clasp-knife out of his pocket and ripped it up. Then he had a fear that he had committed a murder, and dashed away along the street in which he had lived years before. He came upon a panting motorcar and leapt into it, shouting, "Drive quickly." The car started off, and only then for the first time did he notice that the Princess was sitting at the wheel with a leather helmet on her head in which he had not seen her before. At a turning in the road someone threw himself in front of the car, evidently to stop it; there was an unearthly cry, the wheels lurched over something soft, and Prokop woke up.

He realized that he was feverish, got up, and looked about the laboratory for some kind of drug. He found nothing except pure alcohol; he took a good pull at it, burnt his mouth and throat, and again lay down with his head spinning. He saw before him a few formulae, some flowers, Annie, and a confused train journey; then everything became fused, and he fell into a deep sleep.

In the morning he obtained permission to make an experiment on the artillery ground, a fact which caused Carson extraordinary delight. Prokop refused the help of a single laboratory assistant and saw to it himself that a passage was dug in the sandstone as far from the castle as possible, in the part of the ground where there were not even any electrical wires, so that a special fuse was necessary. When everything was prepared he informed the Princess that at four o'clock precisely he would explode her box of powder. He gave particular instructions to Carson to clear the sheds in the vicinity and unconditionally prohibited the presence of anybody within a circle of half a mile; he further demanded that on this occasion he should not be accompanied by Holz. Mr. Carson considered all this fuss to be somewhat excessive, but conceded all Prokop's demands.

A quarter of an hour before the appointed time, Prokop carried the box of powder to the seat of the explosion with his own hands, sniffed for the last time, with a certain satisfaction, at the Princess's scent, and put it in the hole. Then he placed beneath it a mercury capsule, connected with a Bickford cord timed for five minutes, took up his position a short distance away, and waited with his watch in his hand until it should be five minutes to four.

Aha, now he would show this proud girl what he could do. This would be an explosion really worthwhile, something different from the popguns on the White Mountain, when one had to keep one's eye open for a policeman the whole time; it would be a magnificent detonation, a column of fire reaching up to Heaven, a marvellous force, a noise like thunder; the heavens would be cleaved by a fiery power and lightning made by the hand of man.

Five minutes to four. Prokop quickly lit the cord and made off for all he was worth with his watch in his hand, limping slightly. Three minutes; quicker! Two minutes, and then he saw to his right the Princess, accompanied by Carson, making her way to the site of the explosion. For a second he was rigid with terror, and then shouted to them a warning. Mr. Carson stopped, but the Princess went on without even looking round. Carson trotted after her, evidently trying to persuade her to turn back. Overcoming the sharp pain in his leg, Prokop dashed after her. "Lie down," he roared, "for God's sake lie down!" His face was so terribly distorted with anger and horror that Mr. Carson turned pale, made two leaps, and lay down at the bottom of a deep ditch. The Princess continued her way; she was now not more than two hundred yards from the hole. Prokop dashed his watch on the ground, seizing hold of her shoulder. "Lie down," he yelled. The Princess swung round, giving him a terrible look for having taken such a liberty. Then Prokop took her in both his hands, threw her on to the ground, and fell on top of her with all his weight.

Her wiry, lean body wriggled desperately beneath him. "Serpent," hissed Prokop, and breathing heavily forced the Princess back with all the strength of his chest. The body underneath him arched itself and slipped to the side. Strangely enough not a word came through the closed lips of the Princess; she only breathed shortly and quickly, struggling feverishly. Prokop thrust his knees between her legs, so that she should not slip away, and placed his palms over her ears, realizing in a flash that the explosion might break her eardrums. Her sharp nails dug into his neck, and in his face he felt the savage gnawing of four sharp eyeteeth. "Beast," gasped Prokop, and attempted to shake off this aggressive animal; but she would not allow him. A hoarse noise came from her throat, and her body braced itself and undulated in wild convulsions. The familiar, penetrating scent overpowered Prokop's senses; his heart beat agitatedly, and he had a wild desire to jump up, ignoring the explosion which would take place now in a few seconds. Then he felt the struggling knees pressing themselves to his leg, and two arms twined themselves convulsively round his neck; on his face he felt the hot, moist, trembling contact of her lips and tongue. He moaned with agony, and sought the Princess's lips with his own. At this moment there was a frightful explosion, and a column of earth and stones was torn out of the earth. Something gave Prokop a violent blow on the crown of the head, but he hardly realized it, for at that instant he was kissing her mouth, tongue, teeth, her parted and trembling lips. Suddenly, her elastic body collapsed beneath him, shuddering. He had an impression that Mr. Carson had stood up and was watching him, but hastily threw himself on the ground again. Trembling fingers caressed Prokop's neck with wonderful and intolerable sweetness; parched lips kissed his face and eyes with tiny trembling kisses, while Prokop thirstily thrust his lips against the beating warmth of a fragrant neck. "Darling, darling," came a hot whisper into his ears, delicate fingers were passed through his hair, and a soft body pressed its full length against him. Prokop pressed his lips on hers in an endless kiss.

Sss! Thrust away by her elbow, Prokop jumped up and rubbed his forehead as if he were drunk. The Princess sat up and arranged her hair. "Give me your hand," she ordered coolly, hastily looked round, and then quickly pressed the hand which he had stretched out against her burning face. Suddenly, she pushed it away, stood up, and, rigid, gazed with large eyes into the distance. Prokop felt quite embarrassed. He was about to approach her again, but she made a nervous movement with her shoulder, as if she were shaking something off. He saw that she was biting her lips deeply. Only then did he remember Carson, whom he found some distance away lying on his back— but not in the ditch—and gazing up happily at the blue sky.

"Is it all over?" he said, without getting up, and twiddled his thumbs on his stomach. "I'm frightfully afraid of such things. Can I get up now?" He jumped up and shook himself like a dog. "Magnificent explosion," he said enthusiastically and again looked, as it were, casually at the Princess.

The Princess turned round; she was as white as a sheet, but had herself completely under control.

"Was that all?" she asked carelessly.

"My God!" cried Carson. "As if that were not enough! One little box of powder! Man, you're a magician, a devil, the king of hell or someone like that. What? Really. The king of matter. Princess, behold the king! A genius, eh? A unique person. Honestly, compared to him, we're ragpickers. What name have you given to the stuff?" The disconcerted Prokop regained his equilibrium. "Let the Princess christen it," he said, glad to be able to rise to the occasion. "It's...hers."

The Princess trembled. "You might call it 'Vicit,'" she said sharply through her teeth.

"What?" cried Mr. Carson. "Aha! Vicit. That means 'he conquered,' eh? Princess, you're a genius! Vicit! Magnificent. Aha! Hurrah!"

But through Prokop's head there flashed another and a terrible etymology. Vitium. Vice. He looked with horror at the Princess, but it was impossible to read any answer on her strained face.

CHAPTER XXX

Mr. Carson ran ahead to the seat of the explosion. The Princess—evidently on purpose—lingered behind. Prokop thought that she had something to say to him, but she only pointed with her finger at his face. Prokop quickly felt his face; on it he found the bloody traces of her teeth, and, picking up a handful of soil, rubbed it over the marks, as if he had been struck by a clod during the explosion.

The hole in which the powder had been placed had become a crater about fifteen feet across. It was difficult to calculate the power of the explosion, but Carson estimated it at five times that of oxyliquid. "Fine stuff," he said, "but a bit too strong for ordinary usage." Mr. Carson took the whole conversation in hand, slipping adroitly over its serious gaps. Prokop had become conscious of an oppressive weight. On the way back, he took leave of them with an affability that was somewhat too evident, saying that he had this and that to do. What was he to talk about now? For some curious reason, he had the impression that he must not refer in any way to the dark and mysterious happening which took place at the same time as the explosion when "the heavens were cleft by a fiery power." He entertained a bitter and unpleasant feeling that the Princess had coldly dismissed him like a lackey with whom—with whom— He clenched his fists in his disgust, and began to mumble something of secondary interest about the horses; the words stuck in his throat, and the Princess accelerated her step noticeably, evidently wishing to get back to the castle as soon as possible. Prokop limped heavily, but did not let her see that he was doing so. Having reached the park, he wished to take leave of her, but the Princess turned down a side path. He followed her irresolutely; then she drew close to his shoulder, turned back her head, and placed her thirsty lips on his own.

The Princess's chow, Toy, scented the approach of his mistress, and, whining with delight, rushed towards her across the lawn. And here he was! But what was this? He stopped. The Big Unfriendly Person was shaking her, they were biting one another, swaying in a silent and desperate struggle. Oho! His Lady was beaten, her arms sank, and she lay moaning in the arms of the Big Person; now he was crushing her. And Toy began to cry "Help! Help!" in his dog's language.

The Princess tore herself out of Prokop's arms. "Even the dog, even the dog," she smiled nervously. "Let's go!" Prokop's head was spinning; it was only with the greatest difficulty that he could make a few steps. The Princess hung on to him (Insanity! Supposing somebody...), drawing him along, but her legs suddenly failed her; she gripped his arm with her fingers, as if she wished to tear it or something of the sort, drew in her breath sharply, knitted her brows, and a dark light came into her eyes. Then, with a hoarse sob, seeking his lips, she flung her arms round his neck, so that he staggered. Prokop crushed her in his arms; a long breathless embrace, and her body, stretched taut like a bow, collapsed softly and helplessly against him. She lay on his breast with closed eyes. Sweet and meaningless phrases came from her lips; she allowed her face, neck, and hair to be covered with his violent kisses, moving her head as if she were intoxicated and did not know what she was doing. Submissive, half swooning, utterly tender; perhaps happy at this moment with an inexpressible happiness. O God, what a trembling and lovely smile there was on her lips!

Suddenly, she opened her eyes wide and slipped out of his embrace. They were two yards away from the main avenue. She passed her hands over her face, like a person awakening from a dream, moved away, and leaned her forehead against the trunk of an oak. Scarcely had Prokop released her from his rough hands than his heart began to beat violently with emotion, with an emotion of shame and degradation. Christ! For her he was only a servant whom she used to excite her emotions when she had nothing better to do, when she was unable to bear her solitude, or something of the sort. Now she had kicked him away, like a dog, so that...she could do the same thing again with somebody else. He went up to her and placed his hand firmly on her shoulder. She turned round gently with a shy, almost frightened and humiliated smile. "No, no," she whispered, twisting her fingers. "Please, not—"

Prokop's heart swelled with a sudden wave of tenderness, "When shall I see you again?" he asked.

"Tomorrow, tomorrow," she murmured anxiously, and turned back towards the castle. "I must go. Now I can't—"

"When tomorrow?" insisted Prokop.

"Tomorrow," she repeated nervously, drew her cloak more closely round her shivering body, and hurried off, Prokop at her side. In front of the castle she held out her hand to him. "*Au revoir.*"

Her fingers were still twisting feverishly; he would have drawn her again towards him. "You mustn't, you mustn't," she whispered, and left him with a last burning kiss.

No greater damage than this was done by the explosion of Vicit. A few chimneys were knocked over on the adjacent barracks, and the rush of air burst a number of windows. The large windows in Prince Hagen's room were also broken. The crippled old gentleman had, with great difficulty, risen to his feet and stood like a soldier waiting for a further catastrophe.

The company in the castle were sitting over their coffee one evening when Prokop entered, his eyes searching for the Princess. He was unable to bear the devouring torture of uncertainty. The Princess turned pale, but the jovial Uncle Rohn at once grasped Prokop's hand and congratulated him on his magnificent achievement, etc., etc. Even the haughty Suwalski inquired with interest whether it was true that the gentleman was able to turn every substance into an explosive. "Take sugar, for instance," he said, and was simply astounded when Prokop grunted something to the effect that sugar had been used as an explosive even during the Great War. For some time, Prokop was the centre of interest; but he stammered, and, although he answered all the questions that were put to him, was chiefly occupied with trying to interpret the provocative glances of the Princess. His bloodshot eyes were fixed on her with terrible attention. The Princess was as if on thorns.

Then the conversation changed, and Prokop had the impression that nobody any longer took any interest in him. These people understood one another so well, conversed so easily, and touched lightly and with enormous interest on things which he simply did not understand or had never even heard of. Even the Princess became quite animated; there you are, you see, she had a thousand times as much in common with these gentlemen as she had with him! His brow darkened, he did not know what to do with his hands, a blind anger began to rage within him. Then he put down his coffee cup so violently that it cracked.

The Princess turned horrified eyes on him, but the charming *Oncle Charles* saved the situation by telling a story about a sea captain who was able to crush a beer bottle in his fingers. Some fat person, a cousin of sorts, asserted that he could do the same thing. Thereupon they ordered a bottle to be brought in, and one after the other attempted to smash it in this manner. The bottle was a heavy one of black glass, and no one was able to break it.

"Now you," ordered the Princess, with a quick glance at Prokop.

"I shan't be able to," muttered Prokop, but the Princess drew up her eyebrows in such a commanding way that Prokop got up and seized the bottle by its neck. He stood motionless, did not, like the others, contort himself with the effort which he was making, but the muscles in his face stood out as if they were going to burst. He looked like a primitive man who was preparing to kill somebody with a club. His lips were twisted with the strain, his face as it were intersected with powerful muscles, his shoulders loose, as if he were defending himself with the bottle against the attack of a gorilla, and he turned his bloodshot eyes on the Princess. There was a silence. The Princess got up with her eyes fixed upon him. Her lips were drawn back over her clenched teeth, and the tendons stood out on her neck. Her eyebrows drew in, and she breathed quickly, as if she, too, were making a terrible physical effort. They stood opposite one another in this manner, their faces contorted, looking into one another's eyes like two desperate opponents. Convulsive tremors ran through their bodies from head to heel. No one breathed; nothing was to be heard but the hoarse panting of these two. Then there was a crunching sound, the jingle of breaking glass, and the bottom of the bottle fell with a crash on to the floor.

The first to recover himself was *Mon Oncle Charles*, who paced up and down for a moment and then rushed up to the Princess. "Minnie," he whispered rapidly, and lowered her, almost fainting, into an armchair. Kneeling in front of her, by exerting all his strength he opened her convulsively clenched fists; her palms were covered with blood, so deeply had she driven the nails into the flesh. "Take that bottle out of his hand," ordered *le bon Prince*, and drew back one of the Princess's fingers after the other.

"Bravo!" cried Prince Suwalski and began to applaud loudly. Meanwhile, Von Graun had seized Prokop's right hand, which was still grasping fragments of the bottle, and forced open his fingers. "Water," he cried, and the fat cousin, agitatedly looking round, grasped a table cover, soaked it in water and put it on Prokop's forehead.

"Aha-hah!" cried Prokop with relief. The attack was over, but his head was still swirling from the sudden flow of blood and his knees trembled with weakness.

Oncle Charles was massaging on his knees the twisted, quivering fingers of the Princess. "Games of this sort are dangerous," he muttered, while the Princess, completely exhausted, was hardly able to draw her breath. But on her lips there trembled a wry but victorious smile. "You helped him," said the fat cousin, "that's what it was."

The Princess stood up, hardly able to move her legs. "The gentlemen will excuse me," she said weakly, giving Prokop such a burning glance that he grew terrified lest the others should notice it. She left the room on the arm of Uncle Rohn.

It was now necessary to celebrate Prokop's feat somehow or other. The company was a good-natured one, consisting largely of young men who were only too ready to show their appreciation of such a heroic deed. Prokop rose enormously in their estimation due to the fact that he had broken the bottle and afterward demonstrated his ability to consume an incredible quantity of wine and liqueurs without ending up under the table.

By three o'clock in the morning Prince Suwalski was triumphantly kissing him, and the fat cousin, almost with tears in his eyes, was familiarly addressing him as "thou". Then they began jumping over chairs and kicking up a frightful row.

Prokop smiled at everyone, and his head was in the clouds. But when they tried to take him off to the only *fille de joie* to be found in Balttin, he broke free of them, announced that they were drunken cattle, and that he was off to bed.

But instead of executing this sensible project, he wandered into the dark park and for a long time examined the front of the castle, looking for a certain window. Mr. Holz stood dreaming fifteen yards away, leaning against a tree.

CHAPTER XXXI

The next day, it rained. Prokop wandered about the park, angry with himself at the thought that as a result he probably would not see the Princess at all. But she ran out bareheaded into the rain. "Only for five minutes," she whispered, out of breath, and was about to kiss him. Then she caught sight of Mr. Holz. "Who's that man?"

Prokop looked round quickly. "Who?" By this time he was so accustomed to his shadow that he had ceased to realize that it was always with him. "That's...my guard, see?"

The Princess turned her commanding eyes on Mr. Holz, who instantly thrust his pipe into his pocket and retired some distance away. "Come," whispered the Princess and drew Prokop into a summer-house. They sat there, not daring to kiss one another, for Mr. Holz was waiting near by, steadily getting soaked. "Your hand," ordered the Princess quietly, and her passionate fingers grasped the disfigured stumps of Prokop's paw. "Darling, darling," she said, and went on: "you mustn't look at me like that in front of people. I simply don't know what to do. One day I shall throw my arms round your neck in public and then there'll be a scandal, O God!" The Princess was simply aghast at the thought.

"Did you go to those girls last night?" she asked suddenly. "You mustn't, now you're mine. Darling, darling, it's so hard for me—why don't you speak? I've come to tell you that you must be careful. *Mon Oncle Charles* is already on our track. Yesterday you were wonderful!" Her voice betrayed impatience and anxiety. "Do they watch you all the time? Everywhere? Even in the laboratory? Ah, *c'est bête!* When you broke that bottle yesterday I could have come over and kissed you. You were so magnificently angry. Do you remember the night when you broke your chain? Then I went after you blindly, blindly—"

"Princess," Prokop interrupted her in a hoarse voice, "there is something you must tell me. Is all this the whim of a great lady or...?"

The Princess let go of his hand. "Or what?"

Prokop turned his desperate eyes to her. "Are you only playing with me—"

"Or?" she concluded, with evident delight in torturing him.

"Or do you—to a certain extent—"

"—Love you, eh? Listen," she said, placing her hands behind her head and looking at him through half closed eyes, "if at any time it seemed to me that…that I loved you, really loved you insanely, then I should attempt to… destroy myself." She clicked her tongue as she had before on that occasion with Premier. "I should never leave you, if once I fell in love with you."

"You lie," cried Prokop, furious, "you lie! I couldn't bear the thought that this was only…a flirtation. You're not so corrupt as that! It's not true!"

"If you know that," said the Princess with quiet dignity, "why do you ask me?"

"I want to hear you say so," said Prokop through his teeth, "I want you to say…directly…what I am to you. That's what I want to hear!"

The Princess shook her head.

"I must know," said Prokop fiercely, "otherwise—otherwise—"

The Princess smiled wearily and put her hand on his. "No, I beg you, don't, don't ask me to tell you."

"Why?"

"You would have too much power over me," she said quietly, and Prokop trembled with delight.

From outside there came the discreet cough of Mr. Holz, and behind the bushes in the distance could be seen the silhouette of Uncle Rohn. "Look, he's searching for us," whispered the Princess. "You mustn't appear this evening." Their hands grew quiet; the rain hissed on the roof of the summerhouse; they were spattered with cool drops. "Darling, darling," whispered the Princess and put her face near Prokop's. "What a thing you are! A big nose, bad-tempered, covered with scars. They say that you're a great scientist. Why aren't you a prince?"

Prokop made a movement of impatience.

She rubbed her cheek against his shoulder. "You're angry again. And you've called me a beast and worse things. You won't have any mercy for what I do…for what I'm going to do…. Darling," she concluded, and stretched out her hand towards his face.

He bent over her; they kissed in reconciliation. Above the noise of the rain came that of the approaching steps of Mr. Holz.

It's impossible, impossible! The whole day Prokop wandered about trying to catch sight of her. "You mustn't appear this evening." Of course, you don't belong to their society; she feels more free among those swells. It was extraordinary; in the depths of his soul Prokop was aware that he did not really love her, yet he was tortured, full of anger and humiliation. That evening he wandered about the park in the rain thinking of the Princess sitting in the salon in an atmosphere of gaiety and freedom; he felt like a mangy dog which had been kicked out into the rain. There is nothing more painful in life than to be ashamed.

Now we'll put an end to all this, he decided. He ran home, hurried into evening dress and burst into the smoking-room as he had the evening before. The Princess looked very unhappy, but directly she caught sight of Prokop her lips relaxed into a smile of delight. The other young people welcomed him with friendliness; only *Oncle Charles* was a shade more formal. The Princess warned him with her eyes: be careful! She hardly spoke at all, as if somehow she was disconcerted; but nevertheless she found an opportunity to slip into Prokop's hand a crumpled note. "Darling, darling," she had scrawled in pencil in large letters, "what have you done? Leave us." He screwed the piece of paper into a ball. No, Princess, no, I shall remain here. I enjoy seeing your relations with these perfumed idiots. For this passionate obstinacy he was rewarded by a burning glance from the Princess. She began to joke with Sulwalski; Von Graun, with all the men, was malicious, cruel, impertinent, laughing at them all pitilessly. Now and then she gave Prokop a quick glance as if to ask him whether he was satisfied with the bodies of her admirers which she was laying at his feet. But he was not satisfied. He frowned and with his eyes asked for five minutes confidential conversation. Then she stood up and led him to some picture or other. "Be sensible, only be sensible," she whispered feverishly, stood on tiptoe and gave him a warm kiss on the mouth. Prokop was aghast at this insane action; but nobody saw them, not even *Oncle Rohn*, who otherwise noticed everything with his melancholy, intelligent eyes.

Nothing more happened that day. Nevertheless Prokop tossed on his bed, biting the pillows. And in the other wing of the castle the Princess did not sleep the whole night.

The next morning Paul brought Prokop a perfumed note, without saying from whom it came. "My dear friend," it ran, "we shall not meet today. I don't know what I shall do. I am terribly impetuous; please be more sensible than I am. (A few lines were scratched out.) Don't walk past the castle, or I shall run out to you. Please do something to rid yourself of that horrible guard. I've had a bad night. I look terrible and don't want you to see me today. Don't come to us. *Mon Oncle Charles* is already throwing out hints. I shouted at him and am not on speaking terms with him. Dear, advise me: I've just got rid of my maid as they've told me that she has an affair with a groom and visits him. I can't stand that. I could have hit her in the face when she confessed it. She was beautiful and cried, and I enjoyed watching her tears. Imagine, I'd never noticed before the way in which tears come. They well up, run down the cheek quickly, stop and then catch up the others. I cannot cry. When I was small I screamed until I was blue in the face, but I never cried. I drove the girl away an hour ago. I hated her and could not bear her to stand near me. You're right, I'm wicked and full of anger, but how could she dare to do that? Darling, I beg you to speak with her. I'll have her back and behave to her as you'd like me to. I only want to see that you are able to forgive a woman for such things. You know that I'm wicked and filled with envy. I'm so angry that I don't know what to do. I should like to see you but I cannot now. Don't write to me. My love to you."

Prokop read this to the accompaniment of a wild tune on the piano in the wing of the castle. He wrote: "I see that you do not love me. You are inventing all sorts of obstacles and you do not wish to compromise yourself. You are tired of torturing a man who did not force himself upon you. I thought the position was different and now I am ashamed and realize that you wish to end things. If you don't appear in the Japanese summer-house this afternoon, I shall assume that this is the case and do all I can not to bother you any more."

Prokop sighed with relief. He was not used to writing love letters. This one seemed to him to be written sincerely and directly. Mr. Paul ran round with it; the noise of the piano in the other wing was suddenly cut short and all was quiet.

Meanwhile, Prokop had run off to Carson. He met him near the workshops and went straight to the point: Could he be allowed to go about without Holz? He was prepared to take an oath that until further notice he would not attempt to escape. Mr. Carson grinned significantly. But certainly, why not? He could be as free as a bird, aha! go where he liked and when he liked, if he would oblige him in one detail: give up Krakatit. Prokop grew furious: "I've given you Vicit: what more do you want? Man, I've told you that you won't get Krakatit even if you cut my head off!"

Mr. Carson shrugged his shoulders and expressed his regret that in that case there was nothing to be done, since anyone who carried Krakatit under his hat was a public danger, a classical case of preventative supervision. "Get rid of Krakatit, and there you are," he said. "It'll be worth your while. Otherwise…otherwise we shall have to consider sending you somewhere else."

Prokop, who was just about to fall upon him, suddenly stopped, mumbled that he understood, and ran home. Perhaps there's an answer, he said to himself; but there was none.

In the afternoon Prokop began his wait in the Japanese summer-house. Until four o'clock he was filled with anxious, disturbing hope: now—now she may come every moment. After four o'clock he could not bear to sit down any longer; he paced about the summer-house like a jaguar in a cage, picturing himself embracing her knees, trembling with ecstasy and fear. Mr. Holz discreetly retired into the shrubbery. By five o'clock, Prokop was overpowered by a horrible feeling of disillusionment. Then he suddenly thought: perhaps she will come at dusk, of course she will! He smiled to himself. Behind the castle the sun set in its autumnal gold. The branches of the trees stood out sharply and rigidly, one could hear the beetles rustling in the fallen leaves, and, before one realized it, the bright light of day had turned into a golden twilight. The first evening star appeared on the green horizon, the earth grew dark beneath the pale heavens, the bat began its erratic flight and from somewhere the other side of the park could be heard the muffled sound of bells as the cows returned to the farm, filled with warm milk. In the castle one window lighted up after the other. Was it already evening Stars of heaven, how often had not the small boy gazed at you in wonder from the edge of the wild thyme, how often had not the man turned to you, waiting, suffering, sometimes sobbing under his cross.

Mr. Holz appeared out of the darkness. "Are you going?"

"No."

To drink the cup of your humiliation until the morning; for it was clear that she would not come. Now it is necessary to drink this cup of bitterness, at the bottom of which is truth, to intoxicate yourself with pain, to pile up suffering and shame until you writhe like a worm and are stupefied by agony. You tremble in anticipation of happiness; now give yourself up to pain, which is the narcotic of the person who is suffering. It is night, already night, and she does not come.

Prokop's heart was lit up by a sudden ray of joy: she knows that I am waiting (she must know). She will steal out in the night when everyone is asleep and fly to me with her arms opened and her mouth full of the sweetness of kisses. We shall embrace in silence, drinking inexpressible realizations from one another's lips. She will come, pale even in the darkness, trembling with the cold fear which can accompany joy, and give me her bitter lips. She will step out of the black night....

In the castle the lights began to go out....

In front of the summer-house could be discerned the figure of Mr. Holz, his hands in his pockets. His exhausted attitude indicated that "there's been enough of this." Meanwhile in the summer-house, Prokop, with a savage, contemptuous smile on his face, was stamping out the last sparks of hope, hanging on for a desperate minute, for the last minute of waiting would signify the end of everything.

Midnight sounded from the distant town. It was the end.

Prokop rushed home through the dark park, hurrying for no reason at all. He ran bent with dejection. Five paces behind him there trotted, yawning, Mr. Holz.

CHAPTER XXXII

The end of everything. It was almost a relief, at least something certain and restful, and Prokop entered into the fact with his usual thoroughness. Good, it's over. There's nothing to fear now. She remained away on purpose. That's enough, that slap in the face is enough; that's the end. He sat in an armchair, incapable of getting up, continuing to intoxicate himself with his humiliation. A servant who had been given the sack. She was shameless, proud, heartless. She had given him up for one of her admirers. Well, it was over; all the better.

Every time he heard a step in the passage, Prokop raised his head in excited anticipation, the existence of which he would not admit to himself. Perhaps it was a letter. No, nothing. She didn't think him worth even an apology. It was the end.

Mr. Paul shuffled up a dozen times with the old question in his pale eyes: Did the gentleman want anything? No, Paul, nothing. "Wait, have you a letter for me?" Mr. Paul shook his head. "Good, you can go."

Prokop felt as if there was a lump of ice in his chest. This desolation was the end. Even if the door opened, and she herself were standing there, he would still say: The end! "Darling, darling," Prokop heard her whisper, and then he burst out in desperation: "Why have you humiliated me so? If you were a chambermaid, I should forgive you your haughtiness, but as a princess you cannot be excused. Do you hear? It's the end, the end!"

Mr. Paul opened the door: "Does the gentleman require anything?"

Prokop stopped short; he had said the last words aloud. "No, Paul. Have you any letter for me?"

Mr. Paul shook his head.

The day grew more and more oppressive; it was as if he was entangled in a horrible spider's web. It was already evening. Then he heard some voices whispering in the passage, and Mr. Paul entered in delighted haste. "Here is a letter for you," he whispered triumphantly, "shall I turn on the lights?"

"No." Prokop crushed the thin envelope in his fingers and became aware of the familiar, penetrating scent; it was as if he was trying by smelling to see what was inside. The point of ice dug deeper in his heart. Why did she wait until the evening to write? Because she has nothing to say but: You mustn't come to us this evening. All right, Princess, if it's the end, then it's the end.

Prokop jumped up, found in the darkness a clean envelope and placed the letter inside it, unopened. "Paul, take this at once to Her Excellency."

Scarcely had Paul left the room than Prokop wished to call him back. But it was too late and he realized painfully that what he had just done was irrevocable. Then he threw himself on the bed and stifled in the cushions something which was tearing itself out of his mouth against his will.

Mr. Krafft came in, probably as the result of an alarm from Paul, and did all he could to calm and distract his lacerated friend. Prokop ordered some whiskey, drank it, and by an effort recovered himself. Mr. Kraft sipped some soda-water, and assented to everything which Prokop said, although he was agreeing to things which were in direct opposition to his glowing idealism. Prokop cursed, reproached himself, used the most coarse and crude expressions as if it relieved his feelings to besmirch everything, spit on it, trample on it and destroy it. And he overflowed with obscenities, turned women inside out and abused them in the most violent possible terms. Mr. Kraft, sweating with horror, agreed with everything which the enraged genius threw out. Then Prokop's vehemence exhausted itself, he became silent, frowned and drank more than was good for him. Then he lay on the bed, fully dressed, rocking himself from side to side and gazing with large eyes into the swirling darkness.

The next morning he got up, calm and disgusted, and immigrated to his laboratory for good. But he did nothing but lounge about the room, kicking a sponge in front of him. Then he had an idea. He compounded a terrible and unstable explosive and sent it to the office, hoping that a really dramatic catastrophe would follow. Nothing happened. Prokop threw himself on the couch and slept uninterruptedly for sixteen hours.

He awoke like another man, sober, steady and cold. He felt utterly indifferent to what had happened before he fell asleep. He again began to work assiduously and methodically on the explosive disintegration of atoms, and theoretically arrived at such terrible conclusions that his hair stood on end in horror at the nature of the forces among which we live.

Once in the middle of his calculations he was seized by a sudden feeling of restlessness. "Probably I'm tired," he said to himself, and went out into the open air for a bit, bareheaded. Without realizing what he was doing he made his way to the castle, mechanically ran up the stairs and went along the passage to the guests' quarters. Paul was not in his usual seat. Prokop went inside. Everything was as he had left it, but in the air was the familiar scent of the Princess, "Absurd, absurd," thought Prokop. "Suggestion or something of the sort; I've been smelling the strong smells of the laboratory too long." Nevertheless he was painfully excited.

He sat down for a moment and was surprised how far away everything was. All was quiet in the castle, the quietness of the afternoon. And yet had not something changed? He heard muffled steps in the corridor, probably those of Paul, and went outside. It was the Princess.

Surprise and what was almost horror threw her back against the wall, and she stood deathly pale, her eyes wide open, and her lips twisted as if in pain. What did she want in the guests' wing? Perhaps she is going to Suwalski, thought Prokop suddenly, and something in him froze. He made a step forward as if he was going to throw himself upon her, but instead made a noise in his throat and ran out. Did he feel hands pulling him back? You must not look back! Away, away from here! Only when he was a long way from the castle, in the middle of the sandy artillery ground, did he throw himself down on his face. For there is only one pain greater than that of humiliation—that of hatred. Ten yards to the side sat the serious and concentrated Mr. Holz.

The night which followed was heavy and oppressive, unusually black. There was going to be a storm. At such moments people are extraordinarily irritable and unable to control their actions.

About eleven o'clock Prokop burst out of the door of his laboratory and stunned Mr. Holz so thoroughly with a chair that he was able to escape from him into the darkness of the night. A few moments later two shots were heard from the neighbourhood of the factory station. Low down on the horizon there were flashes of lightning, followed by a more intense darkness. But from the top of the wall near the entrance there came a bright ray of violet light which lit up the whole of the station, the trucks, the ramps, and the piles of coal. It also lit up a dark figure which ran in a zigzag path, fell to the ground and then disappeared again in the darkness. The figure then made its way amongst the barracks towards the park; several other figures threw themselves on it. The searchlight then turned on the castle; two more shots, and the running figure plunged into the bushes.

Shortly afterward the window of the Princess's room rattled. She jumped up and at that moment there flew into the room a stone wrapped up in a crumpled piece of paper. On one side of the sheet was something illegible, scribbled with a broken pencil, and on the other a series of reproaches written in a small handwriting. The Princess threw on her clothes, but at that moment another report was heard behind the lake—according to the sound, that of a rifle which was loaded with something more than a blank cartridge. But before the Princess had time to leave the room she saw through the window two soldiers dragging along something dark which struggled and tried to throw them off. He was not wounded, then.

The horizon continued to be lit up with long, yellow flames. But the storm which would have cleared the air did not break.

The sobered Prokop again threw himself headlong into work in the laboratory, or at least forced himself to work. Mr. Carson had just left him. He was in a cold rage and had announced unequivocally that everything pointed to Prokop's being transferred as early as possible to some safer place. If he refused to respond to lenient treatment, they would have to resort to harsher measures. Well, it was all the same, nothing mattered. The test-tube broke in Prokop's fingers.

In the hall Mr. Holz was waiting with his head wrapped in bandages. Prokop offered him some money as a compensation for the injury, but he would not accept it. Well, let him do as he liked. So he was to be transferred somewhere else—very well. Curse these test-tubes! They break one after another.

In the hall there was the sound of someone being awakened suddenly from dreaming. Probably another visit. Prokop did not trouble to turn round from the lamp he was using. The door creaked. "Darling!" whispered somebody. Prokop staggered, gripped the table and turned round as if in a dream. The Princess was standing with her hand against the doorpost, pale, with a dark, fixed look in her eyes, pressing her hands to her breast as if to muffle the beating of her heart.

Trembling all over, he went across to her and with his fingers touched her cheeks and shoulders as if he could not believe that it was she. She placed her cold fingers on his mouth. Then she looked back into the hall. Mr. Holz had disappeared....

CHAPTER XXXIIL

She sat motionless on the couch, her knees drawn up to her chin, her hair falling across her face and her hands clasped convulsively around her neck. He was afraid of what he had done, and kissed her knees, hands, hair, grovelled on the floor and poured out entreaties and endearments; she did not see or hear. It seemed to him that she trembled with revulsion at his every touch.

Then she quietly got up and went over to the mirror. He approached her on tiptoe, hoping to surprise her, but then he caught sight of her reflection. She was looking at herself with an expression so wild, terrible, and desperate, that he was horrified. She turned round and fell on his shoulder.

"Am I ugly? Do I revolt you? What have I done, what have I done?" She pressed her face against his chest. "I'm stupid, you see? I know… I know that you're disappointed. But you mustn't be contemptuous of me, you understand?" She nestled against him like a repentant young girl. "You won't escape, will you? I'll do anything you like, you see? As if I were your wife. Darling, darling, don't leave me to think; I shall become horrible to myself again if once I think; you've no idea what my thoughts are. Don't leave me now—" Her trembling fingers caressed his neck; he raised her head and kissed her, murmuring all sorts of things in his ecstasy. Color came back into her face and she became beautiful again. "Am I ugly?" she whispered, happy and dazed, between his kisses, "I should like to be beautiful for your sake. Do you know why I came? I expected that you would kill me."

"And if you had known what was going to happen," whispered Prokop, rocking her in his arms, "would you have come?"

The Princess nodded. "I am horrible. What must you think of me! But I won't let you think." He embraced her quickly and raised her from the couch. "No, no," she implored, resisting him. But she lay still with moist eyes, her fingers playing with the hair on his heavy forehead. "Dear, dear," she sighed, "how you have tortured me these last few days! Do you?" She did not say the word "love." He assented passionately: "And you?"

"Yes. You should have seen it already. Do you know what you are? You are the most beautiful horrible man that ever had a big nose. Your eyes are as bloodshot as a St. Bernard's. Is it through your work? Perhaps you wouldn't be so nice if you were a prince. Ah! Stop!"

She slipped out of his embrace and went to the mirror to comb her hair. She examined herself attentively and then made a deep bow in front of the glass. "There's the Princess," she said, pointing to her image, "and here," she added, indicating herself, "is your girl, you see? Did you realize that you possess a princess?"

Prokop made an abrupt movement. "What does that matter?" he cried, bringing down his fist heavily on the table.

"You must choose, the princess or the girl. You can't have the princess; you may worship her from the distance but you may not kiss her hand, and you must not ask her whether she loves you. A princess may not do such things; she has behind her a thousand years of noble blood. Did you know that we used to be kings? Ah, you know nothing, but you ought to know at least that a princess lives in a glass case and you may not touch her. But you can have the ordinary woman, this dark girl. Stretch out your hand and she is yours, like anything else. Now you must choose between the two."

Prokop was again chilled. "Princess," he said heavily.

She came over to him and seriously kissed his cheek. "You're mine, you understand? You darling! You see that you have a princess. And are you proud that you have a princess? What a terrible thing the princess must have done to cause anyone to grow haughty for a couple of days! I knew, I knew from the first moment I saw you that you wanted the princess; from anger, from a masculine sense of power or something like that. For this reason you hated me so much that you desired me and I ran after you. Do you think that I am annoyed with myself? On the contrary, I am proud that I have done it. That's something, isn't it? To lower oneself so quickly, to be a princess, a great lady and then to come…to come alone…"

Her words threw Prokop into consternation. "Stop," he begged her and took her into his trembling arms. "I'm not your equal…in birth…"

"What did you say? Equal? Do you think that if you had been a prince I should have come to you? If you wanted me to treat you like an equal I shouldn't have been with you…like this," she cried. "There's a big difference, you understand?" Prokop's hands fell. "You shouldn't have said such a thing," he said through his teeth, recoiling.

She threw her arms round his neck. "Darling, darling, let me speak! Am I reproaching you? I came…alone…because you wanted to escape or to get yourself killed, I don't know what; any girl would have done the same…. Do you think that I was wrong to do it? Tell me! Did I do wrong? You don't understand," she said, wincing, "you don't understand!"

"Wait," cried Prokop. He extricated himself from her embrace, and paced up and down the room. Suddenly, he was blinded by a sudden hope. "Do you believe in me? Do you believe that I shall do something? I can work terribly hard. I've never thought about fame, but if you wished it… I'd exert all my strength! You know that Darwin was carried to his coffin by dukes? If you wished, I could do…tremendous things. I can work—I could change the face of the world. Give me ten years and you'll see—"

It seemed as if she was not listening to him. "If you were a prince it would be enough to look at you, give you one's hand and you would know, you would know, you mustn't doubt—it wouldn't have to be demonstrated to you…ten years! Would you be true to me for ten days! In ten minutes you will become gloomy, dear, and grow angry at the fact that the Princess does not want you…because she is a princess and you are not a prince, see? And then, try as I may to convince you, it will be in vain; no demonstration will be great enough, no humiliation sufficiently deep. He would have me run after him, offer myself to him, do more than any other girl, I don't know what! What am I to do with you?" She came up to him and offered him her lips. "Will you be true to me for ten years, then?"

He seized hold of her, sobbing. "There," she whispered and stroked his hair. "So you're pulling at the chain? And yet I should have remained just as I was. Darling, darling, I know that you will leave me." She sank into his arms. He lifted her up and forced open her closed lips with his kisses.

She lay still with her eyes closed, hardly breathing, and Prokop, bending over her, his heart oppressed, contemplated the inscrutable serenity of her hot, strained face. She extricated herself from his embrace as if in a dream. "What have you got in all those bottles? Are they poison?" She examined his shelves and instruments. "Give me some poison or other."

"Why?"

"In case they want to take me away from here."

Her serious face made him anxious, but to appease her he poured a solution of chalk into a small box, and at that moment she pounced on some crystals of arsenic.

"Don't take that!" he cried, but she had already placed it in her bag.

"I see you will be a great man," she said softly. "I never imagined such things. Did you say that Darwin was carried to his grave by dukes? Who were they?"

"That doesn't matter."

She kissed him. "You are nice! Why doesn't it matter?"

"Well…the Duke of Argyle and…the Duke of Devonshire," he muttered.

"Really!" she considered this, frowning. "I should never have imagined…that scientists were so… And you only mentioned it incidentally!" She put her arms round his shoulders, as if for the first time. "And you, you could—? Really?"

"Well, wait until I am buried."

"Ah, if that were only very soon," she said reflectively with naïve cruelty. "You'd be wonderful if you were famous. Do you know what I like the most?"

"No."

"I don't, either," she said musingly, and turned and kissed him. "I don't know. Whoever and whatever you were—" She moved her shoulders with a gesture of impatience. "It's for always, you understand?"

Prokop recoiled from this relentless monogamy. She stood before him, muffled up to her eyes in her blue fox fur and looked at him in the twilight with glistening eyes. "Oh!" she cried suddenly and sank back into a chair, "my legs are trembling." She smoothed and rubbed them with naïve shamelessness. "How shall I be able to ride? Come, darling, come and see me today. *Mon Oncle Charles* is away today, and even if he weren't it's all the same to me." She got up and kissed him. "*Au revoir.*"

In the doorway she stopped, hesitated, and came back to him. "Kill me, please," she said, her hands hanging limp by her side, "kill me." He put his hands on her: "Why?"

"So that I shan't have to go away…and so that I shall never have to be here." He whispered into her ear: "…Tomorrow."

She looked at him, and submissively bent down her head; it was…a sign of assent.

When she had been gone some time he also went out into the half light. Someone a hundred yards away got up from the ground and rubbed the dirt off his clothes with his sleeve. The silent Mr. Holz.

CHAPTER XXXIV

When he joined the company that evening, still not able to believe what had happened, and in an acute state of tension, he found her looking so beautiful that he scarcely knew her. She was conscious of the burning glance with which he enveloped her, glowed with pleasure, and, indifferent to the presence of the others, gave him ardent looks in return. There was a new guest at the castle, named d'Hémon, a diplomat, or something of the sort, Mongolian in appearance, with purple lips and a short black beard. He was evidently thoroughly familiar with physical chemistry; Becquerel, Planck, Niels Bohr, Milliken and similar names simply poured out of his mouth. He had read about Prokop and was extremely interested in his work. Prokop allowed himself to be diverted, talked at some length and forgot for a moment to look at the Princess. As a result he received such a kick on the shin that he positively jumped and all but returned it. The kick was accompanied by a passionately jealous glance. At that moment, he was obliged to answer a stupid question put by Prince Suwalski regarding the nature of this energy that they are always talking about. He grasped the sugar bowl and gave the Princess such a bitter look that she imagined that he was going to throw it at her. He then went on to explain to the Prince that if all the energy which it contained could be liberated at the same moment it would be sufficient to hurl Mont Blanc and Chamonix into the air; but that, as it happened, such a thing could never take place.

"But you'll do it," said d'Hémon seriously and definitely.

The Princess leaned over towards them: "What were you saying?"

"I was saying that he will do it," repeated Monsieur d'Hémon with perfect simplicity.

"There you are," said the Princess loudly, and sat down victoriously. Prokop grew red and did not dare to look at her.

"And if he does do it," she asked breathlessly, "will he be terribly famous? Like Darwin?"

"If he does it," said Monsieur d'Hémon without hesitation, "kings will consider it an honour to carry his coffin. That is, if there are still any kings."

"Rubbish," muttered Prokop, but the Princess glowed with inexpressible delight. He would not have looked at her for anything in the world; embarrassed, he mumbled something or other, crumbling a piece of sugar in his fingers. Finally, he ventured to lift his eyes. She looked at him directly, with passionate love. "Do you?" she said to him under her breath. He understood only too well what she meant: Do you love me?—but he pretended that he had not heard and quickly looked at the tablecloth instead. God! That girl's mad, or else she deliberately wants.... "Do you?" came to him across the table, still more loudly and urgently. He nodded quickly and looked at her with eyes filled with happiness. Luckily in the midst of the general conversation nobody noticed them; only Monsieur d'Hémon preserved his discreet and remote expression.

The conversation roved all over the place until suddenly Monsieur d'Hémon, evidently an exceptionally well-informed man, began to talk to Von Graun about his genealogy up to the thirteenth century. The Princess listened with extraordinary interest, whereupon the new guest talked instead about her ancestry, without the slightest difficulty. "Enough," cried the Princess when he had reached the year 1007, when the first Hagen founded a barony in Esthonia, having murdered somebody or other; for the genealogical experts had been unable to go back any further. But Monsieur d'Hémon continued: This Hagen or Agen the One-armed was clearly a Tartar Prince, captured in the course of an expedition into the district of Kamsk. Persian history mentions a certain Khan Agan, who was the son of Giw Khan, King of the Turkomans, the Uzbeks, Sards and Kirghiz, while he again was the son of Weiwus, the son of the conqueror Li-taj Khan. This "Emperor" Li-taj is referred to in the Chinese chronicles as the ruler of Turkoman, Altai and Western Thibet, who had slain as many as fifty thousand people, amongst whom was a Chinese Governor, round whose head he had had twisted a wet rope, until the bones broke. Nothing was known of Li-taj's ancestors. More might be discovered if access was ever gained to the archives in Lhassa. His son, Weiwus, who was regarded even by the Mongolians as being rather wild, was beaten to death with tentpoles in Kara Butak. His son Giw Khan depopulated Chiv and extended his activities as far as Itil or Astrachan, where he became famous for having plucked out the eyes of two thousand people and driven them into the Kuban Steppe. Agan Khan continued in his footsteps, having sent out expeditions as far as Bolgar or the Simbirsk of today, where he was taken prisoner, his right hand amputated and kept as a hostage until the time when he was able to flee to Balt among the Livs who then inhabited the district. There he was baptized by the German bishop, Gotilly or Gutilly and—probably through religious zeal—murdered in the cemetery in Verro the sixteen-year-old heir to the Pechorski barony, taking his sister to wife. Through this bigamy he was able to extend his territory as far as Lake Pejpus. See the chronicles of Nikifor, where he is referred to as "Prince Agen," while the Osel Chronicle alludes to him as "Rex Aagen." His descendants, concluded Monsieur d'Hémon quietly, were driven out, but never dethroned.

Monsieur d'Hémon then got up, bowed, and remained standing. His remarks produced an enormous sensation. The Princess simply drank in every one of his words, as if this line of Tartar cutthroats was the finest in the world. Prokop watched her with dismay; she did not even wince at the story of four thousand eyes having been plucked out. Involuntarily he looked for Tartar features in her face. She was extraordinarily beautiful, drew herself up and enveloped herself in her own dignity; suddenly there was such a distance between her and all the others that they all became as formal as if it were a state banquet, not daring to look at her directly. Prokop wanted repeatedly to strike the table, say something rough, disturb this frozen scene. She sat with eyes cast down, as if she were waiting for something, and across her face there flashed something like impatience. The company looked at one another interrogatively, at the dignified Monsieur d'Hémon, and at last one by one rose to their feet. Prokop also stood up, not realizing what was happening. What on earth could it mean? They all stood quite stiffly with their arms at their sides, looking at the Princess. Then she raised her eyes like someone who is expressing thanks for homage, and they all sat down. Only when Prokop was in his seat again did he realize with consternation that they had all just made obeisance to their ruler. He suddenly became so angry that he broke into a sweat. Heavens, that he should have taken part in such a farce! How on earth was it possible that they did not burst out laughing at the ridiculousness of the comedy which they had just played?

He was getting ready to laugh with the others, when the Princess rose. All the others did the same, and Prokop was convinced that now the ice would break. He looked around him and his eyes fell on the fat cousin, who, his arms hanging down at his sides, was approaching the Princess, inclined slightly forwards; surely it must all be a joke. The Princess spoke to him and nodded her head; the fat cousin bowed and retired. What was happening? Now the Princess gave a quick glance at Prokop, but he did not move. The rest stood on tiptoe and watched him fixedly. Again the Princess made a sign with her eyes; still he did not move. The Princess stepped towards an old, one-armed major from the artillery, covered with medals. The major was just drawing himself up when she turned aside and was suddenly quite close to Prokop.

"Darling, darling," she said in a clear soft voice, "do you—? You're getting angry again. I should like to kiss you."

"Princess," said Prokop in a thick voice, "what does this farce mean?"

"Don't shout like that. It's more important than you imagine. Do you know that they now want to give me in marriage?" She trembled with horror. "Darling, go away now. Go down the passage to the third room on the right and wait there for me. I must see you."

"Listen," Prokop wanted to say, but she only inclined her head and moved suavely across to the old major.

Prokop could not believe his eyes.

Could such things happen? Was it not really a carefully arranged performance? Were the different people taking their roles seriously? The fat cousin took him by the arm and discreetly led him aside. "Do you know what this means?" he whispered excitedly. "The old Hagen is paralyzed. It's a ruling family! Did you see that heir to a throne? There was to be a marriage, but it didn't come off. That man is certainly sent here purposely. God, what a pedigree!" Prokop got free of him. "Excuse me," he mumbled, walked down the passage as slowly as possible and went into the appointed room. It was a sort of little boudoir for drinking tea, with shaded lights, everything lacquered, black porcelain and other rubbish. Prokop strode about this miniature apartment with his hands behind his back, buzzing like a blowfly which hits its head against the glass of a window-frame. *Sacra*, things were altered and for the sake of a lousy Tartar pedigree which a decent person would be ashamed of.... A nice reason! And on account of a handful of such Huns these idiots crawled along on their bellies and she, she herself... The blowfly butted the glass in a frenzy. Now.... This Tartar princess would come in and say: Darling, darling all is over between us; you must realize that the granddaughter of Li-taj Khan can't love the son of a cobbler. Tap, tap; he heard in his head the noise of his father's hammer and he could almost smell the odour of the leather and of the cobbler's wax; and his mother, in a blue apron, was standing, flushed, over the stove....

The blowfly buzzed desperately. "We shall see, Princess! What have you let yourself in for, man? When she comes you must knock your forehead on the floor and say: Pardon, Tartar princess, I shall not show myself in your presence again...."

In the little room there was a faint smell of quince, and the light was dull and soft. The desperate fly continued to strike its head on the glass and complain in a voice that was almost human. What have you let yourself in for, idiot?

The Princess suddenly glided noiselessly into the room. At the door she reached out for the switch and turned out the light. In the darkness Prokop felt a hand which lightly touched his face and then passed round his neck. He took the Princess in his arms; she was so supple and almost incorporate, that he touched her fearfully as if she were something fragile. She covered his face with her aerial kisses and whispered something which he could not catch; he felt his hair being delicately stroked. Then he felt her sinuous body yielding, the arm round his neck pressed him more closely and her moist lips moved on his own, as if they were speaking voicelessly. Trembling all over, she grasped Prokop more and more firmly, pulled down his head, pressed herself to him with her breasts and knees, twined both her arms round him; a passionate, agonizing embrace, the moaning of a creature which is being suffocated; they staggered in a convulsive, insane embrace. Never to leave go. To devour one another! To fuse into one being or to die! She was sobbing helplessly, but he freed himself from the terrible grip of her hands. She swayed as if she were intoxicated, pulled a handkerchief out of her bosom and wiped her lips, and without saying a word passed into the adjacent room.

With a splitting head, Prokop remained in the darkness. This last embrace seemed to him to mean farewell.

CHAPTER XXXV

The fat cousin was right. The old Hagen was becoming more and more paralyzed, though he had not yet succumbed to the disease. He now lay helpless, surrounded by doctors, trying to open his left eye. Uncle Rohn and his relations were suddenly sent for; and the old Prince tried once more to open his eye so as to look again at his daughter and make some signal.

She ran out of the room, bareheaded, and rushed outside to Prokop who had been waiting for her in the park for some time. Completely ignoring Holz she kissed and clung to him passionately. She made hardly any allusion to her father and Uncle Charles, absorbed in something, harassed and affectionate. She pressed herself against him and then suddenly became distant and preoccupied. He began to poke fun at the Tartar dynasty...a little too pointedly. She gave him an expressive look and changed the conversation, talking about the previous evening. "Until the last moment I thought that I wouldn't go to you. Do you know that I am nearly thirty? When I was fifteen I fell terribly in love with our chaplain. I went to him to confess, simply in order to get a nearer sight of him, and because I was ashamed to say that I had stolen or lied I told him that I had been unchaste; I didn't know what that meant, and the poor man had a lot of work to find out the truth. Now I couldn't confess," she concluded quietly, and made a bitter movement with her mouth.

Prokop was disturbed by her continued self-analysis, in which he saw a morbid desire for self-torture. He tried to find something else to talk about and discovered to his consternation that if they did not speak about love they had nothing to say to one another. They were standing on the bastion. It gave the Princess a certain relief to return to her past, to confess small but important things about herself. "Soon after I confessed we had a dancing master who fell in love with my governess, a stout woman. I heard about it and... saw them. It disgusted me. Oh! But all the same I spied on them and... I couldn't understand. And then one day when we were dancing I suddenly understood, when he pressed himself against me. After that I wouldn't let him touch me; in the end... I fired a shotgun at him. We had to dismiss them both.

"At that time... I was terribly worried by mathematics; I simply hadn't a head for it, you see? My teacher was a famous man, but unpleasant; you scientists are all extraordinary. He set me an exercise and looked at his watch;

it had to be done in an hour. And when I had only five, four, three minutes left and I had still done nothing…my heart began to thump and I had such a horrible feeling—" She dug her fingers into Prokop's arm and drew in her breath. "Then I got to like those lessons.

"When I was nineteen they selected a husband for me; you wouldn't believe it. And because by that time I understood everything I made my fiancé promise that he would never touch me. Two years later he died in Africa. I pined so much—through being romantic or something of the sort—that they never tried to make a match for me again. I thought that I'd got the question settled forever.

"And I forced myself, you know, to believe that I had some obligation to him and that I ought to be true to him even after his death, until finally I grew to believe that I had been in love with him. Now I see that all the time I was only acting to myself and that I had never felt anything more than foolish disillusion.

"It's curious, isn't it, that I'm telling you all these things about myself? You know, it's a great relief to speak about oneself like this without keeping anything back.

"When you arrived I thought to begin with that you were like that professor of mathematics. I was even frightened of you, darling. He'll give me an exercise to do, I thought, and my heart began to beat again.

"A horse simply intoxicated me. When I was on a horse I felt that I didn't need love. And I rode insanely.

"I always imagined that love was something vulgar and…terribly revolting. You see, I still can't deal with it; at the same time it frightens me and masters me. And now I'm glad that I'm like any other woman. When I was little I was afraid of water. They showed me the strokes of swimming on dry land, but I would not go near the lake; I got the idea that it was full of spiders, and one day I was suddenly seized by some sort of courage or desperation, shut my eyes, cried out and sprang in. Don't ask me how proud I was afterward; it was as if I had passed an examination, as if I knew everything, as if I had changed into another person. As if I had grown up at last.…"

That evening she came into the laboratory, uneasy and worried. When he took her into his arms she said agitatedly: "He's opened his eye, he's opened his eye, oh!" She was thinking of the old Hagen; in the afternoon she had had a long conversation with Uncle Rohn but would not speak about it. It seemed that she was striving to get away from something; she threw herself into Prokop's arms so passionately and devotedly that he had the impression that she wanted to blot everything out at all costs. Finally, she lay still, her eyes closed, completely limp. He thought that she had fallen asleep but then she began to whisper: "Darling, I shall do something terrible, but you mustn't leave me. Swear to me, swear to me," she insisted wildly and sprang to her feet, immediately, however, getting control of herself again. "Ah! No. What could you swear to do? I've read in the cards that you will go away. If you want to, do it now before it's too late."

Prokop naturally jumped up, saying that she wanted to get rid of him, that her Tartar pride had rushed to her head, and similar things. She became very excited and charged him with being base and harsh, saying that he would answer for it, that...that... But scarcely had she said it than she flung her arms round his neck, repentant: "I'm a beast. I wasn't thinking of that. You know, a princess ought never to shout, but I shout at you...as if I were your wife. Strike me, I beg you. Wait, I'll show you that I'm capable...." She released him and suddenly, as she was, began to tidy up the laboratory, wetting a cloth under the tap and cleaning the whole floor on her knees. She meant it for an act of repentance, but somehow she found the work pleasant, became radiant, worked with a will, humming to herself a song which she had picked up somewhere from the servants. He wanted to raise her to her feet. "No; wait," she defended herself, "there's a bit over there." And she crawled with the cloth underneath a chair.

"Come here," she said in a moment, surprised. Still mumbling reproaches he sat down next to her. She was squatting, her arms clasped round her knees. "Just see what a chair looks like from underneath. I've never seen such a thing before." She placed on his face a hand which was still damp from the wet rag. "You're as rough as the under side of this chair; that's the most lovely thing about you. I've only seen other people on their smooth, polished side, but you, when one first looks at you, you're like a beam with cracks in it—everything that holds the human frame together. If one runs one's finger over you one gets a splinter in it, but all the same you're beautifully made. One begins to realize something else...something more important than what one gets from the smooth side. That's you."

She nestled against him. "I feel as if I were in a tent, or a log hut," she whispered, entranced. "I never used to play with dolls, but sometimes... secretly... I used to go out with the gardener's boys and climb trees with them.... Then they wondered at home why my clothes were torn. And when I used to climb with them my heart beat with fear so wonderfully. When I'm with you I have the same wonderful fear that I had then.

"Now I'm thoroughly hidden," she said happily, leaning her head against his knees. "Nobody can find me, and I'm rough, like the bottom of that chair; an ordinary woman, not thinking about anything, only being soothed.... Why is a person so happy when he's hidden? Now I know what happiness is: One must close one's eyes and become tiny...quite tiny, waiting to be discovered...."

She rocked herself to and fro contentedly while he smoothed her dishevelled hair; but her widely opened eyes looked past his head into the distance.

Suddenly, she turned her face to him. "What were you thinking about?"

He moved his eyes away shyly. He could not tell her that he saw before him the Tartar princess in all her glory, a proud and commanding figure which now…in pain and yearning.…

"Nothing, nothing," he muttered, looking down at the happy and contented face against his knees, and stroked her dark cheek, which flushed with tender passion.

CHAPTER XXXVI

HE would have done better if he had not come that evening, but he compelled himself to because she had forbidden him to appear. *Oncle Charles* was particularly charming to him. By an unlucky accident he had seen the two of them on an inappropriate occasion pressing one another's hands; finally he had put up his monocle to see better, upon which the Princess snatched her hand away and blushed like a schoolgirl. Oncle Charles came across to her, drew her aside, and whispered something into her ear. After that she did not return, but Rohn appeared instead and engaged himself in conversation with Prokop, evidently trying to sound him. Prokop behaved like a hero, and betrayed nothing, which at least appeared to please the old gentleman. "In society one must be extremely careful," he concluded, rebuking and advising him at the same time. Prokop was greatly relieved when he was left alone to reflect on the significance of this last remark.

The worst of it was that something was evidently being prepared behind the scenes; the older members of the family were positively bursting with importance.

When the next morning Prokop was walking round the castle he was approached by a chambermaid who informed him breathlessly that he was wanted in the birch wood. He made his way there and waited for a long time. Finally, the Princess arrived, moving with the long, beautiful steps of a Diana. "Hide yourself," she whispered rapidly. "Uncle is following me." They ran off hand in hand and disappeared behind the thick foliage of a lilac bush; Mr. Holz, after having searched for them for some time, sat down on the grass, resigned. Then they caught sight of the light hat of Uncle Rohn. He was walking quickly, looking out on both sides of him. The Princess's eyes glistened with delight, like those of a young faun. In the bushes there was a damp and musty smell; the twigs and leaves were covered with spiders' webs. Without even waiting for the danger to pass, the Princess drew Prokop's head towards her. Between his teeth he felt her kisses, like wild berries, bitter and yet pleasant. The game was so delightful, new and surprising that it was if they were seeing one another for the first time.

And that day she did not come to him; beside himself with every sort of suspicion, he made his way to the castle. She was waiting for him, walking with her arms round Egon's neck. Directly she caught sight of him she let go of the boy and came up to him, pale, distraught, mastering a certain desperation. "Uncle knows that I've visited you," she said. "God, what will happen! I think that they will send you away. Don't move now; they're watching us from the window. I spoke this afternoon with…with…" she shivered… "with the manager, you know. We quarrelled… *Oncle Charles* wanted me simply to leave you, to let you escape or something of the sort. The manager was furious and wouldn't hear of such a thing. It looks as if they are sending you somewhere else.… Darling, come here tonight; I'll come out to you, I'll evade…them.…"

And she actually came, breathless, sobbing with dry and anxious eyes. "Tomorrow, tomorrow," she wanted to say, but at that moment a firm and friendly hand descended on her shoulder. It was Uncle Rohn. "Go back, Minna," he ordered sternly. "And you wait here," he added, turning to Prokop. Putting his arm round her shoulder he led her back into the castle. A moment later he came back again and took Prokop by the arm. "My friend," he said sympathetically, "I understand you young people only too well and… I feel with you." He made a gesture of hopelessness with his hand. "Something has taken place which should not have happened. I don't wish to…and of course I can't reproach you. On the contrary, I realize that…obviously.…" Clearly this was a bad beginning and *le bon prince* tried another road. "My dear friend, I respect you and I really like you very much. You are an honest man and…a genius; an unusual combination. I have rarely felt such sympathy for anybody. I know that you will go a long way," he said with relief. "You believe that my intentions are friendly?"

"Nothing of the sort," said Prokop calmly.

Le bon oncle became confused. "I am sorry, extraordinarily," he jerked out, "because I cannot tell you what I want to say unless we have the fullest possible confidence in one another.…"

"*Mon prince*," Prokop interrupted him politely, "as you know, I am not here in the enviable position of a free man. I think that under the circumstances I've no cause to have faith.…"

"Y-yes," sighed *Oncle Rohn*, pleased with the turn that the conversation had taken. "You're perfectly right. You are up against the painful fact that you're a prisoner, eh? You know, that's just what I was going to speak about. My dear friend, as far as I'm concerned… From the very beginning… I passionately condemned this idea of keeping you…in captivity. It's illegal, brutal and…in view of your importance, simply inexcusable, I took various steps…some time ago, you understand," he added quickly. "I intervened in the highest places but…in view of a certain international tension the higher officials are in a panic. You are confined here under the accusation of espionage. Nothing can be done," and the Prince bent down to Prokop's ear, "unless you can succeed in escaping. Trust me, and I'll provide the means. I give you my word."

"What means?" Prokop threw out carelessly.

"I shall simply…arrange it myself. I'll take you in my car—and they can't stop me, you understand. The rest later. Where do you want to go?"

"Leave it; I don't want to go away," answered Prokop definitely.

"Why?" said *Oncle Charles*, surprised.

"To begin with… I don't want you, Prince, to take any risks. A person like yourself—"

"And in the second place?"

"In the second place I'm beginning to like it here."

"And further, further?"

"Nothing further," smiled Prokop, enduring the serious, scrutinizing glance of the Prince.

"Listen," said *Oncle Rohn* after a moment, "I did not mean to tell you. But the point is that in a day or so you are to be transferred elsewhere, to a fortress. Still under the accusation of espionage. You mustn't imagine…. My dear friend, get away while there is still time!"

"Is that true?"

"Honestly it is."

"Then…then I am obliged to you for warning me."

"What do you propose to do?"

"Well, I shall make my arrangements," said Prokop bloodthirstily. "*Mon prince*, you may inform HER that it isn't done…as easily as that."

"What? What do you mean?" stammered *Oncle Charles*.

Prokop made a gesture in the air with his hand as if he were throwing something imaginary in front of him. "Bang," he said.

Oncle Charles drew back. "You intend to defend yourself?"

Prokop said nothing, but stood with his hands in his pockets, frowning darkly and reflecting.

Oncle Charles, pale and fragile in the nocturnal darkness, stepped up to him. "Do you…love her as much as that?" he said quickly, gulping with emotion.

Prokop did not answer. "You love her," repeated Rohn, and embraced him. "Be strong. Leave her and go away! You can't stay here, you must realize that. What would it lead to? For God's sake have pity on her. Save her from a scandal. Can you really imagine that she could ever be your wife? It may be that she is in love with you but—she is too proud; she wouldn't forgo the title of Princess…. Oh, it's impossible, it's impossible! I don't wish to know what there was between you, but if you love her, go away! Go at once, this very night! In the name of love, go away, friend, I beg you in her name. You've made her the most unhappy woman—isn't that enough? Protect her if she's not able to protect herself! Do you love her? Then sacrifice yourself!"

Prokop stood motionless, his head bent, and *le bon prince* felt that this black rough trunk was splitting inside with pain. His heart was torn in sympathy, but he had still one more card to play; if it was not successful he would have to give in.

"She's proud, fantastic, wildly ambitious; she's been like that from childhood. And now we have received the valuable information that she's a princess whose pedigree is equal to that of anyone else's. You don't realize what that means to her. To her and to us. It may be prejudice but…such things are our life. Prokop, the Princess is going to be married. She is marrying a Grand Duke without a throne—a decent and amenable person—but she, she will fight for the crown, for fighting is her nature, her mission, her pride. At last her lifelong dream is being realized. And now you're standing between her and her future. But she's already decided; she's only torturing herself with reproaches—"

"Aha!" cried Prokop. "So it's that way, is it? And—you think that I shall give way now? Wait and see!"

And before *Oncle Rohn* could realize what was happening he had hurried off in the darkness to the laboratory. Mr. Holz silently behind him.

CHAPTER XXXVII

When they reached the laboratory he wanted to slam the door in Holz's face, so as to fortify himself inside, but Mr. Holz just had time to whisper the words: "The Princess."

"What's that?" said Prokop, turning round sharply.

"She has instructed me to remain with you."

Prokop was unable to disguise his delighted surprise. "Has she paid you?"

Mr. Holz shook his head and for the first time a smile passed across his parchment-like face. "She gave me her hand," he said respectfully. "I promised her that nothing should happen to you."

"Good. Have you got the gun? Now you shall watch the door, Nobody must come in, you understand?"

Mr. Holz nodded and Prokop made a thorough strategical examination of the laboratory, considered as a fortress.

Fairly satisfied, he collected on the table all the metal vessels and boxes which he could get together, and further, to his great delight, discovered a heap of nails. Then he set to work.

The next morning Mr. Carson, with a fine assumption of casualness, wandered down to Prokop's laboratory. When some distance away he made him out standing in front of the building, evidently practising throwing stones. "A very healthy sport," he shouted cheerfully.

Prokop hastily put on his coat again. "Healthy and useful," he answered readily. "What do you want me for?"

The pockets of his coat bulged out and something rattled inside them. "What have you got in your pockets?" asked Mr. Carson carelessly.

"Nitric acid," said Prokop. "And explosives."

"H'm. Why do you carry it in your pockets?"

"Oh, just for a joke. Is there anything you want to say to me?"

"Nothing at the moment. Particularly not at this moment," said Mr. Carson uneasily, keeping at a fair distance. "And what have you got in those—those boxes?"

"Nails. And here," he said, bringing a little box out of his pockets, "is some Benzoltetraoxozonid, a novelty, the *dernier cri*. Eh?"

"Don't wave it about," said Mr. Carson, retreating to a safer distance. "Is there any request you have to make?"

"Request?" said Prokop pleasantly. "I should be obliged if you would tell THEM something. To begin with, that I'm not going."

"Good. That's to be understood. And further?"

"And further, if anybody should inadvertently attack me…or try to make an assault on me… I hope that it isn't your intention to murder me."

"Certainly not. Honestly."

"You can come nearer."

"You won't go up in the air?"

"I shall be careful. I only wanted to ask you to stop anybody entering my fortress while I'm away from it. There's an explosive fuse on the door. Be careful; there's a trap behind you."

"Explosive?"

"Only Diazobenzolperchlorate. You must warn people. Nobody's to come near here, see? Further, I've certain reasons…to believe that I'm in danger. I should be grateful to you if you would arrange for Holz to protect me personally…against every sort of attack. And he should be armed."

"No," said Carson loudly. "Holz will be transferred."

"What?" protested Prokop. "I'm afraid to be alone, you understand? Kindly instruct him." So saying he approached Carson threateningly, rattling as if he was made of nothing but tin and nails.

"All right then," said Carson hastily. "Holz, you are to look after Mr. Prokop. If anybody wishes to approach him Devil take it, do what you like. Is there anything else you want?"

"Nothing for the moment. If I want anything I'll come to you."

"Thank you very much," said Carson, and quickly removed himself from the dangerous area. The first thing he did was to dash to his office and tele-phone the necessary instructions in all directions. But there was a rattling in the corridor and Prokop burst into the room, fully charged with bombs.

"Listen," said Prokop, white with anger. "Who gave orders that I should not be allowed into the park? If that order isn't withdrawn immediately—"

"Just keep a little farther off, yes?" cried Carson, holding on to his desk. "What do I care about the park? Go—"

"Wait," Prokop interrupted him and compelled himself to explain pa-tiently: "Let us take it that there are occasions when…when a person is not absolutely indifferent as to what happens," he said quickly. "You understand me?" Rattling and clattering he crossed over to the calendar on the wall. "Tuesday, today is Tuesday! And here, here I have—" he searched feverishly in his pockets and finally brought to light a porcelain soap box carefully tied up with a piece of string. "So far four ounces. You know what it is?"

"Krakatit? You're bringing it to us?" said Mr. Carson, his face lit up with a sudden hope. "But then, of course—"

"Nothing of the sort," grinned Prokop, and he put the box back in his pocket. "But if you irritate me, then…then I shall strew it about where I want to, see?"

"See?" repeated Carson mechanically, completely crestfallen.

"Well, just see that that lad is removed from the entrance. I want to go into the park."

Mr. Carson cast a rapid glance over Prokop and then spat on the floor. "Bah!" he said with feeling, "I've arranged this badly!"

"You have," agreed Prokop. "But it didn't occur to me before that I had this card in my suit. Well?"

Carson shrugged his shoulders. "For the present, God! This is no small matter! I am extremely glad that I'm able to assist you. Honestly, extremely glad. And you? Will you give us six ounces?"

"I won't. I shall destroy it myself but…to begin with I want to see whether our old treaty still holds. Free movement, and all the rest, eh? You remember?"

"The old agreement," roared Mr. Carson. "The devil take the old agreement. At that time you weren't—you hadn't yet relations with—"

Prokop sprang towards him, rattling loudly. "What did you say? What hadn't I?"

"Nothing, nothing," Mr. Carson hastened to say, blinking his eyes quickly. "I don't know. Your private affairs are nothing to do with me. If you want to walk about the park that's your affair, eh? Only for God's sake go and—"

"Listen," said Prokop suspiciously, "No cutting off the current to my laboratory. Because—"

"Good, good," Mr. Carson assured him. "The *status quo*, eh? Good luck. —Ugh! A cursed fellow," he added irritatedly when at last Prokop had left the room.

Still rattling, Prokop made his way to the park, as heavy and solid as a howitzer. In front of the castle was standing a collection of gentlemen, but no sooner had they caught sight of him in the distance than they retired in some confusion, evidently having been informed of this highly charged and furious individual; their backs expressed the highest degree of indignation that such a thing should be allowed. Then Prokop came upon Mr. Krafft walking with Egon and giving him peripatetic instruction. As soon as he saw Prokop, he left Egon and ran across to him. "Will you shake hands with me?" he asked, and grew red at his own heroism. "I shall certainly be dismissed for this," he said proudly. Prokop learnt from Krafft that the report had spread through the castle like lightning that he, Prokop, was an anarchist, and that the heir to the throne was expected that very evening…. That they proposed to telegraph to His Excellence to postpone his arrival, and were holding a big family council about it.

Prokop approached the castle. Two flunkeys in the passage flew out of his path and pressed themselves against the wall, allowing this charged, clanging assailant to pass without a word. The family council was being held in the large hall. *Oncle Rohn* was anxiously walking up and down, the elder members were tremendously excited about the perversity of anarchists, the fat cousin was silent, and some other gentlemen were warmly advocating that soldiers should be sent against this wild person: he would either have to give himself up or be shot. At that moment the doors opened and Prokop crashed into the room. His eyes sought the Princess. She was not there, but all the rest of the company stood up rigid with terror, awaiting the worst. Prokop addressed Rohn in a hoarse voice: "I've only come to tell you that nothing will happen to the royal heir. Now you know." He nodded sharply and walked out of the room as solid as a statue.

CHAPTER XXXVIII

The passage was empty. He crept along as quietly as he was able to the Princess's apartments and waited in front of the door, motionless as the knight in armour downstairs in the vestibule. A chambermaid came out, screamed at the sight of the scarecrow and hastily retired. A moment afterward she opened the door again and, scared out of her life, and careful to keep out of his way, silently motioned him in, after which she again disappeared. The Princess came forward to meet him. She was wearing a long cloak and had evidently only just got out of bed. The hair over her forehead was tangled and damp as if she had just removed a cold compress. She was extremely pale and not looking attractive. She put her arms round his neck and put forward a pair of lips which were feverishly dry. "You are good," she whispered, half swooning. "I've got the most frightful headache! I hear that your pockets are full of bombs! I'm not frightened of you. Go away now, I'm looking ugly. I'll come to you at mid day; I shan't go down to dinner. I'll tell them I'm not well. Go." She touched his mouth with her sore, peeling lips and hid her face so that he should not see her.

Accompanied by Mr. Holz, Prokop returned to the laboratory; everybody whom he encountered stopped and then took to flight, some at times even taking shelter in a ditch. He again threw himself into his work as if possessed, mixed materials together which nobody would have dreamed of associating, armed with a blind certainty that he could convert them into explosives. He filled flasks, matchboxes, tins for preserved food, everything that came into his hands. The table, window-ledges and the floor were covered with them and he went on until he simply had nowhere to put the stuff. In the afternoon the Princess appeared, veiled and wrapped up to the eyes in her cloak. He ran towards her and would have taken her in his arms, but she repulsed him. "No, no, today I'm ugly. Please go on working; I'll watch you."

She sat down on the edge of a chair directly opposite to the frightful arsenal of explosives. Prokop with set lips was rapidly weighing and mixing something which hissed and smelt bitter. Then he filtered it with the greatest care. She watched him, her hands motionless, her eyes burning. Both were thinking that the royal heir was to arrive that day.

Prokop was looking for something on a shelf on which were ranged various acids. She stood up, raised her veil, put her arms round his neck and placed her dry, closed lips against his mouth. They swayed about between the rows of bottles containing unstable oxozobenzol and terribly powerful fulminates, dumb and convulsed, but again she pushed him away and sat down, covering her face with her hands. Prokop set to work again still more quickly, like a baker making bread, and this time it was to be the most diabolical substance which man ever prepared, a violent and frightfully sensitive oil, the incarnation of swiftness and inflammability. And now here it was, transparent as water and fluid as ether; a terrible and incalculable destructive agent. He looked round to see where he had placed the flask containing this nameless substance. She laughed, took it out of his hand and held it clasped in her hands on her lap.

Outside, Mr. Holz suddenly cried "Stop!" to somebody. Prokop ran out. *Oncle Rohn* was standing extremely near the explosive trap.

Prokop went up to him. "What do you want?"

"Minna," said *Oncle Charles* sweetly, "she's not well and so—"

Prokop made a face. "Come and fetch her," he said and led him in.

"Ah, *Oncle Charles!*" The Princess greeted him kindly. "Come and look, this is frightfully interesting."

Oncle Rohn looked carefully at her and about the room and was evidently relieved. "You shouldn't have come, Minna," he said reproachfully.

"Why not?" she objected innocently.

He looked helplessly at Prokop. "Because…because you are feverish."

"I'm better now," she said quietly.

"But still you shouldn't…" said *le bon prince*, frowning seriously.

"*Mon Oncle*, you know that I always do what I want to," she said, making an end to this family scene. At that moment Prokop was removing from a chair a little box containing some explosives. "Do sit down," he said politely to Rohn.

Oncle Charles did not seem to be pleased at the situation. "I'm not… stopping you in your work?" he asked of Prokop aimlessly.

"Not in the least," said Prokop, rolling some substance in his fingers.

"What are you doing?"

"Making explosives. Please, that bottle," he said, turning to the Princess.

She gave it him and added openly and provocatively, "Do you—?" *Oncle Rohn* recoiled as if he had been struck but soon gave himself up to contemplating the rapid, though extremely cautious, way in which Prokop was pouring some drops of a yellow liquid on to a piece of clay.

He coughed and asked: "How do you ignite that?"

"By shaking it," answered Prokop shortly, continuing to pour out the liquid.

Oncle Charles turned to the Princess. "If you are frightened, Uncle," she said dryly, "you needn't wait for me." He sat down resignedly and tapped with his stick on a tin box which had once contained Californian peaches. "What does that contain?"

"That's a hand-grenade," explained Prokop. "Hexani trofenyl methylnitramin. Feel the weight of it."

Oncle Rohn become flurried. "Wouldn't it perhaps be better to be a little more careful?" he asked, twisting in his fingers a matchbox which he had picked up from the desk.

"Certainly," agreed Prokop and took it out of his hand. "That's chlorargonat. Not to be played with."

Oncle Charles frowned. "All this gives me a rather disturbed feeling," he said sharply.

Prokop threw the box down on the table. "What? And I also had a disturbed feeling when you threatened to send me to a fortress."

"...I can say," said Rohn, accepting the reproach, "that all that...made no impression on me."

"But it made an enormous impression on me," said the Princess.

"Are you afraid that he will do something?" said *le bon prince*, turning to her.

"I *hope* that he will do something," she said optimistically. "Do you think that he's not capable of it?"

"I have no doubt about it," said Rohn. "Shall we go now?"

"No. I should like to help him."

Just then Prokop was breaking a metal spoon in his fingers. "What's that for?" she asked him curiously.

"I've run out of nails," he said gruffly. "I've nothing to fill the bombs with." He looked round in search of something made of metal. Then the Princess stood up, blushed, hastily peeled off one of her gloves and removed a gold ring from her finger. "Take this," she said softly, her eyes cast down. He took it, wincing; it was almost a ceremony...as if they were being betrothed. He hesitated, weighing the ring in his hand; she raised her eyes to him in urgent and burning inquiry. Then he nodded seriously and placed the ring at the bottom of a tin box.

Oncle Rohn blinked his birdlike eyes with melancholy concern.

"Now we can go," whispered the Princess.

That evening the heir to the throne arrived at the castle. At the entrance was drawn up a ceremonial escort; there were official greetings and other functions; the park and the castle were specially illuminated. Prokop sat on a small mound in front of his laboratory, and watched the castle with sombre eyes. Nobody entered it; save for the lights coming from the windows all was quiet and dark.

Prokop heaved a deep sigh and stood up.

"To the castle?" asked Mr. Holz. He transferred his revolver from the pocket of his trousers to that of his everlasting mackintosh.

Prokop nodded, and they set off. When they passed through the park, the lights in it had already been extinguished. On two or three occasions some being or other retired into the bushes on their approach and about fifty paces behind them they could hear all the time the sound of someone following them over the fallen leaves. Otherwise all was deserted, terribly deserted. But in one wing of the castle the large windows stood out a bright yellow.

It was autumn, already autumn. Was the water still dripping into the well at Tynice with a silver note? There was not even a wind, yet there was a sort of chill which seemed to run either along the ground or through the trees. Up in the sky a falling star traced a red band of light.

A number of gentlemen in evening dress, magnificent looking and satisfied with themselves, came out on to the terrace at the top of the castle steps, yawned, smoked and laughed a little and then retired. Prokop sat motionless on a seat, twisting a little metal box in his disfigured fingers. Now and then, like a child, he rattled it about. Inside was the broken spoon, the ring and the nameless substance.

Mr. Holz approached cautiously. "She can't come today," he said respectfully.

"I know."

Lights appeared in the windows of the guest's suite. They were those of the "Prince's apartments." And now the whole castle was illuminated, aerial and unsubstantial as in a dream. Everything was to be found within: unheard of wealth, beauty, ambition, fame and dignity, breasts covered with orders, amusements, the art of living, delicacy, wit and self-regard—as if they were different people, different from the like of us....

Again Prokop rattled his little box like a child. Gradually the lights went out in the windows. That light which was still on belonged to Rohn, and that red one to the bedroom of the Princess. Uncle Rohn opened the window to enjoy the cool of the evening and then began to pace from the door to the window, from the window to the door, uninterruptedly. No movement was to be seen in the room of the Princess.

Then even Uncle Rohn put out his light and there was only one left. Would human thought find a means of forcing its way through this hundred or two metres of dumb space and reach the waiting mind of another being? What message have I for you, Tartar Princess? Sleep, it is already autumn; and if some sort of God exists, may he smooth your feverish brow.

The red light went out.

CHAPTER XXXIX

The next morning, he decided not to go into the park; he felt rightly that there would be difficulties there. He took up a position in a rather low-lying and deserted part of the grounds in which the direct path from the castle to the laboratory was intercepted by an old, overgrown rampart. He climbed on to the top of it whence, more or less hidden, he could see the corner of the castle and a small part of the park. He liked the place and buried there some of his hand-grenades. He divided his attention between watching the path, a beetle running at his feet, and the sparrows perched on the swinging branches. Once a robin settled there for a moment, and Prokop, holding his breath, gazed at its dark neck; it piped a note or two, twitched its tail and *f-r-r*—it was gone. Below in the park, the Princess was walking along by the side of a tall young man while they were followed at a respectful distance by a group of gentlemen. The Princess was looking to the side and moving her hand as if she had in it a switch and was flicking the ground with it. Nothing more was to be seen.

An hour later Uncle Rohn appeared with the fat cousin. Then again nothing. Was it worth while waiting there?

It was almost mid day. Suddenly, round the corner of the castle there appeared the Princess, heading straight in his direction.

"Are you there?" she called in a subdued tone. "Come down and then to the left."

He slid down from the rampart and pushed his way through the bushes in the direction indicated. There against the wall was a heap of all sorts of objects: rusty hoops, tin pots full of holes, old top hats, filthy rags; God knows how such things had accumulated in the castle. And in front of this miserable pile was standing the Princess, fresh and beautiful, and childishly biting her fingers. "I used to come here to be angry, when I was little," she said. "Nobody knows of the place. Do you like it here?"

He saw that she would be annoyed if he was not pleased with it. "I like it," he said quickly.

Her face glowed with pleasure, and she put an arm round his neck. "You dear! I used to put an old pot on my head, you know, as a crown and pretended to myself that I was the reigning princess. 'What may Her Excellency deign to want?' 'Harness the four-in-hand; I'm going to Zahur.' You know,

Zahur, that was the place I'd invented. Zahur, Zahur! Darling, is there really such a place in the world? Come, we'll go to Zahur! Discover it for me, you who know so much—"

She had never been so fresh and joyful as today. So much so that it filled him with jealousy, with a passionate suspicion. He took her in his arms and pressed her to him. "No," she defended herself, "don't. Be reasonable. You are Prospero, the Prince of Zahur, and you've only disguised yourself as a magician in order to abduct me. I don't know. But Prince Rhizopod has come for me from the Kingdom of Alicuri-Filicuri-Tintili-Rhododendron, a horrible, horrible man with a church candle instead of a nose and cold hands. Hu! And I'm just going to become his wife when you suddenly appear and say: 'I'm the Magician Prospero, the hereditary Prince of Zahur.' And my Uncle Metastasio will fall on your neck and they will begin to ring bells, blow trumpets and fire—"

Prokop realized well enough that her playful chatter conveyed something very, very important, so refrained from interrupting her. She kept her arm round his neck and rubbed her fragrant face against his rough one. "Or wait; I'm Princess of Zahur and you are the Great Prokopo-Kopak, King of Spirits. But I'm under a curse, they've said over me the words: 'ore ore baléne, magot malista manigoléne' and so I'm to be given to a fish, a fish with fishy eyes and fishy hands and fishy in its whole body. And he's going to take me away to the fishes' castle. And then the Great Prokopo-Kopak arrives on his magic carpet and carries me off—*Au revoir!*" she concluded suddenly and kissed him on the lips. She was still smiling, clear and rosy as she had never been before, and left him to brood gloomily over the ruins of Zahur. And in God's name, what did it all mean? She clearly wanted him to help her; pressure was being put on her and she relied on him…expected him somehow to save her! Heavens! What was he to do?

Deep in thought, Prokop wandered back to the laboratory. Clearly… nothing was left but the Big Attack, but where was he to begin it? He had already reached the door and was feeling in his pocket for the key. Then he suddenly recoiled and broke into curses. The outer door of the building was barricaded with iron crosspieces. He pulled at them in a frenzy but could not move them.

To the door was affixed a piece of paper on which were the words: "In accordance with the instructions of the Civil Authorities this building is closed on account of having been used irregularly for storing explosives without the required precautions having been taken. Par. 216 & 217 d.lit.F tr.z. and No. 63,507. M.1889." Underneath was an illegible signature and below that, written with a pen, the words: "Mr. Eng. Prokop is to report at the quarters of Sgt. Gerstensen, Barrack No. III."

Mr. Holz carefully examined the barricade with the eye of an expert but finally only whistled and thrust his hands into his pockets; there was absolutely nothing to be done. Prokop, white with rage, walked all round the building. The explosive trap had been dug up and, as before, there was a grille in front of each window. He hastily took stock of all his munitions; five small bombs in his pockets, four larger ones buried in the Zahur rampart; one could not do much with them. Beside himself with anger, he hurried to the office of that cursed Carson: "Wait, you louse, and see what I'll do with you!" But on arriving there he was told by a servant that the manager was away and was not returning. Prokop pushed him out of the way and penetrated into the office. Carson was not there. He quickly went through all the offices, causing consternation among all the officials, down to the girl at the telephone. Carson was nowhere to be seen.

Prokop ran back to the Zahur rampart, so that he could at least save his bombs. And then he found that the whole rampart, including the tangle of brushwood and the rubbish heap, was surrounded by a fence of barbed wire; a real entanglement of the type used in the War. He tried to loosen the wire but only succeeded in tearing his hands. Sobbing with anger, he somehow succeeded in getting through it, to find that his four large bombs had been removed. He nearly cried with helplessness. To make matters worse, an unpleasant drizzle began to fall.

He crawled back, his clothes torn to rags and his hands and face bleeding, and hurried to the castle in the hope of finding there the Princess, Rohn, or the heir to the throne. In the vestibule he was stopped by the blond giant he had encountered once before, who was determined this time to be torn to pieces rather than let him pass. Prokop took one of his little boxes of explosives out of his pocket and shook it threateningly. The giant blinked his eyes but did not yield. Suddenly, the giant dashed forward and seized Prokop round the shoulders.

Holz struck him in the chest with his revolver with all his strength. The giant roared and let go, and three men, who had appeared suddenly, as if out of the earth, and were about to hurl themselves on Prokop, hesitated for a moment and then stepped back against the wall.

Prokop stood with the box in his raised hand, ready to throw it under the feet of the first one who moved, and Holz, who was definitely on the side of revolution, waited with his revolver ready. In front of them were four pale men, inclined a little forward, three of them with revolvers in their hands. There was evidently going to be a fight. Prokop moved strategically to the stairs and the four men also moved in the same direction.

Behind, someone ran away. There was a deathly silence. "Don't shoot," whispered one of them sharply. Prokop could hear the ticking of his watch. From the floor above came the sound of cheerful voices; no one there knew what was happening. As the exit was still open, Prokop retired towards the door, covered by Holz. The four men near the steps remained as motionless as if they were carved out of wood and Prokop made his way back into the open.

There was still a cold and unpleasant drizzle. What was he to do now? He rapidly considered the situation and decided to fortify himself in the swimming bath on the lake. But from there he could not watch the castle. As the result of another sudden decision, Prokop ran off to the quarters of the guard, with Holz behind him. He broke into them just at the time when the old doorkeeper was having his dinner. The old man was completely unable to realize why he was being driven away "by force and under a threat of death"; he shook his head and went to the castle to complain about it. Prokop was extremely satisfied at having captured this position. He closed the iron gates leading to the park and finished the old man's dinner with the greatest relish. Then he collected everything which he could find in the house that resembled chemicals: coal, salt, sugar, glue, dried paint and other materials and considered what he could make of them. Meanwhile, Holz spent his time in looking out and converting the windows into portholes—a rather unnecessary step in view of his having only four cartridges. Prokop set up his laboratory in the kitchen; there was a frightful smell but in the end he had succeeded in making a small quantity of high explosive.

The enemy did not launch any attack; they evidently did not want to cause a scandal while they still had such a distinguished guest in their midst. Prokop racked his brains to think of a way of wiping out the castle. He cut off the telephone, but there still remained three gates, without counting the road to the factory by the Zahur rampart. He was forced to abandon the plan of surrounding the castle on all sides.

It rained unceasingly. The window of the Princess's room opened and a white figure wrote large characters in the air with its hand. Prokop was unable to decipher them but nevertheless stood in front of his own little house and wrote provocative messages in the air, waving his arms like a windmill. In the evening Dr. Krafft ran across to the rebels. In his lofty excitement he had forgotten to arm himself in any way; his mission was a purely moral one. Later on Mr. Paul shuffled over, bringing with him in a basket a magnificent cold supper and quantities of champagne and red wine; he asserted that he had not come on anyone else's behalf. Nevertheless Prokop carefully impressed upon him that he was to say—he did not say to whom—that "he thanked them and would not give himself up." At their splendid supper Dr. Krafft ventured to drink wine for the first time, probably to show his manliness; the result was that he became idiotically dumb, while Prokop and Mr. Holz began to sing military songs. It was true that they sang different songs in different languages, but from a distance, especially in the rain and darkness, they achieved a sort of melancholy harmony.

Finally, someone in the castle opened his window to hear better and then attempted to accompany them on the piano. But soon he began to play the Eroica instead and then to strike chords aimlessly. When the lights in the castle had gone out, Prokop erected an enormous barricade in front of the door, and the three heroes quietly went off to sleep. They were awakened the next morning by the knocking of Mr. Paul, who arrived with three cups of coffee on a tray.

CHAPTER XL

It continued to rain. Armed with a white flag, the fat cousin arrived to propose to Prokop that he should give in; in return he should get back his laboratory. Prokop announced that he would not do so, that before that he would allow himself to be blown into the air. Further, that he was going to do something; let them wait and see! On receiving this dark threat, the cousin withdrew. In the castle they were evidently very displeased at the fact that the proper entrance was blockaded, but did not make a fuss about it.

Dr. Krafft, the pacifist, was overflowing with wild and belligerent proposals. He wanted to cut off the current from the castle and cut off their water supply; to manufacture some sort of poison gas, and release it in the castle. Holz had discovered a lot of old newspapers; he produced a pair of pince-nez from some mysterious pocket and spent the whole day in reading, looking extraordinarily like a university lecturer. Prokop was painfully bored; he was burning to take some military step but did not know how to set about it. Finally, he left Holz to guard the little house and went out with Krafft into the park.

There was nobody to be seen in it; the enemy's forces were concentrated in the castle. He walked round it to the side on which it was adjoined by the sheds and stables. "Where's Whirlwind?" he suddenly asked. Krafft indicated a small window about nine feet from the ground. "Lean against the wall," whispered Prokop, climbed on to his back and then stood on his shoulders so as to look inside. Krafft nearly fell under his weight, and to make matters worse, Prokop was dancing on his shoulders—what was he doing? A heavy window-frame fell on the ground and a quantity of rubble crumbled down from the wall. Suddenly, a beam also dropped and the terrified Krafft raised his head to see two legs disappearing through the window.

The Princess was just giving Whirlwind a piece of bread and looking reflectively at his beautiful eyes when she heard the noise in the window and saw in the twilight of the stable the familiar mutilated hand which was removing the wire screen from the window. She placed her hands on her mouth to prevent herself crying out.

Head first, Prokop fell on to Whirlwind's back, jumped down, and there he was, certainly torn, but intact, out of breath and attempting a smile. "Quiet," said the Princess fearfully, for there was a groom just behind the door.

Then she threw her arms round his neck: "Prokopokopak!" He pointed to the window outside. "Where?" whispered the Princess, kissing him.

"To the doorkeeper."

"You stupid! How many are there of you?"

"Three."

"You can see it's no good!" She stroked his face. "Don't attempt it."

Prokop considered whether there was any other way of abducting her, but it was dark inside the stable, and the smell of a horse is somehow exciting. Their eyes gleamed and they kissed passionately. Suddenly, she broke away and recoiled, whispering: "Go away! Go!" They stood opposite one another trembling and with a feeling that the passion which possessed them was an unclean one. He looked away and idly turned a rung in the ladder; only then did he regain control of himself. He swung round towards her and saw that she was biting her handkerchief. She pressed it to her lips and handed it him without a word, as a reward or as a souvenir. And he kissed his arm on the place where her distracted hand had rested. Never had they loved one another so wildly as at that moment, when they were unable to speak and feared to touch one another.

Then there was the sound of steps grating in the gravel outside. The Princess made a sign to him. Prokop swung himself up the ladder, seized some hook or other in the ceiling and, feet first, slipped out of the window. When he had reached the ground again Dr. Krafft threw his arms round him in delight. "You've cut the horses' tendons, eh?" he whispered bloodthirstily; he evidently considered this as a necessary military precaution.

Prokop silently made his way back to the guard's house, impelled by anxiety regarding Holz. When still some distance away, he saw the terrible thing that had happened: two men were standing in the gate, a gardener was erasing from the sand the traces of a struggle, the gate was half open—and Holz was gone. But one of the men had a handkerchief tied round his hand; Mr. Holz had bitten him seriously.

Prokop returned to the park, gloomy and speechless. Dr. Krafft imagined that his superior was concocting another offensive plan and therefore did not disturb him; but Prokop, sighing deeply, sat down on a stump and became absorbed in the contemplation of some torn rag or other. On the path there appeared a workman, pushing in front of him a wheelbarrow full of dead leaves. Krafft, seized with suspicion, set on him and gave him a most terrible beating, in the course of which he lost his spectacles. Then he took the wheelbarrow, representing the spoils of the victory, and hurried back with it to Prokop. "He's run off," he announced, and his shortsighted eyes shone with triumph. Prokop only grunted and continued to examine the snow-white object which fluttered in his hands. Krafft occupied himself with the wheelbarrow, trying to think what the trophy would be good for. Finally, it occurred to him to turn it upside down: "We can sit on it!"

Prokop picked himself up and went towards the lake, Dr. Krafft following him with the wheelbarrow, probably for the transport of the future wounded. They established themselves in a swimming bath built out on posts over the water. Prokop went round the cubicles. The largest was that belonging to the Princess and still contained a mirror, a handful of hair, a couple of hairpins, a shaggy bathing-robe and some sandals, intimate and abandoned objects. He forbade Krafft to enter it and settled down with him in the men's cubicle on the other side. Krafft was radiant; he now possessed a fleet consisting of two Rob Roys, a canoe and a tub-shaped boat which was relatively a super-dreadnought. Prokop spent a long time in silently walking up and down the platform over the grey lake and then disappeared into the Princess's cubicle, sat down on her couch, took the shaggy bathing-gown into his hands and buried his face in it. Dr. Krafft, who, in spite of his incredible lack of observation, had some inkling of his secret, respected his feelings, and went about the place on tiptoe, baling out the water from the warship with a tin and getting together some suitable oars. He displayed considerable military talents, ventured on to the bank and carried stones of all sizes to the bathing-place, including huge ones torn out of a neighbouring wall. Then, plank by plank, he tore up the bridge connecting the bathing-place with the bank. From the material which he thus obtained he was able to barricade the entrance, and he further discovered some priceless rusty nails which he bent into the blades of the oars, points upwards. In this way he obtained a powerful and really dangerous arm.

Having put everything in order and seen that it was all right, he wished to report to his superior what he had done, but Prokop was still shut up in the Princess's cubicle and was so quiet that it seemed as if he were not breathing. So Dr. Krafft remained alone on the floating platform, which splashed coldly on the surface of the water. Now and then there was a *plop!* as some fish leapt out of the water and fell back again, and sometimes a rustling in the rushes. Dr. Krafft began to feel uneasy in the midst of this solitude.

He coughed in front of his leader's cubicle and now and then said something under his breath to attract his attention. Finally, Prokop came out with his lips set and a wild look in his eyes. Krafft showed him over the new fortress, and pointed out everything, finally demonstrating to him when the enemy would come within range of a stone; in indicating this he very nearly fell into the water. Prokop said nothing but put his arm round his neck and kissed him, and Dr. Krafft, quite rosy with delight, would have done ten times as much for him as he had already.

They sat down on a seat near the water, at the spot where the Princess used to bask in the sun. Clouds began to get up in the west, and a sickly strip of yellow sky appeared an infinite distance away. The whole of the lake began to glow, broke into ripples, and became suffused with a pale and gentle light. Dr. Krafft developed impromptu a completely new theory of eternal warfare, the control of power, and the salvation of the world through heroism. Everything that he said was in painful contrast with the torturing melancholy of this autumnal twilight, but luckily Dr. Krafft was shortsighted, and in addition, an idealist, and, as a consequence, completely independent of the influence of his chance surroundings. Apart from the cosmic beauty of the moment, they were both conscious of being cold and hungry. And then on the land they heard the short, quick steps of Mr. Paul, who approached with a basket on his arm, looking to the right and left and periodically calling out in his little old voice: "Cuckoo! Cuckoo!" Prokop went across to him on the warship and tried to force him to say who had sent him. "Nobody, please," asserted the old man; "but my daughter Elizabeth is the housekeeper." He would have talked further about his daughter Elizabeth, but Prokop stroked his white hair and told him to tell this nameless person that he was well and strong.

That day Dr. Krafft drank alone, gossiped, philosophized, and again expressed his contempt for all philosophy; action, he maintained, was everything. Prokop sat trembling on the Princess' seat and all the time kept his eye on one star. God knows why he selected that particular one, which was a yellow one in the constellation of Orion. It was not true that he was well; he had pains in the places in which he had suffered from them in Tynice, his head was spinning and he was trembling with fever. When he wanted to say anything his tongue somehow failed him, and his teeth chattered so much that Dr. Krafft became sobered and almost uneasy. He hastily stretched Prokop out on the couch in the cubicle and covered him with all sorts of things, including the Princess's bathing-gown. He also placed a cold compress on his forehead. Prokop asserted that he had a cold.

About midnight, he went off to sleep, semi-delirious and a prey to the most terrible dreams.

CHAPTER XLI

The next morning the first to be woke up by Paul's calling was Dr. Krafft. He wanted to jump up but found that he was stiff all over, as he had been frozen the whole night and had slept curled up like a dog. When he finally somehow pulled himself together, he found that Prokop had gone; one of the boats of his fleet was rocking against the bank. He became very anxious about his superior and would have set out to look for him if he had not been afraid of deserting the fortress which he had barricaded so carefully. He improved it as best he could and looked round for Prokop with his shortsighted eyes.

Meanwhile, Prokop, who had awakened absolutely prostrated with a taste of mud in his mouth, chilly, and a little dazed, had been for some time high in the foliage of an old oak in the park, from which he could see the whole of the front of the castle. He felt very giddy, held on to the branches firmly and was afraid to look straight below him for fear of falling.

This part of the park was evidently regarded as being safe; even the older members of the family ventured at least as far as the castle steps, the gentlemen went about in groups of two or three and a cavalcade of them was making its way along the main road. The old doorkeeper was again at his post. Soon after ten o'clock the Princess herself came out, accompanied by the heir to the throne, and set out for the Japanese pavilion. Prokop suddenly felt giddy; it seemed to him that he was falling head downwards; he convulsively clutched at the branches, trembling all over. Nobody followed them; on the contrary, all the rest quickly left the park and collected together in front of the castle. Probably a definitive conversation or something of the sort. Prokop bit his lips so as not to cry out. It took an immense time, perhaps an hour or even five hours. And then the heir ran back alone, his face red and his fists clenched. The party of gentlemen in front of the castle broke up and they drew back to make way for him. The heir ran up the steps without looking either to the right or to the left. At the top he was met by the bareheaded Uncle Rohn. They spoke together for a moment, *le bon prince* passed his hand across his forehead and both went inside. The gentlemen in front of the castle again gathered into groups, thrust their heads together and finally stole away one by one. Five automobiles drew up before the castle.

Prokop, clutching at the branches, slipped down the tree until he hit the ground heavily. He wanted to run to the Japanese pavilion, but he was almost comically incapable of controlling his legs; his head was swimming, he felt as if he were wading through dough and somehow he couldn't find the pavilion, as everything in front of his eyes was dull and shifting about. At last he reached it. The Princess was sitting inside, whispering something to herself with severe lips and swishing her switch through the air. He collected all his strength so as to come in as cavalierly as possible. She rose and came to meet him: "I was expecting you." He sat down next to her, very nearly on top of her, since he saw her as being a great distance away. He laid his hand on her shoulder, forcibly holding himself straight, swaying a little and biting his lips; he thought that he was talking. She also said something, but he could not understand her; everything was taking place as if under water. Then came the sound of the horns of the departing cars.

The Princess made a sudden movement, as if her legs had failed her. Prokop saw before him a white, vague face, in which were two dark cavities. "This is the end," he heard close and clear, "the end. Darling, I've sent him away!" Had he been in full possession of his senses he would have seen her as if carved out of ivory, frozen, beautiful in her pain at the highest moment of her sacrifice; but he only blinked, trying to master the trembling of his eyelids, and it seemed to him that the floor was rising beneath his feet and tilting over. The Princess pressed her hands to her forehead and staggered; he wanted to take her into his arms, to carry her, to support her in her exhaustion after her great deed, but instead he fell without a sound at her feet, collapsing as if he was nothing but a heap of rags.

He did not lose consciousness; his eyes wandered about; he tried to understand where he was and what was happening to him. He had the idea that someone, trembling with fear, was raising him up; he wanted to help himself, but could do nothing. "It's only…entropy," he said, and it seemed to him that this characterized the situation and he repeated the word several times. Then something began to run about inside his head making a noise like a weir; his head slipped heavily out of the trembling fingers of the Princess and crashed on to the ground. The Princess jumped up wildly and ran for help.

He had no clear idea of what happened next. He felt that three people were lifting him and slowly dragging him along as if he were made of lead. He heard their heavy, dragging steps and quick breath and was surprised that they could not carry him with their fingers alone, like a rag. Someone held his hand the whole time; he turned round and recognized the Princess. "You are good, Paul," he said to her gratefully. Then began a confused, breathless movement; they were carrying him up the steps, but Prokop thought that they were all falling together to the bottom of an abyss. "Don't push so," he roared and his head spun so much that he ceased to take anything in.

When he opened his eyes he found that he was again in the guest's quarters and that Paul was undressing him with trembling fingers. At the head of the bed was standing the Princess, with widely opened eyes. Prokop's mind was hopelessly confused. "I fell from a horse, eh?" he muttered. "You... were...there, eh? Bang, ex-explosion. Litrogly—nitrogry—mikro—Ch$_2$ On$_2$ O$_2$). Com—pli—cated fracture." He felt the touch of a small, cool hand on his forehead and became quiet. Then he caught sight of the butcher-doctor and dug his nails into somebody's cold fingers "I don't want you," he roared, for he was afraid that there would be pain again, but the butcher only placed his head on his chest and breathed heavily. In front of him he saw a pair of dark and angry eyes which fascinated him. The butcher got up and said to somebody behind: "Influenza and pneumonia. Take Her Excellence away. It's infectious." Someone spoke as if under water and the doctor answered: "If it develops into inflammation of the lungs—then—" Prokop realized that he was lost and that he would die, but the knowledge left him completely indifferent; he had never imagined that it would be so simple. "A hundred and five," said the doctor. Prokop had one wish: that they would let him sleep until the time came for him to die, but instead they wrapped him up in something cold—ugh! At last they began to whisper. Prokop closed his eyes and knew no more about anything.

When he woke up, two dark, elderly gentlemen were standing over him. He felt very much better. "Good morning," he said and tried to raise himself up. "You mustn't move," said one of the gentlemen and gently pushed him back into the pillows. Prokop obediently lay still. "But I'm better, am I not?" he asked contentedly. "Naturally," said the other gentleman evasively, "but you mustn't move about. Quietness, you understand?"

"Where's Holz?" asked Prokop suddenly.

"Here," came a voice from the corner, and Mr. Holz appeared at the end of the bed with a terrible scratch and a blue mark on his face, but otherwise as dry and skinny as ever. And behind him was Krafft, Krafft, who had been forgotten in the bathing-place, with red and swollen eyes as if he had been howling for three days. What had happened to him Prokop smiled at him to comfort him. Then Mr. Paul came up on tiptoe, holding a napkin to his lips. Prokop was delighted that they were all there. His eyes wandered about the room, and behind the two dark gentlemen he caught sight of the Princess. She was deathly pale and was looking at Prokop with melancholy expression which somehow frightened him.

"I'm all right now," he whispered, as if excusing himself. She questioned one of the gentlemen with her eyes and he gave a resigned nod. Then she came up to the bed.

"Do you feel better?" she asked softly. "Darling, are you really better?"

"Yes," he said uncertainly, somewhat oppressed by the serious behaviour of everybody. "Almost completely recovered, only—only—" Her steadfast gaze filled him with confusion and almost with anxiety; he felt uncomfortable and constrained.

"Do you want anything?" she asked, bending over him.

Her glance filled him with a terrible fear. "To sleep," he whispered, so as to be free of it.

She looked inquiringly at the two gentlemen. One of them gave a brief nod and looked at her—with curious seriousness. She understood and turned still more pale. "Sleep now," she said in a strangled voice and turned to the wall. Prokop looked round him in surprise. Mr. Paul had his napkin pressed to his lips, Holz was standing like a soldier, blinking his eyes, and Krafft was simply blubbering, leaning against a cupboard and blowing his nose noisily.

"But what?" cried Prokop, and tried to raise himself up, but one of the gentlemen placed on his forehead a hand which was so soft and kind, so reassuring and pleasant to the touch, that he at once calmed down and sighed with relief. A moment later he was asleep.

He awoke in a curious state of semiconsciousness. There was no light but that of the lamp on the table, and beside the bed the Princess was sitting, dressed in dark clothes, looking at him with gleaming, bewitching eyes. He quickly closed his own so as not to see her, so much was he embarrassed.

"Darling, how are you?"

"What's the time?" he asked confusedly.

"Two."

"In the day?"

"In the night."

"Really," he said in surprise, and began to weave again the dark thread of sleep. At moments he just opened his eyes, glanced at the Princess and went off again. Why was she looking at him so hard? Someone moistened his lips with a spoonful of wine; he swallowed it and mumbled something or other. Finally, he fell into a deep, heavy sleep.

He awoke to find that one of the gentlemen in black was carefully listening to his heart. Five others stood round.

"Incredible," said the dark gentleman. "He has a heart of iron."

"Shall I die?" asked Prokop suddenly. The dark gentleman almost jumped with surprise.

"We shall see," he said. "If you've been able to get through such a night. How long have you been going about with it?"

"With what?" asked Prokop, astonished.

The dark gentleman waved his hand. "Quiet," he said, "only quiet." Prokop, although he felt miserably ill, could not help smiling; when doctors have no idea what to do they always prescribe quiet.

Then the one with the pleasant hands said to him: "You must believe that you will get better. Faith works miracles."

CHAPTER XLII

He started out of his sleep covered with a terrible sweat. Where—where was he? The ceiling undulated and swung to and fro above him; no, no, no, it was falling, descending with a screwlike motion, slowly coming down like a gigantic hydraulic press. Prokop wanted to shout, but was unable to do so, and now the ceiling was so low that he could distinguish a transparent fly which was resting on it, the grain of the material with which it was covered, every inequality on its surface. And still it continued to descend and Prokop watched it with breathless horror, unable to make any sound louder than a hiss. The light went out, and black darkness took its place; now it would crush him. Prokop already felt the touch of the ceiling on his hair and uttered a voiceless cry. Aha! Now he had found the door, pulled it open and dashed outside. Even there there was the same darkness, or rather not darkness, but fog, fog so thick that he was unable to breathe and began to suffocate, hiccoughing with horror. Now I'm being strangled, he thought, and took to flight in terror, treading upon—upon—some sort of living bodies, which were still writhing. He bent down and felt beneath his hands a young breast. That—that was Annie, he thought, and passed his hand over her head; but instead of a head she had a box, a por-ce-lain box containing something slimy and spongy like a lung. He felt utterly revolted and tried to draw his hand away, but the thing adhered to it, attached itself and began to creep up his arm. It was Krakatit, a damp and resinous sepia with the gleaming eyes of the Princess, which were fixed on him agitatedly and passionately; the thing moved about his naked body looking for a place on which to sit down upon him. Prokop was unable to breathe, struggled with it, dug his fingers into this yielding, sticky matter—and woke up.

Mr. Paul was bending over him and placing a cold compress on his chest.

"Where's—where's Annie?" mumbled Prokop with relief and closed his eyes. Breathless and perspiring he found himself running across a ploughed field. He did not know where he was going in such a hurry but he hastened along until his heart was nearly splitting with the strain and he groaned with anxiety lest he should arrive too late. And here at last was the house; it had neither doors nor windows, only above it a clock, the hands of which marked five minutes to four. And Prokop knew in a flash that when the big hand reached twelve the whole of Prague would be hurled into the air. "Who's stolen my Krakatit?" he roared, and tried to climb up the wall so as to stop the hand at the last minute. He sprang up and dug his nails into the plaster, but only slid down, leaving a long scratch on the wall. Screaming with horror, he flew off somewhere to get assistance. He burst into the stables, to find the Princess standing there with Carson. They were making love to one another with abrupt, mechanical gestures, like those of marionettes. When they saw him they joined hands and began to jump quicker, quicker and ever quicker.

Prokop looked up and saw the Princess bending over him with closed lips and burning eyes. "Beast!" he grunted with dull contempt and quickly closed his eyes again. His heart beat wildly and rapidly. His eyes were stung with sweat and he felt a salty taste in his mouth. His tongue was stuck to his palate and in his throat was a blind, dry thirst. "Do you want anything?" asked the Princess, very close to him. He shook his head. She thought that he was again sleeping, but after a while he said hoarsely: "Where's that parcel?"

She thought that he was delirious and did not answer. "Where's that parcel?" he repeated, knitting his brows authoritatively. "Here, here," she said quickly, and thrust between his fingers a piece of paper which she happened to have in her hand. He quickly crumpled it into a ball, and threw it away.

"That's not it. I—I want my parcel. I—I want my parcel."

As he continued to repeat these words and began to rage, she sent for Paul. Paul remembered having seen somewhere a dirty parcel tied up with string, but where was it? They found it in a cupboard; there you are! Prokop clasped it in both hands and held it to his breast. Appeased, he fell into a deep sleep. Three hours later he again began to sweat profusely; he was so weak that he scarcely breathed. The Princess at once sent for the doctors. His temperature fell lower and lower and his pulse almost stopped. They wanted to give him a camphor injection at once, but the local doctor, who felt very shy and provincial amongst such mandarins, was of the opinion that if they did the patient would never wake up. "At any rate he would pass out in his sleep, eh?" said the famous specialist. "You are right."

The Princess, completely exhausted, went to lie down for an hour on being told that nothing more could be done. Dr. Krafft remained with the patient, having promised her that he would let her know the position in an hour's time. He sent no message and the agitated Princess came to see for herself. She found Krafft standing in the middle of the room waving his arms and talking at the top of his voice about telepathy, quoting Richet, James and somebody else, while Prokop was listening to him with clear eyes, now and then interposing the objections of a scientific and limited sceptic. "I've resurrected him, Princess," shouted Krafft, forgetting everything, "I concentrated my mind on the fact of his recovery; I—I made passes over him with my hands, see? But that sort of thing exhausts one! I feel as weak as a fly," he announced, and thereupon emptied a full glass of the benzine which was kept for washing bandages, evidently taking it for wine, so excited was he by his success. "Tell me," he shouted, "have I made you well or not?"

"You have," said Prokop with friendly irony.

Dr. Krafft collapsed into an armchair. "I myself did not realize that I have such a powerful aura," he said contentedly. "Shall I pass my hands over you again?"

The Princess looked from one to another of them in consternation. Then she smiled and suddenly her eyes filled with tears. She stroked Krafft's ruddy hair and ran out of the room.

"Women can't stand anything," said Krafft proudly; "you see, I'm absolutely calm. I felt a fluid oozing out of my fingertips. It could certainly have been photographed. A sort of ultra-radiation."

The specialists returned, sent Krafft out of the room in spite of his protests and again took Prokop's temperature, felt his pulse and all the rest of it. His temperature was higher, his pulse ninety-six, and he had developed some sort of an appetite. After this the mandarins retired to the other wing of the castle where their services were needed, for the Princess was in a fever, and had completely collapsed after sixty hours of watching by Prokop's bedside. In addition she was extremely anemic and ill in several other ways.

The next day, Prokop was already sitting up in bed and receiving visits. Almost all the company had already left; only the fat cousin remained alone in boredom. Carson arrived rather agitated, but the meeting turned out all right. Prokop made no allusion to what had passed, and finally Carson announced that the terrible explosives that Prokop had invented during the last few days had shown themselves to be as dangerous as sawdust. In short Prokop must have already been feverish when he prepared them. The patient accepted this information quite calmly and smiled, in fact, for the first time. "Well," he said affably, "all the same I frightened you all pretty thoroughly."

"You did," admitted Carson willingly. "I've never been so frightened about myself and the factory before."

Krafft dragged himself into the room pale and exhausted. He had spent the night celebrating his possession of a miraculous gift by drinking large quantities of wine and now he felt utterly miserable. He lamented the fact that his power had left him forever and announced that he had decided for the future to devote himself to yoga.

Uncle Charles also arrived, very friendly and subtly reserved. Prokop appreciated the fact that he had fallen back into the style of a month before, again addressing him in the plural. Only when the conversation turned on the Princess did the atmosphere become a little strained.

Meanwhile, in the other wing of the castle, the Princess was coughing painfully and receiving a report from Paul every half hour as to what Prokop was eating, saying and doing.

He again became feverish and his terrible dreams returned. He saw in front of him a dark shed containing an endless row of casks of Krakatit. In front of the shed an armed soldier was marching to and fro, to and fro; nothing more, but it was terrible. It seemed to him that he was again in the war; before his eyes there stretched a vast field, covered with dead. They were all dead and he was dead too, and frozen to the ground. Only Mr. Carson trotted over the corpses, cursing between his teeth and looking impatiently at his watch. From the other side with awkward, convulsive movements there approached the crippled Hagen; he was moving with amazing rapidity, jumping like a pony.

Carson greeted him carelessly and said something to him. Prokop strained his ears to catch what they were saying but could not hear a single word. Perhaps the wind was carrying them away. Hagen pointed to the horizon with a preternaturally long and shrivelled hand; what were they saying? Hagen turned round, put his hand to his mouth and took out a golden set of teeth and his jaws as well; now instead of a mouth he had a great black hole which giggled voicelessly. With the other hand he extracted one enormous eye from its socket, and, holding it in his fingers, held it close down to the faces of the dead. Meanwhile, the gold set of teeth in his other hand was screeching: *"Seventeen thousand one hundred and twenty-one, one hundred and twenty-two, one hundred and twenty-three."*

Prokop was unable to move, as if he were dead. The horrible bloodshot eye touched his face and the horse's set of teeth counted: "Seventeen thousand one hundred and twenty-nine." Now Hagen disappeared in the distance, still counting, and across the corpses there jumped the Princess, with her skirts drawn up shamelessly high. She approached Prokop waving in her hands a Tartar bunchuk, as if it were a whip. She stood over Prokop, tickling him under the nose with it, and sticking the point of her shoe into his head, as if trying to find out whether he was dead. The blood trickled down his face, although he was really dead, so dead that he felt within him his heart frozen as hard as a bone; all the same he could not bear the sight of her well-shaped legs.

"Darling, darling," she whispered, pulled down her skirt, knelt down by his head and passed her hands lightly across his chest. Suddenly, she pulled out of his pocket that carefully tied-up parcel, jumped up, and angrily tore it into pieces which she threw into the air. Then with her arms stretched out she began to whirl round and round, passing over the dead until she disappeared into the darkness of the night.

CHAPTER XLIII

From the time when the Princess fell ill, he did not see her any more, but several times a day she wrote him short and passionate notes which hid more than they revealed. He heard from Paul that she was again able to move about her rooms and could not understand why she did not come and visit him. He himself was already out of bed and waited every minute for her to send for him. He did not know that meanwhile she had developed tuberculosis seriously and was actually spitting blood. She did not write to him about it, evidently fearing that it would make him turn from her at the thought that on his lips there were still burning the traces of the kisses which she had once given him. And principally, principally she was afraid of not controlling herself and again kissing him with passionate lips. He had no idea that the doctors had discovered traces of infection in his own lungs, a fact which had driven the Princess to desperation and self-condemnation. He knew nothing, grew angry at the fact that she was so evasive now that he was completely well, and became frightened when another day passed without the Princess expressing the wish to see him. I've made her tired of me, he thought; I've never been anything more for her than a momentary distraction. He suspected her of all sorts of things, did not want to descend to insisting on a meeting, hardly wrote to her and did nothing but wait in an armchair for her to come, or at least to let him know what had happened. There were a few sunshiny days and he ventured into the park, wrapped up in a rug. He wanted to wander about by himself with his dark thoughts near the lake, but there were always with him Krafft, Paul, Holz, Rohn, or the charming and dreamy poet Charles, who always had something on the tip of his tongue but never said it. Instead, he discoursed on science, personal courage, success and heroism and God knows what else. Prokop listened with one ear; he had the impression that the Prince was making a special effort for some reason or other to interest him in ambition. Then one day he received a roughly scrawled note from the Princess, telling him to wait and not to be shy. Directly afterward Rohn introduced him to a laconic old gentleman in whose bearing everything revealed the officer disguised as a civilian. The laconic gentleman inquired of Prokop what he proposed to do in the future. Prokop, somewhat nettled by his tone, answered sharply and magnificently that he was going to exploit his inventions.

"Military inventions?"

"I'm not a soldier."

"Your age?"

"Thirty-eight."

"Occupation?"

"None. And yours?"

The laconic person became rather confused. "Do you intend to sell your inventions?"

"No." He felt that he was being examined and sounded officially. This irritated him and he answered very shortly and only here and there would he give them a fragment of his erudition and this only because he saw that it pleased Rohn particularly. Actually the Prince was radiant and was all the time looking at the laconic gentleman, as if to ask him: "Well, what do you say to that miracle?" But the laconic gentleman said nothing and finally took leave of them politely.

The next day, Carson appeared very early in the morning, rubbing his hands and evidently full of something extremely important. He babbled all sorts of nonsense, all the time trying to sound Prokop. He threw out all sorts of vague words, like "future," "career" and "splendid success," but would say nothing more, while Prokop did not like to ask any questions. And then there arrived a strange and important letter from the Princess: "Prokop, today you will have to make a decision. I have done so and do not regret the fact. Prokop, at this last moment I assure you that I love you and will wait for you as long as may be necessary. And even if we must separate for a time—and this must be so, since your wife may not be your lover—even if we separate for years, I shall always be your dutiful betrothed. I am already so happy about it, that I simply cannot speak of it; I walk about my room overpowered and repeat your name. Darling, darling, you cannot imagine how unhappy I've been since this happened to us. And now do what is necessary for me to be able really to call myself your W."

Prokop couldn't understand what it all meant; he read it several times and simply was unable to believe that the Princess meant quite simply…he wanted to run round to see her but was too agitated and bewildered. Was this again some feminine extravagance which was not to be taken literally and which he really didn't understand? While he was reflecting like this Uncle Charles entered, accompanied by Carson. Both looked so…official and serious that it flashed through Prokop's head: "They've come to say that they're sending me away to that fortress; the Princess has been plotting, and now here we are!" He looked round for some weapon, in case it should come to force, selected a marble paperweight and sat down, mastering the beating of his heart.

Uncle Rohn looked at Carson, and Carson looked at Rohn with the mute question of who was to begin. Then Uncle Rohn said: "What we've come to tell you is…to a certain extent…" He was beginning as usual hesitatingly, but suddenly he pulled himself together and continued more confidently: "My dear friend, what we have come to tell you is something very important…and discreet. It is not only in your interests that you should do this… but on the contrary… To put it shortly, it was first of all *her* idea and…as far as I am concerned, after careful consideration…in any case we must leave her out of it; she is self-willed and passionate. Apart from that, it appears that she's taken it into her head…in fact from every point of view it would be better to find a suitable way out of the difficulty," he concluded with relief. "The General Manager will explain the position."

Carson, as the General Manager, put on his spectacles very seriously. He looked quite disturbingly important and very different from what he had ever been like before. "I consider it an honour," he began, "to interpret to you the wishes of our highest military circles, who wish you to connect yourself with our army…naturally only with the highest technical service, with duties which are related to your work, and that straight away in the capacity of—so to speak… I mean to say, that it is not a military custom to employ civilian specialists apart from war, but in your case, in consideration of the fact that the present situation approximates very closely to that of war, and with special regard to your exceptional significance, which is enhanced by the present conditions, and…and taking also into consideration your peculiar position or rather, to put it more precisely, your extremely private obligations—"

"What obligations?" Prokop asked hoarsely.

"Well," stammered Carson, somewhat embarrassed, "I mean…your interests, your relation.…"

"I never spoke to you about any interest," said Prokop sharply.

"Aha!" said Mr. Carson, as if refreshed by this rudeness, "of course you didn't; there was no need to. We didn't flaunt that up at the castle. Of course not. Purely personal considerations, that's what I mean. Powerful intervention, you understand? Of course you're a foreigner—but that's been arranged," he added quickly. "It'll be enough if you put in a demand to become a citizen of our State."

"Aha!"

"What did you say?"

"Nothing, only aha!"

"Aha! That's all, eh? All you have to do is to make a formal demand and…apart from that… Well, you will understand of course that…that we should demand some guarantee, eh? You will have to earn the right to the honour which is being bestowed on you…for exceptional services, eh? Let's assume that…that you hand over to the Army Council…you understand, that you hand over…"

There was a dead silence. The Prince looked out of the window and Carson's eyes disappeared behind the glitter of his glasses. Prokop was deeply uneasy.

"…that you hand over…simply hand over…" gulped Carson, also breathing with difficulty.

"What?"

Carson wrote a large K in the air with his finger. "Nothing further," he said, relieved. "The next day, you'll get a document nominating you as an *extra statum* captain in the engineers…stationed in Balttin. Straight away. So."

"That is to say only a captain to begin with," said Uncle Charles. "We haven't ventured any farther. But we have been given a guarantee that if it should suddenly come to a war—"

"Within a year," cried Carson, "within a year at the latest."

"—as soon as war breaks out—whenever and with whomever it may be—you will be appointed a general in the engineers. And should—as the result of the war—the form of government be changed you would also be given the title of Excellence and…in short at least a baronetcy to begin with. Even with regard to this…we have been given an assurance…from the highest quarters," concluded Rohn almost inaudibly.

"And who told you that I should like that?" said Prokop icily.

"But my God!" cried Carson, "who wouldn't? They've promised me the rank of knight; it doesn't mean anything to me, but it's not given me on my own account. But for you it would have quite special significance."

"So you expect," said Prokop slowly, "that I shall hand you over Krakatit."

Mr. Carson would have sprung into the air, but Uncle Charles restrained him.

"We take it," he began seriously, "that you will do everything, or…it may be…make every sacrifice, to save Princess Hagen from any sort of illegal and…impossible position. Under certain conditions…the Princess is allowed to marry a soldier. As soon as you are a captain your position will be regularized…by a strictly secret engagement. The Princess will of course go away and return as soon as she can secure a member of the ruling house as bridegroom for the wedding. Until then…until then we expect you to earn the right to a marriage which we feel to be good both for you and for her. Give me your hand. You need not decide just yet. Consider the matter carefully, consider what your duties are and the sacrifices which you have to make. I could appeal to your ambition, but I am speaking only to your heart. Prokop, she is suffering beyond her strength and bringing to love a greater sacrifice than any other woman. And you too have suffered. Prokop, you are suffering with your conscience, but I will not try to exert any pressure on you because I have confidence in you. Consider the matter carefully, and tell me later…"

Mr. Carson nodded his head, this time really deeply touched.

"That's so," he said. "I don't come of any sort of family myself, but I must say that…that… I tell you, that woman has race. God! One can see straight away…" He struck the region of his heart with his fist and blinked his eyes. "Man, I'd throttle you if you weren't worthy…"

Prokop was not listening. He sprang up and marched up and down the room with his face distorted with rage. "I—I must, eh?" He ground out hoarsely. "So I must? Good. If I must…you've cheated me! But I didn't want—"

Uncle Rohn stood up and quietly put his hand on his shoulder. "Prokop," he said, "you must decide yourself. We don't want to hurry you; consult with the best that there is in you. Ask God, love or conscience or feeling or I don't know what. But remember that this does not only concern you but her who loves you so much that she's ready to…" He waved his hand hopelessly. "*Au revoir!*"

CHAPTER XLIV

It was an overcast day and rain was falling in a fine drizzle. The Princess continued to cough and was alternately hot and cold, but she could not stay in bed. Impatiently she awaited Prokop's answer. She looked out of the window to see if he might be coming, and again sent for Paul. The answer was always the same: Mr. Prokop was walking up and down his room. And did he say anything? No, nothing. She dragged herself from one wall to the other and then sat down again, rocking her body to and fro to calm her feverish anxiety. Oh, it was too much to be borne! Suddenly, she began to write to him a long letter, entreating him to marry her, and saying that he must not give up a single one of his secrets, that she would enter his life and be faithful to him, whatever might happen. "I love you so much," she wrote, "that there is no sacrifice which is too great for me to make for you. Test me, remain poor and unknown; I will follow you as your wife and never be able to return to the world which I left. I know that you only love me a little and that with a small part of your heart; but you will get used to me. I have been proud, wicked and passionate; now all is changed, all my familiar surroundings are strange to me, I have ceased to be—" She read the letter through and then tore it into pieces, moaning softly. It was evening. There was still no news of Prokop.

Perhaps he will come without announcing himself, she thought, and in impatient haste she put on her evening clothes, terribly agitated. She stood in front of her mirror and examined herself with burning eyes, horribly dissatisfied with her clothes, the way her hair was dressed, and everything possible. She covered her heated face with a thick layer of powder, and bedecked herself with jewels. But she seemed to herself to be ugly, impossible and awkward, "Hasn't Paul come?" she asked every moment. At last he arrived: Nothing new; Mr. Prokop was sitting in darkness and had not ordered the lights to be lit.

It was already late and the Princess, utterly exhausted, was sitting in front of her glass. The powder was peeling off her burning cheeks, she looked positively grey and her hands were numb. "Undress me," she ordered her maid weakly. The fresh, sturdy girl took off one ornament after another, loosened her clothes and wrapped her in a diaphanous *peignoir*. Just as she was about to begin combing the loose hair of the Princess, Prokop burst into the room, unannounced.

The Princess recoiled and became even more pale. "Go, Marie," she breathed and drew the *peignoir* over her thin chest. "Why...have you come?"

Prokop leaned against a cupboard, his face pale and his eyes bloodshot. "So," he said through his teeth, "that was your plan, eh? You arrange things for me nicely!"

She stood up as if she had been given a blow: "What—what are you saying?" Prokop ground his teeth. "I know what I'm saying. The idea was that... that I should give you Krakatit, eh? They're getting ready for a war, and you, you," he cried, "you are their tool! You and your love! You and your marriage, you spy! And I—I was to be lured into it so that you could kill, so that you could avenge yourselves—"

She sank into a chair with her eyes wide open with horror; her whole body was shaken by a terrible dry sob. He wanted to throw himself upon her, but she prevented him with a movement of her frozen hand.

"Who are you?" Prokop ground out. "You are a princess? Who persuaded you to this? Do you realize, you worthless creature, that you would have killed thousands and thousands of men, that you would have helped them to destroy cities, and that our world, our world and not yours, would have been obliterated! Obliterated, smashed to fragments, wiped out! Why did you do it?" he cried, and fell on his knees and crawled towards her. "What did you want to do?"

She raised to him a face full of horror and aversion and edged away from him. He bent his face over the spot where she had been sitting and began to cry with the heavy, crude sobs of a raw youth. She would have knelt next to him, but controlled the impulse to do so and retreated still further, pressing her convulsively twisted fingers to her breast. "So," she whispered, "this is what you think?"

Prokop was being suffocated by the weight of his pain. "Do you know," he cried, "what war is? Do you know what Krakatit is? Have you never realized that I'm a man? And that—I have a contempt for you! That is why I was good to you! And if I had given up Krakatit it would all have been over; the Princess would have gone away, and I—" He sprang up, beating his head with his fists. "And to think that I wanted to do it! A million lives for the sake of—no, two million dead! Ten million dead! That—that for the sake of a marriage with a princess, eh? To lower oneself so far for that! I was mad! Aa-ah!" he roared, "I loathe you!"

He was terrible, like some monster, with froth on his lips, swollen face and the eyes of a madman. She pressed herself to the wall, deathly pale, with staring eyes and lips twisted with horror.

"Go," she wailed, "go away!"

"Don't be afraid," he said hoarsely, "I shan't kill you. I always loathed you; even when—even when you were mine, I was horrified and didn't believe you even for an instant. And yet, yet I—I shan't kill you. I—know quite well what I'm doing. I—I—" He looked round, picked up a bottle of *eau de Cologne*, poured a generous quantity of it over his hands and rubbed it on his forehead. "Aha!" he cried, "aha-ha! Don't be afraid! No—no—"

He calmed down a little, sat down on a chair and put his face in his hands. "Now," he began hoarsely. "Now, now we must talk, eh? You see that I'm quiet. Not even...not even my fingers are trembling...." He stretched out his hand to show her, but it trembled so that it was frightful to look at it. "We can...undisturbed, eh? I'm quite calm again. You can dress. Now...your uncle told me that...that I'm obliged...that it's a question of honour for me to make it possible for you...to repair your slip and that I must...simply must... earn the right to a title...sell myself, and pay for the sacrifice which you—"

She got up deathly pale and wanted to say something. "Wait," he interrupted her. "I haven't yet— You all thought...and have your own ideas about honour. But you made a terrible mistake. I'm not a nobleman. I'm...the son of a cobbler. That doesn't matter much, but... I'm a pariah, you understand? An absolutely commonplace person. I haven't any honour. You can drive me away like a thief or send me off to a fortress. I won't give it up. I won't give Krakatit up. You may think...that I'm base. You can tell them...what I think about war. I was in the war and I saw poison gases...and know what people are capable of. I won't give up Krakatit. Why should I trouble to explain it all to you? You won't understand me; you're simply a Tartar princess and too lofty.... I only want to tell you I won't give it up and I humbly thank you for the honour—incidentally, I'm engaged already; I certainly don't know her, but I've betrothed myself to her—that's my baseness again. I'm sorry that... I'm not worthy of your sacrifice."

She stood as if petrified, digging her nails into the wall. It was painfully quiet. He got up slowly and heavily: "Have you anything to say?"

"No," she said quietly and her large eyes continued to gaze into the distance. She looked exquisitely young and tender in her *peignoir*; he would have knelt down and kissed her trembling knees.

He approached her, wringing his hands.

"Princess," he said in a controlled voice, "now they'll take me away as a spy or something of the sort. I shan't try to defend myself. I am prepared for whatever happens. I know that I shall never see you again. Have you anything to say to me before I leave?"

Her lips trembled, but she said nothing. Oh God! Why was she staring like that into the distance?

He drew near her. "I loved you," he said, "I loved you more than I am able to say. I am a base and rough man, but I can tell you that...that I loved you differently... I took you...and held on to you through fear that you might not be mine, that you would escape me; I wanted to make sure; I could never believe it; and so I—" Not realizing what he was doing, he placed his hand on her shoulder; she trembled under the thin *peignoir*. "I loved you...desperately..."

She turned her eyes on him. "Darling," she whispered and her pale face was flushed for a moment. He bent down and kissed her trembling lips; she made no resistance.

"What," he ground his teeth, "I love you now?" With rough hands he tore her from the wall and enveloped her in his embrace. She struggled as if she were mad, so powerfully that if he had released his grip she would have fallen on the floor. He held her more closely, staggering himself through her desperate resistance. She writhed with clenched teeth and hands pressed convulsively against his chest; her hair fell over her face and she bit it to prevent herself shrieking and tried to push him away as if she was having an attack of epilepsy. It was incredible and horrible; he was conscious of only one thing: that he must not let her fall on the ground and that he must avoid knocking any chairs over. What...what would he do if she evaded him? He would sink through the earth for shame. He drew her to him and buried his lips in her tangled hair; he encountered a burning forehead. She turned away her head with revulsion and tried still more desperately to free herself of the iron grip of his arms.

"I'll give up Krakatit," he heard his own voice say, to his horror. "I'll give it up, you hear? I'll give up everything! A war, a new war, millions of dead. It's all the same to me. Do you want me to? Say one word—I'm telling you, that I'll give up Krakatit! I swear that I'll... I love you, do you hear? What...whatever happens! Even...even if I had to destroy the whole world—I love you!"

"Let me go," she wailed, struggling.

"I can't," he groaned, his face buried in her hair. "I'm the most miserable man on earth. I'm a traitor to the whole world. To the whole human race. Spit in my face, but don't dr—drive me away! Why can't I let you go? I'll give you Krakatit, you hear? I've sworn to; but then forget me! Where—where's your mouth? I'm a monster, but kiss me! I'm lost—" He swayed as if he were about to fall and now she could slip out of his grasp. He stretched out his arms vaguely and she threw the hair back from her face and offered him her lips. He took her in his arms, quiet and passive, and kissed her closed lips, her burning cheeks, her neck, her eyes; he was sobbing hoarsely and she made no effort to defend herself. Then he grew frightened by her motionless passivity, let her go and drew back. She staggered, passed her hand over her forehead, smiled weakly—and put her arms round his neck.

CHAPTER XLV

They sat together, their eyes staring into the semi-darkness. He could feel the feverish beating of her heart; for these hours they had not spoken; she had kissed him insatiably and then wrenched herself away. Now she had turned her face away and was gazing feverishly into the darkness.

He sat with his hands clasped round his knees. Yes, lost; caught in a trap, fettered, he had fallen into the hands of the Philistines. And now that which must take place would take place. They were putting the weapon into the hands of those who would use it. Thousands upon thousands would perish. Look! Was there not in prospect an endless waste covered with ruins? This was a church and that a house; there were the remains of a man. Force was a terrible thing and all evil came from it. A curse on force, the unregenerated spirit of wickedness. Like Krakatit, like himself.

Creative and industrious human weakness, all that is good and noble comes from you. Your work is to bind and link together, to assemble parts and preserve what has been built up. Cursed be the hand which liberates force! Cursed be he who loosens the fetters which bind the elements! Humanity is only a little boat on an ocean of forces; and you, you have let loose a storm, the like of which has never been seen.

Yes, he was letting loose a storm of a kind which has never been known before; he was handing over Krakatit, liberating an element which would blow the boat of humanity into pieces. Thousands upon thousands would perish. Towns and peoples would be wiped off the face of the earth. There would be no limit to the power of anyone who had this weapon in his hands and a corrupted heart. He, Prokop, had done it. Passion is terrible, the Krakatit of human hearts; and all evil comes from it.

He looked at the Princess—without contempt, torn by disturbing passion and sympathy. What was she thinking about now, motionless and as if in a trance? He bent down and kissed her shoulder. It was for this that he was giving up Krakatit. He would give it up and go away so as not to see the terror and shame following his defeat. He would pay the terrible price for his love and go away.

He made a gesture of helplessness. Why did they let him go? What was the use of Krakatit to them while he was still able to give it to others? Ah, that was why they wanted to keep him a prisoner forever! Ah, that was why he must sell himself to them soul and body! He would remain here, here, fettered by passion, and forever he would hate this woman; he would struggle in the throes of cursed love, and all the time he would be inventing hellish devices…and he would be serving them.…

She turned to him with a breathless look. He sat motionless, the tears running down his coarse, rough face. She looked at him with a fixed stare, her eyes full of painful scrutiny; he did not realize that she was doing so, half closed his eyes and remained stupefied by his defeat. Then she quietly got up, turned on the light over the dressing-table and began to dress.

He was recalled to her existence by her throwing a comb down upon the table. He watched her with surprise as with both her arms raised she braided her dishevelled hair. "Tomorrow…tomorrow I will give them it to them," he whispered.

She did not answer; she was holding some hairpins in her mouth and rapidly coiling her hair round her head. He followed all her movements. She hastened feverishly, again blushed and looked down at the ground, then tossed her head and set to work again all the more quickly. Then she stood up, carefully examined her reflection in the glass, and powdered her face as if there was nobody else in the room. She went into the next room, returning with a scarf over her head. Sitting down again, she rocked her body to and fro in meditation; then she nodded her head and again went into the next room.

He got up and softly went over to her dressing-table. God! What a collection of curious and charming objects! Scent-bottles, lipsticks, little boxes, creams, every possible sort of toy. Here was woman's trade: eyes, smiles, strong and disturbing scents— His mutilated fingers passed trembling over all these fragile and mysterious objects; he experienced a sort of irritation and excitement, as if they were touching something which was forbidden.

She came back into the room wearing a leather coat and cap. She was pulling on a heavy pair of gloves. "Get ready," she said in a colourless voice, "we're going."

"Where?"

"Where you like. Get together what you need, but quickly, quickly!"

"What does this mean?"

"Don't waste time asking questions. You mustn't remain here, you see? They won't let you go. Are you coming?"

"For…how long?"

"Forever."

His heart began to thump. "No…no, I won't go!"

She came up to him and kissed his face. "You must," she said quietly. "I'll tell you when we're once outside. Come to the front of the castle, only quickly, while it's still dark. Now go, go!"

He went back to his room as if in a dream, collected all his papers, his priceless and endless notes, and quickly looked round. Was that all? "No, I won't go," flashed through his head, and leaving the papers where they were he ran outside. In front of the castle was standing a throbbing car with the lights turned off; the Princess was already at the wheel. "Quickly, quickly," she whispered. "Are the doors open?"

"They are," answered the sleepy chauffeur in a hoarse voice, pulling down the hood of the car.

A shadow appeared from the back of the car and stopped in front of them.

Prokop stepped up to the open door of the car. "Princess," he said in a hoarse voice, "I've…decided that I'll…give up everything and stay."

She was not listening. Inclined forwards, she was staring attentively at the spot where that shadow fused with the darkness. "Quickly," she said suddenly, seized Prokop by the arm and pulled him into the car beside her. A single movement and the car had begun to slide forward. At that moment a light appeared in one window of the castle and the shadow sprang out of the darkness. "Halt!" it cried and threw itself in front of the car; it was Holz.

"Out of the way," cried the Princess, closed her eyes and opened the throttle full. Prokop raised his hand in horror; there was an inhuman roar and the wheels lurched over something soft. Prokop was about to spring out of the car, but at that moment it swung round the corner of the drive, so that the door slammed to by itself and the machine hurled itself into the darkness. With horror he turned round to the Princess. He could scarcely recognize her with her leather cap, bent forward over the wheel. "What have you done?" he cried.

"Quiet," she said sharply through her teeth, still inclined forward. He caught sight of three figures in the distance on the white road. She slowed down and drew up close to them. It was the military guard.

"Why are your lights off?" asked one of the soldiers. "Who are you?"

"The Princess."

The soldiers raised their hands to their caps and drew back. "The password?"

"Krakatit."

"Please put on your lights. Who have you with you, please? Your pass, please."

"One moment," said the Princess calmly and went into first speed. The car simply jumped forward; the soldiers were only just able to get out of the way.

"Don't shoot," cried one of them as the car flew into the darkness.

The Princess went round a sharp corner and continued almost in the opposite direction. Two soldiers approached the car.

"Who's on duty?" she asked coldly.

"Lieutenant Rohlauf," answered the soldier.

"Send for him!"

Lieutenant Rohlauf came running out of the guardhouse, buttoning up his uniform.

"Good evening, Rohlauf," she said amicably. "How are you? Please let me out."

He stood still respectfully, but looked doubtfully at Prokop: "Delighted, but…has the gentleman a pass?"

The Princess smiled. "It's only a bet, Rohlauf. To Brogel and back in thirty-five minutes. You don't believe me? Don't make me lose my bet." Stripping off her glove, she gave him her hand from the car. "*Au revoir*, yes? Look in some time."

He clicked his heels and kissed her hand, bowing deeply. The soldiers opened the barrier and the car moved off. "*Au revoir!*" she called back.

They whirled along an endless avenue. Now and then there flashed past the light of some human habitation; in a village a child was crying, behind a fence a dog became excited at the dark, flying car. "What have you done?" cried Prokop. "Do you know that Holz has five children and a crippled sister? His life is worth five times as much as yours and mine! What have you done?"

She did not answer. With knitted brows and clenched teeth she was watching the road, raising her head higher every now and then to see better. "Where do you want to go?" she asked suddenly at a crossroads high above the sleeping countryside.

"To hell," he said through his teeth.

She stopped the car and turned round to him seriously. "Don't say that! Do you think that I haven't wanted a hundred times to crash us both into some wall or other? Let me tell you that we should both go to hell. I know that there's a hell. Where do you want to go?"

"I want…to be with you."

She shook her head. "That's no good. Do you remember what you said? You're engaged and…you want to save the world from something terrible. Well, do it. You must keep yourself pure; otherwise…otherwise it'll be bad. And I can't…" She passed her hand along the steering wheel. "Where do you want to go? Where do you live?"

He clasped her in his arms with all his strength. "You've…killed Holz! Don't you…"

"I know," she said quietly. "Do you imagine that I can't feel? It seemed as if my own bones were being crushed and I see him in front of me all the time, all the time the car is rushing at him, and again and again he runs forward—" she shivered. "Well, where? To the right or the left?"

"Is this the end?" he asked quietly.

She nodded. "It is the end."

He opened the door, sprang out of the car and stood before it. "Go on," he said in a hoarse voice. "Drive over me."

She reversed and drove back a few yards. "Come, we must go farther. I'll take you at least to the frontier. Where do you want to go?"

"Back," he said through his teeth, "back with you."

"With me you can't either go back or go forward. Don't you understand? I must do this to see, to be certain that I love you. Do you think that I could hear what you told me again? You can't go back; you would either have to give up…what you don't want to give up and mustn't, or they'd take you away, and I—" She let her hands fall into her lap. "You see, I've thought of what it would mean if I were to go on with you. I should be able to, I should certainly be able to, but…you've got a *fiancée* somewhere—go to her. Do you know it never occurred to me to ask you about her. When one's a princess one thinks that one's alone in the world. Do you love her?"

He looked at her with eyes which were full of torture; yet he couldn't deny—

"There you are," she breathed. "You darling, you simply cannot lie! But listen. When I considered— What was I to you? What was it that I did? Did you think of her when you were in love with me? How you must have hated me! No, say nothing! Don't take away from me the strength to say these last words."

She wrung her hands. "I loved you! I loved you, man, as much as I could ever love more. And you, you were so loath to believe it that finally you shattered even my faith. Do I love you? I don't know. When I see you there I could thrust a knife into my breast; I should like to die and I don't know what else, but do I love you? I—I don't know. And when you took me into your arms…for the last time I felt something…impure in me…and in you. Forgive my kisses; they were…unclean," she breathed. "We must part."

She was not looking at him and did not listen to what he said in reply. Suddenly, her eyelashes began to tremble, and then her eyes filled with tears. She wept silently, her hands on the wheel. When he tried to approach her she moved the car away.

"Now you're no longer Prokop," she whispered, "you are an unhappy, unhappy man. You see, you pull at your chain…as I do. It was…a wrong sort of link that joined us, and yet when one tears oneself away it is as if one left everything behind, one's heart, one's soul…. Can there be good in a man when he is so empty?" Her tears fell more quickly. "I loved you, and now I shall never see you again. Out of the way, I'm turning round."

He did not move.

She drew the car close up to him. "Good-bye, Prokop," she said softly, and began to go backwards along the road. He ran after her, but the car began to retire more and more rapidly.

Then it vanished altogether.

CHAPTER XLVI

He stood still and strained his ears in terror, fearing to hear the sound of the car crashing off the road somewhere at a corner. Was not that the sound of a motor in the distance? Was that terrible and deathly silence the end? Beside himself, Prokop dashed down the road after her. Running down the serpentine road, he finally reached the end of the slope. But not a trace of the car was to be seen. He rushed back again, examining the road on each side, clambered down, tearing his hands whenever he caught sight of anything conspicuous, but it always proved to be only a stone or a bush, and he again scrambled up and pounded along the road, staring into the darkness, in case he should come upon a pile of wreckage, and under it...

He was again back at the crossroads; it was here that she had begun to disappear into the darkness. He sat down on a milestone. It was quiet, utterly quiet. Above him were the cold stars. Was the dark meteor of the car flying along somewhere? Would there never be a sound, the cry of a bird, the barking of a dog in a village, some sign of life? But everything was bathed in the majestic silence of death. And this was the end, the silent, dark and icy end of everything—a desert surrounded by darkness and silence—an icy desert in which time stood still. If only it were the end of the world! The earth would open and above the noise of the tempest would be heard the words of the Lord: I take you back to myself, weak and miserable creature; there was no purity in you and you set free evil forces. Loved one. I will make you a bed out of nothingness.

Prokop began to tremble beneath the crown of thorns of the universe. And now human suffering was nothing and had no value; he was a tiny, shrivelled up, trembling bubble at the bottom of an abyss. Good, good; you say that the world is infinite, but if I could only die!

In the east the sky began to go pale. The road and the white stones could already be seen clearly. Look, here were the marks of wheels in the dead dust. Prokop picked himself up, numb and cold, and started to walk. Downhill, towards Balttin.

He went on without stopping. Here was a village, an avenue lined with blackberries, a little bridge over a dark and silent river. The mist disappeared and the sun began to shine through; again a grey and cold day, red roofs, a herd of cows. How far might it be to Balttin? Sixteen, sixteen kilometres. Dry leaves, nothing but dry leaves.

A little after mid day he sat down on a pile of pebbles; he could go no farther. A peasant's cart approached; the driver drew up and looked at the exhausted man.

"Can I give you a lift?"

Prokop nodded gratefully and sat down next to him without a word. Later the cart drew up in a little town.

"Here we are," said the peasant. "Where exactly are you going?"

Prokop got down and went on by himself. How far might it be to Balttin?

It began to rain, but Prokop could go no farther and remained leaning against the wall of a bridge. Underneath was a cold, foaming current. Suddenly, a car approached the bridge, slowed down and then stopped. Out of it sprang a man in a leather coat who came up to Prokop.

"Where are you going?" It was Mr. d'Hémon, with goggles over his Tartar eyes and looking like an enormous shaggy beetle. "I'm going to Balttin; they're looking for you."

"How far is it to Balttin?" whispered Prokop.

"Forty kilometres. What do you want there? They've issued a warrant for your arrest. Come along. I'll take you away."

Prokop shook his head.

"The Princess has left," continued Mr. d'Hémon quietly. "Early this morning, with Uncle Rohn. Chiefly so that she should forget…a certain unpleasant experience in connection with running over somebody."

"Is he dead?" breathed Prokop.

"Not yet. In the second place, the Princess, as you possibly know, has consumption seriously. They're taking her to somewhere in Italy."

"Where?"

"I don't know. Nobody knows."

Prokop stood up, swaying. "In that case—"

"Will you come with me?"

"I don't…know. Where?"

"Where you like."

"I should like to go…to Italy."

"Come along." Mr. d'Hémon helped Prokop into the car, threw a fur rug over him, and slammed the door. The car started off.

And again the countryside began to unroll itself, but curiously, as if in a dream and backwards; a little town, an avenue of poplars, pebbles, a bridge, a village. The snorting car climbed zigzag fashion up a long hill; and here was the crossroads where they had parted. Prokop raised himself up and would have jumped out of the car, but Mr. d'Hémon drew him back, and put the car into top speed. Prokop closed his eyes and now they were no longer going along the road but had mounted into the air and were flying. He felt the pressure of the air on his face and the impact of scraps of cloud like rags. The noise of the motor became a deep, prolonged roar. Below there was still probably the earth, but Prokop was afraid to open his eyes and see again the flying avenue. Quicker! To be smothered! Quicker still! His chest was constricted by terror and dizziness, he could hardly breathe, and gasped with delight at the wild way in which they tore through space. The car slipped up and down hills and valleys while from somewhere beneath their feet there came the cries of people and the whining of a dog. Sometimes they turned almost lying over on their sides, as if they had been caught up by a tornado. Now again they were flying straight ahead, pure speed, whizzing across country like an arrow.

He opened his eyes. Misty darkness, a row of lights shining through it, lights of a factory. Mr. d'Hémon drove the car in and out of the traffic in the streets, slipped through a suburb which seemed to be in ruins and they were again in the open. In front of the car stretched two long antennae of light which fell on rubbish, mud, stones. The car whirled round corners, the exhaust drumming like a machine gun, and then threw itself at a long stretch of road as if it were winding it in. To the right and the left was a crisscross pattern of narrow valleys between hills. The car turned off into it and plunged into woods, noisily twisting its way upwards and dropping head first into further valleys. The villages breathed rings of light into the thick fog and the car flew on, roaring and leaving behind it clouds of sparks, rushing down hills, and climbing in spirals higher, higher, higher. At last it jumped over something and lurched. Stop! They pulled up in black darkness; no, it was a house. Mr. d'Hémon stepped out of the car, breathing heavily, knocked at the door and engaged some people in conversation. A moment later he returned with a can of water and poured its contents into the hissing radiator; in the bright light of the car's lamps he looked in his fur coat like a devil from some story for children. Then he went round the car, felt the tyres, raised the hood and said something, but Prokop, utterly exhausted, was already half asleep. Then he again became conscious of the everlasting rhythmic vibration and fell asleep in the corner of the car, having no idea what was happening beyond the continuous shaking. He only recovered consciousness when the car had stopped in front of a brightly lighted hotel amongst stretches of snow. The air was sharp and cold.

He woke up numb and worn out. "Th—this isn't Italy," he stammered, surprised.

"Not yet," said Mr. d'Hémon, "but come and have something to eat." He led Prokop, who was dazzled by so many lights, to an isolated table. A white tablecloth, silver, warmth, a waiter like an ambassador. Mr. d'Hémon did not even sit down, but walked up and down the room looking at the tips of his fingers. Prokop, heavy and sleepy, dropped into a chair; it was a matter of complete indifference to him whether he ate or not. All the same he drank some hot soup, poked at one or two dishes, scarcely able to hold the fork, twisted a glass of wine in his fingers and burnt his throat with some scalding coffee. Mr. d'Hémon still did not sit down but went on walking up and down the room, every now and then taking a mouthful as he went along. When Prokop had finished eating he gave him a cigar and lit up himself. "So," he said, "and now to business.

"From now," he began, still walking up and down, "I shall be for you simply… Comrade Daimon. I will introduce you to our people; they're not far away. You mustn't take them too seriously; amongst them there are desperadoes, people evading justice from all the corners of the world, fanatics, babblers, doctrinaires and dilettante salvationists. Don't ask them for their programme; they are only material which we use for our purposes. The chief thing is that we can put at your disposal an extensive secret international organization which has its branches everywhere. The only programme is direct action. Through this we'll get hold of everybody without exception. They're already crying for it, like children for a new toy. Anyway they'll find the fascination of a 'new programme of action,' 'destruction inside the head' irresistible. After the first successes they'll follow you like sheep—especially if you weed out from their leaders the people I shall indicate to you."

He spoke smoothly like an experienced orator, that is to say thinking all the time about something else, and with such self-evident truth that he made doubt or resistance impossible. It seemed to Prokop that he had heard him on some occasion or other before.

"Your situation is unique," Daimon continued, still walking up and down the room. "You have already rejected the proposal of a certain Government, and you behaved like a sensible man. What can I offer you compared to what you can obtain by yourself? You'd be mad to hand over your secret to anybody. You have in your possession a means by which we can overcome all the powers of the earth. I have unlimited confidence in you. Do you want fifty or a hundred million pounds? You can have them within a week. It is enough for me that at present you are the sole owner of Krakatit. Our people have fourteen and a half ounces in their possession, brought by a Saxon comrade from Balttin, but these fools haven't the slightest understanding of what your chemistry means. They keep it like a sacred relic in a porcelain box and three times a week nearly come to blows over the question of what government building they are going to blow up into the air. Anyway, you'll hear them. There's no danger to you from that quarter. There's not a scrap of Krakatit in Balttin. Mr. Thomas is evidently near to abandoning his experiments—"

"Where is George—George Thomas?" asked Prokop.

"At the Powder Works in Grottup. But they are already sick of him there with his everlasting promises. And even if by chance he does succeed in preparing it he won't derive much benefit from the fact. I can answer for that. In short, you alone have Krakatit in your power and you won't give it to anybody. You will have at your disposition human material and all the ramifications of our organization. I will give you a printing press which I maintain myself. And finally you will also have the use of what the newspapers refer to as the 'Secret Wireless Station,' that is, our illegal wireless station which, by means of so-called anti-waves or extinguishing sparks, causes your Krakatit to explode at a distance of from one to two thousand miles. Those are your cards. Do you want to play?"

"What…what do you mean?" said Prokop. "What am I to do with it all?"

Comrade Daimon stopped and looked at Prokop fixedly. "Do what you like. You will do great things. Who can suggest anything further to you?"

CHAPTER XLVII

Daimon drew up a chair and sat down. "Yes," he began reflectively, "it's almost impossible to believe it. There's simply no analogy in history to the power which you have in your hands. You will be able to conquer the world with a handful of people, as Cortez conquered Mexico. No, that's not the right image. With Krakatit and the wireless station you can checkmate the world. It's amazing but it's true. All you need is a handful of white powder and you can blow up what you like any instant you please. Who can stop you? Actually, you are the uncontrolled master of the world. You will be able to give orders, without anyone even seeing you. It's amusing. You can attack Portugal or Sweden; in three or four days, they will ask for peace and you will dictate contributions, laws, frontiers, anything that occurs to you. At that moment, there's only one controlling force, and that's you yourself.

"You think that I'm exaggerating? I've a lot of very efficient fellows here, capable of everything. You decide for a lark to make war on France. One day at midnight there go up in the air the ministries, the Banque de France, the post offices, power stations, railway stations and a few barracks. The next night you explode aerodromes, arsenals, iron bridges, munition factories, ports, lighthouses and main roads. At present we have only seven aeroplanes; you sprinkle Krakatit where you like, then you turn on a switch in the station and there you are. Well, would you like to try?"

Prokop felt that it was all a dream. "No! Why should I do such a thing?"

Daimon shrugged his shoulders: "Because you must. Force...will out. Why should some State do it on your account, when you can do it yourself? I don't know what you couldn't do; you must begin to experiment. I can assure you that you'll acquire a taste for it. Do you want to be the ruler of the world? Good. Do you want to blow up the world? You can. Do you want to make it happy by forcing upon it continual peace. God, a new order, a revolution or something of the sort? Why not? You've only to begin. It doesn't matter about the programme. Finally, you will only do what you are compelled to do through the conditions which you have yourself created. You can destroy banks, kings, industrialism, armies, eternal injustices or what you like; as you go along you will see what you want to do. Begin where you like and the rest will follow by itself. Only don't look for analogies in history. Don't ask yourself what you may do; your situation is unprecedented. There is no

Dzhinghiz Khan or Napoleon to tell you what you have to do or to say what your limits are. Nobody will be able to give you advice; nobody will be able to abuse your power. You must be alone if you want to take things to their limits. Don't let anybody come near you who would set you any boundaries or suggest any particular line of action."

"Not even you. Daimon?" asked Prokop sharply.

"No, not even me. I am on the side of power. I am old, experienced and rich; all I want is that something should be done along lines laid down by a man. My old heart will be contented with what you will do. Think out the most daring, beautiful, heavenly schemes you can and impose them by the right of your power; this will reward me for serving you."

"Give me your hand. Daimon," said Prokop, full of suspicion.

"No, it would burn you," smiled Daimon. "I've an old, agelong fever. What was I saying? Yes, one of the possibilities of strength is force. Force has the capacity for setting things in motion; you would not be able to help the fact that everything finally revolves round yourself. Get used to this beforehand; regard people merely as your instruments or as instruments of the ideas which you evolve. You want to do an enormous amount of good; as a result you will be extremely severe. Stop at nothing in your efforts to achieve your magnificent ideals. Incidentally that will come by itself. At present it seems to you that it would be beyond your strength to rule the Earth—I don't know in what way. You will, and this will not be beyond the strength of your instruments; your power will go further than any sober reflection.

"Arrange your affairs in such a way that you are dependent on nobody. This very day I shall have you elected as the President of the Intelligence Commission. This will mean that you will have the secret station in your own hands; in any case it is situated in a plant which is my own private property. In a moment you will see our various comrades; don't frighten them by announcing any great plans. They are expecting you and will receive you with enthusiasm. Give them a few phrases about the good of humanity or anything you like; otherwise you will become involved in the chaos of opinions which are usually described as political convictions.

"You must decide for yourself whether your first attacks will be on political or economic lines, that is to say whether you will begin by bombarding military objects or factories and railway lines. The first is more effective and the second more fundamental. You can begin a general attack all round or you can choose one sector. You can cause a revolution either privately or publicly, or you can declare war. I don't know what your proclivities are; anyway, it doesn't matter about the form as long as you reveal your power. You are the highest court of appeal in the world; you can pass judgment on anybody you like and our people will execute it. Do not consider human lives. Work on a large scale; there are millions of lives in the world.

"Listen. I'm an industrialist, a journalist, a banker, a politician, anything you like. In short, I'm accustomed to calculate, consider the circumstances, and work on limited possibilities. Just for this reason I must tell you—and this is the only advice which I propose to give you before you assume power—don't make calculations or look round you. The moment you look back you will turn into a pillar like Lot's wife. I am reason; but if I cast my eyes upwards I at once want to become insane and irresponsible. Everything which exists inevitably collapses out of the chaos of limitlessness into nothing, and this by way of number. Every powerful force is opposed to this progressive decline; everything which is noble wants to become limitless. The force which does not flow beyond its original frontiers is doomed. You have in your hands the possibility of achieving enormous things; are you worthy of utilizing or are you simply going to play about with it? I'm an old, practical man and I tell you: You will think of wild and frenzied deeds, of action on an unprecedented scale, of incredible demonstrations of human power. In actuality you will only achieve half or a third of what you propose to do, but that which you succeed in doing will be tremendous. Attempt the impossible so that at least you will achieve something which has never been thought possible before. You know what a tremendous thing experiment is: good, the thing which all the rulers of the world fear most is that they should have to do something new, something unheard of, something perverse. There's nothing more conservative than ruling over human beings. You are the first man in the world who can regard the whole world as his laboratory. This is the High Place of temptation; everything is given you not simply for you to exercise your power on it, but that you may transform it and create something better than their miserable, cruel world. There is need again and again of a creator of the world, but a creator who is only a ruler is a fool. Your thoughts will be orders; your dreams will be historic revolutions, and, if you do no more than make yourself remembered, that will be enough. Take what is yours.

"And now we must go. They are waiting for us."

CHAPTER XLVIII

Daimon started the engine and jumped into the car.

"We shall be there in a moment."

The car dropped down from the Hill of Temptation into a broad valley, flew through a silent night, flashed past a number of country houses and drew up in front of a long wooden house surrounded by alders; it looked like an old mill. Daimon sprang out of the car and led Prokop to the foot of some wooden steps, but here their path was barred by a man with his collar turned up.

"The password?" he asked.

"One Piece," said Daimon and removed his goggles. The man stepped back and Daimon hurried on. They came into a large, low room, which looked like a schoolroom; two rows of seats, a platform, a desk and a blackboard. The only difference was that the place was full of smoke and noise. The benches were crammed with people who were wearing their hats. They were all quarrelling with one another; some red-haired lout was shouting something from the platform, while at the desk there stood a dry, pedantic old man, desperately ringing a bell.

Daimon went straight up to the platform and mounted it.

"Comrades," he cried, and his voice was as inhuman as that of a seagull. "I have brought someone to you—Comrade Krakatit."

There was a dead silence and Prokop felt himself seized and mercilessly examined by fifty pairs of eyes. As if in a dream, he stepped on to the platform and looked round the smoky room not knowing what to do.

"Krakatit. Krakatit," there resounded below and the noise grew into a shout: "Krakatit! Krakatit! Krakatit!"

In front of Prokop there was standing a beautiful tousled girl who gave him her hand: "Good luck, comrade!" A brief, hot pressure, eyes with a burning glance which promised everything, and immediately afterward a dozen other hands: rough, firm and dried up by the heat, moist and cold, spiritualized. Prokop found himself surrounded by a chain of hands which seized his own.

"Krakatit! Krakatit!"

The pedantic old man rang his bell like a madman. When this failed to achieve anything he rushed up to Prokop and shook his hand; it was dry and leathery, as if made of parchment, and behind his cobbler's glasses there shone an enormous joy. The crowd roared with enthusiasm and then grew quiet.

"Comrades," said the old man, "you have greeted Comrade Krakatit with spontaneous delight…with spontaneous and living delight, delight which I should also like to express in my capacity of president. We also have to greet President Daimon…and to thank him. I invite Comrade Krakatit to take his seat…as a guest…in the president's chair. I invite the delegates to declare whether the meeting is to be presided over by me…or by President Daimon."

"Daimon!"

"Mazaud!"

"Daimon!"

"Mazaud! Mazaud!"

"To the devil with your formalities. Mazaud," cried Daimon. "You are presiding and that's enough."

"The meeting continues," cried the old man. "Delegate Peters has the floor!"

The red-headed man again began to address the meeting. It appeared that he was making an attack on the English Labour Party, but nobody took any notice of him. All eyes were resting on Prokop. There in the corner were the large, dreamy eyes of a consumptive; the bulging, blue ones of some old, bearded gentleman; the round and glittering glasses of a professor; sharp little eyes peering out of great clots of grey hair; careful, hostile, sunken, childish, saintly and base eyes. Prokop's glance wandered about the tightly packed benches. Suddenly, he looked away sharply as if he had burnt himself; he had encountered the glance of the tousled girl, a glance which could have only one meaning. He looked instead at an extraordinarily bald head beneath which hung a narrow coat; it was impossible to tell whether the creature was twenty or fifty years old, but before he had decided the point the whole head was furrowed by a broad, enthusiastic and respectful smile. One look tormented him the whole time; he looked for it among the others but could not find it.

Delegate Peters stutteringly finished his speech and sank down on to a bench, very red in the face. All eyes were fixed on Prokop in tense and compelling expectation. Mazaud muttered a few formal words and bent down to Daimon. There was a breathless silence, and then Prokop rose to his feet, not knowing what he was going to do. "Comrade Krakatit has the floor," announced Mazaud, rubbing his dry hands.

Prokop looked round him with dazzled eyes: What ought he to do? Speak? Why? Who were these people? He caught sight of the gentle eyes of the consumptive, the severe and scrutinizing gleam of spectacles, blinking eyes, curious and strange eyes, the bright, melting glance of the beautiful girl who in her absorption had opened her hot, sinful lips. In the front bench the bald and furrowed little man hung upon his words with attentive eyes. Prokop gave him a smile.

"Friends," he began quietly and as if in a dream, "last night... I paid a tremendous price. I lived through...and lost..." He made an effort to pull himself together. "Sometimes one experiences...such pain that...that it ceases to be one's own. You open your eyes and see. The universe is overcast and the earth holds her breath in agony. The world must be redeemed. You would be unable to bear your pain if you only suffered alone. You have all gone through hell, you all—"

He looked around the room; everything had become fused into a sort of dully glowing subterranean vegetation. "Where have you got Krakatit?" he asked, suddenly irritated. "What have you done with it?"

The old Mazaud carefully took up the porcelain relic and put it into his hand. It was the very box which he had once left in his laboratory hut near Hybsmonka. He opened the lid and dug with his fingers into the granulated powder, rubbed it, triturated it, smelt it, put a speck of it on his tongue. He recognized its strong, astringent bitterness and tasted it with delight. "That's good," he said with relief and pressed the precious object between his palms, as if he were warming on it his numbed hands.

"It is you," he said under his breath, "I know you; you are an explosive element. Your moment will come and you will liberate everything. That's good." He looked about uneasily from under his eyebrows. "What do you want to know? I only understand two things: The stars and chemistry. It's beautiful...the endless stretches of time, the eternal order and steadfastness, the divine architecture of the universe. I tell you...there's nothing more beautiful. But what do I care about the laws of eternity? Your moment will come and you will explode. You will liberate love, pain, thought, I don't know what. Your greatest triumph will last only for a second. You are not part of the endless order or of the millions of light years. Explode with the most lofty flame. Do you feel yourself shut in? Then burst to pieces the mortar. Make a place for your sole moment. That's good."

He himself did not clearly understand what he was saying, but he was carried on by an obscure impulse to express something which immediately evaded him again. "I... I'm only a chemist. I know matter and...understand it; that's all. Matter is broken up by air and water, splits, ferments, rots, burns, absorbs acid or disintegrates; but never, you hear, never with all that gives up what it contains. Even if it goes through the whole cycle, even if some fragment of earth becomes incorporated in a plant and then in living flesh and then becomes a cell in the brain of a Newton, dies with him and again disintegrates, it still does not give up its power. But if you compel it...by force... to split up and liberate its strength, then it explodes in a thousandth of a second, then at last it exercises the force which it contains. And perhaps it was not even asleep; it was only bound, suffocated, struggling in the darkness and waiting for its moment to come. To release everything! That is its right. I, I must release everything. Have I not only to expose myself to corrosion and wait…ferment in an unclean way…disintegrate and then…all at once…release the whole man? Best of all…best of all in one supreme moment…and through everything…. For I believe that it is good to release everything. Whether it's good or bad. Everything in me is interfused; good and bad and the highest. That is the redemption of man. It doesn't lie in anything which I have done, it's become a part of me…like a stone in a building. And I must fly to pieces…by force…like an explosive charge. And I won't ask what it is that I may be bursting. There's a need in me…to liberate the highest."

He struggled with words, endeavouring to express the inexpressible, lost it with every word, furrowed his brow and examined the faces of his listeners to see if anyone had any idea of what he was trying, and failing, to express. He found a glowing sympathy in the clear eyes of the consumptive, and concentrated effort in the entranced blue ones of the shaggy giant at the back. The shrivelled little man drank in his words with the complete devotion of a believer, and the beautiful girl, half lying down, received them with tender shudderings of her body. But the other faces gaped at him unsympathetically, inquiringly, or with increasing indifference. Why, exactly, was he talking to them?

"I have lived through," he continued hesitatingly and already somewhat irritated, "I have lived through…as much as a man can live through. Why am I telling you this? Because that alone is not enough for me, because…so far I am not redeemed; the highest was not in it. That's…buried in a man like energy in matter. You must disturb matter to make it release its force. You must free man, disturb him, split him up for him to flame up to his highest. Ah, that would…that would be too much…for him not to find that…he had reached…that…"

He began to stammer, became morose, threw down the box containing the Krakatit and sat down.

CHAPTER XLIX

There was a moment of tense silence.

"And is that all?" said a mocking voice from the middle of the hall.

"That's all," said Prokop, disgusted.

"It is not all." Daimon stood up. "Comrade Krakatit assumed that the delegates would be good enough to understand—"

"Oho!" there resounded from the middle of the hall.

"Yes, Delegate Mezierski must have patience and let me finish. Comrade Krakatit has graphically explained to us that it is necessary," and Daimon's voice again was like the screeching of a bird, "that it is necessary to inaugurate a revolution without paying attention to the theory of stages; a levelling and disruptive evolution in the course of which humanity will release the highest which is hidden within. Man must explode to release everything. Society must explode to find the highest good within itself. You here have spent years in disputing the question of the highest good of humanity. Comrade Krakatit has shown us that it is sufficient to cause humanity to explode in order for it to flame up higher than you have wished it to in your debates. And we must not bother about what is destroyed by the explosion. I say that Comrade Krakatit is right."

"Yes, yes, yes!" There was a sudden burst of shouting and clapping. "Krakatit! Krakatit!"

"Silence!" shouted Daimon. "And his words," he continued, "have all the more weight because they are supported by the actual power of bringing about this explosion. Comrade Krakatit is not a man of words, but of deeds. He has come here to convert us to direct action. And I tell you that it will be more terrible than anyone has dared to dream. And the explosion will take place today, tomorrow, within a week!"

His words were drowned in an indescribable confusion. A wave of people poured from the seats and surrounded Prokop. They embraced him, seized his hands and cried: "Krakatit! Krakatit!" The beautiful girl struggled wildly, her hair loose, trying to make a way for herself through the crowd of people. Thrown forward by the pressure from behind, she pressed herself against his breast. He tried to push her away, but she put her arms round him and passionately whispered something in a foreign language.

Meanwhile, on the edge of the platform, a man wearing spectacles was slowly and quietly demonstrating to the empty benches that theoretically it was not permissible to deduce sociological conclusions from inorganic matter. "Krakatit. Krakatit," roared the crowd. No one would sit down although Mazaud was ringing his bell all the time like a dustman. Suddenly, a dark young man sprang on to the platform and waved the box of Krakatit above their heads.

"Silence," he roared, "and down with you! Or I will throw it under your feet!"

There was a sudden silence; the crowd evacuated the platform and drew back. Above there was left only Mazaud, his bell in his hand, confused and at a loss what to do, Daimon, leaning on the table, and Prokop, on whose neck there was still hanging the dark-haired Mænad.

"Rosso," cried a number of voices. "Down with him! Down with Rosso!" The young man on the platform looked wildly round the room with his burning eyes. "Let nobody move! Mezierski wants to shoot at me. I shall throw it," he shouted and flourished the box.

The crowd recoiled, growling like an enraged animal. Two or three people put up their hands, and others followed them. There was a moment of oppressive silence.

"Get down," shouted old Mazaud. "Who gave you permission to speak?"

"I shall throw it," threatened Rosso, taut like a bow.

"This is against the regulations," said Mazaud excitedly. "I protest and… leave the chair." He threw the bell on the ground and stepped down from the platform.

"Bravo, Mazaud," said an ironical voice. "You've helped him."

"Silence," cried Rosso, and threw back the hair from his forehead. "I'm speaking. Comrade Krakatit has told us: Your moment will come and you will explode; make room for this unique moment. Good, I've taken his words to heart."

"It wasn't meant like that!"

"Long live Krakatit!"

Someone began to whistle.

Daimon caught Prokop by the arm and dragged him to a door somewhere behind the blackboard.

"Hiss away," continued Rosso mockingly. "None of you hissed when this foreign gentleman stood in front of you and…made room for his moment. Why shouldn't anyone else try?"

"That's right," said a satisfied voice.

The beautiful girl stood in front of Prokop to protect him with her body. He tried to push her away.

"That's not true," she shouted with burning eyes. "He…he is…"

"Be quiet," said Daimon.

"Anyone can preach," said Rosso feverishly. "As long as I have *this* in my hand I can preach too. It's all the same to me whether I go out or not. Nobody may leave this room! Galeasso, watch the door! So, now we can discuss matters."

"Yes, now we can discuss matters," echoed Daimon sharply.

Rosso turned round to him like lightning, but at that moment the blue-eyed giant dashed forward with his head lowered like a ram's; and, before Rosso could turn round, seized his legs and pulled them from under him. Rosso fell from the platform head first. In the middle of a tense silence he rolled over and struck his head against the floor while the lid of the porcelain box rolled under the benches.

Prokop rushed across to the unconscious body; Rosso's chest, and face, the floor, the pools of blood beneath him, were all covered with the white dust of Krakatit. Daimon held him back and at that moment there was a loud cry and several people rushed on to the platform. "Don't tread on Krakatit, it will explode," ordered some cracked voice, but the people had already thrown themselves on the ground and were collecting the white powder into matchboxes, struggling, writhing in a heap on the ground.

"Shut the door," roared somebody. The lights went out. At that moment Daimon kicked open the little door behind the blackboard and dragged Prokop out into the darkness.

He turned on a pocket electric lamp. They were in a windowless hovel, with tables piled on top of one another, trays for beer, a lot of musty clothing. He quickly dragged Prokop on further: the unsavoury black hole of a staircase, black and narrow steps leading downwards. Halfway down them they were overtaken by the tousled girl. "I am going with you," she whispered, and dug her fingers into Prokop's arm. Daimon led them out into a yard, turning the light of the pocket lamp about him; around there was black darkness. He opened a gate and they found themselves on the road. Before Prokop could reach the car, struggling to throw off the girl, the motor had begun to throb and Daimon was at the wheel.

"Quickly!"

Prokop threw himself into the car, and the girl jumped in behind him. There was a jerk and the car flew into the darkness. It was icily cold and the girl shivered in her thin clothes. Prokop wrapped her up in a fur rug and himself settled in the other corner. The car was racing along a bad, soft road, tossing from one side to another, pulling up and then noisily accelerating again. Prokop was angry and moved away whenever the motion of the vehicle threw him against the girl. But she nestled against him.

"You're cold, aren't you?" she whispered, opened the rug and wrapped him in it, pressing herself against him. "Get warm," she breathed with a lewd smile and pressed herself against him with her whole body. She was hot and yielding, as if she were naked. Her loose hair exuded a wild and bitter scent, tickled his face and fell across his eyes. She spoke to him in some foreign language, repeating something again and again more and more softly. Then she took the lobe of his ear between her delicately chattering teeth, and suddenly she was lying on his chest and placing her lips on his in a moist, unclean, sophisticated kiss.

He pushed her away roughly. She drew back deeply offended, sat farther away from him, and with a movement of her shoulder jerked off the fur rug. There was an icy wind blowing; he took up the rug and again passed it round her. She threw herself about wildly, tore off the rug and let it fall on the floor of the car. "As you like," growled Prokop, and turned away.

The car turned into a firm stretch of road and immediately accelerated. Of Daimon nothing was to be seen but the back of his shaggy coat. Prokop sobbed with the coldness of the wind and looked round at the girl. She had twined her hair round her neck and was shivering with cold in her thin clothes. He was sorry for her, and again took the rug and threw it over her. She pushed it away in fury and then he wrapped her up in it from her head to her heels, as if she were a package, and clasped her in his arms: "Don't move!"

"What are you up to?" threw out Daimon casually from the wheel. "Well…"

Prokop pretended that he had not heard this piece of cynicism, but the package in his arms began to giggle quietly.

"She's a good girl," continued Daimon calmly. "Her father was an author." The package nodded and Daimon told Prokop a name so famous, so sacred and pure that he was positively aghast and involuntarily relaxed his grasp. The package twisted round and bounced on his lap; from beneath the rug there projected a pair of beautiful, wicked legs, which childishly kicked about in the air. He drew the rug over her so that she should not be cold, but she seemed to regard this as a game, was convulsed with laughter, and went on kicking her legs about. He held her as firmly as he could, but her hands slid out from the rug and played over his face, pulled his hair, tickled his neck and found their way in between his lips. At length he let her go on; she felt about his forehead, found it severely furrowed, and drew back as if she had been burned. Now it was a venturesome child's hand which did not know what it was allowed to do. It gently and surreptitiously approached his face, touched it, drew away, touched it again, smoothed it and at last timidly rested on his rough cheek. From the rug there came the sound of deep breathing.

The car slid through a sleeping town and shot into the open country. "Well," said Daimon, turning round, "what do you think of our comrades?"

"Quietly," whispered the motionless Prokop, "she's asleep."

CHAPTER L

The car drew up in a dark, wooded valley. Prokop made out in the half light some large towers and slag heaps. "Well, here we are," muttered Daimon. "This is my mine and forge; that's nothing. Out you get!"

"Am I to leave her here?" asked Prokop softly.

"Who? Ha, ha! Your beauty. Wake her up, we're stopping here."

Prokop carefully stepped out of the car, carrying her in his arms. "Where am I to put her?"

Daimon unlocked the door of a desolate-looking house. "What? Wait. I've got a few rooms here. You can put her... I'll show you."

He turned on the light and led him along a number of cold passages through some offices. Finally, he turned into a room and switched on the light. Prokop found himself in a repulsive, unventilated room containing an unmade bed. The blinds were drawn down. "Aha!" said Daimon, "evidently some friend of mine has spent the night here. It's not very beautiful, eh? Well, put her down on the bed."

Prokop carefully deposited the heavily breathing package. Daimon was walking up and down the room, rubbing his hands. "Now we'll go to our station. It's on the top of the hill, about ten minutes away. Or would you rather stay here?" He stepped over to the sleeping girl and lifted the rug so that she was uncovered as far as the knees. "She's beautiful, eh? It's a pity I'm so old."

Prokop frowned and covered her up again.

"Show me your station," he said shortly. A smile trembled on Daimon's lips. "We'll go."

Daimon led him through the yard. There were lights in the factory, and there was to be heard the throbbing of machinery. About the yard there sauntered the fireman, his sleeves rolled up and a pipe in his mouth. To the side was a belt with a row of trucks for the mine, the girders of its supports standing out like the ribs of a lizard.

"We've had to close three pits," explained Daimon. "They didn't pay. I should have sold them a long time ago if it hadn't been for the station. This way." He began to ascend a steep footpath leading up through the wood to the top of the hill. Prokop could only follow him by sound; it was a black night, and from time to time heavy drops fell from the branches of the pines.

Daimon stopped, breathing with difficulty. "I'm old," he said, "I can't get my breath as I used to. I've got to depend on people more and more…. There's no one at the station today; the telegraphist has remained below with the others…but that doesn't matter. Come on!"

The top of the hill was cut about as if it had been the scene of a battle; abandoned towers, a wire cable, enormous deserted slag heaps and on the top of the largest of them a wooden shed with an aerial above it. "That's… the station," panted Daimon. "It stands on forty thousand tons of magnesia. A natural condenser, you see? The whole hill…is an enormous network of wires. Some time or other I'll explain it to you in detail. Help me up." He scrambled over the loose surface of the slag heap, the heavy gravel tumbling noisily under his feet, but here at last, anyway, was the station.

Prokop drew back, unable to believe his eyes; it was his own laboratory shed at home in the fields near Hybsmonka! The same unpainted door, a pair of planks, lighter in colour, where repairs had been made, knots in the wood which looked like eyes. As if in a dream he felt the wall: yes, the same bent, rusty nail which he himself had once driven in! "Where did you get this from?" he cried excitedly.

"What?"

"This shed."

"It's been here for years," said Daimon indifferently. "Why are you so interested in it?"

"Nothing." Prokop ran round the shed feeling the walls and windows. Yes, there was the crack, the fault in the wood, the broken pane in the window, the place where the knot had fallen out and the piece of paper stuck over the inside of the hole. With trembling hands he examined all these wretched details; everything was as it had been, everything….

"Well," said Daimon, "have you finished your inspection? Open the door, you've got the key."

Prokop felt for the key in his pocket. Of course, he had with him the key of his old laboratory…there at home. He thrust it into the padlock, opened it, and went inside. There, as if at home, he mechanically reached out to the left and turned on the light; instead of a button there was a nail—again as at home. Daimon followed him in. God, there was his sofa, his wash-stand, the jug with the broken rim, the sponge, the towel, everything. He turned round and looked into the corner; there he saw the old green stove with its pipe mended with wire, the box with coal dust at the bottom, and the broken armchair with failing legs, with the wire and tow still sticking out of it. There was the same tack projecting from the floor, the burnt plank and the clothes cupboard. He opened it, and there fell out an old pair of trousers.

"It's not very magnificent," said Daimon. "Our telegraphist is a—well, strange sort of fellow. What do you think of the apparatus?"

Prokop turned to the table as if in a dream. No, that wasn't there, no, no, no, that didn't belong there. Instead of the chemical apparatus there stood at one end of the bench a powerful wireless apparatus, with condensers, a variometer, and a regulator. A pair of ear phones lay on the table. Under the table was the usual transforming apparatus and at the other end...

"That's the normal station," explained Daimon, "for ordinary conversation. The other is our extinguishing station. With it we send out those anti-waves, contra-currents, magnetic storms, or whatever you like to call them. That's our secret. Can you understand it?"

"No." Prokop quickly looked over a piece of apparatus which was completely different from anything he had ever seen. There was a quantity of resistances, a sort of wire screen, something resembling cathode pipe, several isolated drums or something of the sort, an extraordinary coherer and a taster with contacts; he could not make out what it all meant. He left the apparatus and looked up at the ceiling to see if there was on it that extraordinary marking on the wood which always at home recalled to him the head of an old man. Yes, it was there. And there also was the little mirror with the corner broken off....

"What do you think of the apparatus?" asked Daimon.

"It's...your first model, eh? It's still too complicated." His eyes fell on a photograph which was supported on an induction spool. He took it up and examined it; it represented the head of an extraordinarily beautiful girl, "Who's this?" he asked hoarsely.

Daimon looked at it over his shoulder. "Surely you recognize her? That's your beauty whom you carried here in your arms. A lovely girl, eh?"

"How did she get here?"

Daimon grinned. "Well, probably our telegraphist worships her. Wouldn't you like to turn on that large switch? That one with a lever. He's that shrunken little man. Didn't you notice him? He was sitting in the front row."

Prokop threw the photograph down on the table and turned on the switch. A blue spark ran across the metal screen. Daimon's fingers played on the taster and short blue sparks began to flash all over the apparatus. "So," said Daimon in a satisfied tone, watching the display motionlessly.

Prokop grasped the photograph with burning hands. Yes, of course, it was the girl down there below; there could be no doubt about that. But if... if, for instance, she had a veil and was wearing a fur covered with drops of moisture...and little gloves—"

Prokop ground his teeth. It was impossible that she should resemble her so! He half closed his eyes in the effort to catch a retreating vision. Again he saw the girl with the veil, pressing to her breast the sealed package and now, now she turned on him a pure and desperate glance.

Beside himself with excitement, he compared the photograph with the form in his mind's eye. Good heavens, what exactly did she look like? He didn't know, he thought, with sudden fear. He only knew that she was veiled and beautiful. She was beautiful and veiled, and he had noticed nothing more, nothing more. And this picture here with the large eyes and delicate and serious mouth, was that the one…the one asleep down there? But she had her lips half open, sinful and half opened lips and loosened hair and didn't look like that, didn't look like that. Before his eyes was the veil covered with rain drops. No, that was nonsense; it could not be the girl down there, it was nothing like her. This was the face of the girl with the veil who came in anguish and consternation; her brow was calm and her eyes darkened with pain. Against her lips there was pressing her veil, a thick veil with drops of moisture on it. Why didn't he raise it, so as to see what she was like?

"Come along. I have something I want to show you," said Daimon, and dragged Prokop outside. They stood on the top of the slag heap. Beneath their feet the sleeping earth stretched out of sight. "Look over there," said Daimon, pointing to the horizon, "do you see anything?"

"Nothing."

"No, there's a tiny light. It's shining faintly."

"Do you know what it is?"

Then there was a faint sound, like the moaning of the wind on a still night.

"That's that," said Daimon triumphantly, and took off his hat. "Good night, comrades."

Prokop turned to him inquiringly.

"Don't you understand?" said Daimon. "The noise of the explosion has only just reached us. Fifty kilometres as the crow flies. Exactly two and a half minutes."

"What explosion?"

"Krakatit. Those idiots collected it in matchboxes. I don't think we shall be bothered with them any more. We'll call a new conference…elect a new committee—"

"Did—you—?"

Daimon nodded. "It was impossible to work with them. Up to the very last moment they quarrelled about tactics. There's certainly a fire there."

A faint red light was to be seen on the horizon.

"The inventor of our apparatus was there as well. They were all there. Now you can take it into your own hands. Listen how quiet it is. And yet from these wires a silent and exact cannonade is going out into space. Now we have interrupted all wireless communications and the telegraphists are hearing in their ears, crack, crack! Let them rage. Meanwhile, Mr. Thomas, somewhere in Grottup, is trying to complete the preparation of Krakatit.

He'll never do it. And if he did! At the moment at which he had completed his synthesis it would be the end. Work away, station, send out your sparks secretly and bombard the whole of the universe. Nobody, nobody beside yourself will be the ruler of Krakatit. Now there is only you, you alone." He put his hand on Prokop's shoulder and silently indicated in a circle the whole world. Round them was a deserted and starless darkness; only on the horizon was there to be seen the dull glow of a conflagration.

"Ah. I'm tired," yawned Daimon. "It was a good day. We'll go down."

CHAPTER LI

Daimon hurried along. "Where exactly is Grottup?" asked Prokop on a sudden impulse, when they had descended.

"Come," said Daimon, "I'll show you." He led him into the factory office to a map hanging on the wall. "Here," and he indicated on the map with his enormous nail a little circle. "Wouldn't you like to drink something? This sort of thing warms you up." He poured out a glassful of some jet-black liquid for Prokop and himself. "Your health." Prokop tossed down his portion and gulped; it was red-hot and as bitter as quinine; his head began to spin dizzily. "Any more?" said Daimon through his yellow teeth. "No? A pity. You don't want to keep your little beauty waiting, eh?" He drank glass after glass. His eyes flashed with a green light, he wanted to babble but could not master his tongue. "Listen—you're a good chap," he said. "Get to work tomorrow. Old Daimon will give you everything you ask for." He rose unsteadily and made Prokop a low bow. "Now everything's in order. And now—w-w-wait—"

He began to talk all possible languages at once. As far as Prokop was able to understand, it was unutterable filth. Finally, he hummed some senseless song, threw himself about as if in a fit and lost consciousness. Yellow foam appeared on his lips.

"Hey, what's the matter with you?" cried Prokop, shaking him.

Daimon opened his glassy eyes with difficulty.

"What…what's up?" he muttered, raised himself up a little and shook himself. "Aha! I'm… I'm… That's nothing." He rubbed his forehead and yawned convulsively. "Yes. I'll show you to your room, eh?" He was horribly pale and his Tartar face had suddenly grown flabby. He walked uncertainly as if his limbs were numbed. "Come then."

He went straight to the room in which they had left the girl sleeping. "Ah," he cried from the doorway, "the beauty has woke up. Come in, please."

She was kneeling by the hearth. Evidently she had just lit the fire and was looking into a crackling flame. "Look how she's arranged it," said Daimon appreciatively. Certainly the stuffy and depressing aspect of the room had disappeared in the most extraordinary way; it was now pleasant and unpretentious like a room in one's own home.

"How clever you are," said Daimon admiringly. "Girl, you ought to settle down." She stood up and became red and confused. "Don't be frightened now," said Daimon. "Here's the comrade you like."

"Yes. I like him," she said simply and went over and closed the window and pulled down the blinds.

The stove threw a pleasant heat into the bright room. "Child, you've made everything very nice," said Daimon, gratified, warming his hands. "I should like to stay here."

"Please go away," she cried quickly.

"At once, my dear," said Daimon, grinning. "I... I feel lonely without people. Look, your friend seems to be struck dumb. Wait. I'll talk to him."

She suddenly became angry. "Don't say anything to him! Let him behave as he wants to!" He raised his bushy eyebrows in surprise. "What? what? You don't mean to say that you lo—"

"What's that to do with you?" she interrupted him, her eyes flashing. "Who wants you here?"

He laughed quietly, leaning against the stove. "If you knew how that suits you! Girl, girl, has it really at last happened seriously to you? Show me!" He tried to take hold of her chin. She drew back, pale with rage, showing her teeth.

"What? You even want to bite? Who were you with yesterday, that you are so— Aha! I know. Rosso, eh?"

"That's not true," she cried with tears in her voice.

"Leave her alone," said Prokop sternly.

"Well, well, it doesn't matter," muttered Daimon. "Anyway. I mustn't interfere with you, eh? Good night, children." He stepped back, pressed himself to the wall and before Prokop realized the fact, had disappeared.

Prokop drew a chair up to the crackling stove and stared into the flames without even looking round at the girl. He heard her walking about the room hesitatingly on the tips of her toes, putting something straight. He did not know what she was doing. She was now standing still silently. There is an extraordinary power in flames and flowing water; you stare at them, become bewildered, cease to think, know nothing, and are unable to recollect anything, but before you there is represented everything that has ever happened without form and outside time.

There was the sound of one slipper being thrown down after the other; evidently she was taking her shoes off. Go to sleep, girl, when you are asleep we shall see who it is whom you resemble. Very quietly she crossed the room and then stopped. Again she arranged something. God alone knew why she wanted to have everything so clean and tidy. And suddenly she knelt down in front of him, stretching out her comely arms to his feet. "Shall I take off your boots for you?" she said gently.

He took her head between his palms and turned it towards him. She was beautiful, submissive and extraordinarily serious. "Did you ever know Thomas?" he asked in a hoarse voice.

She reflected and then shook her head.

"Don't lie! You...you... Have you a married sister?"

"I haven't!" She tore herself sharply out of his grasp. "Why should I lie? I'll tell you everything deliberately so that you shall know—I'm a fallen girl." She hid her face against his knees. "They all...so that you shall know—"

"Even Daimon?"

She did not answer but only shivered. "You...you may kick me... I'm... don't touch me... I'm...if you knew..." She was unable to go on.

"Leave that," he cried in pain and raised her head by force. Her eyes were wide open with desperation and anxiety. He let go her head again and moaned. The resemblance was so striking that he gulped with horror. "Be quiet, at least be quiet," he said in a strangled voice.

She again pressed her face against him. "Let me... I must tell you everything... I began when I was thir...thirteen..." He covered her mouth with his hands; she bit it and continued her terrible confession through his fingers. "Be quiet," he cried, but the words tore themselves out of her, her teeth chattered, she trembled and went on. Somehow he managed to silence her. "Oh," she moaned, "if you knew...the things that people do! And everyone, everyone is so rough with me...as if I was...not even an animal, not even a stone!"

"Stop," he said, beside himself, and, not knowing what to do, smoothed her head with the trembling stumps of his fingers. Appeased, she sighed and became motionless; he could feel her hot breath and the beat of the artery in her neck.

She began to giggle quietly. "You thought that I was sleeping, there, in the car. I wasn't asleep. I did it on purpose...and expected you to behave... like the others. Because you knew the sort of thing I was...and...you only became angry and held me as if I were a little girl...as if I were something sacred..." Although she was laughing, tears suddenly came into her eyes. "Suddenly—I don't know why—I was more happy than I had ever been— and proud—and frightfully ashamed, but...it was so beautiful—" With trembling lips she kissed his knees. "You...you didn't even wake me up...and laid me down...as if I were something precious...and covered my legs, and said nothing—" She burst into tears. "I'll, I'll wait on you, let me... I'll take your boots off.... Please, please don't be angry that I pretended that I was asleep! Please—"

He wanted to raise her head; she kissed his hands. "For God's sake, don't cry!" he gulped out.

She drew herself up, surprised, and stopped crying. "Why are you reproaching me?" He tried to raise her face; she defended herself with all her strength and entwined herself round his legs. "No, no, no," she gasped, laughing, and at the same time frightened. "I'm plain—I've been crying. You, you wouldn't like me," she breathed gently hiding her face. "It was so long…before you came! I'll wait on you and write your letters…. I'm learning to use a typewriter and I know five languages. You won't drive me away, will you? When you took such a long time to come I thought what I would do…and he spoilt everything and spoke as if…as if I were… But that isn't true… I've already told you everything. I'll… I'll do what you tell me…. I want to be decent—"

"Stand up. I beg you!"

She squatted down on her heels, folded her hands in her lap and looked at him as if entranced. Now… She was no longer like the one with the veil; he recalled the sobbing Annie. "Don't cry any more;" he said gently and uncertainly.

"You are beautiful," she whispered admiringly. He grew red and muttered something or other. "Go…to bed," he gulped and stroked her burning cheek.

"Do you hate me?" she whispered, blushing.

"No, nothing of the sort." She did not move, and gazed at him with anxious eyes. He bent down and kissed her. She kissed him back clumsily, in confusion, as if she were kissing a man for the first time. "Go to bed," he muttered, worried, "I've still…something which I must think out."

She got up obediently and quietly began to undress. He sat down in a corner so as not to disturb her. She took off her clothes without any shame, but also without the least frivolity. Simply, without hurrying, she laid aside her underclothes, slowly took the stockings off her strong and well-shaped legs. She became reflective, looked down on the ground, like a child began to observe her long toes, and glanced at Prokop. She laughed and whispered: "I'm being quiet." Prokop in his corner was hardly breathing: it was again she, the girl with a veil; this powerful, beautiful and developed body belonged to her; she would lay aside her clothing piece by piece in the same lovely and serious way, her hair would fall like that over her composed shoulders, she would reflectively stroke her full arms in the same manner…. He closed his eyes, his heart beating violently. Have you never seen her, closing your eyes in the most complete solitude, seen her standing in the quiet light of the lamp amongst her family, turning her face towards you and saying something which you couldn't somehow catch? Have you never, rubbing your hands between your knees, seen beneath your eyelids the constrained movement of her hand, a simple and noble movement in which was the whole of the peaceful and silent joy of home? Once she appeared to you, seen from behind, her head bent over something, and on another occasion you saw her reading by the light of the evening lamp. Perhaps this now was only a continuation and would disappear if you were to open your eyes, and you would be left with nothing but solitude.

He opened his eyes. The girl was lying in bed, covered up to her chin, her eyes turned towards him in passionate and submissive love. He came over to her, and bent over her face, studying her features with sharp and impatient attention. She looked at him interrogatively and made room for him at her side. "No, no, no," he muttered and stroked her lightly on the forehead. "Go to sleep." She obediently closed her eyes and hardly seemed to breathe.

He returned to his corner on tiptoe. No, she's not like her, he assured himself. He had an idea that she was watching him through her half closed eyes. This tortured him; he could not even think. He became irritated, and turned his head away. Finally, he sprang up and crossed the room softly to look at her. Her eyes were closed and she was breathing very quietly; she was beautiful and unresisting. "Sleep," he whispered. She made a tiny movement of assent with her head. He turned out the light, and rubbing his hands returned on tiptoe to his corner near the window.

After a long, painful interval he crept to the door like a thief. Would she wake? He hesitated with his hand on the catch, opened it with a beating heart, and stole out into the yard.

It was not yet day. Prokop looked about amongst the slag heaps, and then climbed over the fence. He dropped on to the ground, brushed the dirt off his clothes and made for the main road.

It was all that he could do to see his way. He looked about him, trembling with cold. Where, where exactly should be go? To Balttin?

He went on for a few steps and then stopped, looking down at the ground. Now to Balttin? Assailed by a fit of rough, tearless crying he turned back.

To Grottup!

CHAPTER LII

The paths of the world twist in a curious way. If you were to follow out all your steps and all the journeys you have made, what an intricate design they would make! For by his steps everyone traces out his map of the world.

By the time that Prokop found himself standing in front of the grille before the factories at Grottup, it was already evening. The factory consisted of a great stretch of sheds, illuminated by the dull globes of arc lamps; the lights were still showing from one or two windows. Prokop thrust his head through the bars of the grille and cried: "Hallo!"

The doorkeeper, or perhaps the guard, came up. "What do you want? It's forbidden to enter."

"Excuse me, is Mr. Engineer Thomas still with you?"

"What do you want with him?"

"I must speak to him."

"…Mr. Thomas is still in the laboratory. You can't see him."

"Tell him…tell him that his friend Prokop is waiting for him…that he has something which he wishes to give him."

"Get farther away from the grille," muttered the man, and called someone.

A quarter of an hour later someone in a long white coat came up to the grille.

"Is that you. Thomas?" cried Prokop in a low voice.

"No. I'm the laboratory assistant. Mr. Thomas can't come. He has important work. What do you want?"

"I must speak with him urgently."

The laboratory assistant, a stout and active little man, shrugged his shoulders.

"I'm afraid it's no good. Mr. Thomas isn't free today even for a second."

"Are you making Krakatit?"

The assistant snorted evasively. "What's that to do with you?"

"I must…warn him of something. I've something to give him."

"You can give it to me. I'll take it to him."

"No. I'll… I'll only give it to him. Tell him—"

"All the same, you could leave it with me." The man in the white coat turned on his heel and went off.

"Wait," cried Prokop. "Give him this. Explain to him…explain to him…." He drew out of his pocket the crumpled package and passed it through the grille. The assistant took it suspiciously with the tips of his fingers and Prokop felt as if he had torn himself away from something. "Tell him that…that I'm waiting here and that I should like him to…to come here!"

"I'll give it to him," said the assistant and went away.

Prokop squatted down on his heels. On the other side of the partition a silent shadow continued to watch him. It was a frosty night, the bare branches of the trees stretched into the fog, there was a slimy and chilly feeling in the air. A quarter of an hour later someone came up to the grille—a pale youth, evidently suffering from lack of sleep, with a face the colour of curds.

"Mr. Thomas says that he thanks you very much and that he can't come and that you mustn't wait," he announced mechanically.

"Wait," said Prokop impatiently through his teeth. "Tell him that I *must* see him, that…that it's a question of his life. And that I will give him anything that he wants if…if he will only let me know the name and address of the lady from whom I brought him the parcel. You understand?"

"Mr. Thomas only told me to say that he thanks you very much," repeated the lad in a sleepy voice, "and that you are not to wait."

"But—the devil," groaned Prokop through his teeth, "I'll explain when he comes and shan't move until then. And tell him that he must leave his work or that…he'll go up in the air, see?"

"Please," said the youth dully.

"Ask him to come here! And to give me that address, only that address, and say that then I'll give him everything, have you understood?"

"Please."

"Well, go then, quickly, for heaven's—"

He waited in feverish impatience. Was that the step of a human being within? He had a sudden vision of Daimon, twisting his violet mouth and staring at the blue sparks of his apparatus. And this idiot Thomas didn't come! He was preparing something over there where one could see the lighted window and had no idea that he was being bombarded, that with his quick hands he was digging a grave for himself. Was that a step? No one came.

Prokop was rent by a hoarse cough. I'll give you everything, madman, if you will only come and tell me her name! I want nothing, nothing except to find her. I'll give you everything if you will only tell me this one thing! His eyes stared into the distance and now she was standing in front of him, veiled, with dry leaves at her feet, pale and extraordinarily serious in this darkness. She twisted her hands on her breast and had already given him the parcel. She looked at him with deep, attentive eyes; her veil and fur were covered with drops of moisture. "You were unforgettably kind to me," she said softly in a muffled voice. She raised her hands to him and again he was convulsed by a fierce cough. Oh, was nobody coming? He threw himself at the grille, trying to force his way through.

"Stay where you are or I'll shoot!" cried the shadow from the other side. "What do you want here?"

Prokop drew back. "Please," he said desperately in a hoarse voice, "tell Mr. Thomas…tell him…"

"Tell him yourself," the voice interrupted him illogically, "but keep away."

Prokop again squatted down on his heels. Perhaps Thomas would come when his experiment again missed fire. Certainly, he would not be able to discover how Krakatit was prepared; then he would come and call Prokop…. He sat hunched up like a beggar. "Look here," he said at length. "I'll give you…ten thousand if you'll let me through."

"I'll have you arrested," answered the voice sharply and inexorably.

"I… I…" stammered Prokop. "I only want to know that address. See? I only want to know that… I'll give you anything if you will only get it for me! You…you're married, and have children, but I… I'm alone…and I only want to find…"

"Keep quiet," scolded the voice. "You're drunk."

Prokop became silent and rocked himself on his heels. "I must wait," he reflected dully. "Why does nobody come? I'll give him everything. Krakatit and everything else if he'll only… You were unforgettably kind to me.' No. God preserve me. I'm a bad man, but you, you awakened in me the passion of tenderness. I would do anything in the world to earn a look from you; you know why I'm here. The most beautiful thing about you is that you have the power of making me serve you. That's why, you see. I can't help loving you!"

"What's up with you?" came the voice from the other side of the grille. "Are you going to be quiet or not?"

Prokop stood up: "Please, please tell him—"

"I'll set the dog on you!"

A white figure, accompanied by the glowing end of a cigarette, sauntered up to the partition. "Is that you, Thomas?" cried Prokop.

"No. Are you still here?" It was the laboratory assistant. "Man, are you mad?"

"Is Mr. Thomas coming, please?"

"He wouldn't dream of such a thing," said the assistant contemptuously. "He doesn't need you. In a quarter of an hour we shall have it ready, and then, *gloria victoria*! Then I shall have a drink."

"Please tell him that…that I want that address!"

"That's already been dealt with by the boy," said the assistant. "Mr. Thomas tells you to go to hell. Do you think that he'll leave his work just now when the great moment is being reached? We're on the point of making it and then—there we are."

Prokop screamed out in horror: "Run and tell him—quickly—that he mustn't turn on the high frequency current! He must stop it! Or—something will happen—run as fast as you can! He doesn't know...he doesn't know that Daimon—for God's sake stop him!"

"Pooh!" the assistant broke into a short laugh. "Mr. Thomas knows what he's doing and you—" Here the butt of the cigarette flew through the partition. "Good night!"

Prokop sprang to the grille.

"Hands up," came a cry from the other side, and the guard's whistle sounded piercingly. Prokop took to flight.

He ran along the main road, jumped over the ditch at the side, and ran over the soft ground, stumbling over a ploughed field. He fell over, picked himself up, and dashed on. He stopped with a beating heart. All around him was darkness and deserted fields. Now they wouldn't be able to catch him. He listened; all was quiet. He could hear nothing but the sound of his own breath. But what—what if Grottup should be blown into the air? He clutched his head and ran on further, descending into a deep valley, scrambling up on the other side, and then limping over more ploughed fields. He felt the acute pain of his old wound and a burning sensation in his chest. He could go no further, sat down on a stone and looked at Grottup, mistily glowing with its arc lamps. It seemed like a bright island in the midst of boundless darkness. It was oppressively dark, and yet within a radius of thousands and thousands of miles a terrible and unremitting attack was being launched. Daimon on his Magnetic Hill was precisely and silently bombarding the whole world. In all directions waves were being sent out which would ignite the first grain of Krakatit which they encountered anywhere in the world. And there, in the dead of night, bathed in this pale light, an obdurate, wrongheaded man was working, bending over a secret process of transformation. "Thomas, look out!" cried Prokop, but his voice was lost in the darkness like a stone thrown into a pond by some childish hand.

He sprang up, trembling with fear and cold, and dashed on further, as far as he could from Grottup. He found himself in the middle of some swampy place and stopped. Had he heard the noise of an explosion? No, all was quiet, and with a new access of terror he clambered up a slope, slipped on to his knees, sprang up again and dashed on, rushing into some bushes, tearing his hands, slipping about, and then descending again. He drew himself up, brushed away the sweat with his bleeding hands, and ran on.

In the middle of a field he came across something white—a cross which had been overturned. Breathing heavily, he sat down on its vacant support. He was now a long way from the ruddy glow over Grottup, which was already on the horizon; it now seemed to be on the surface of the ground. Prokop breathed a deep sigh of relief; there was no sound; perhaps Thomas's experiment had failed and the terrible thing would not happen. He listened cautiously; no, nothing was to be heard but the cold dripping of water in some gutter underground and the beating of his heart.

Then an enormous black mass was thrown into the air over Grottup and all the lights went out. The next moment, as if the darkness had been torn asunder, a pillar of fire leapt into the air, spread terribly and liberated a tremendous body of smoke. Directly afterward came an impact through the air, something cracked, the trees began to rustle, and—crash! A terrible blow, as with a whip, an uproar, a shattering blow. The earth trembled and torn-off leaves whirled through the air. Snatching for air, and holding on with both hands to the support of the cross, so as not to be swept away. Prokop stared wildly at the roaring furnace.

And the heavens shall be cleaved by a fiery power and the voice of God shall be heard in the thunder.

Two more masses went up, one after the other, and were broken up by a band of fire. Then came the sound of a still more terrible explosion—evidently the ammunition stores. A roaring mass flew into the air, exploded, and came down in the form of a ray of sparks. The roar changed into a pounding bombardment; in the stores there were exploding rockets which flew up like sparks from an anvil. A purple fire glowed on the horizon, and there was a continuous succession of reports like the noise of a machine gun. A fourth and fifth explosion followed with the noise of a howitzer. The fire spread on both sides and soon half the horizon was a flame.

Only then could he distinguish the sound of the crackling of the timber in Grottup, but this was still nearly obscured by the explosion of the arsenal. A sixth explosion resounded firm and clear—evidently kresylite. As a sort of accompaniment, came the deeper note of the explosion of casks filled with dynamite. A huge flaming projectile flew halfway across the sky, leaving an enormous trail of flame behind it. Another flame sprang up, went out, and reappeared a short distance away, but the noise of the explosions only arrived a few seconds later. For a moment it was so quiet that one could hear the crackling of the fire, like that of broken brushwood. Then there was a further rending explosion and above the Grottup factories there sprang up a flame which spread to the town of Grottup.

Aghast with fear, Prokop picked himself up and staggered on further.

CHAPTER LIII

He ran along the main road, breathing heavily, passed over the top of the hill, and descended into a valley. The ruddy flow disappeared behind him. There disappeared also the objects lit up by the dull glow and the shadows thrown by it. It was as if everything was drifting confusedly away, motionless, as if it were being carried on the breast of an immense river, a river untroubled by any wave and unvisited by any bird. He grew afraid of the beat of his own feet in the midst of this silent and immense flux of everything; he relaxed his pace, trod more softly, and went on through the milky darkness.

In front of him on the road he saw the twinkling of a light. He wanted to avoid it, stopped and hesitated. A lamp on a table, the remains of fire in a stove, a lantern looking for a path, while some wornout moth beat its wings against the flickering light. He approached it without hurrying, as if not sure of himself. He stopped, warmed himself from a distance at the unsteady fire, came nearer with a fear that he would again be driven away. A short distance away he stopped again; it was a cart with a covering of cloth. On one of the shafts was hanging a lighted lantern which threw trembling handfuls of light on to a white horse, white stones, and the white stumps of birch trees at the side of the road. On its head the horse had a rough sack and was crunching some oats. It had a long, silver mane and a tail which had never been clipped. At its head there stood a little old man with a white beard and silver hair. He also in colouring was coarse and pale, like the covering over the cart. He stamped about, reflecting, saying something to himself and twisting the white mane of the horse in his fingers.

Then he turned round, looking blindly into the darkness, and asked in a trembling voice: "Is that you, Prokop? Come along. I've been waiting for you."

Prokop was not surprised, but only inordinately relieved. "I'm coming," he said, "but I've been running!"

The old man stepped up to him and took hold of him by the coat. "You're quite wet," he said reproachfully. "You mustn't catch cold."

"Old man," said Prokop hoarsely, "do you know that Grottup has exploded?"

The old man shook his head regretfully. "And what a lot of people must have been killed! You ran away, eh? Sit down on the coachbox. I'll give you a lift." He stumped over to the horse and slowly removed the sack of oats. "Hi, hi, that's enough," he mumbled. "We must get along, we've a guest."

"What have you got in the cart?" asked Prokop.

The old man turned round to him and smiled. "The world," he said. "Haven't you ever seen the world?"

"No. I haven't."

"Then I'll show you—wait." He put the nosebag away and, without hurrying, began to undo the covering on the other side. Then he threw it back, revealing a box into which had been inserted a spyhole covered with a glass. "Wait a moment," he said, looking for something on the ground. He picked up a small branch, squatted on his heels over the light, and lit the wick, all this slowly and seriously. "Now, burn nicely, burn," he said to it, sheltering it with his hands. Then he placed it inside the box, lighting it up. "I use oil," he explained. "Some of them have carbide...but that carbide hurts the eyes. And then one day it explodes and there you are; besides, you might hurt somebody. And oil, that's like in a church." He bent down to the little window, and peered through it with his pale eyes. "You can see nicely," he whispered, delighted. "Have a look. But you must bend down, so as to be...little...like a child. That's right."

Prokop stooped down to the spyhole. "The Grecian Temple in Girgent," began the old man, "on the island of Sicily, dedicated to God or to Juno. Look at those pillars. They are made so carefully that a whole family can eat on each stone. Think what work that means! Shall I go on turning?—The view from the Mountain of Penegal in the Alps at sunset. Then the snow is lit up with a strange and beautiful light, as it's shown there. That's an Alpine light and that other mountain is called Latemar. Further?—The sacred city of Benares; the river is sacred and cleanses the sinful. Thousands of people have found there what they sought."

The pictures were carefully drawn and coloured by hand. The colours had faded a little and the paper had a tinge of yellow, but the charming, variegated effect of the blues, greens, yellows and reds of the people's clothing and the pure azure of the sky remained; every blade of grass was drawn with love and care.

"That sacred river is the Ganges," concluded the old man reverently, and turned the handle further. "And this is Zahur, the most beautiful castle in the world."

Prokop simply glued his eye to the hole. He saw a magnificent castle with graceful cupolas, lofty palms, and a blue waterfall. A tiny figure with a turban in which was stuck a feather, with a purple coat, yellow pantaloons, and a Tartar sabre was greeting with a low bow a lady dressed in white, who was leading by the bridle a prancing horse. "Where...where is Zahur?" whispered Prokop.

The old man shrugged his shoulders. "Somewhere over there," he said uncertainly, "where it is most beautiful. Some find it and some do not. Shall I go on?"

"Not yet."

The old man drew away a little and stroked the leg of the horse. "Wait, no no no, wait," he said gently. "We must show it him, see? Let him enjoy himself."

"Turn on, grandfather," said Prokop. He saw in succession the harbour at Hamburg, the Kremlin, a polar landscape with the Northern Lights, the Volcano of Krakatau, Brooklyn Bridge, NotreDame, a native village in Borneo, Darwin's house, the wireless station in Poldhu, a street in Shanghai, the Victoria Falls, the Castle of Gernstein, the petroleum wells in Baku. "And this is the explosion in Grottup," explained the old man, and Prokop saw coils of reddish smoke being thrown high up in the air by a yellow flame. In the midst of the smoke and flames could be discerned fragments of human bodies. "More than five thousand people perished. It was a great disaster," sighed the old man. "That's the last picture. Well, have you seen the world?"

"No. I haven't," muttered Prokop, stupefied.

The old man shook his head in disappointment. "You want to see too much. You will have to live for a long time." He blew out the little lamp and, muttering to himself, slowly covered the box up again. "Sit down on the coachbox, we'll go on." He pulled off the sack which was covering the horse's back and put it over Prokop's shoulders. "So that you shan't be cold," he said, and sat down next to him. He took the reins in his hand and whistled quietly. The horse set off at a gentle trot. "Hi! Now then," sang the old man.

They passed along an avenue of birches, by cottages half drowned in the mist, a serene and sleeping countryside. "Grandfather," Prokop found himself saying, "why has all this happened to me?"

"What?"

"Why have I come up against so many things?"

The old men reflected. "It only seems like that," he said finally. "What happens to a man comes out of himself. It all winds out of you as if from a skein."

"That isn't true," Prokop protested. "Why did I meet the Princess? Grandfather, perhaps...you know me. You know that I've been looking for... that other one, you understand? And yet it happened that—why? Tell me!"

The old man considered this, munching with his soft lips. "It was your pride," he said slowly. "Sometimes it happens to a man like that, he doesn't know why, but it's because he has it in him. And he begins to throw himself about—" He illustrated what he was saying with the whip, so that the horse became uneasy and increased its pace. "P-r-r-r, what, what?" he cried to it in a thin voice. "You see, it's the same as when some little chap gives himself airs; he upsets everybody. And there's no need to make such a fuss. Sit still and watch the road and you'll get there all right."

"Grandfather," cried Prokop, half closing his eyes in pain, "have I done wrong?"

"Yes and no," said the old man cautiously. "You've hurt people. If you had been sensible you wouldn't have done it. One must be sensible. And a man must realize the meaning of everything. For instance…you can burn a hundred crown note, or use it to pay your debts. If you burn it it looks more, but…it's the same with women," he concluded unexpectedly.

"Did I behave badly?"

"What?"

"Was I wicked?"

"…You weren't clean inside. A man…must think more than feel. And you threw yourself at everything."

"Grandfather, that was through Krakatit."

"What?"

"I… I made a discovery—and through that—"

"If it hadn't been in you it wouldn't have been in the discovery. A man does everything out of himself. Wait and consider; think and try and remember what your discovery came from and how it was made. Think about that carefully and then say what you know. Hi, no, no, no!"

The cart rumbled over the rough road, the white horse moving its legs in a tremulous and quaint trot. The light danced over the ground, lighting up trees and stones, while the old man bumped up and down on his seat, singing softly to himself. Prokop was rubbing his forehead. "Grandfather," he whispered.

"Well?"

"I've forgotten!"

"What?"

"I… I've forgotten how to…make… Krakatit!"

"There you are," said the old man calmly. "So you have found out something."

CHAPTER LIV

To Prokop it was as if they were passing through the quiet countryside in which he had spent his childhood, but it was very foggy and the light from the lantern penetrated no further than the side of the road, beyond which there was a silent and unknown land.

"Ho-ho-hot," cried the old man, and the horse turned off the road right into that veiled, silent world. The wheels dug into soft grass. Prokop made out a shallow valley, on each side of which were leafless thickets, between which was a beautiful meadow. "P-r-r-r," cried the old man and slowly got down from the coachbox. "Get out," he said, "we've arrived." He slowly undid the traces. "Nobody will come after us here."

"Who?"

"…The police. There must be order…but they always want all sorts of papers…and permits…and where you are coming from…and where you are going. It's all more than I can understand." He unharnessed the horse, saying to him quietly: "Keep quiet and you shall have a piece of bread."

Prokop stepped down from the cart, numbed by the journey. "Where are we?"

"Over there where there's that hut," said the old man vaguely. "You will sleep it off and be all right." He took the lantern from the shaft and threw its light on to a small wooden shed, for hay or something of the sort, but decrepit, poor and crazy. "And I'll make a fire," he said in his singing voice, "and get you some tea. When you've sweated you'll be well again." He wrapped Prokop up in the sack and put down the light in front of him. "Wait while I fetch some wood. Stay here." He was just on the point of going off when something occurred to him. He thrust his hand into his pocket and looked at Prokop interrogatively.

"What is it, grandfather?"

"I…don't know if you would like to… I'm a star reader." He brought his hand out of his pocket again. Through his fingers there was peering a little white mouse with red eyes. "I know," he babbled on quickly, "that you don't believe in such things, but…he's a pretty little chap—Would you like to?"

"I should."

"That's good," said the old man, delighted. "S-s-s-s—ma—la, hop!" He opened his hand and the little mouse nimbly ran along his sleeve up to his shoulder, sniffed delicately at his hairy ear and hid in his collar.

"He's a beauty," breathed Prokop.

The old man's face glowed with pleasure. "Wait and see what he can do," and he ran to the cart, rooted about in it, and returned with a box full of tickets arranged in series. He gave the box a shake, gazing with his shining eyes into the distance. "Show him, mouse, show him his love." He whistled between his teeth like a bat. The mouse sprang up, ran along his arm, and jumped on to the box. Holding his breath, Prokop watched its rosy little paws searching among the tickets. Finally, it took one in its little teeth and tried to pull it out. Somehow or other it succeeded, shook its head and at once seized the next one, pulling that out also. Then it sat up on its hind legs, gnawing at its tiny paws.

"This is your love," whispered the old man, elated. Out with it."

Prokop took hold of the ticket and bent over the light. It was the photograph of a girl…the one whose hair was all loose; her lovely breast was bare, and the eyes were the same, passionate and deep—Prokop recognized her. "Grandfather, that's not the one!"

"Show me," said the old man with surprise, taking the picture out of his hand. "Ah, that's a pity," he croaked regretfully. "Such a beauty! Lala. Lilitko, that isn't the one, nanana ks ks ma—la!" He put the photograph back in the box and again softly whistled. The little mouse looked about with its red eyes, again took the same ticket in its teeth and tugged with its head. But the ticket would not come out; instead it pulled out the next.

Prokop took up the picture; it was Annie, a photograph taken in the village; she did not know what to do with her arms, had her Sunday clothes on and stood there silly and beautiful—"That's not her," whispered Prokop. The old man took the picture from him, smoothed it and appeared to be saying something to it. He looked at Prokop uneasily and sadly and again gave a faint whistle.

"Are you angry?" asked Prokop shyly.

The old man said nothing and looked musingly at the mouse. Again the little creature tried to pull out the same ticket; but no, it was impossible and it extracted the next one instead. This was a picture of the Princess. Prokop moaned and let it fall on to the ground. The old man silently bent down and picked it up.

"Let me try myself," cried Prokop hoarsely, and thrust his hand into the box. But the old man stopped him: "That's not allowed!"

"But she…she's there," said Prokop through his teeth. "The right one's there!"

"Everybody's there," said the old man, caressing the box. "Now you shall have your planet." He whistled quietly, and the mouse ran along his arm and drew out a green slip of paper. A moment later it was back again; evidently Prokop frightened it. "Read it to yourself," said the old man, carefully putting the box away. "I'll be fetching some wood—and don't be worried."

He stroked the horse's side, stowed the box away in the bottom of the cart and set off for the thicket. His light-coloured coat disappeared in the darkness. The horse watched him for a moment and then jerked his head and followed him. "Ihaha," the old man could be heard saying, "so you want to come with me? Ah! Hotty, hotty-hot, ma-ly!"

They disappeared in the fog and Prokop remembered the green ticket. "Your planet," he read by the flickering light. "You are an honourable man, with a good heart and more learned than others in your profession. You will have to suffer a lot of opposition, but if you avoid impetuousness and arrogance you will obtain the respect of your neighbours and an exalted position. You will lose much but you will later be rewarded. Your unlucky days are Tuesdays and Fridays. Saturn Conj. b. b. Martis. DEO gratias."

The old man loomed out of the darkness with his arms full of sticks. Behind him appeared the white head of the horse. "Well," he whispered tensely and with a certain amount of the shyness of an author, "did you read it? Is it a good planet?"

"It is, grandfather."

"There you are," said the old man, relieved, "everything will turn out all right, praise be to God." He put down the armful of brushwood and, muttering happily, lit a fire in front of the hut. Then he again rummaged in the cart, produced a kettle and stumped off for some water. "In a minute, in a minute," he murmured. "Boil, boil, we have a guest." He ran about like an agitated hostess. In a moment he had come back again with some bread and bacon, at which he sniffed with delight. "And salt, salt," he cried, slapping himself on the forehead. He ran back to the cart. At last he had settled down by the fire. He gave Prokop the larger portion and himself slowly munched every mouthful. Prokop was suffering from smoke in the eyes or something of the sort; tears ran down his face as he ate. The old man gave every other mouthful to the horse, whose head was bent over his shoulder. And suddenly, through a veil of tears, Prokop recognized him: it was the old, wrinkled face which he had always seen on the wooden ceiling of his laboratory! How often had he not looked at it when going off to sleep! And, in the morning when he woke up it was completely different—nothing but knots, dampness and dust.

The old man smiled. "Does it taste good? Ah, at last it's boiling!" He bent over the kettle, raised it with an effort and limped off to the cart. In a moment, he was back with a couple of mugs. "Just hold it a minute." Prokop took one of the mugs; on it was painted in gold the name "Ludmila," surrounded with a garland of forget-me-nots. He read the name twenty times and tears came into his eyes. "Grandfather," he whispered, "is…that…her name?"

The old man looked at him with sad, tender eyes. "So that you know," he said softly, "it is."

"And…shall I never find her?"

The old man said nothing but only blinked rapidly. "Hold it out," he said uncertainly, "I'll give you some tea."

Prokop held out the mug with a trembling hand and the old man carefully poured into it some strong tea. "Drink it while it's warm," he said gently.

"Th—thank you," sobbed Prokop and took a sip of the sharp-tasting drink.

The old man stroked his long hair reflectively. "It's bitter," he said slowly, "it's bitter, isn't it? Wouldn't you like a bit of sugar?"

Prokop shook his head. He felt the bitter taste of tears, but his breast was filled with a generous warmth.

The old man sipped at his mug noisily. "And now look," he said, so as to make things easier, "what I've got painted on mine." He handed him his mug; on it was depicted an anchor, a heart and a cross. "That's faith, love and hope. Don't cry any more." He stood over the fire with his hands clasped. "Dear one, dear one," he said softly, "you will not achieve the highest and you will not release everything. You tried to tear yourself to pieces by force, but you have remained whole and you will neither save the world nor smash it to pieces. Much in you will remain closed up, like fire in a stove; that is good, it is sacrifice. You wanted to do too great things, and you will instead do small ones. That is good."

Prokop knelt down in front of the fire, not daring to raise his eyes. He knew now that it was God the Father who was speaking to him.

"It is good," he whispered.

"It is good. You will do things which will help people. He whose thoughts are full of the highest turns away his eyes from people. Instead you will serve them."

"That is good," whispered Prokop, on his knees.

"Now you see," said the old man, pleased, and squatted down on his heels. "Tell me, what's this—what do you call it? Your invention?"

Prokop raised his head. "I've…forgotten."

"That doesn't matter," the old man reassured him. "You'll take up other things. Wait a moment, what was it I was going to say? Aha! Why was there such a great explosion? That's more people injured. But look about and search; perhaps you'll find…well, perhaps only such *pf-pf-pf*," he said, blowing out his soft cheeks. "You see? So that it should only be *puff-puff*…and do something which will work for people, do you understand?"

"You mean," muttered Prokop, "some sort of cheap energy, eh?"

"Cheap, cheap," agreed the old man, delighted. "So that it could be very useful. And shine, and warm, you understand?"

"Wait," said Prokop reflectively, "I don't know—that would mean experimenting all over again…from the other end."

"That's it. Start from the other end and there you are. There, you see, you've something to begin with right away. But leave that other. I'll get your bed ready." He got up and limped off to the cart. "Hato hot ma-ly," he sang, "we're going to bed." He returned with a rough mattress. "Come along," he said, took the lantern and led the way into the wooden shed. "There's straw enough," he croaked as he made the bed ready, "for all three of us. Praise be to God."

Prokop sat down on the straw. "Grandfather," he cried, amazed, "look!"
"What?"

"There, on the wall." On each of the planks forming the side of the hut there had been written large letters in chalk. Prokop read them by the flickering light of the lantern: K… R… A… K… A… T…

"That's nothing, that's nothing," muttered the old man reassuringly and quickly rubbed them out with his cap. "That's all over. Just lie down and I'll cover you with a sack. So."

He went to the doorway. "Dadada ma-ly," he sang in his trembling voice and the horse thrust its beautiful silver head through the door and rubbed its nose against the old man's coat.

"Come in, come in," he said, "and lie down."

The old horse ambled into the shed, scratched the opposite wall with its hoofs, and knelt down. "I'll find a place between you," said the old man, "he'll breathe on you and you'll be warm. So."

He sat down quietly near the door. Behind him could still be seen the glow of the dying fire, and the pale blue eyes of the horse, turned on him. The old man muttered something to him, nodding his head.…

Prokop closed his eyes in bliss. "Why…why, it's my old father," he said to himself. "God! How old he's grown! His neck's become scraggy—"

"Prokop, are you asleep?" whispered the old man.

"No," answered Prokop, trembling with love.

The old man began to sing gently a strained and quiet song: "Lalala hou, dadada pan, binkili bunkili hou tata.…"

Then Prokop fell into a sweet and healing sleep, free from all dreams.

www.ingramcontent.com/pod-product-compliance
Lightning Source LLC
Chambersburg PA
CBHW011717240626
47153CB00009B/2889